# ELIZABETH

Book Two
The Sacred Women's Circle

Judith Ashley

Windtree Press
Portland, Oregon

Windtree Press
818 SW 3$^{rd}$ Avenue #221-2218
Portland OR 97204-2405
http://windtreepress.com
email: windtreepress@windtreepress.com

Publisher's Note: This is a work of fiction. Names, characters, places, and incidents are a product of the author's imagination. Locales and public names are sometimes used for atmospheric purposes. Any resemblance to actual people, living or dead, or to businesses, companies, events, institutions, or locales is completely coincidental.

Cover Design – Christy Caughie www.GildedHeartDesign.com

Book Layout ©2013 BookDesignTemplates.com

Editing by Kelly Schaub
http://www.the-efa.org/dir/memberinfo. php?mid=8345

Ordering Information:
Quantity sales. Special discounts are available on quantity purchases by corporations, associations, and others. For details, contact the "Special Sales Department" at the address above.

Elizabeth/Judith Ashley. -- 1st ed.

ISBN 9781940064536

## Acknowledgements

No book becomes a reality without the support and assistance of many people. My own sacred women's circle (Heather, Kris, Michele), my romance writing sisters, Helen and Sarah, and the inspiration of the #RCRWFTB group as well as the mentoring and encouragement of Maggie Lynch have kept me at the computer on days when polishing this story seemed daunting. And a special "thank you" to Terrel Hoffman for her coaching on formatting for the print version of this book.

Reminiscing with my long time Glasser friend, Judith, who I traveled with in Ireland was critical to bringing the essence of that experience to this story. While we did talk to sheep, we never met Michael.

*Author's Note: For those of you who are familiar with international travel, please note ahead of time that I did not include the realities of Elizabeth's travel visa in the story using my omnipotent power as the author to make it a non-issue when in real life it would need to be dealt with.*

# 1   Ireland At Last

**The Hotel Lir**
**Limerick, Ireland**

Elizabeth Elliott froze in mid-step. Her blue eyes wide, her mouth agape in awe, her gaze took in the stunning statue of the Children of Lir morphing from humans to swans in the center of the hotel lobby.

One minute she was agog at the sight before her, the next she was stumbling forward hands grasping for something, anything to catch herself.

Nothing.

Heart pounding, a scream froze in her throat as she pitched forward.

Instead of landing on the hard marble-tiled floor, she landed against a hard masculine chest. Her racing heart slowed. Her oxygen-starved lungs gulped familiar-scented-air.

She tilted her head and caught a glimpse of the man still clutching her.

Him—Michael Murphy, the funniest, kindest, sexiest man she'd ever met and her seatmate on the long flight from Cincinnati, Ohio to Limerick, Ireland. The firm hold on her body eased.

"It may be grand, but that doesn't give you leave to just stop," he growled, hauling her to the side.

"Wha… ," she stammered.

"We're blocking the door," he said nodding toward the entrance.

People streamed past.

"Oh, I'm sorry, I… ," she stopped in mid-apology drawn back to the stunning sculpture. "I-They-Words-." She gestured toward the towering statue.

"Words fail you?"

Elizabeth nodded. "It's exquisite," she whispered. She leaned toward the monument and he let her go, steadying her until she got her balance. "It's, it's fantastic," Elizabeth said, in a dreamy awe-struck tone. "This alone is worth the trip." Her carry-on bag forgotten, she walked slowly toward the lobby's star feature.

She passed large leather chairs and sofas set in conversation groups around the scene, her fingers trailed across side tables fashioned to look like crystal rocks. Behind her, flanking the entrance were crystal stands with large vases of fresh flowers their fragrance filling the air and adding to the atmosphere.

Michael added her carry-on to his and followed. "If this hotel lobby alone is worth the trip, then you're certainly in for one hellofa experience." He chuckled and nudged her forward. "Go on, take a closer look."

Standing next to the ten foot tall, eight-foot diameter sculpture, she felt small and inconsequential. Set on a bluish-mirror-like surface that simulated a reflecting lake, the statue was carved from granite and marble. Sand-like grains of crystal covered some surfaces casting rainbows around the room.

A plaque told the story of the Children of Lir who were transformed into swans by their jealous stepmother, Aoife. According to legend, the children of the King of Lir were cursed by Aoife to spend three hundred years as swans in Westmeath on Loch Derravaragh; three hundred years in the strait of Moyle; and three hundred years on the open seas. This statue depicted their transformation to swans on Loch Derravaragh.

Elizabeth circled the work of art, looking closely at the details on each piece. One was already a swan, the details of the feathers such that if she touched it she knew she'd feel warmth and softness. One was human from the knees down; the rest of her body, a swan. The one who was mostly human still featured the head, neck, and upper torso of a swan. The fourth child was half swan and half human. Each of the Children of Lir was adorned with a strand of gold and diamonds draped around her neck, a large diamond atop her head.

Even in the middle of the bustle, the business of a large hotel lobby, there was something sacred about this space and this legend about the dangers of jealousy. *Interesting. I believe swans represent family because they mate for life and are devoted parents. In The Circle we see swans are about life-long relationships, inner beauty, and power— not jealousy.*

The familiar twinge of yearning ached in her chest. *Family. To have one, I created my own—my sacred women's circle is my family now. They've supported my dream to follow visions of The Lady. With their encouragement, I've come to*

*Ireland to find her and I pray five weeks is enough time.* Elizabeth closed her eyes. The Lady shimmered before her, arms opened wide in welcome. And as had happened so many times, seconds passed and She was gone.

Michael watched her, watched the emotions flicker across her face, and watched her tuck memories away. Fragile was the word he'd use to describe her. His need to protect her roused.

"Need more time?"

"Oh, you don't need to wait on me," Elizabeth said, her eyes never leaving the scene before her.

"I don't mind," Michael replied, slouching down in one of the comfortable leather armchairs.

*What is it about her?* He let his mind wander back to the flight from Cincinnati. They were seat partners and he enjoyed listening to her enthusiasm for this trip. She'd fallen asleep at one point and he smiled remembering her flustered poise when she woke. He rubbed his left shoulder and arm where her head had lain.

*What is it about her?* Curly blue-black hair, tied back at the nape with a blue ribbon, cascaded mid-way down her back. Her slim build was casually dressed. Her scent lingered in the air. He'd asked her about it because he couldn't readily identify it. The base was bergamot, not bergamont she'd emphasized, with other essential oils. Her own special blend.

*What is it about her?* Comfortable. Something about her was comfortable. So comfortable he'd fallen asleep, his head resting on her shoulder, his hand on her thigh. A slender, well-muscled thigh—his hand twitched.

She'd been a pleasant companion chattering about her travel plans. And more than once during that long flight he told himself he deserved a wee bit of a break once he got home, more than once he was tempted to offer to show her around, and more than once lust surged through him.

"It's amazing!" she said turning away.

"That it is," he said, gracefully gaining his feet. "What's next?"

"Check in, shower, something to eat, in that order, I think," she said, tipping her head to one side.

"This way," Michael said. His hand on her elbow, he guided her across the lobby to check in.

"Oh, my luggage," Elizabeth halted, scanning the lobby for her carry-on.

"Taken care of," he said, pointing to a young man who'd retrieved their carry-ons and added them to a luggage cart.

"Thank you, I'm usually much more organized, more on top of things," Elizabeth explained.

"Jet lag," he said and smiled. "No need to explain or apologize – just smile and say "jet lag"."

"That's it? All will be forgiven? Forgotten?" Puzzlement creased her forehead.

"Surely in your line of work you've heard of sleep deprivation."

"Not at all," she responded, a note of spunky sarcasm in her voice. "You do know it isn't nice to throw people's words back at them."

He grinned down at her. "Now, luv."

"And who gave you permission to call me that? I do have a name," she tossed back.

"Next," the desk clerk called.

"You first, luv," Michael said and winked.

Nose in air, Elizabeth sailed forth to the counter.

"Your name?"

"Elizabeth Elliott. I have a reservation for two nights in a no smoking room."

"I don't see it," the desk clerk replied, his fingers clicking over the keys.

Michael heard the conversation. A vision of her in his bed flashed through his mind his body responded in kind. He was motioned forward to the other desk clerk. "Michael Murphy," he stated.

"Oh yes, Mr. Murphy. I've got your reservation right here. And, if I may add, congratulations on your win," the young desk clerk gushed.

"Thanks, Mary," he said using the name on her badge. "I wasn't the one running, you know." She laughed and he saw an invitation to more in her eyes.

He shifted, leaned towards Elizabeth, unashamedly listening to the conversation. She wasn't getting anywhere in sorting out her room reservation. His room key in hand, he turned toward the elevator. He wanted that hot shower and something to eat but the desperation in her voice stopped him.

"What's happening here?" he asked the desk clerk. He stood close; her hair brushed his chin, caught in his stubble, bergamot wafted.

"This lady's reservation is lost or," the clerk looked directly at Elizabeth, "was never made."

He rested a hand on her shoulder. "And you have no rooms to let?"

"We do, but she insists she has a reservation."

"I've got the confirmation number here somewhere," Elizabeth said as she continued to rummage through her bag.

"The important thing is to have a room, get that hot shower, and hot meal," he said in a soothing voice, his hand stroking her shoulder and arm. "Let's just see what else he has for you."

She nodded.

Michael handed the desk clerk his reservation. "What do you have near here?"

"Mr. Murphy, sir," the desk clerk jerked to attention. "I'm sure I can take care of this little problem." His fingers flew across the computer's keys. "Why, with your permission, if I can move your room down one, you and the lady will have adjoining rooms."

"You do that," Michael said turning Elizabeth to face him. "All taken care of." *Why did I change my room? I don't need a connecting room to have her in my bed. There's something about her – something more than getting her into my bed.*

"I don't understand," Elizabeth said, her expression perplexed, her voice tired.

A few minutes later, the desk clerk handed room keys to each of them. "Enjoy your stay, Mr. Murphy."

Michael's brow raised and he stared at the clerk. "Enjoy your stay, Ms. ..." the clerk paused and looked at the computer screen, "Elliott."

Elizabeth let Michael lead her to the elevator. His cocky grin belied the look in his eyes: a look that took her breath away; a look of bright burning desire. Standing next to him waiting for the elevator, his scent tantalized, her toes curled and her face flushed pink. Energy thrummed between them, an energy she'd never experienced with her ex-boyfriend, Jeremy. Her breath hitched, heat pooled in her belly. The intense feelings of arousal disconcerted. She'd never acted on these feelings before because she'd never even felt them. *What if I step out-*

*side myself, allowed a night of passion, get to know him in the Biblical sense? The nuns would have me on my knees.*

The elevator arrived. She stepped forward, stumbled. Strong hands grabbed her upper arms and steadied her.

"I-I-I must be more t-t-tired than I feel," Elizabeth stuttered as heat prickled her skin where Michael's hands still gripped her.

He pulled her close, tucked her against his side, and guided her into the waiting elevator. A bellman pushed the luggage cart inside. The young man at the elevator's control panel pushed the button for the Eighth floor. The elevator started its upward climb.

"Congratulations on winning the Preakness, Mr. Murphy, sir," one young man said with enthusiasm.

"Thanks."

"Maybe next year you'll win another of the Triple Crown races," the other bellman added with relish.

"That would be something," the first bellman said.

"Sure and it would," Michael responded.

"Brian Boru, you will race him in the Breeders Cup, now," the first bellman added.

"Thinkin about it. Twill depend on how well he recovers from the races he's just run."

Elizabeth listened carefully and realized that her seat partner on the flight and her rescuer at the front desk was famous in horse racing circles in Ireland.

When the doors opened, the young men gestured them out. One took control of the luggage cart, the other ushered them down a long hall while talking about sights to see near the hotel. Stopping in front of one of the rooms, he opened the door, and stepped aside gesturing for Elizabeth and Michael to enter. A polite knock on the door jamb announced the arrival of the luggage cart.

"This is my luggage," Elizabeth said pointing to her three suitcases.

Michael stepped forward. "The rest in the room next door." He handed the young man unloading Elizabeth's suitcases onto the racks next to the closet a tip before turning to the first young man, "My room key, please." He held out a folded bill and exchanged it for his room key which he tucked in his pocket. "That'll be all."

"Thank you, Mr. Murphy, sir," both young men spoke at once. "We'll be about our duties then. Give us a call if you need anything. I'm Sean," the first young man said pointing to himself. "That there's Liam," he gestured to the second young man still standing in the doorway.

"Anything at all, Mr. Murphy," Liam chimed in. "Just let us know and we'll get it for you."

"Thanks, lads. If either Ms. Elliott or I need something we'll ask for you. Now get those bags in my room and be off to your duties."

"Yes sir," they chorused as the door shut behind them.

In the stillness, the air sizzled with repressed energy. Michael lounged against the desk, hands resting on the surface behind him, ankles crossed, his eyes, lids lowered, never left her.

Elizabeth nervously chewed her bottom lip, looking everywhere except at the man whose presence filled the room. Doubts flooded her mind. She'd come to Ireland on a quest to find The Lady. That purpose now warred with a longing to put her conservative life aside and live for the moment. Primal desire flared. *One night with this man can't hurt, can it?* Blue eyes met blue eyes and she knew a lifetime of memories were hers.

He crossed the short distance. Her breath caught as he drew her into his arms. His heart beat beneath her cheek, the hint of sandalwood and something else unique to him filled her lungs, his muscled arms held her close against his hard chest, the texture of his linen shirt smooth beneath her hands. His heat invaded her body, her mind slowed down, her knees weakened. She leaned into him. One finger grazed her chin finding its way down her throat to that sensitive indentation at the base of her neck, resting there before traveling back up to tilt her head back against his arm. He was so beautiful with his blue-black hair mussed, his face etched with stubble, his eyes burning with desire – for her.

His lips brushed hers. "I've wanted to do this for hours," he whispered. His lips continued to brush against hers, nibbling at the corners of her mouth, when he sucked her lower lip her knees wobbled. She clutched his shirt at the onslaught of sensations filling her before sliding her hands up and over his shoulders, pressing against him.

His beard abraded her skin. It didn't matter she'd be marked. Passion curled in her core and she rose on her toes to receive more of him.

He eased back; back to brushing his lips against hers; back to holding her without an inch of space between them. His hands stroked up and down her back from her waist to her neck. She trembled beneath his touch. He took a small step back.

Elizabeth drew her hands from his shoulders, cupped his face, smiled and rising up on her tiptoes, pulled his head down to hers, and gently kissed him. His hands tightened on her arms before he stepped back and released her. Every cell in her body felt the loss of his heat and strength.

It wasn't that she'd never been held or kissed before. It wasn't that she had tons of experience but she wasn't a virgin. It wasn't that she'd never been in a serious relationship; she'd been engaged to Jeremy for three years before he broke it off. But nothing she'd experienced with Jeremy or the few boys she'd dated in high school and college had affected her like this. Still in Michael's arms, one of his hands caressing her back, it dawned on her that while she'd been upset when Jeremy broke their engagement, her distress was really because it meant she wouldn't be married, she wouldn't have a family and children of her own.

The memories of Jeremy faded. Elizabeth shifted in Michael's arms, his grip loosened. She searched his eyes. *How does he do that? How does he affect me more than any man I've ever known?* His eyes, a sky blue, lighter than her own, were studying her, taking her measure.

"Well, I need to unpack." He took another step back, dropping his hands to his side as he did so. Instead of going to the hall door, Michael turned and walked to a door in the wall, unlocked it, and left it unlatched.

"W-wha-what are you doing?" she stammered. "W-what?" her lips moved but no further words emerged.

"At the time connecting rooms seemed a good idea."

Her mouth moved, no sounds came out.

He ran his hand through his already tousled hair and around to stroke his unshaven face. "Let's get ourselves unpacked and see about a meal. We can talk while we're eating." He turned, crossed the room to the hall door, and without waiting for a reply, left. The door was barely closed, when Elizabeth found her voice. Hands fisted at her side, breathing strained, she shook her head in exasperation and muttered, "What is it about him that makes me stutter, stammer?" She sank to the chair, her head in her hands, "Oh Goddess, I hope I'm not making a horrible mistake."

# 2 An Altar and A Choice

Stepping out of a long hot shower, Elizabeth slathered a special cream on her face because her skin was reddened from the roughness of Michael's beard. She dabbed on a little eye shadow to highlight the natural color of her eyes, added a touch of mascara to thicken her dark lashes, and pulled her hair back from her face, securing it with a scrunchy. Make-up in place, she dressed casually in a rose red pair of slacks, a matching blouse, a simple necklace of turquoise beads around her neck.

Next? Set up her altar.

"Yes, this will do nicely," she said to herself as she cleared off the north-facing desk. A cigar box, a piece of cloth, a candle, and matches were retrieved from her tote. Unfolding the square of light-summer-green cloth, she placed it on the diagonal. Lighting the candle, she swirled it around her body, saying prayers of cleansing and protection, repeating the process with the cigar box, its contents, and the cloth.

"Goddess, Great Spirit, bless these objects, imbue them with their highest purpose, may they represent Your presence here." Each piece was passed through the candle's heat before she placed it on the cloth. A small brass bowl graced the center.

Pieces of gold calcite and citrine and a carved robin went on the right side of the cloth, the east, the place of beginnings. In the south, the point closest to her, she placed a piece of carnelian and a raw, tumbled ruby along with a small basket containing a variety of herbal seeds representing abundance, the bounty of mother earth. The point on the left, the west or the void, received lapis lazuli and sodalite along with a feather from a raven and carving of an orca. In the north, at the top of the cloth, she placed a four inch wand of selenite, a double terminated phantom crystal and a fetish of a barn owl also known as the ghost owl. Midway between these points she place an apache tear asking the spirits sacred to her to guard and protect her on this journey. When all was in place she stepped back and raised her arms in prayer.

"Oh Goddess, Great Spirit, the One who is All. Watch over, guide and protect me as I go forth on this journey of my soul. Let me see with certainty that I'm going in the direction of my highest good. May The Lady who drew me to this land, continue to be by my side. Blessed Be." Elizabeth stood silent before her altar, the sacred space she created for this room, and gazed unseeing at her creation. Lost in herself she didn't hear the connecting door behind her open, the sharp intake of breath, or the door quietly closed.

Michael leaned against his side of the connecting door lost in a furor of feelings. His eyes closed, he shook his head trying to clear the picture etched in his brain the words ringing in his ears. His head bent as if a weight hung from his forehead. A frustrated groan escaped as he pushed away from the wall, and strode across the room to stand in front of the windows and stare out into the night. *What do I do now?* Deep calming breaths helped ease the tension from his body. He walked slowly around the room, lost in thought, sorting out what he'd seen and heard when he'd opened the door to Elizabeth's room.

The surge of energy spent, he flopped in the chair, put his feet on the hassock, closed his eyes, and rested his head on the back of the chair. *Don't know why I'm so surprised. After all The Lady called her to come. Well, that puts an interesting wrinkle in things.* Michael was quiet and still on the outside, his mind awhirl within. He felt such a strong attraction to Elizabeth, not just one of lust but also one of protection. And he enjoyed her company, seeing her discombobulated before she realized he was teasing her, hearing her laugh, watching her expressions change mirroring her emotions. *Her energy and unique scent? I'd recognize her in the dark. Ah, hell.* He sighed. *Why fight it. Just go with it.* He rose and crossed the room to the adjoining door. *See what happens.* With that thought upper-most in his mind, he knocked.

# 3   DINNER AND THEN?

"You look ready to eat." A wide smile on her face, her eyes aglow with welcome, Elizabeth laughed and walked toward him, her hands loose at her side.

An impulse to step back quashed before it became action, his breath caught in his throat. He was in deep trouble if he thought he had much control around her. She was stunning. Unable to think of a witty rejoinder, he said, "I am ready, how about you?"

"Oh, yes. I'm starved." She was close enough her scent drifted around him. He wanted to reach out and pull her tight against him, feel her curves press along his already rousing body. Instead, he gently clasped her hands in his.

"There's a great pub not too far from here; great bar menu. Irish stew is their specialty."

"Let's go, then." Elizabeth disengaged, turned and picked up a small bag on the dresser. Looking back over her shoulder, she said, "Are you coming? I really don't know where to go without you, you know."

"I'm right behind you," Michael started toward her. "Right beside you now." He caught her by the elbow and guided her out the door.

Elizabeth's skin tingled. It was as if his hand wrapped around her bare skin. She wobbled a moment as the sensations rushed through her. His hand tightened on her elbow. She found her footing.

"Are you okay?" he said, bending low and speaking softly.

Her whole body shivered as the heat from his words feathered across her ear and the side of her neck. Glancing up, for a moment she was lost in Michael's passionate sky-blue gaze. She looked away and took a steadying breath.

"I've been told it's jet lag," she said, the grin on her face sounding in her voice.

The elevator arrived and Michael chatted with the young man at the controls for the few moments it took to reach the lobby. He kept his hand on her elbow, turned them to the left as they walked out the hotel lobby door, and started to talk about the sights they could see along the street.

"Along here are shops to look at. There are better buys when you aren't so close to the hotel. Look here, though," he stopped in front of a shop with a display of crystal in the window. "Here's some Galway Crystal. It isn't as well-known as Waterford but some master craftsmen from Waterford started the company so you know the quality of the work is good."

"I do want to shop. My friends and I have a tradition of picking up something for each other when we travel, a way of bringing back a bit of the energy of the place. My challenge will be to figure out what represent the energy, the sacredness of Ireland." She paused and looked further into the shop. "I think this would be a wonderful place to just spend some time. Can you feel the energy of the place? So sparkling!"

"Is the energy of the place filling your stomach? I just heard it asking for food, not sparkling energy," Michael said and chuckled.

"On to the pub, then, oh mighty leader." As Elizabeth turned away from the shop she caught their reflection in the glass. Her heart stuttered and she swayed. A shimmering light encircled them, the same light that surrounded The Lady. *I'm tired and must be seeing things.* Glad for his steadying hand, she continued down the street.

The carved and painted sign above the pub door had a figure astride a horse that Michael told her was a faerie king. He opened the heavy, darkened oak door to The King's Pub and Elizabeth stepped into another world. The music sprightly, the singing loud, and smells enticing. Behind her she could feel Michael's hard body pressed against hers. She took another step and another step until her legs loosened and she walked into the center of the bedlam.

"Hey, Mick."

"How ya doing, Mick?" a shout of welcome boomed over the noise. She looked around for "Mick" and then she heard Michael's answering voice.

"Hey, Paddy, what're you doing here? Thought you'd be home nursing your wounds, ole man." Laughter swelled at the banter between the two men. Elizabeth looked to her right and saw a bear of a man coming toward them, a glass of dark liquid in hand. He stopped, reached over her and clapped Michael on the back. She tensed, thinking Michael'd be pushed into her but he withstood the assault with good-natured ease.

"And who is this pretty miss, you've got with ye?" the big man asked giving her a wink and a smile.

"If you think I'm going to introduce you to her, you've another think coming, Paddy," Michael's bantering tone had a bit of an edge beneath it.

"Ahh, 'fraid I'll steal her from you," he said and laughed.

Elizabeth watched in fascination as the two men exchanged taunts and insults for a couple of minutes. Paddy shoved his glass at Michael who instinctively grabbed it before he caught her up in his big hands and lifted her into the air until she was eye-to-eye with him, looking into grass-green eyes that held a wealth of humor.

"I'm Padraig O'Cochran, I am. I've got me own stud farm, winners, a big house and it can all be yours if you toss him over for me," his voice boomed and Elizabeth could feel her cheeks redden with embarrassment as the noise quieted and eyes turned her way.

She tried to squirm but his hands held her firmly and he didn't seem inconvenienced or even put upon holding her up in the air, waiting for her answer. She looked again at the giant of a man and realized she'd nothing to fear as the amusement twinkling in his eyes spoke of his desire to taunt Michael and had nothing to do with her.

"I'm afraid, Mr. O'Cochran, that I'm just visiting in Ireland and have no need for my own stud farm, winners, and a big house. However, I am hungry and Mr. Murphy was kind enough to bring me here for a meal. Perhaps you'd be gentlemanly enough to put me down, now? Before, that is, I'm forced to hurt you."

"Hurt me?" the big man chuckled. "What could you possibly do to hurt me?"

"This," Elizabeth smiled sweetly as she positioned her right foot inches from his crotch.

"Mick, you've got yerself some kind of filly here, ye do at that," Paddy said while gently lowering her to the floor. "Hey, Sarri. How bout a table for these two. They look ready to topple over from hunger," he bellowed.

Elizabeth stepped back as soon as her feet touched the floor and felt Michael's hard chest against her back. An arm snaked around her waist and pulled her tight against him. She relaxed and leaned back, soaked up his warmth. "How'd I do?" she tilted her head to the side and smiled up at him.

Michael's breath stirred her hair along the side of her face as he leaned over to speak to her. "You saved him from a beating. But I didn't see what you did. Just saw the astonished look that came over his face before he quickly lowered you to the floor."

"I showed him the disadvantage of having someone so short held up in the air. It was easy enough to maneuver my foot where it could do some damage," she said a satisfied smile on her face.

Michael looked at her and burst into laughter. "My God, but you're a feisty one at that. Come on, I see Sarri has a table for us over this way." He gestured to his left, nudging her along from behind.

The pub special was a big bowl of Irish stew and homemade bread with fresh butter. Paddy sent a pitcher of Guinness over and she tried the dark brew. The initial bitter taste disappeared after a few sips and with the stew and bread, it was divine. A corner of the pub had a large stone fireplace and to one side a small stage on which a trio of musicians sat. Two played fiddles and one an Irish drum called a bodhran. Everyone joined in singing and Elizabeth found herself humming along and singing softly to herself from time to time.

Michael seemed to know everyone at this place and it was a wonder he got his meal eaten with all the interruptions. A constant stream of people stopped by and congratulated him on his recent victory. A couple of women who stopped by flirted outrageously with him and eyed her with some interest. She noted that he was polite, friendly even, but did not encourage the double-entendre-laden conversations nor did he introduce her to them.

For her part, she relaxed and enjoyed the atmosphere, thinking ahead to what she wanted to write in her journal. Of course, her encounter with Paddy would be included as well as her first impression of Guinness, the wonders of the Irish stew, the taste of the fresh butter. While all that would take up a few paragraphs, she knew the people and their music would take up pages.

Everyone, well almost everyone, was so friendly and welcoming. There were men who were surreptitiously flirting with her when they thought Michael wasn't looking. But, somehow he always knew and sent a fierce glare in their direction. She'd never had quite this experience before—being seen as attractive and having someone else guarding her. *Jeremy got jealous and always blamed me if someone flirted.* She couldn't remember a time when someone had truly claimed her in the elemental way that she felt claimed by Michael.

The remnants of the long trip crept over her. She barely got her hand up to stifle a yawn before Michael was leaning toward her asking if she wanted to go. She nodded and soon found herself on her feet, moving through the crowded room. A few bawdy comments were tossed out by unseen patrons as Michael escorted her out the door.

Out on the sidewalk, they stopped and breathed in the fresh air, the stillness a relief from the noise of the pub. In the dim glow of the lone street light she was glad for Michael's arm as they started back to the hotel.

In the elevator, Michael dropped his hand from her elbow and leaned back against the rail. Liam was on duty but other than inquiring about their evening remained silent.

"Are you okay?" she asked, her voice soft. Her hand on his arm, she looked up and into eyes glittering with desire. Out of the corner of her eye she could see his hand drifting slowly upward toward her face. She was held, transfixed by his gaze. And then the ping and the sound of the elevator doors opening broke the trance. Elizabeth turned and walked out of the elevator, Michael close behind her.

At her door, she stopped and took the room key from her bag.

"Good night," she managed before words evaporated.

Michael's hands were planted on the wall on each side of her head, his stance wide. Soft hot lips brushed across her forehead, her right check and then her left. He lingered a moment on the tip of her nose before moving to the tip of her chin. When he reached her mouth, when he kissed her fully and deeply, his tongue slid in to discover her taste, her heat, her wetness.

The door knob pressed into the middle of her back. She stretched up on her toes to meet him, her tongue curling around his, and then following it back to explore him as he'd explored her. He tasted of Guinness and Irish stew. They jerked apart at the sound of a door opening, voices, and laughter. Michael's breathing was labored as if he'd just sprinted a mile. Elizabeth's breathing sounded fractured as if she couldn't quite catch her breath.

Michael grabbed the room key from her hand, reached around her, and with a deft movement opened the door, and pulled her inside. The door closed behind them and she was back in his arms, his mouth greedily plundering hers, his hands roaming her body.

A moan – was it hers or his? She felt encompassed by his body, his arms tight around her. She could feel the thickness of his arousal press against her abdomen and her own body's answering surge. Heat coiled through her starting deep in the core of her being. Her breasts seemed to swell and her nipples tightened when his hands brushed over them on their way to unbuttoning her blouse.

"Hell!" The word tore from his throat. "Ah, luv, you're like a candle's flickering flame drawing the moth inexorably to you." He pulled her close and rested his chin on the top of her head. "And, I'm the moth doomed to burn and die in your fire."

Elizabeth allowed herself to lean against Michael's body and catch her breath. "You are the faerie king, luring me to temptation. I've never felt this—desperate before." Her voice held a note of exasperation. She leaned back from his chest; her lower body pressed against the ridge tenting his pants and looked up into blue eyes blazing with passion. "What are we going to do about this?" she asked innocently, her arms curling around his neck.

"Don't have protection. Never thought.... But then, I hadn't met you."

Michael held her tight. *There's more than one way to have sex. Or I could get condoms. Or I can let her go.*

Elizabeth wiggled out of his arms. The internal debate was written on his face. "What are you thinking about?"

"Options."

"Such as?"

"Now, luv."

"Michael, my name is Elizabeth as you well know. You use "luv" like a-a-a throw-away word. If you don't want to spend the night, just say so." Her face flamed with embarrassment. *This is very different than discussing a couple's sex life during an adoption study.* She stood her ground, maintained eye contact, and prepared herself for rejection. *Why else would he have stopped other than he doesn't want me – well, that isn't exactly true. His pants are still tented. But that doesn't mean he wants me.*

"Elizabeth, while we've spent the better part of the past twenty-four hours together, that doesn't mean you know me well-enough to invite me to spend the night. Hell, that sounds preachy even to me. Let me rephrase that by asking a question.

"When was the last time you engaged in a one-night-stand?"

She swallowed hard. *So that's it. I'm not experienced enough for him.* "I'm not going to answer that impertinent question."

He smiled. Not one of triumph, but one of tender sadness. "Ah, but you have answered." His hands rested on her shoulders as he bent down and brushed a soft kiss across her forehead. "And, for your information, I do want you – badly. But, I don't think jumping into bed tonight is the way to go so here's an idea.

"I'm going to take a cold shower and cool down. Then bed and sleep, hopefully 'til morning. I'll knock on your door around 8:30. We'll have breakfast, see some sights. Tomorrow night, if we're still attracted to each other after we've gotten to know each other a wee bit better, we'll see what happens." A mischievous grin tugged his mouth, a twinkle sparked in his eyes. "You can be sure I'll have that protection."

"Are you sure," Elizabeth's reply was cut short by his very thorough kiss.

"Yes, very sure." He turned away, strode to and through the connecting door without stopping. In his room, he turned back and stared at the blank surface. *Long night ahead of me.*

# 4 Swan Feathers and The River Shannon

It had been a restless night with vivid, sensual dreams. Back home there were times a faceless man came to her in dreams. Last night, he'd come again but this time he had a face – Michael's. In that hazy dream time just before waking, The Lady appeared, inordinately pleased with something.

The thin blade of sunlight slicing the room announced another day, her first full day in Ireland. Stretching, aware of every inch of her body, aware of her own sexuality in a very different way, she reached high above her, pointed her toes and gently pulled her joints apart. *I could stay here in this bed for a week.* A smile touched her mouth. *I'd be tempted if Michael were here with me.*

As if summoned, Michael came through the connecting door, showered, shaved, and dressed. "Ah, there you are."

The lilt in his voice held promises she'd like to explore.

"Nay, ye can't get me in there, Elizabeth. That's why I'm staying clear over on this side of the room. You're a bewitching piece. And, I promised to show you the sights, can't do that if we spend the day in this room."

Michael's Irish brogue was more pronounced at times and "why?" teased at her mind.

He took two steps into the room, retreating, she noticed when she scooted to sit up on the bed. It wasn't that he wasn't tempted, Elizabeth realized as she watched him battle with himself; starting into the room, stopping; his eyes burning her skin with their smoldering gaze. The slight bulge in his trousers showed he definitely was tempted but he was staying strong in his determination to keep his promise to her; to show her the sights of Limerick; to give them time to get to know each other a little better. She sighed, tossed the covers aside, and stood. Midnight blue silk slipped down covering her exposed legs, coal black hair tumbled down her back. She sauntered to the bathroom door, turned and, a saucy grin on her face, said, "I'll be ready in twenty minutes, luv."

True to her word, twenty minutes later, he was standing at the elevator with Elizabeth by his side. Dressed in jeans, a dark blue tank top, and a lighter blue camp shirt she wore as a jacket, her tote was slung over a shoulder. She'd taken her cue from his own jeans and t-shirt ensemble and he'd teased her about "going native", enjoying the pink flush on her cheeks. As they ambled out the lobby door, he took her elbow in his hand. He liked the feel of her skin, soft, smooth and full of a life force all her own. He liked the way her elbow fit in the palm of his hand, the way she fit him, all of him. He shook his head, dispelling the licentious thoughts now swirling in his mind.

Before breakfast, they decided to walk along the River Shannon. On their way, Michael kept up a running monologue about the sights. At the park near the bridge, they stopped and watched the swans. The regal water birds were his favorites. *She has a white feather on her altar. Wonder if it's from a swan.*

"Would you like to see if we can find a couple of swan feathers, luv?"

Elizabeth glared.

*She's right. Tis a throw away word.* He shook his head. *Except, not with her.*

They leaned on a railing, watched the swans, river, and people feeding them for several minutes before she answered.

"I'd love to. What a great gift that would be for my circle sisters. That is if we can find seven feathers," she said with a smile.

"You planned on being in Limerick for two days so we can always check back tomorrow if you don't find what you want today."

Excitement shone in her eyes as Elizabeth nodded in reply and ducked under the railing, her tote still on her shoulder. On the other side of the rail she stopped for a moment, closed her eyes, and centered herself. *Spirit of swan, I ask you for seven feathers, one for me and one to take to each of my circle sisters. Know that your feathers will be held sacred. Blessed Be.*

"Careful," he called out after her. "You don't want to get too close. They're powerful fierce birds."

"I know," she called back over her shoulder as she carefully picked her way across the grassy expanse, avoiding the large bird's droppings, toward what looked to be a flight feather. Like a hunting dog in search of pheasants, Elizabeth sniffed the air as she searched for seven perfect feathers. After each find she stopped, closed her eyes, and said a prayer of thanks. *Spirit of swan, thank you for the gift of this feather. May you always know how sacred you are.*

Elizabeth had three flight feathers and two beautiful breast feathers tucked in her tote. Two more and her quest would be filled. She stood and refocused on the area around her spying two feathers near a stand of reeds. Making her way to the spot, she crouched to check them out.

The sound of a loud hiss and the beating of wings caught her attention. Looking up she saw a swan bearing down on her. *I'm too close to a nest.* She remained bent, eyes closed, and brought the vision of a swan to mind.

*Spirit of swan, I call to you. Spirit of swan, I ask for your protection. Spirit of swan, we are one.* She held the image of merging with the swan strong and clear in her mind, opened her eyes, and looked into the eyes of an adult swan with wings spread wide bathed in shimmering light.

"Don't be afraid. I won't hurt you or your children," she whispered. "We are one, you and I. Did you not hear my prayer asking permission to gather seven feathers? Is my request too much? If it is, please accept my apology, for I do not wish to take more than can be spared."

The swan undulated its neck before stretching it toward her. Elizabeth remained stooped. The swan retracted its neck and watched her. She heard people calling out. The swan hissed and wings flapped.

Elizabeth pulled her errant thoughts back to the here, the now, back to the vision of her and swan being as one. It was imperative to communicate she meant no harm.

"Two" resonated in her mind. The swan stretched to its full height, bent its long neck and plucked two feathers from its wings, letting them fall at Elizabeth's feet.

Stunned, it took several seconds before Elizabeth recovered and nodded her head in a respectful gesture. "Thank you," she whispered. Slowly she reached for the two feathers, picked them up, and without breaking eye contact or losing the vision in her mind, stood. She took a step back and paused, another step back and another pause continuing until she was several feet away. It was only then she turned and strolled away still seeing the swan and her morphed together similar to the Children of Lir's statue in the hotel lobby.

Michael was under the rail and striding toward her as she approached. He reached for her, took her elbow as was now his habit, and led her to the railing. The group of people he'd held back started to rush forward, one look from him and they stopped. He guided her under the railing and to the walkway beyond. A glance down and he saw she was still under the influence of a trance. *Shit.*

"Shows over folks," Michael said to the crowd still hanging around as he kept a protective arm around her. When she leaned heavily into him, he was glad he had a firm grasp and tucked her closer to his side.

*She's here and yet she isn't. That's what being in a trance does to a person.* He rubbed her arms and tightened his grip in an effort to connect with her.

"Thank you," she said snuggling into his embrace. "Would you just hold me for a moment while I get my bearings again?"

"For as long as you want." Michael pulled her closer, one arm holding her tight, the other running up and down her back in a gentle caress.

Moments passed. "Better?" he asked.

"Yes, much better," she said, her nose wrinkling. "Is that me I smell?"

"It is at that. You stepped in swan poop on your adventure."

Leaning back against his arms, Elizabeth looked up into Michael's face seeing concern but no confusion. *What does he know?* She wondered as she searched for the answer deep in his eyes. *Something. He knows something, I'd swear it.*

Pulling back from his embrace, Elizabeth sniffed and said, "I'd love to clean up before seeing more of Limerick." She looked around and pointed down the street. "The hotel is that way, isn't it?"

He nodded, cupped her elbow, and off they went.

Cleaning up took the form of a shower and a change of clothes after washing swan poop off her shoes. An hour later, Elizabeth, now dressed in a skirt and blouse and sandals, found herself in Michael's car, a picnic basket stowed in the back seat. When they'd returned to the hotel, she hadn't been hungry so agreed to his Plan B. Plan B was a drive through Limerick, out along the River Shannon to see some of the countryside, and to have lunch on the way.

Elizabeth enjoyed the scenery flying by as Michael sped down the road even though her mind was full of answers to his unasked questions. She had no illusions he didn't have them and that his idea of a picnic in the countryside was to be alone with her. What did surprise her was when he pulled his car onto a grassy verge on the side of the road and turned off the motor, he sat still, staring straight ahead.

Then his eyes closed and he rested his head against the seat back. From what she could see of his face and read in his posture, he was girding himself for a battle. He opened his eyes and turned toward her.

"Are you okay? You don't look like yourself."

"I'm fine." He took the key from the ignition, opened his door, and got out, extracting the picnic basket and blanket from the backseat. As he started around to her side, Elizabeth opened her own door and got out.

"Let me carry something." She reached out and took the blanket from his arm. A bright smile on her face she looked up, "Where to, oh great leader?" she quipped.

Michael smiled back but she noticed it didn't quite reach his eyes. "This way," he said and gestured. "There's a quiet spot over by those trees with a clear view of the river."

Together they walked the short distance to the patch of grass enclosed by a semi-circle of trees and bushes. The lush greens of the trees, bushes, and grass were a backdrop to the view of the river. Here, the Shannon's slow moving waters reflected the serene scene from the opposite bank of weeping willows, verdant fields, a splash of red from the bank of wild fuchsias and the cloud bedecked sky. The blanket spread out, the picnic basket in the center, Elizabeth stood mesmerized by the picturesque landscape before her.

"Be right back," Michael said as he turned and trotted back to the car.

The sounds of him getting something from the car dimly registered as she sank to the blanket, her eyes never leaving the sight of the river.

Moments later he was back, plopping down on his side of the blanket, a bottle of wine in his hand. "Forgot this. It's a great light white wine that should go well with our lunch." He opened the basket and began setting the containers out.

Elizabeth watched him intently for a moment and then shrugged. *All happens in its own time.* Over the years she'd learned things went better when she held that thought. *Better but not always easy,* she admitted to herself before joining in unpacking the basket and arranging the fare on the blanket.

As they took lids off containers, her nose feasted on the variety of smells. Rosemary and thyme chicken; a savory meat pie; sliced cucumbers and cherry tomatoes with a blue cheese dip; a loaf of fresh bread and creamy butter; a bowl of fresh strawberries with a chocolate cream mousse to dip them in. And then there was the wine, a fruity bouquet wafted in the breeze when Michael opened it.

"And this feast is just for the two of us?" Elizabeth's mouth watered as she sniffed the aroma of the various dishes and unpacked the plates and silverware from the basket.

"Thought we'd be hungry since we didn't have breakfast and it's been an eventful day so far. Be right back." He scrambled to his feet and took off in the direction of the car. She heard the same sounds and chuckled to herself wondering what he could possibly have forgotten. Her question was quickly answered as Michael returned and handed her a crystal goblet.

"Much better than paper or plastic cups, don't you think?" he asked as he poured. "Take a sip and see what you think?" He crouched down and waited while Elizabeth raised the glass, tilting it toward him in a salute, and then brought it to her lips. His breath caught while he watched the glass tilt and the clear liquid slip between her rosy lips. Her eyes slightly closed, he watched her swallow, savor the wine.

"Nice, very nice," her voice took on a sultry tone as she lowered the glass. She smiled. "Aren't you going to have any?" she asked her eyes wide in question, her voice devoid of seduction.

Michael stood, crossed to his side of the blanket, and sat. He filled his wine glass a third full before adding more to Elizabeth's. Picking up his plate and piling food on it, he gestured for her to follow suit.

Plates full, they savored the spread before them, their conversation focused on the tastes, textures, and pleasures of a good meal. When her plate was finally empty, Elizabeth set it down, hugged her knees and looked at the river.

"One of my circle sisters, Sophia, has a big garden every year. She grows fruits and vegetables and every week she shares the bounty of her garden with us. We had fresh strawberries from her yard for my circle sister, Lily's wedding to Jackson a few days ago. She didn't have enough for the entire gathering so made a special bowl for the seven of us with berries picked just that morning." Even with the essence of Michael surrounding her, she missed the other women in The Circle. She had things on her mind, things to sort out, and these women always had time to listen.

They'd been there an hour. Elizabeth grew more and more edgy. The leftovers were packed back in the basket and they sipped the last of the wine. Michael looked the picture of ease as he leaned back on his elbows, long legs crossed casually at the ankles, looking out at the Shannon. Even though they'd just met, she knew something bothered him, and it was more than what had happened this morning. She'd kept up a patter of polite chatter saying nothing of substance unless you counted her tales of Sophia's garden, vignettes of something she and one of The Circle had done, waiting for him to start and he hadn't.

"About this morning," Elizabeth plunged into the unease, hoping her voice sounded strong and sure and didn't reflect the trembling inside.

"What about his morning," Michael answered without looking at her.

"Nothing really, I just wondered if you had any questions. Well, not questions really. There wasn't anything to question. But, well, I didn't know if you had anything to say. You know if you wanted to say something? Some people might, that's all. I just thought I'd bring it up, just in case there ...." *E,* she screamed in her mind, *be quiet. Stop nattering.*

"Well, now that you mention it, I do have a question or perhaps two that could use some answers." Michael's voice was deceptively calm, his body still.

Elizabeth wasn't fooled for a minute that he was using his considerable self-control to appear calm and keep himself still.

A moment later when he did move, he was across the blanket in a thrice, pinning her beneath him. His face contorted in a combination of anger and pain, his hands gripped her upper arms and one of his long thighs was pressed between her legs. This wasn't about loving or even sex. It was something much more and somehow darker.

"What did you do, witch? What did you do to that swan? Cast a spell?" His voice was soft, the thread of steel giving it a menacing quality. "Do you know what it was like to watch that swan come after you, a swan that can break a man's arm with its wings? Hell, Elizabeth, it gave you two fucking feathers." He was yelling now, his face inches from hers, his eyes blazing with emotions: fear, anger, panic.

Elizabeth saw the shimmer of light surround Michael. One part of her mind registered his words knew his fear of anything more than nasty bites was unfounded and felt his emotions. The other part was connected to the source of light, The Lady. She felt Her energy and even though she couldn't see Her, Elizabeth knew all would be all right because The Lady was with her. With a certainty, she knew she was where she needed to be, with someone she needed to be with. Everything was as it should. A soul-deep calmness claimed her and she reached up as best she could and touched his face, ran her fingers over his lips even as he shouted at her. Finally lifting her head she touched her mouth to his, her lips stilling the words.

"This is a sacred space, Michael. Right here. Right now." She spoke in a soft commanding voice. "Hundreds of years before us, people came and set up camp, did ceremony, prayed. All of that was done right here on this exact same spot. I know you can feel the sacredness, Michael. It's why you chose it for us today," her gentle voice feathered across his lips. "And since you know about sacred spaces, Michael, you know what happened this morning." She rested her head once again on the blanket and looked him in the eyes. "If you need me to put it all into words, I will. But, you should understand Michael, I know you already have the answers."

"I want to hear it from your own lips, Elizabeth. I need to know why you are here, and what you want from me." He released her arms, sat back but did not move away.

Elizabeth scooted back so she could sit up, look at his face and into his eyes as she talked.

"It's a fairly long story, Michael, but the highlights are I was raised in the Catholic Church. When The Lady began coming to me in dreams, I remember them from when I was four or five, I saw Her as the Virgin Mary. Except She wasn't the mother of Jesus and I knew that in some way. Looking back I think it was because there was never an aura of sadness about Her and I don't believe the Virgin Mary would not feel sad for the loss of her son, Jesus. And, She never mentioned God or Jesus. She did talk to me about love and the blessings that come from living a life of love, being kind to others, seeing the sacred in all things. There have been times in my life when She's frequently come to me in visions as well as dreams and then there've been times when She hasn't.

"When I finished college She was there and led me to apply for a position with a private adoption agency. I've been with them for ten years. Over seven years ago, She showed me to the group of women I now call my circle sisters. We're like family. Other than a period of one year when one of our members went off to realize a dream and the occasional meeting when someone is gone due to illness or like now, my trip, we come together every other week. We create sacred space wherever we are, whether alone or together.

"In high school The Lady began calling me to come to Ireland. It's taken me more than fifteen years to pull everything together and come. I'm not sure why She called me, what I'm to do here. I only know that I feel a sense of urgency to be here." Elizabeth sat quietly, hands lightly clasped in her lap, and waited. She'd seen a myriad of guarded emotions slip across Michael's face so it was hard to know what he thought of her story.

"Has the call been consistent since high school?" He studied her face as he spoke appearing to look for some sign.

"No, for over a year, The Lady seldom came to me, but in the Spring, just over a year ago, She reappeared in my dreams and came to me in visions that were so strong I felt like I could reach out and touch Her. I don't know what happened, why the connection was weakened. I never felt it was lost, only fragile for that period of time."

"And since you've been here in Ireland? Has She come to you? Have you seen Her?" Again his gaze searched her face, urgency laced his voice.

"I've felt Her, seen the shimmering light that always surrounds Her. She was with me this morning, or perhaps more accurately she was with the swan. I could see Her shimmering light surround the swan." Elizabeth leaned forward, reached out and touched the side of Michael's face with one hand, the other rested lightly on his knee. "I've seen Her light surround you, too, Michael."

Elizabeth rose onto her knees, leaned forward, and gently kissed him. "She is with you as She is with me," she whispered against his lips, her breath mixing with his. "Is that what you want to confirm, Michael? Is that what you want to know?" Her hand slipped from his face to the back of his neck, her other hand joined it. She held him lightly, pressed against him, reveling in his heat and hardness, hearing the catch in his breath. Coaxing his mouth open, she slipped her tongue inside to mate with his as the shimmering light of The Lady surrounded them.

# 5 THE LOVERS

Michael was in a tunnel of light with flames licking, kissing him everywhere. He reached for Elizabeth, for something to hold on to, and knew he was even more lost when he caught her close. All he felt was cool air on his skin, the condom on his penis, the rougher texture of the blanket on his back, the slippery grass beneath his feet, and Elizabeth.

Drawn deep within her, she sucked on his tongue with her mouth and his erection with her feminine muscles. Her hands roamed his body teasing, touching, taunting.

He tried to take control, to rise up and turn her, lay her under him, put himself in control. He didn't manage that. What he did manage was responding to her and that was enough.

She was astride him now, riding him hard, calling him to come with her as her own release neared. "Now, Michael. Please Michael. Come with me now." As she shattered, he surged with his own release.

Sprawled on top of him, their limbs tangled, their bodies pasted together with sweat, he was aware of her pulsing essences and his own throbbing climax. Breathing slowed, heartbeat settled, brain engaged.

She looked like the proverbial cat who'd eaten the canary or lapped the bowl of cream, a combination of perched and sprawled on top of his body, a smug, self-satisfied smile on her face.

As he slipped from her body, he automatically tightened one arm around her waist, and cupped her head to his chest with the other. *I know in my soul, The Lady sent her to me. Something holds me back from telling her about my connection with Her.*

Deep in her eyes he saw the flickers of a fire that would keep him warm the rest of his life. *You're mine!* roared through his mind as his penis roused. *All mine, forever mine.* He pulled her down to him, ravishing her mouth with his kiss, rolling her over on her back, and thrusting into her in a single, fluid motion.

"You're mine, Elizabeth. All mine, forever mine," he murmured in her ear as his hands sought her sensitive places. "Always, for always," he said as her body responded. "As it is now, it will forever be. Know it. Acknowledge it." He raised himself on his elbows pressing himself more fully into her. "Look at me, look at me, Elizabeth. Look at me now," he exhorted.

She opened her eyes, looked deeply into his passionate gaze.

"Say it, Elizabeth. Say it. Say you know you are mine, forever, for always. Say it. Say it. Say it." He was frantic with the need to hear her acknowledge his ownership.

"I am yours, Michael as you are mine, here, and for now." Elizabeth wrapped her legs tighter around his hips, her arms around his neck. She pulled his head down and dragged him into a deep, soul searching kiss as she worked her inner muscles to bring them to release. "For now Michael. I'm yours for now. Come with me to the stars," she implored as she began to shatter.

He flew with her to the heavens; saw her shimmer as she shattered around him, held her as time passed and they returned to earth, to this small piece of land, surrounded by trees, overlooking the River Shannon, this sacred space.

Neither spoke as they dressed, put the crystal goblets in the picnic basket, gathered up the blanket and walked hand in hand to the car. Michael slipped the picnic basket onto the floor of the back seat. Elizabeth dropped the blanket on top. He took her hand and gestured for her to get in, dropping a kiss on her knuckles, and letting go. Rounding the car, he slid behind the wheel. The powerful engine churned to life and they were on the road, speeding back to Limerick. As soon as he'd shifted to driving speed, Michael reached over and took Elizabeth's hand, raising it to his lips, he pressed soft kisses on the back and then on the palm, working his way up to her wrist.

"Ah, luv. I don't think I'll ever get enough of ye." He murmured against her palm. "You're a part of me now, under my skin, in my heart, deep in my soul."

Elizabeth was glad Michael was driving and couldn't see her face. She knew her time in Ireland was limited. If she wasn't careful, very, very careful her heart would be irreparably broken. A shiver passed through her. *It doesn't seem possible I only met Michael yesterday on the plane. It's like I've known*

*him forever.* Elizabeth gazed unseeing at the countryside sliding by. *I'm only in Limerick another day. We'll be going our separate ways then.* Her free hand pressed her stomach as a sharp pain lodged there. She leaned her head against the back of the seat. An awareness of his thumb stroking her palm in sensual circles, creating swirls of pleasure that drifted up her arm and dispersed throughout her body distracted her from contemplating the reality of the limited amount of time she had with him. Her eyes drifted shut. Before her was The Lady.

*I am with you, Elizabeth* the musical voice sounded in her mind. *Enjoy the moment. The future will take care of itself. You were meant to be here in Ireland. You were meant to be with Michael at this time. All is as it should be, Elizabeth. Know that. Trust that your highest good is being served in this moment.* The light surrounding The Lady dimmed. She vanished.

Anchored by Michael's touch, his thumb making lazy circles in her palm or on her inner wrist, Elizabeth felt safe, protected, cherished. Tears sprung up behind her still closed eyelids. She struggled to keep them from falling but they were determined and escaped. Michael's hand left hers. The car slowed and stopped.

She opened her eyes to see Michael leaning over her, concern coloring his handsome features. She reached up and touched his lips, tracing them with her fingertips. Michael gently pushed her hand to the side and kissed her; a tender, tentative kiss that left her lips and roamed her cheeks, drying the tears with its warmth.

"Is it better yet?" His voice drifted across her skin leaving an invisible trail of sensation.

"Yes," she whispered. "I'm okay. A bit emotional right now, but really I'm okay." She wanted to cling to him but knew she needed to keep some distance right now so she kept her hands resting on his arms. He pulled back a ways and looked at her, his blue eyes searching her own.

"If I was home," she began, "I'd be getting ready to spend time with my circle sisters. I'd tell them about you, how I feel when with you … ." She paused, the blush reddening her skin from her toes to her hair, as she took in the incredulous look on his face. "Well, not everything, of course. Well, what I mean is I'd tell them we were lovers." She began to stammer as his eye brows shot up. "I-well, I-what I mean is we talk about things." She pushed him back into his seat. "Oh stop it Michael," her voice huffy. "It isn't as if I'd tell them any details. But honestly, they know me so well, one look at me and they'd know anyway. We really don't have secrets. We all knew the first time Lily and Jackson became lovers. We could just tell. Actually we knew when she fell in love with him and that was long before she realized much less admitted it. That's just how it is with circle sisters."

Elizabeth stopped. The noise she heard was Michael choking back a chuckle. She scowled at him and he burst out laughing. "Ah, Elizabeth, I look forward to meeting these circle sisters of yours. If they're anything like you they must be a sight."

"Actually, I'm one of the meekest, tamest of the lot," she said primly.

Night was beginning to fall. They'd spent more time along the Shannon than Elizabeth had realized. Perhaps it was time to call it a day.

As if reading her thoughts Michael said, "Since we've enough food left in the basket to munch on for supper, I'm suggesting we return to the hotel. I'll order another bottle of wine and you can tell me what you want to see in Limerick and where else you are headed. I can go over your itinerary and make sure you see some of the lesser known sights. That is if you'll allow me to be your tour guide."

Elizabeth looked at his sober mien. "You have the time to show me around?" Her heart flipped at his nod. The Lady's words ... *trust your highest good is being served in this moment.* She hadn't been tired and seeing things last night. It had been The Lady's shimmering light surrounding their reflection in the store window. She was to spend more time with him. Why? She couldn't fathom an answer. A bittersweet tingle tantalized, more time with Michael would mean more pain when they parted.

# 6 Crystal, Castles, and Lily

Michael was a consummate tour guide. The next day he took Elizabeth to little known parts of Limerick where they browsed through shops, had tea at the stroke of five, and a late dinner at an exclusive restaurant along the river.

Her fourth day in Ireland, they rose early, had a hearty Irish breakfast of eggs, sausage, bacon, scones, porridge, and potatoes along with steaming cups of Bewley's Irish Breakfast tea. Michael drank his black; Elizabeth added fresh cream and sugar to hers.

As they checked out of the hotel, headed north to Galway and a surprise destination, Elizabeth noticed Michael talking to the two young men they'd met when checking in. He took something from his pocket and handed it to them. Whatever he said appeared to be humorous as they laughed, glanced at her, and smiled. *It's something more than a tip, why else would they laugh?* Her cheeks redden as it dawned on her where he'd got the condoms they'd been using. By the time he took her elbow, she was spitting mad.

"You asked those young men to get the condoms?" she said in a lowered voice trembling with rage and embarrassment.

They reached the car. Liam stood holding the door open.

"Thank you for staying at Hotel Lir." He bowed as Michael handed Elizabeth into the car and stepped around to the driver's side. "Enjoy the remainder of your time in Ireland," he added as he shut her door and stepped back.

Michael gave a slight nod in acknowledgement, saw a knowing grin cross Liam's face. Resigned to the inevitable, Michael opened his door and got in.

"How could you embarrass me so, Michael?" Elizabeth knew her voice was shrill and she didn't care. Her face animated in anger, her expressive hands slashed the air, she sputtered her fury. "How could you!

They'd stopped at a light and he took the opportunity to grab one of her wildly waving hands and bring it to his lips. "Ah, Elizabeth, I know you're upset and I don't blame you. If it helps, I can promise you it'll never happen again." He turned her hand over and brushed soft kisses into her trembling palm working his way to her wrist. He licked the tender softness of the bend in her elbow.

"Why should I believe you?" she said in a voice laced with irritation and want.

"Because I've bought them by the carton to make sure we never run out. Why, if you open the glove box, you'll see a few in there." A horn sounded behind him and Michael realized the light was green. He shifted gears and started through the intersection before he reached for her hand, held it as if it was fragile. "You caught me by surprise. I never expected to meet you. I admit I was attracted to you but that doesn't mean I thought it would go as far as it has."

He paused and concentrated on maneuvering the car through traffic. Once around the turnabout he added, his voice low, its tone unforgiving. "I'm not some green lad. I'm always in control of myself. Always." His hands gripped the steering wheel so tight the knuckles in his hands turned white. "From the beginning it's been different with you. The urge to be with you is overwhelming."

He glanced her way. She was sitting ramrod straight looking out the side window. Sighing, he covered her hands folded primly in her lap with his left one, his voice full of apology when he spoke. "I'm sorry if you were embarrassed by how I went about getting the condoms."

"Making love with someone, with you," Elizabeth began, her eyes averted. "It's well; with you it's been special." She looked down at her lap, his hand covering hers. "I've never felt this way with anyone else." Her stomach churned. Talking about this was harder than she thought it would be. But it was important for him to know so she took a deep breath and proceeded. "Having sex with someone," she saw his eyebrow arch and the corner of his mouth tighten and hastily added, "or making love with someone is private. While people may know, unless they've watched you, it is their assumption, not certain knowledge."

"Are you ashamed of having been with me?" Michael's voice was deceptively neutral.

"Oh no, Michael. No, not ashamed. Not ashamed at all. Definitely not ashamed. It's just the idea of those two young men knowing that we were," she cleared her throat and lowered her voice, "together, you know, involved."

"Lovers?" Michael queried. "Is that the word you were looking for?"

She cleared her throat again. "Yes, that's the word."

They rode in silence for several minutes. Elizabeth tried to focus on the scenery flowing by the window but there was one more thing she needed to say, to put this issue behind her. "What we have together is beyond my ability to put into words. I'm not ashamed of, of our being lovers." She took a deep breath struggling for words. "I don't want to lose; that is I'll be leaving in a few weeks and you, you have a life here. Whatever time we have now, I don't want to lose it."

Michael let her words sink in relieved she knew what they had was special. What she didn't know was she was his forever and always. Then there was The Lady. What did She have to do with it all?

Time was what he needed. Time for Elizabeth to understand this is where she belonged. Time for her to see, to experience what their future held.

For now, he was her tour guide and with that in mind he told her about Galway, the first stop on today's trip.

"Hi there, Mick," was a familiar salutation every place they stopped as they traveled north. The view of stone-hedged fields dotted with sheep was the backdrop to her musings. *Why is man with an apparently successful stud farm and racing stable spending his time showing me around?* It wasn't a complaint, just a shadow question that from time to time shifted into the light.

His hand sought hers, held it loosely, his thumb stroked her palm, her eyes drifted closed. *The Lady said I am where I'm meant to be.* She turned her hand, laced her fingers with his, brought their joined hands to her lips, and brushed a kiss over his knuckles. A smile tugged the corners of her mouth. *She also said to enjoy the moment. I will cherish this time with him before I go home.*

Late in the afternoon, they arrived at the Galway Crystal Factory. Michael's eyes raked her body as, once out of the car, she stretched. He claimed her elbow and escorted her inside.

"Hi there, Mick," the young clerk said when they entered. He immediately went to a door behind the counter. Opening it, he'd called in "Mick Murphy's here, sir." Moments later the manager came out. A hearty slap on the back for Mick and a gracious welcome for her had started a fantastic visit. Treated like royalty, she'd been given a private tour, fascinated to watch master craftsmen carve intricate designs in glass.

"Ohh, Michael, it's all so lovely. I can't seem to make up my mind," she said and sighed. Holding the goblets, glasses, and vases up to the light, she oohhed and aahhed as the light refracted rainbows around the room. No high-pitched tinkling from the bell, a clear moderate to deep tone reverberated through the room and echoed in her bones.

"Do you want it to be useful or decorative?" Michael asked her in an attempt to help her decide.

"Anything from here would be decorative and what I'm looking at would be useful also," she turned back to the display on the counter and smiled at the manager who was personally waiting on them. "I'm so sorry to be in such a dither about this, Mr. O'Connell."

"That's all right Ms. Elliott. Happens all the time," he smiled indulgently at her and winked at Michael. "Just take your time. Remember, we can ship it home for you so you don't need to worry about that."

"I know. That will be such a help, too." She turned to Michael standing patiently by her side. "You see," she gestured to the display on the counter, "the goblets or glasses can be used in ceremony or even for a meal. The vases can be used on our altars or to hold flowers from Sophia's garden. And the bells? Well, we use bells to cleanse space because the sound from the bells moves the air and relieves a place of any stagnation." She leaned against his arm and sighed. "Since I can't seem to make up my mind, maybe I'm not supposed to get anything here."

Mr. O'Connell interjected, "Now Ms. Elliott, you've certainly picked some fine pieces of crystal here. If I might suggest, we have a special on the goblets and bells right now. Perhaps, that information will assist you in making a decision?" He wrote some figures on a piece of paper for Elizabeth to view.

"Oh, my, yes. That certainly narrows things a bit." She stood lost in thought, her mind imaging her circle sisters opening the gift. "The goblets," she said at last. "Yes, I think the goblets will be the best." That decision made, she turned her face to gaze at Michael. "You've been very patient with my dithering. Thank you," she rose on her tip toes to brush her lips against his.

Michael's arm wound around her waist bringing her closer to his side as he leaned over and whispered, "That's only a down payment on my full bill for this experience." Her response was a laugh as she twirled out of his arms and across the display room. Seeing that she was now engaged in an animated conversation with the young sales clerk and other customers, he leaned over the counter to Mr. O'Connell, "James, I think I'll take one of those bells."

"Of course, Mick, in one of our display boxes, I'd imagine."

"Right you are, James," Michael said drawing the money from his wallet and handing it to the other man. "And, be discreet." With that Michael walked over to join Elizabeth.

That night they stayed at the Ashford Castle on Loch Corrib. After a gourmet dinner, they savored an Irish Coffee nightcap in the castle's study which was now a lounge.

Their room was in the front of the castle with a view of the river. Elizabeth leaned on the marble windowsill of one massive windows and watched two swans and a pair of goslings gliding on the water. *Swan energy is following me.* On either side of the slowly flowing waterway were expansive well-manicured lawns, old gnarled trees and beds abounding with colorful flowers. She thought they were impatiens and wished Sophia was there to identify everything for her.

"Michael?" she called over her shoulder. "Do you know what the flowers are along the walks toward the river?"

"Can't say that I do," he said coming to stand next to her. "Maybe impatiens?"

"That's what I thought." She leaned back against his broad chest and sighed as his arms came around her waist, his chin resting on the top of her head.

"You seem very content right now."

His breath stirred her hair and his arousal pressed against her back. "I am." She put her hands over his and held him close. "Very content."

"You do remember that you owe me from the Galway Crystal Shoppe," Michael said, his voice husky.

"Actually, I'm a bit hazy on that. Why do I owe you anything? I had planned on stopping at the Waterford Crystal Factory," she murmured seductively.

Michael turned her in his arms. "Without me, you'd never known about the Galway Crystal Shoppe or had the private tour. So, what do you think it's worth?"

"Well, I did give you a kiss. Perhaps one more would be enough?" She slid her arms up his chest and around his neck.

"Never," he growled as he pulled her tight against him. "One kiss will never be enough."

The next morning they sat down to another magnificent Irish breakfast. Elizabeth had taken a bite of one of the best scones she'd ever eaten when she heard a familiar voice. Turning she spied Lily and Jackson sitting down at a table across the room. While she debated whether to approach the newly-weds or not, she heard her name called out. Lily, a welcoming smile on her face, her hands outstretched, started toward them. Jackson followed close behind.

Wrapped in Lily's embrace, tension eased, and Elizabeth was connected to home.

"I didn't know you'd be here," Lily exclaimed turning to cast a blinding smile over her shoulder at her new husband. "Did you know E would be here, Jackson?"

"No," her husband said eyeing the man standing possessively by. As the two women continued to hug and talk, Jackson stuck out his hand. "Jackson Montgomery," he said, his voice formal, his brow arching in a question.

"Michael Murphy," Michael returned, shaking the offered hand.

"You'd think these two haven't seen each other in months. Believe it or not, they were together less than a week ago at our wedding." Jackson grinned at his new wife. "Lily my love." he laid his hand on her shoulder.

"Yes," she turned and smiled. "Can you believe it, Jackson? Elizabeth is here. The Goddess is good." Lily pivoted back to her friend. She hadn't missed the young man standing beside Elizabeth and now looked at her friend, an eyebrow raised.

Blushing, Elizabeth took Michael's hand and formally introduced him to Lily and Jackson. "He's been wonderful, taking time to show me some of the country." Elizabeth's hope her friend wouldn't sense the truth of her relationship with Michael was immediately dashed with one look at Lily and the glint in her eye. A soft rosy pink flooded her cheeks and she averted her eyes.

"Would you care to join us?" Michael said, deciding to make the best of things. He could stand here listening to Elizabeth and her friend talk and make idle conversation with the husband, or invite them to sit down. Mentally he rearranged the plan for the day which had been to head out after breakfast. *Time to play it by ear.*

An easy conversation with Jackson was a pleasant surprise. They'd quickly dispensed with the formal "Mr." and were on a first-name basis. Leaving the women to chat, they went to the buffet and loaded their plates. Michael explained the ingredients in the more traditional Irish fare such as blood and black sausages.

Breakfast eaten, the two couples strolled the grounds, the women in front, the men trailing behind. Michael found himself subjected to an inquisition of sorts as Jackson questioned him. The easiness gone, his answers were short and as uninformative as he could make them without being rude.

It struck a nerve that, for some reason, Jackson believed he had the right to pass judgment on him and his suitability for Elizabeth. The only scrutiny he had to pass was Elizabeth's. He inwardly scowled. His feelings for Elizabeth ran deep and included the unfamiliar need to possess and protect.

He looked again at the two women. Lily glowed and there was a look on Jackson's face when he looked at his wife, and he did that almost continuously, that telegraphed his love for her. Was he jealous? Jealous of a newly married man obviously in love with his wife? Jealous of the commitment they shared?

Michael observed the two women, arms linked, amble along the path through the formal gardens. Their heads together, Lily's blond hair contrasted with Elizabeth black. Both were on the petite side and blue-eyed. Their connection to each other was obvious as they talked non-stop. *I see what Elizabeth meant when she said they just know things about each other.* Jackson's inquisition seemed to be over. *It can't hurt to get better acquainted.* To that end he started up a conversation about the sights to see in the area.

They took their lunch on an outside terrace, conversation easy between the four of them. While he'd always got along with people, Michael was surprised that in such a short time, he and Jackson were genuinely comfortable and friendly with each other.

The not-so-subtle interrogation and the suggestions on what to see and do in the area over, they easily found topics of common interest to keep them occupied while the two women talked. Sometime after lunch, Jackson claimed jet lag and after a round of hugs and good-byes, he ushered Lily off to their room.

The day half gone, Michael modified their plans although kept the part about moving on. They drove north and west, stopping at Kylemore Abby and touring the castle's rooms. Strolling the grounds, Elizabeth drew him off the well-worn path to an old well behind the kitchen garden. Another sacred place she'd found because she was sensitive to the energies. They spent some time sitting on the moss-covered ground beside crumbling walls of the old spring. If pressed, he'd admit the spiritual energy calmed and soothed. She didn't press.

They spent two nights at a bed and breakfast in the seaside town of Clifton where she had reservations. Their en suite room was spotless but small. The first night they dined at a local tavern where she tried the local fish fried in a Guinness beer batter.

Over the next two days they toured a peat bog, took in the local sights, walked the cliffs, and talked about how the Great Famine was a loss to Ireland but a boon to the United States. The third day they drove north to Sligo just because Elizabeth wanted to see a town with that name. Several times they stopped along the roadside so she could take pictures of the sheep.

The last time, Elizabeth giggled as she took pictures of sheep crowded around an empty phone booth. This time the sheep were standing next to a waterfall of fuchsia blossoms and she like the contrast of the red fuchsia and the grey of the sheep. He had limits though and he'd adamantly refused to allow her to bring wisps of smelly wool in his car.

"Did you hear them, Michael?" she chattered excitedly as she climbed back in the car. "They talked to me."

"People will think you're touched in the head if you keep talking like that." He shook his head, a fond smile on his face. He loved looking at her, so excited at the ordinary things, flowers on the side of the road, the shadows of clouds moving across the fields, the fields themselves with the stone fences, and then there were the sheep and cows. He'd stopped at least a dozen times in the last two days so she could take pictures of the beasts and "talk" to them.

This part of their travels was nearing an end. They'd spend the night in Galway and tomorrow head south - toward The Manor near Kinslow. He'd spent a lot of time thinking about how to handle things once they got closer. Maybe Paddy would help. They'd been friends since childhood, rivals too, but the friendship was deeper.

There was a risk he'd lose her when she found out about his relationship with The Lady. *Maybe with more time together it won't matter so much.*

It was a week ago they'd met on the trans-Atlantic flight, his life forever altered. *She's more important to me than my horses.* How did he know that? It was the middle of the season and he still wasn't home from the Triple Crown races in America. Twice a day he called and checked in with his head groom but this—this wasn't like him. *I haven't made it to where I am in the racing world by taking a week off in the middle of the season. Time to get back to it.*

The question was how,

and keep Elizabeth by his side,

and keep her from finding out about The Lady.

The car door opened jigging him out of his musing. Just seeing Elizabeth slide into her seat, her face infused with such happiness, such joy, his own mood lifted from its somber state and he smiled.

"Thank you, Michael, you're a prince among men." A wide grin on her face, she shifted closer, reached over, pulled him to her and kissed him. Kissed him with such passion he clutched the steering wheel for grounding and to keep from imploding. "Thank you so very much, Michael," she whispered against his lips. "You've made this trip more than I ever dreamt it could be. For that I'll always be grateful." Another kiss – this one a long, lingering meeting of lips and tongue. When she pulled away, the loss of her closeness rumbled deep inside like thunder. He wanted, wanted her with an urgency that struck like lighting. Control—he struggled to gain some semblance of control.

His knuckles white from griping the steering wheel, he focused on breathing through his mouth, until his grasp relaxed, and his ardor subsided. A glance at their surroundings and his desire changed to chagrin. What was he thinking? To take her in his car on the side of a public road or against the rock wall? Insanity – sheer insanity.

Opening his car door, he got out, pushing it closed as he walked to the back of the car. He stretched his arms high and took a deep breath before swinging them wide and then back as if hugging himself. "I'm in control. I can keep my hands off of her. I can do this," he muttered to himself as he now did a couple of deep knee bends. Breathing deeply, he continued to exert himself physically for a few more minutes feeling his body calm.

The next four days passed in a whirlwind of sights, sounds, and experiences. Michael took Elizabeth to the Cliffs of Mohr, Tralee, and around the Ring of Kerry. Dusk the fourth day, they pulled into the parking lot of a pub in the small town of Kinslow an hour or so from Killarney.

The Winner's Circle, fashioned of local stone, with a bright red door flanked on each side by two sets of mullioned windows, was a lively place. The door and windows were wide-open to the mild July evening and the sounds of voices and laughter spilled out. As they crossed the threshold, she saw wood tables, chairs, and benches burnished to a low shine that reflected the lights overhead. Along the back wall was the bar, the display of bottles reflected in the mirror, the brass and ceramic taps of Guinness stood proud. The air was redolent of the smell of fresh baked bread and Elizabeth's mouth watered.

While she was no longer surprised that Michael was greeted almost everywhere they went, the atmosphere here was different. Unlike in other places, everyone here was paying particular attention to her. He introduced her in a different manner she couldn't quite put her finger on. And, while he seemed to know everyone, he led her to a table in the corner where their view of the door was unobstructed. Her curiosity was pricked.

"I'd like to freshen up," she'd said and he'd given her directions. Obviously he knew this place.

Michael motioned Peter O'Leary, the barman over, and ordered them each a Guinness.

"Have someone take our bags upstairs," he said and handed the keys to his car over to the now outstretched hand before him. "She'll be staying here and I expect she'll be taken care of properly."

"Not a problem, boss." Peter quipped and winked.

"And, none of that "boss" stuff. She doesn't know I own this place."

"What does she know?"

"Only that I have a stud farm nearby and race horse. That's how I want it for now, understand?"

"Not really, but if that's how you want to play it." Peter shrugged, backed away from the table, and called a lad of about sixteen over. He quietly spoke to the young man, handed him the keys, and went back to his job of listening to the customers, bantering with the regulars, and keeping the drinks flowing.

# Kinslow and The Dance

"Gotta go," Michael whispered his voice husky.

Elizabeth felt his hands drift over her hip as she roused. "Oh," she groaned making a move to toss back the covers and get up.

"Not you. Stay and sleep. I'll be back at eleven and we'll have lunch."

Elizabeth reached up and pulled his head down for a sleepy kiss before rolling over. She heard the door click shut and that was all until, as was her habit, she woke at seven. Following her old morning routine, she took a quick shower and dressed.

During her morning prayers at the altar she'd set up on the window sill, she asked for guidance about whether she was to stay here for a few days or continue on her journey. While she and Michael had no spoken agreement and she could leave at any time, it felt right to be here in the bustling little town where The Lady's energy was strong. In the quiet moment at the end of her prayers, The Lady appeared. Her message? She was where she needed to be - in the moment with Michael.

What was different from her morning routine at home was going downstairs to have breakfast with Peter; a breakfast she didn't cook; a breakfast she didn't clean up after. It was really quite decadent to have potatoes, meat, eggs, scones, tea and no dishes to do once she'd finished. No cooking, cleaning up, or housework were additional gifts when on vacation.

Curiosity to see more of the town, followed fulfillment of her first task, getting her film developed. She was old-fashioned not yet fully into the digital age. There was something about the look and feel of real photographs, reliving her adventures when she made albums she wasn't ready to give up.

Walking around town, she looked in all the shops and got a feel for the place. She knew she'd be here at least two days because that was how long it would take to get her pictures back. Kinslow was such a friendly, welcoming town she knew she'd enjoy her stay. Every shopkeeper chatted with her, asked how long she'd be staying, told her about things to do and sights to see. The Dance outside of town was now at the top of her list.

Michael was waiting when she arrived back at the pub a few minutes after eleven. He turned when Peter call out to her as she came in the door. His eyes followed her every move as she made her way to the where he stood at the bar. A shiver shuddered through her and the rest of the room, the rest of the people disappeared from her awareness. All she could see was Michael bathed in shimmering light.

That afternoon after Michael returned to his stables, she finished her exploration of Kinslow. She'd been in every shop and wandered the residential streets looking at the neat cottages with their gaily colored flower gardens and Irish lace curtains. The fresh air, full with the profusion of scents from those very same gardens, surrounded her. Friendly people called out a few words of welcome as she ambled by.

While she'd expected the shop keepers to be friendly, these women were working in their yards, hanging out wash, or sitting on their porches with a glass of lemonade or what looked like tea. By the time she returned to the pub with another roll of film from her ramblings, she'd become thoroughly enchanted with the town.

As he's told her he would, Michael returned around five. Dinner in the cozy apartment tasted delicious. Another kind of delicious? Passion that overtook them on the couch before they made it to the bed. In the dark before dawn, Michael gathered her close and made slow, sweet love to her before tucking the covers around her, showering, and leaving.

Her second day in Kinslow started as had her first, only this time after breakfast Elizabeth walked down a road past fields of grain, breathing deeply and enjoying the fresh air. She was entranced by more grazing sheep and found herself stopping and talking to them for minutes at a time. For their part, the sheep watched her, not scurrying away and some even approaching.

Lunch with Michael then another stroll along another road after he went back to the stables, taking more pictures of the countryside, the green rolling hills, the fields of waving grass, the bright blue sky above. Perched on a rock wall, she reveled in the reality there was nothing for her to do except be in this time and space, be in the now. And the now had no future, no past, only the present.

A routine developed. Breakfast with Peter after a shower, dressing, and morning prayers; lunch with Michael in the pub;

dinner in the apartment above, catching up on each other's day while the music from the small band seeped through the floor boards, making love to the beat, and falling asleep in each other's arms.

On this third day, after she picked up her pictures, Elizabeth sat at the table in front of the window, her Journal open and a second Journal to her left. One Journal was about where she was, what she was doing, her spiritual connection to the people and land, and thoughts about The Lady and The Sacred Grove. The second Journal was about her growing feelings for Michael. On some level she knew he withheld a piece of himself, had a secret he wasn't sharing. Without anyone from The Circle to talk to, she used this second Journal and the depth of their connection to sort things out.

Of course she was curious about what his stud farm and racing stables looked like but she was also aware of her need to keep some distance. She would be returning to Fremont, to The Circle. In some ways the less she knew about Michael's life the better.

That evening while looking at her pictures, Michael informed her in a solemn tone he was psychic.

Initially surprised, she sensed something "off". "Oh, really?"

Michael, with drama in his movements, turned the remaining pictures image side down. "Sheep," he intoned and with a sweeping gesture turned the picture over.

"Sheep," he intoned again, turning a picture of a sheep over.

"I swear I'll not take another picture of sheep as long as I'm here," she vowed between gales of laughter when he'd turned over yet another photo of the wooly beasts.

Another fit of mirth engulfed her when Michael arched an eyebrow, a skeptical mien on his face. When he pulled her onto his lap, her laughter was effectively doused as he proceeded to banish all thoughts of sheep from her mind.

Finding the dance or stone circle Peter and a few other people had mentioned was her focus on her fourth day. She'd waited until today because Michael had work to do with his horses and wouldn't be joining her for lunch. No time constraints made it a perfect day to explore the ancient sacred space. With her Journal, camera, and bottle of water tucked in her tote, she set off. Walking through town, she stopped and asked one of the children for directions to the stone circle.

"The dance, it is ye want?" he'd asked her with large green eyes and carroty hair.

"Yes, the dance, the stone circle. Which way is it?"

"Just keep going on this road. You're already going in the right direction. Just keep going along there," he said pointing down the road she was on.

"Thank you." Smiling at the young boy, she gave a quick wave and started out at a brisk walk until she passed the last of the houses when she slowed her pace. As she strolled alongside the road, Elizabeth stopped for brief periods and search with her mind for the energy she believed would signal she'd found the ancient sacred space.

An hour passed before the invisible pull of sacred energy thrummed through her body. She scanned the road and fields on either side but saw nothing. The tug seemed more intense to her right. Following her instincts, Elizabeth crossed the verge, clamored over the stone wall, strode off across the field, and up the slope. At the top of the rise, she looked down and saw what she was looking for - the dance.

As she looked down at the stone circle a vision of people coming from all four directions, dressed in ceremonial gowns and capes, carrying baskets of fruit, nuts, grains, flowers and jugs of water, wine and ale was so real she shook herself to dispel it.

For several minutes she sat in the grass on the rise, taking in the scene before her, letting the images come. Time morphed and the past shifted to the present when she made her way down to the stone circle.

Walking around the outer stones, taking in the feel of the place, she visualized how it once had been: all the stones upright, with lintels over the entrances from the north, south, east and west. A stone slab on the grass in the middle: the altar.

From where the sun stood in the sky, Elizabeth calculated she entered the dance through the West gate, coming out of the void into this sacred space. As she approached the altar, the humming grew louder until it was all she heard. She stood before this sacred center stone, her arms rising as energy and sound swirled around her.

"Goddess, the divine feminine, spirits of this sacred place. I come to you offering myself to serve you in this place this day. I stand before you awaiting your instruction."

Elizabeth turned toward the sun. Her arms still upraised her head back, her eyes closed. The light of the sun bathed her, the energy of the dance permeated every cell. A message came to her. Lowering her arms, she crossed them over her chest and bent her head. "To the best of my ability, I will do as you wish."

Righting things was her task. Pieces of litter that had blown into the dance were quickly picked up and tucked into the pocket of her skirt. Weeding took longer. She knelt around each stone and pulled the long pieces of grass away. Her ball-point pen helped dig out recalcitrant roots. A corner of her skirt served as a cloth so she could scrub some scribbling away. The last of her drinking water was used to wash the stone altar.

Even with the improvements from her labor, more needed to be done. She returned to the road to gather flowers, pick a few berries, and find four small smooth stones. Back in the circle, she placed her bounty on the altar placing the stones on each corner and the flowers and berries in the center.

*Much better.* Elizabeth turned slowly seeing the majesty of the place. *I could come back tomorrow with tools and make things look even better.* She smiled and her face glowed. *I know in my soul the reason I was called to Ireland by The Lady has something to do with sacred spaces.* She looked around the dance, her eyes coming to rest on the altar. *How wonderful to be able to have my own private ceremony in this ancient sacred space.*

Elizabeth stood, her heels touching the altar, facing East. She raised her arms in prayer, felt the warmth of Grandfather Sun envelop her body, and golden yellow energy swirl behind her closed eyes.

"Spirits of this place. Spirits of the East. Hear my prayer. May you look upon your place on this land and see the possibilities of sending forth the energy of new beginnings to the world." The golden yellow color deepened until it was a burnished old gold. "Many people in the world need the energy of hope to help them move forward with their lives. Hope good things will come to them; hope they will be okay; hope they have the strength to survive, to find the gifts in pain."

Her arms dropped to her side. Elizabeth remained standing, head back, eyes closed, as the burnished old gold color faded to golden yellow and faded yet again to a pale yellow. When the light behind her eyes was almost clear, she opened them, and blinked a few times to focus.

Because it was her tradition, she turned to her right, circled the center stone, and stopped when she was in the South. She positioned her feet, heels touching the altar, facing South, arms raised in prayer, eyes closed. This time the energy, the color swirling behind her eyes, was a rose red.

"Spirits of this place. Spirits of the South. Hear my prayer. May you look upon your place on this land and see the possibility of sending the energy of abundance throughout the world." The rose red deepened and became more vibrant, fiery, with flickering flames replacing the swirls. "Many people in the world need the energy of abundance, to see the world as having enough for everyone, to see the difference between what is needed and what is wanted, to know with a certainty you will always bestow your bounty wherever you are honored."

Once again her arms dropped to her side. She remained standing, head back, eyes closed as the vibrant fiery red faded, the flickering flames turning to soft swirls of rose red and then fading yet again to a pale pink. When the light behind her eyes was almost clear, she opened them and blinked a few times to focus.

Circling the altar stone, she stopped when in the West. Her heels touching the altar, she faced West, arms raised in prayer, eyes closed. This time the energy, the color swirling behind her eyes, was the turquoise blue of a tropical sea.

"Spirits of this place. Spirits of the West. Hear my prayer. May you look upon your place on this land and see the possibility of sending the energy of contemplation throughout the world." The turquoise blue shifted and waves of colors surged, deepening, darkening until reaching the color of the night sky. "Many people in the world need the energy of contemplation, time to reflect, to consider, to process all that is in their life at this time. To know the seasons of life, whether in each day, in each moon cycle or in each year, provide the time to contemplate, to discover the secrets of life."

Arms at her side, Elizabeth remained standing, head back, eyes closed as the midnight blue ebbed, the waves shifting colors until the clear turquoise blue dominated. A moment later the color faded yet again to a pale blue. When the light behind her eyes was almost clear, she opened them, blinking a few times to focus.

Circling the altar, she stopped in the North, her heels yet again touching the altar stone. Her arms raised in prayer, her eyes closed, the energy, the color of this direction swirled and she was enclosed in a brilliant white.

"Spirits of this place. Spirits of the North. Hear my prayer. May you look upon your place on this land and see the possibility of sending the energy of remembering throughout the world." Pale grey shadows infused the swirling white. "Many people in the world need the energy of remembering, to connect with their ancestors, to remember the past and bring those lessons forward to the present, to have the voices of wisdom echoing in their minds when problems arise, when conflict appears in their lives."

When the prayer ended her arms dropped to her side. She remained standing, head back, eyes closed as the swirling white stopped and then faded to nothing. This time the light behind her eyes became clear and she opened them seeing the aura of the stones and surrounding area.

Her prayers having activated the stone circle, Elizabeth continued with her Ceremony. She turned to her right, circling the stone altar three times honoring the phases of the Devine Feminine, Maiden, Mother, Crone. On her fourth circuit she stopped and bowed at each gate in honor of the four directions.

"Oh my, this is spectacular," she breathed. "I feel so alive." The energy in the dance shifted, the humming she hadn't heard while in prayer was noticeable, and a beat joined the sound. Her feet moved. A joyous rapture claimed her and she danced, danced with abandon, danced with energy flowing rampant throughout her body.

So caught up in the moment, Elizabeth danced and danced. Even when she grew hot, tired, and thirsty, she danced. She collapsed in the cool, sweet grass, one arm across the altar, looked after by Grandfather Sun with the spirits of the place surrounding her.

Colin, the young lad who worked in the pub, found Michael about three in the afternoon. The short message: *Elizabeth isn't back from her morning walk. A search party is out looking for her.*

Peter had waited to alert him because he expected her to walk through the door any moment.

Out in the far paddock, working with his best stallion, Brian Boru or B.B. for short, when he got the word Michael kicked B.B. in the side and leaning over the big black's neck, galloped for town.

First stop: the pub and checking in with a sober Peter.

"No, she isn't back yet. No, no one has any idea where she is," he reported.

Michael took the steps to the apartment two at a time. He stood in front of her altar, closed his eyes, calmed his racing heart, and concentrated on her. There was a definite energy but he couldn't tell if it came from her altar or directly from her. He charged down the stairs checking to see if the energy was different. It wasn't.

*Find her, Michael.*

Dashing back up the stairs, he grabbed a bottle of water from the refrigerator and snatched a blanket from the bed. Instincts roaring, he tore down the stairs and out to where B.B. stood, his reins held by one of the local boys. "I'm heading out O'Leary's road," he called out to Peter as he galloped off.

Once out of town, Michael slowed and concentrated on Elizabeth. *Where are ye, luv? Let me know where ye are.* He cantered now and a couple of miles passed by before he heard the hum and felt the energy. Reining B.B. to a halt, he looked around and got his bearings.

"Hell," he muttered as he realized the old dance, the stone circle, was just over the rise. Michael tied the stallion to a bush, vaulted the dry stacked stone wall, and jogged up the rise. His heart leapt in his throat at the sight before him.

Elizabeth lying on her back, the coal black of her hair contrasting with the brilliant green of the grass and the grey of the lichen-spotted stone. From this distance he couldn't see if she was breathing, but she wasn't moving. Fear ripped through him, froze him to the spot.

One second he was still as a statue, the next he was racing down the hill, crossing through the nearest space in the stones to kneel by her side. *Thank God she's breathing.* His fingers feathered her neck, finding her pulse beating strongly. A sheen of perspiration covered her face; her damp blouse and skirt clung to her body.

"Elizabeth, Elizabeth," he croaked, his own voice hoarse. "Elizabeth," his voice stronger now, he gently shook her shoulders. "Elizabeth. Wake up. It's me, Michael. Wake up. Wake up, Elizabeth." His voice held an edge of panic as he watched her intently for any sign of response.

Eye lashes fluttered. She stirred.

"Michael? Is that you?" her slurred voice sounded like she'd been drugged.

"Elizabeth, are you hurt?" Michael leaned over her, his fingers gently checking her limbs and joints.

"I don't think so," her raspy voice was stronger. "I'm very thirsty, though."

Michael carefully eased one arm under her shoulders and the other beneath her legs. "Does it hurt when I do this, luv?"

"No."

Picking her up, Michael started to carry her out of the dance. As he crossed through the circle of stones, he saw Paddy start down the rise.

"Bring me water and the blanket, Paddy. They're with B.B," he hollered to his friend. With Elizabeth in his arms, Michael turned back to stare at the dance. It made sense it was Elizabeth who'd recently taken care of it: tidied up the place, set up the altar with berries, flowers and smooth stones on the corners.

What didn't make sense? The grass within the circle was crushed as if hundreds of feet had trampled it. He looked down at Elizabeth's bare feet just showing below the hem of her skirt. They were stained green. "Where're your shoes, luv?" he whispered.

Paddy made his way down the rise, water and blanket in hand.

Elizabeth still in his arms, Michael started up the slope towards Paddy. "How'd you know to find me here?"

"One of the lads said that "the new lady" asked which way the dance was. Here, let's get her wrapped up in the blanket," Paddy said shaking the blanket out and holding it up. "You can trust me for the moment it'll take to wrap her up in this, you know." He cocked his head, a knowing smile on his face.

Michael didn't respond to the gentle teasing of his old friend, he just put Elizabeth in Paddy's outstretched arms, folded the blanket around her and then took her back. Paddy reached into his pocket and drew out the water bottle, opening the cap, he held it to her lips and let a bit of the cool liquid dribble on her mouth. Like a little bird waiting for food from its parents, Elizabeth's mouth opened, and her tongue licked the cool water from her lips. Michael shifted her so she was more upright and Paddy gave her another small drink.

"Her tote's back there. See if you can find her shoes, will you Paddy?" Michael asked. The worry for Elizabeth plain on his face, he added, "I need to get her back home."

Paddy started walking back up the rise. "I'll see to things here, Mick. You just take care of her. Come, I'll walk with you to B.B. and help you get settled."

Paddy took Elizabeth from Michael for the few seconds it took while he mounted. Gently lifting her into Michael's outstretched arms, he admonished, "Off with you. I'll check things out here and then come along to see how she's doing."

"Thanks," Michael choked out as he swung the stallion around and rode off to town. "You'd better be okay, Elizabeth," he warned softly as they rode. "You'll face my wrath if you've hurt yourself this day." He kissed the top of her head and held her close.

"Michael? Am I on a horse?" Elizabeth's voice held a hint of anxiety. "Michael? What's going on? Where am I? What happened?" She struggled in the binding blanket trying to get her arms free.

"Elizabeth, dear God, I was so worried," Michael pulled his horse to a halt, tipped up her chin and kissed her soundly. "Don't you ever worry me like that again," he scolded. He kissed her forehead, nestling her head under his chin. "You know they have a search party out for you?"

"A search party? What for? I'm okay. Please let me out of this blanket. Michael?"

"I'm not letting you loose yet, young lady," his voice was stern, as if lecturing a recalcitrant charge. "You have no idea how terrified I was. You must promise me, Elizabeth. Never do anything like that again. I forbid it, actually."

She smiled and snuggled close. "You forbid me, Michael?" she said a smile in her voice. "Really, how very daring of you." She laughed and wriggled, tipping her head up, kissing his neck, just below his ear as that was as far as she could reach.

"Behave yourself, Elizabeth. We're here now." Michael's tone was gruff, another sign of his relief. He loosened the blanket enough that he could help Elizabeth slide off B.B. He dismounted and handed the reins to Peter who'd come out of the pub when he'd heard the news they'd been spotted. "Take care of him for me," Michael said before he tightened the blanket around her shoulders, swept her into his arms, and strode to the side stairs leading up to the apartment.

"Not one word, Elizabeth. Not one word until we're inside," he warned.

# 8   THE NECKLACE

At the top of the stairs, Michael set Elizabeth on her feet, still battling the utter panic he'd felt when he'd found her crumpled in the dance. With a purposeful intensity, he loomed over her, trapping her between his body and the door. His hand shook as he reached behind her and, opening the door, herded her into the apartment. A modicum of tension eased as the door clicked shut.

"Never again, Elizabeth, never again," he said his face a fierce scowl; his words a growl; He had to touch her again, to know she was all right. His body brushed hers. She didn't move. He reached out, pulled her tight against him. His left arm slipped around her waist, his hand dipping to cup her buttocks, his right slid up her back to her shoulder, his fingers whispered against her neck, her throat. Her arms moved up his chest and wrapped around his neck, one leg snaked around his ankle. He tilted her chin up until her eyes were focused on his face. Connected, locked in an embrace as much through their eyes as through their bodies.

A knock on the door startled them. His arm still around Elizabeth, Michael turned and opened the door to see Paddy standing there, Elizabeth's tote and shoes in one hand, something else in the other.

Paddy handed Michael her tote as he stepped past him and stood before Elizabeth, who shivered and grew paler. "Here're your shoes." He held them out to her. Paddy reached out and put his hand on her shoulder. Tremors racked her. Keeping his hand on her, he held out what looked like a necklace. "I found this, too. Is it yours?"

"I'm so cold." Elizabeth hugged herself looking at Paddy. "Why am I so cold?" her fading voice shook.

Paddy's voice was gentle. "Are these your shoes, Elizabeth?" He moved them in front of her face again.

Elizabeth shook her head trying to clear the fog that was clouding her mind. "Yes, yes, they are."

"What about the necklace?"

"No, I've not seen it before," she whispered and swayed on her feet.

Michael had already moved to stand behind her when Paddy'd started questioning her. When Elizabeth swayed, he pulled her back against his chest. "Where'd you find it?"

"Under her shoes. When I picked them up, I saw a flash, glanced down, and there it was." Paddy held up the necklace for Michael and Elizabeth to see. The pendant was round, about two inches in diameter. In the center was a large cabochon of gold citrine. Two holes were punched at one side and a strand of links made up a chain. Around the outer edge, varying designs, faded with time and wear, were hammered into the metal. Four cabochons, slightly smaller than the gold citrine, were set at the top, bottom, and sides. One appeared to be garnet, another hematite, the other two different colors of calcite. All these stones were native to the British Isles and would have been used in trade, Michael's mind raced with thoughts as he held Elizabeth close.

"Over the years hundreds if not thousands of people have been to that dance." It was Paddy talking again. He held the necklace out to her. "It's meant to be yours, Elizabeth. I know that as sure as I know the sun comes up in the East. This is yours."

Michael thanked God he already had a hold of her when she sagged against him. Swinging her up in his arms he took the few steps to a chair. He sat down, holding Elizabeth on his lap, calling to her to look at him, talk to him. She was in the same condition as when he found her at the dance. If he was right, she was susceptible to the energy of the ancient sacred places and that worried him. While she was drawn to naturally occurring sacred places and created her own whenever possible, he worried she didn't have the strength and didn't know how to handle the old energy.

He rubbed her back and arms and continued talking to her, urging her to open her eyes, look at him, come back to him. It seemed to take forever before she began to stir and snuggle closer to him. "Elizabeth, open your eyes. Let me see those beautiful blue eyes, Elizabeth." He brushed his hand over her forehead and cheek to her chin. "Look at me, luv," there was urgency in his voice. "Now, Elizabeth, open your eyes. Now," he ordered.

Wrapped in Michael's arms, the heat from his body banishing the cold from hers, Elizabeth opened her eyes, looked deeply into his and smiled. When she tried to sit up her smile turned to a frown. She wiggled to get upright.

"Wh - wha - what happened? Michael? What happened? One minute you were holding me and then I got so cold and, and couldn't think." Her confused looked switched from Michael to Paddy. "Wha - What ha – ha - happened to me?" she said, her voice tinged with apprehension.

"Hey, Paddy. Where's the necklace?" Michael looked up at his friend. His arms were now holding her tightly, his chin resting on the top of her head. "I'd like to see it again." He shook Elizabeth gently. "Tell me what happens when you look at the necklace, okay?"

She nodded her agreement.

Paddy pulled the necklace from his pocket and held it by the chain. The pendant twirled with the stones glowing when they caught the light. "Do you want me to move closer, Mick?"

"Slowly," Michael responded his voice low and serious. "Elizabeth, how do you feel?"

"Very tired, Michael. Like I need to sleep," she yawned.

"Turn away for a moment, Paddy," Michael requested. When his friend's body was between Elizabeth and the pendant, he asked, "How do you feel now, Elizabeth?"

"A little better." Elizabeth looked puzzled. "Michael, do you think the necklace is making me tired?"

"Yes, I do; but I'm not sure why." His focused shifted to his friend standing a few feet away still holding the necklace. "If you'd wrap it in the towel on the counter and put it on the table by the door that might help."

"Sure thing, Mick." Paddy grabbed the towel quickly securing the necklace inside as he walked toward the small table by the door. He turned back to Michael and Elizabeth, a smile on his face. "Well, if you two won't be needin me, I've a racing stable to see to." He shoved his hands in his back pockets, stood and watched as Elizabeth wriggled and writhed to get off Michael's lap. "Hey, Mick, why don't you bring Elizabeth along to the meet this week? She can learn how to muck out a stall, haul hay, clean tack. All kinds of useful things she can do." He winked at Elizabeth and grinned at Michael.

"That's a great idea, Paddy," Elizabeth squirmed around until she was facing Michael, precariously perched on his lap. "Don't you think so, Michael?" Seeing the frown on his face she turned and looked over her shoulder. "Can I come with you, Paddy, if Michael doesn't want me along?"

"Sure thing," Paddy watched the fire blaze in Michael's eyes. He smiled and rocked back on his heels adding, "I'm leaving at 7 a.m., be ready and I'll take you along with me. That is, if Mick hasn't figured out what to do with you." Paddy chuckled to himself.

Michael glared at his friend and then gave it up with a sigh. "Do you want to come to the races with me?" he murmured in her hair.

"Oh yes, Michael. I very much want to come with you." Elizabeth wound her arms around Michael's waist and snuggled closer. "I'll stay out of the way; really, I will. I'll not be underfoot at all. I'll do anything you say. I'm sure I can learn to do whatever you call it in the stalls and with the hay." She felt the tremors in his chest. "You don't have to laugh at me, Michael. Really, sometimes you are not a gentleman. Like right now for example." She tried pushing away, stiffening her posture, indignation in her voice. Looking up she saw Michael's face creased with smiles, laughter dancing in his eyes; a glance over her shoulder showed Paddy's wide smile.

"Really, Michael!" Her tone was prim and prissy. "Really, Paddy," she huffed. "I thought the two of you better than this." She'd never admit it, but her position on Michael's lap was tenuous as her ramrod-straight-posture caused her to tee-ter.

The room filled with their loud belly laughs. She slipped off Michael's lap when his grip loosened and stood. Clutching the blanket at her waist, she watched the friends hold their sides, no longer trying to contain their laughter. Her nose turned up, she "harrumphed" with distain; her actions bring-ing on another bout. With her nose in the air, her spine rigidly straight, she dropped the blanket and walked into the bath-room. Closing the door, she took one look at herself in the mirror. "I'll show them. I'll keep up. I'll —. First things first." She glared at the door before turning on the water for a hot shower.

The next morning Elizabeth was up, dressed, packed and waiting when Michael pulled his truck up in front. After the two men had left, she'd rested. Later after a light meal of Irish stew from the pub, she'd decided to spend time working with the energy of the necklace.

Remembering what she needed to do to keep herself grounded had been the first step.

She'd also called upon The Lady and when within The Lady's shimmering light, she could touch the necklace, hold it in her hands. While she wasn't ready to wear it, the time would come when she could. Right now it was wrapped in a piece of red cloth and tucked into the middle of her bag be-tween the jeans and tops she'd packed.

Michael stowed her bag in the back of the truck, climbed in and they were off. Elizabeth, sensitive to his energy, knew he was tired and soon learned he'd only managed three hours of sleep. While she knew he was behind, she didn't understand how much. Even now she took him at his word that what needed to get done was done. *I still need to keep some distance from him. My time in Ireland is half over and I'm already so drawn to him. To be more involved in his life here will only make it harder to leave.* During the two hour drive, she interspersed times of quiet with times of conversation talking when his energy lagged in effort to energize him.

The stable was the first stop. Even though Michael's expressed wishes were that she stay "out of the way" she helped unload things from the truck. While he made sure everything was in order, she chatted with the stable hands, met Dickens the head groom, who started her education about horses and racing. Only when the horses were settled to Michael's satisfaction did they check in at a hotel close to the barns and raceway.

"Go take a shower." Elizabeth pointed toward the doorway that led to the bathroom. "You need some rest before going back to check on the horses. Go on now." She made shooing motions with her hands while walking toward him. "Don't argue with me about this, Michael. I'm serious. You look dead-on-your-feet." She was about two feet from him when his long arm reached out and curved around her waist pulling her against him. Shifting, he hauled her up under one arm and started into the bathroom.

"Put me down! I mean it! Right now, put me down!" Elizabeth screeched, watching as his free hand reach for the shower controls and turned the water on. "Michael," her voice had notes of panic and pleading. "Don't, Michael. Don't do this." She sputtered as water splashed over her head; she was flipped and pulled against a hot, hard, wet chest.

"Don't fuss with me, luv. I'm doing what you wanted. I'm taking a shower," he grinned down at her, his hands slipping under her shirt and peeling it off her wet body. Next to go was her bra. It was flung somewhere; she heard it land with a splot. His hands roamed her body; his thigh pressed between her legs; his rough beard scraped her skin. "I missed you last night," he murmured. "Missed you so much." His hands pushed her jeans off her hips, down her legs. His arm went around her, lifting her off her feet. Braced against the shower wall, he used a foot to finish taking them off.

Except for her socks, she was naked standing in the shower, her hair plastered to her head and back, her body thrumming with life as his hands, Michael's hands, worshipped every inch of her. She didn't know and really didn't care when his shirt and pants came off. Hot water sluiced off their bodies as they soaped and washed each other.

Michael loved to soap her hair and then watch the streaks of bubbles woven through it stream down her back as the water rinsed through it; she loved to watch her hands make soap designs on his chest, his back and feel his muscles tense and bunch under her fingertips.

His hands caught her buttocks, lifted her, and slid her up his torso. "Put your legs around my waist," he commanded.

Her back pressed against the shower wall, she wrapped them tight, crossing her ankles to hold her close. He and the wall were the only things holding her up. When his hands left her, she felt him roll on a condom. *He must have had one in his jeans pocket.* His hands on her buttocks, he let her slide down a few inches. His erection probed seeking her heat. She wriggled and he let her slide another inch. *Almost, almost, almost* she chanted. There wasn't another teasing inch. There was only Michael, Michael filling her, Michael moving in an ancient rhythm, holding her close, murmuring words she didn't understand, words from the old language, words she could feel in her soul.

The world came crashing around them as they sought their release; colors blinded them to anything other than each other. Still breathing hard, clinging to each other as if they were all they had left in this world, they returned to this room, the water pummeling them. Slowly their breathing returned to a normal pace, he softened and slipped from her. She uncrossed her ankles and let her legs slide toward the floor. He set her gently on her feet, holding her secure until she could stand on her own. Lukewarm water pulsed down on them.

"Okay, I took my shower," he leaned back to look her fully in the face pressing his lower body more closely into her. "Satisfied?" He smiled a pleased, well-sated smile as he reached to turn the water off.

The routine of the next three days: four a.m. Michael got up, dressed, went off to the barns to check on his horses and oversee their morning workout. Four hours later, he was back at the hotel. Elizabeth got up an hour before Michael returned and worked with the energy from the necklace. When he came back, they showered together, had breakfast and returned to the barns by 10 a.m. Elizabeth spent a few hours each day with Paddy, watching how he did things, questioning why he did some things different than Michael.

"I thought horses need the same things, Paddy. But you and Michael don't do everything the same. Why is that?" Elizabeth asked the third morning.

"It's like this Elizabeth. We're both people and we both eat breakfast, right?"

"Yeess,"

"So, what did you have for breakfast?"

"Scones, eggs and hot chocolate. I can't seem to get enough scones. They are especially delicious here in Ireland."

"What'd Michael have?"

"I see your point, Paddy. You and Michael most likely had similar things to eat than you and I or Michael and I. So part of it is you train the mares and fillies different from the stallions, colts, and geldings?"

"And the jumpers from the racers, Elizabeth. Did ye see the horses are built differently depending on what they do? Jumpers are bigger, stronger, have more endurance. Racers are quicker, their muscles more streamlined. What they all have in common is a love of running and a sense of competition. They all like to win."

"But only one can win. How do the horses who don't win handle losing?"

"Drown their sorrows in a bag of oats," Paddy said and laughed. "Ah, Elizabeth, here comes your better half." He gestured toward the open barn door where Michael stood.

He sauntered over to join them.

"You are way too full of yourself, boyo," Elizabeth said with mock severity, a hint of an Irish brogue in her voice . "Overstepping yourself, you are."

"Way too much levity here." Michael pulled her back against his chest and rested his chin on her head. "What's so funny?"

"Ah, Mick, if you ever decide to give this one the boot, boot her over my way, will ya?" Paddy's laugh was now only a chuckle. "She's priceless, she is."

Elizabeth felt Michael stiffen and pull her even closer. He wasn't dealing well with Paddy's banter this morning and she wasn't sure why. "Don't hold your breath, boyo," Michael responded. "But I do agree she is a woman worth more than her weight in gold and gems. So what were you two laughing about?"

"I wasn't laughing, Michael," Elizabeth pointed out. "All I was doing was asking some simple questions," she said with a sniff and her nose in the air.

"She wanted to know how the horses who lost handled not winning." Paddy was already losing the battle with the burble of laughter.

"He told me they drown their sorrows in a bag of oats," Elizabeth said primly. "I don't see what's so funny. Michael? Michael? Are you laughing at me?" She felt his chest moving. "You are laughing at me, Michael Murphy. You- you- you awful man." She stomped her foot, caught Michael's boot with her heel. His guard dropped and she spun out of his arms and now faced him. His blue black hair tousled, blue eyes lit with laughter, mouth open but no sound came out. And then he caught his breath and the laughter exploded forth. Elizabeth, arms folded, foot tapping, stood between these two men who were now leaning on each other, holding each other up, and laughing at her.

*Actually they do look rather ridiculous standing there like that* she smiled and then the moment caught her up as well and she joined them. *Laughter is like that. I remember times when one of my circle sisters would laugh and then we'd all be laughing and not even know why.*

The fourth day was a race day and while Michael was still up at 4 a.m. and off to the barns, the rest of the day's routine was different. When he returned around 8 a.m., he showered, shaved, and dressed in a suit. He'd had something to eat at the track; Elizabeth was too nervous to eat. They went to the barns, checked on the horses, and then Michael led Elizabeth to the owner's boxes, introduced her to the people around them and was off. She saw a different Michael now. He was all business, serious. Gone were the smiles and laughter they'd shared until one of his horses won the first race.

"Come along, Elizabeth. We're off to the winner's circle," he'd said after twirling her around and kissing her senseless. "Come on, luv." The boyish grin on his face, the excitement in his eyes, as well as the strong arm around her waist drew her along beside him.

In the winner's circle, Michael introduced Elizabeth to the race officials and sponsors. He owned as well as trained this horse. The official picture included Elizabeth, Michael's arm around her waist, his other hand on the horse's neck. Elizabeth was comfortable enough around horses now to pat his nose. "What a brave one, you are," she crooned. "The fastest of the lot." The horse, for his part, nudged her with his nose and sent her stumbling back, caught just before she toppled over by the Jockey Club president, Mr. Charles Mallory.

"Brought me luck, today," Michael rescued her from 'Chuck' and nuzzled her ear.

"Michael, we're in public?" Elizabeth's face was pink with embarrassment.

Michael chuckled and then laughed a deep hearty laugh.

"What's so funny, Michael?"

"I was just thinking about the conversation you and Paddy had yesterday. You know about what horses do when they lose?"

"So, what does that have to do with anything? Your horse won."

"Right. My horse won." Michael pulled her tight against him, her soft body molded to his. He resisted lowering his hand to her buttocks, but nuzzled her ear and nibbled his way to her mouth. After what he considered to be a fairly thorough kiss, he looked down at her passion-glazed eyes and her well-kissed mouth. "This, luv, is what the owner and trainer does when he wins," he murmured and kissed her again.

Between Michael and Paddy, they won five of the eight races that day. The second day of racing together they won six. Over the two days, Paddy'd won six races and Michael five. They'd gone out for a celebratory dinner and had good-naturedly argued over who was paying for the meal. Elizabeth had tossed the coin and Paddy had won. Michael had paid for the dinner and they'd left the restaurant in high spirits.

"Thought any more about my suggestion, Mick?" Paddy asked as they strolled down the street in the direction of their hotel.

"The one about New Grange?" Michael smiled to himself as Elizabeth came alert at his side. "Since I lost to you at this meet, boyo, I'd better get back and start working on a new training program. Can't let you get big ideas. That'd never do."

"As if a few hours can help you now," Paddy bantered back. "You're on the downhill side of things, Mick. Accept your fate. You'll be losing to me on a regular basis now."

"New Grange?" Elizabeth's voice was eager and she strained to see both men's faces. Visiting the ancient burial ground was another destination on this trip. The proverbial clock was ticking, time was running out and if she wanted to spend as much time with Michael as she could before going home, this might be her only opportunity to visit the sacred place. "What were you suggesting about New Grange?"

Both men stopped, bringing her to a halt also. She looked expectantly between their two faces. Paddy and Michael had identical grins, amusement danced in both of their eyes, they were proud as peacocks about something. Elizabeth stood her ground, watched them intently, her foot tapping out an impatient beat.

Michael cleared his throat. "Well, Paddy and I know you'd like to see New Grange and we were talking about how as it's a couple hours off a road leading back home, it was a doable side-trip." He watched her excitement build until the energy glowed around her. *It's better this way than a tour. At least Paddy will be there to protect her if she has problems with the energy.*

"Really, Michael, really? I'm really going to get to see New Grange? Paddy, are you sure? Oh, my, goodness," she gasped as the realization dawned that she was to visit this most sacred site. She squealed with delight and flung herself first at Paddy, covering his face with kisses and then at Michael, who held her close after a thorough kiss. "Tomorrow? Do we go tomorrow?"

"Tomorrow, I leave at first light." He watched her face as the word "I" registered. "Paddy will be taking off at eight and has agreed to stop by New Grange on the way home." Elizabeth stood, expectation still on her face, waiting for the rest to be said. "I'm sorry. But I've gotten more behind than I can afford right now. I've got to get back."

"Tell her the rest, Mick." It was Paddy's soft voice.

"Paddy'll bring you out to my place. I want you to move to The Manor so I can keep up with things better and still have the time I want with you. That is if that's okay with you." Michael held his breath as he witnessed a myriad of emotions flit across her face. He didn't want to guess at what moving in with him would entail, what he'd be forced to tell her. *I've at least another day before I have to face the truth with her.*

Elizabeth turned to Paddy. "Are you sure you have the time, that it's okay for you to go to New Grange?"

"Haven't been in years," Paddy answered. "I can spare the few hours it'd take to stop by there. Tomorrow'd not be a working day for me, anyway. I'd just see my horses back to my place and kick back the rest of the day. Our horses will travel together and Mick'll see them to my stable. Since they're leaving at first light, there'll be enough time for him to see that they get to their stalls as well as take care of his own. My lads are good ones, they know what to do and I'll be there before dark. The question is, Elizabeth, do you want to go with me as your guide?"

Both men were watching her expectantly. Although Elizabeth was disappointed not to have Michael with her when she visited the ancient burial mound, she heard The Lady whisper now was the time for her to go. She'd just made up her mind when she heard Paddy say, "You can always go on a tour."

Elizabeth looked at Paddy and noted his nervousness. She didn't blame him after what he'd witnessed at the stone circle and with the necklace. Humbled that he was willing to take her she knew it was because of his friendship with Michael. "My own personal tour guide," she smiled. "Thank you, Paddy, for your offer. I'll be ready." She started down the sidewalk toward the hotel. Calling back over her shoulder, she said, "If you'll excuse me, I've things to do to prepare for this adventure, gentlemen."

"Wait up," Michael called out as he went after her. "Coming, Paddy?"

"Go on with you, Mick. I think I'll have a nightcap at that little place across the way." He smiled to himself, seeing that his friend had already caught up with Elizabeth, had his arm around her, and was kissing her. "Way to go, Mick," he said softly to himself. "I'll take real good care of her for you tomorrow."

# 9  NEW GRANGE

Michael stood in the semi-darkness staring down at the lithe form stretched out on the bed wondering what had taken her from their bed for so long last night. His middle finger trailed lightly down her spine, the softness of her skin like warm silk beneath his caress. She shifted as his finger traced down her back and the tug of desire began to burn. *Will I ever get enough of this woman?* He paused, his head tilted to the side and regarded her from a different angle as if that would give him a different answer. *No, I don't expect I ever will.* He stepped back from the bed and picked his bag up from the nearby chair. *By the end of today, it might not matter.* With one last look at Elizabeth's sleeping form, he turned and with determination in his stride exited the room.

The wake-up call came at seven. Elizabeth grumbled hearing the cheery voice announcing the hour and the weather outside. Dragging herself into the bathroom and into the shower, she turned the temperature on hot and let the water pummel her body awake. Sleep washed from her mind. She smiled.

The work she'd done in the middle of the night was worth the tiredness now sluicing down the drain. Dressed, Elizabeth dabbed on a bit of make-up. Her packing was done except for taking down her altar. Picking the items up from the sacred space, she moved them to the bed adding the cigar box, its contents, cloth, and bags she used in packing everything.

Elizabeth sat cross-legged on the bed and took her time looking over the stones littering the spread. *The Lady told me I needed to protect myself, pay attention to the energies around me, and stay grounded in order to keep myself present and safe on this visit to New Grange.* Her hands drifted over her collection. With deliberation she moved them back and forth, up and down, sensing the different energies, seeing which stones "called" to her. A small red mesh bag peeked from under the cigar box. Plucking it up, she opened it.

"For protection I'll take you," she reached out and picked up a small piece of turquoise, dropping it in the bag, "and you" she added the piece of labradorite to the bag. Her hand hovered over the fire agate before she plucked it up. "You'll do nicely." The tourmaline joined the fire agate still in her hand. Elizabeth paused a moment before electing to add amethyst to the collection in her hand. With great care she tumbled the stones into the bag. Another sweeping glance over the stones in front of her and she opted to add the hematite to the bag before pulling the ties and closing it.

Next, Elizabeth placed the bag near her lap and began the task of packing up her altar supplies. "Supplies," she grinned, "I wonder where that came from. You all are anything but mundane supplies. You are the source, the power, what makes my altars come alive with energy." With everything packed up and the cigar box tucked away in her suit-case, Elizabeth held the bag in her hand feeling the energy within.

Scrambling off the bed, she paced to where her altar had been. One item remained: the necklace. She tucked the bag in her bra and held the necklace up to her as if it were around her neck. She was pleased she could be this close to it and stay centered. The work she'd done over the last few days night had paid off. She lowered the necklace, wrapping it carefully in a piece of red velvet and tucking it away in the middle of her suitcase. With everything packed, she turned to the window, lifted her arms and said her morning prayers moving her arms and hands in the age-old ritual.

"The gifts of the Goddess are to think, to speak, to feel, to create, to give and receive the gifts of the Goddess which are to think, to speak, to feel, to create, to give and receive the gifts of the Goddess which are to think, to speak, to feel, to create, to give and receive the gifts of the Goddess for I am the Goddess, for I am the Goddess, for I am the Goddess, Blessed Be." Her arms outstretched, she bent low at the waist before righting herself, standing tall, eyes still closed.

Elizabeth took a deep breath and visualized white light coming from the heavens, flowing through her, leaving her feet to go deep into the center of the earth. Although she was standing in a room on the fourth floor of a hotel, the energy she received from her prayers was substantial; more than strong enough to begin this day.

A knock on the door signaled Paddy's arrival. Elizabeth turned from the window, a smile on her face, a sparkle in her eyes, ready to see what adventure awaited her.

After a leisurely breakfast, they started toward New Grange. Elizabeth loved the varied greens of the Irish countryside and never tired of the play of light and shadows across the landscape. Paddy knew a great deal about the area, was an excellent tour guide, and a consummate story teller. It was eleven when they reached the road leading to New Grange.

Paddy turned his truck onto the access road and Elizabeth quieted her body and mind to more clearly feel the energy of this holiest of sacred places. As they made their way toward the ancient burial ground, the energy flowed over her, growing stronger, pulling her into trance.

"Look, Elizabeth, you can see it from here," Paddy's quiet voice was strong, a touchstone with the present.

The massive burin, a parking lot full of cars, and buses filled her vision. New Grange was a busy popular place. Paddy found a parking place well away from the crowd and they sat in comfortable silence for several minutes just taking in the scene before them.

Dismay settled in Elizabeth's heart. To these people, New Grange was a tourist destination: something to see when in Ireland. It was not a sacred place. In her imagination she saw these same people outraged, if their holy places were desecrated with dogs relieving themselves on the grounds, children and adults yelling, arguing, fighting, complaining, and criticizing. Her shoulders hunched, a frown marred her face.

"Are you okay?" concern laced Paddy's voice. "You look upset, almost angry."

"It's just —" She shook her head and sighed. "It's just that this is an ancient sacred place. I know most of these people would be appalled if these same behaviors were enacted in their churches, synagogues, temples — their sacred places." Elizabeth took a deep cleansing breath while looking around the parking lot. "It is how it is," she said softly before turning to Paddy.

"Since I can't change anything, I need to let my dismay go. Maybe when I'm closer, I'll have a cleaner experience of the energy. I'm curious to see whether it has its own unique imprint or if it's similar to the dance, a place Michael and I stopped at along the Shannon, or the old well at Kylemore Abbey. So far, what I've experienced is a different energy in each place."

"Can't you feel the energy of the place from here?" Paddy asked puzzled.

"Yes, I can, but it is layered with noise and confusion. I don't know if what I feel is the essence of this place," Elizabeth confessed. "I'd really like to get closer. Are you okay with my exploring a bit?"

"Of course I am." Paddy exited and quickly rounded the front of the truck to assist Elizabeth to the ground. Side-by-side they walked across the parking lot toward the ancient burial mound.

When Elizabeth drew closer to the burin, a wave of energy flowed around her and stopped her in her tracks. Paddy halted beside her. Closing her eyes she inwardly called upon The Lady for guidance. Light shimmered behind her eyelids as The Lady appeared, Her arm pointing to one side of the mound. As quickly as She appeared, She faded away. When Elizabeth opened her eyes and looked in the direction The Lady had pointed, she saw nothing but vehicles with New Grange looming in the distance.

"Let's go this way," Elizabeth said gesturing to one side. A few yards in the new direction, a new surge enveloped her. The bag of grounding and protecting stones tucked in her bra didn't seem to be working very well. She turned away from Paddy, drew the bag from her bra and clutched it tight in her hand. Her fingers surrounding the bag of stones, made a difference. "I'm ready," she said smiling at Paddy before walking on.

Minutes later, strolling in the direction The Lady had indicated, they were across the parking lot away from the main entrance. A faint trail leading around the base of the large burin was partially hidden by low growing bushes. Without hesitation as soon as she spied it, she started forward, her steps purposeful. The narrow path started a slow inexorable climb. In the lead, Elizabeth stopped when she reached the top.

"We've done it," she gasped awestruck. She'd come to Ireland to find The Lady but at the top of her list was seeing New Grange. In her dreams she was with a tour group, shuffling through the main entrance, having a tour guide telling her about this place. The reality of being on top of New Grange was more than she thought possible. Turning slowly, looking out over the countryside, it seemed she should be able to see to the Irish Sea and the Atlantic Ocean. "This is wonderful!" she said turning in a slow circle, taking in the view spread out before her like a feast for a starving man.

"Look over there," he said pointing across the mound to a faint indentation in a field in the distance. "Do you see the markings in that field?"

Elizabeth followed where Paddy's fingers were pointing and saw the faint shadows. "What are they?"

"The remains of an old stone dance, darlin."

"Oh my. You've been here before, haven't you?"

"Many times, but not with someone who has the gift like you do. You seem to be doing well though."

"I'm keeping my mind busy and I've brought protection to help me stay grounded, and I've stayed physically close to you. All these things are helping me stay here and not drift off. And," she leaned closer to him and tapped him on the arm, "I'm not so foolish as to think I can go within myself, take the risk of going deep into a trance. But," she sighed softly, "I do wonder what it would be like to let my guard down a little."

"Go ahead, I'm right here. I won't let anything happen to you. If need be, I'll carry you down to the truck and drive away. Once you're away from the place you'll be fine."

"I'm a bit heavy to carry from here to the truck, Paddy. I can't do that to you. I'm okay with things as they are." She smiled at the big man and turned to look out again at the spectacular views.

Even with her protection and mental guards, the energy of New Grange called. The hum of the energy vibrated through her. Kicking off her shoes, she took the piece of hematite from her bag and placed it on the ground curling her toes around it. Shaking the other stones into her hand, she tucked the fire opal and amethyst in her bra. Immediately she felt the heat, the energy of the stones against her skin. Under her other foot, she placed the labradorite, curling her toes around it. The turquoise and tourmaline she held in her hands.

Looking at where the sun was in the sky, Elizabeth knew she faced North, the direction of wisdom and the ancestors. *How fitting that on this burial mound, I find myself standing in their direction.* Her arms slowly lifted from her sides to above her head. She looked somewhat like an 'X' with her arms over her head and her legs slightly spread. From her center source she let the energies flow through her to find expression in words. Within her the shimmering light grew and she was bathed in its burning brightness.

"Oh Spirits of this place. Those who've gone before, who hold the wisdom of ancient times, ancient peoples, and ancient ways. I stand before you, to honor you, to remember you, to hold you foremost in my prayers at this time. May you always know that this, your final resting place, is sacred space. May you always know there are people all over the world, some who have come to see you and some who will never be able to stand in this space with you, who believe that is so. May you always find peace here amidst the comings and goings of so many. May you always know what you've left behind for us to see, to come to know, to feel in our souls is sacred. Blessed Be."

Calmness wafted over her, the energy of New Grange less intense. The urge to lie down on the grass and sleep was strong. Fighting the pull, she stayed in the present and soaked up the energy and sensations of this place. The connection grew so intense, she swayed. A hand touched her arm, the connection faded.

When she stood strong on her own, it was done. Her arms drifted down to her sides. Her toes gripped the stones, her connection with the energy weakened. Pulling the red mesh bag from her skirt's waistband, one-by-one she dropped the stones into it. A surge of energy from the ground traveled up her legs and suffused her with its power when she picked up the labradorite and hematite. Grasping the stones and the bag in her hands, she slipped on her shoes.

Between her shoes and the stones, the energy was muted enough that she was clearly in the present. She spied Paddy several yards distant, talking to three young women who'd obviously taken the path to the top of the mound. He looked up and waved her over.

The young women, in their early twenties, were from the United States, Ohio to be exact. They'd come to visit relatives in Ireland. Paddy had explained to them she was saying prayers and they had listened to her words.

"How do you know what to say?" one of the young women asked.

"The words come," Elizabeth answered.

"Don't you like, write them out, like a sermon? You know, memorize them?" asked another of the trio.

"No, I don't even think about what to say. I know in my soul that the words that need to be said will come. It's always been that way." *It's like faith. You either believe, have that certain knowing, or you don't.*

Conversation was limited as the five of them walked single file down the path. They found a table and benches below and continued visiting for almost an hour. It was obvious to Elizabeth these young women were sensitive to energy. They had questions about sacred spaces other than New Grange. Answering their questions, she also added information about the energy of the different directions and how to create personal sacred space.

"Setting up an altar is as simple as finding a few inches and placing objects that have special meaning to you there," she explained.

"What do you say when people ask about your altars?" one of the women asked.

"That's a very good question; a question that requires some soul-searching. You see, there are people in this world who do not believe everything is sacred and connected to the divine source, that there is a divine feminine as well as a divine masculine, that there is a Goddess as well as a God. You don't have to believe all of that to have a sacred space, an altar. You just need to know what you believe and have a sense of who the person is who's asking the question. A vague answer is "it's a collection of things that have meaning to me".

A more specific answer is "it's my altar, a sacred space in my home."

The sun was showing the time to be mid-afternoon. More time had passed than she'd realized. With their permission, she gave each of the young women a hug and wished them well.

They were on the road to Kinslow when Paddy broke the silence. "You were wonderful, Elizabeth. Have you thought of teaching people about the sacred?"

"I don't know about that." Elizabeth shook her head in denial. "They were amazing young women and anything I did that helped them find their spiritual path I'm grateful for." She sighed, leaned her head on the back of the seat and watched the countryside slide by. "Thank you for bringing me here today. I will remember and treasure this day for the rest of my life." *So this is what it feels like to be around people who know and accept you and your beliefs. Considering I've only felt this way when with The Circle or at a 14$^{th}$ Moon Gathering, this is an added blessing. Maybe it is being here in Ireland but I've felt so comfortable in my spirituality here. I will miss this connection when I return to Fremont.*

The day was coming to a close when they passed between two stone columns that marked the entrance to The Manor, Michael's home. Each column was topped by a horse. One in mid-air astride a fence and the other stretched out as if crossing a finish line. *If my circle sisters were here they'd agree that horse is either Michael's personal or house totem.*

Paddy pulled the truck into a parking area between the house and the barns. Elizabeth, her mouth open in awe, looked at the castle-like structure Michael called home. Out of the corner of her eye, she caught movement coming from the barn. Turning, she watched Michael striding towards the truck, a big smile on his face.

"What in the hell!" exploded from Paddy's mouth as he helped Elizabeth down from the vehicle.

Elizabeth looked from Paddy's red, furious face to Michael, who looked confused and then startled when he turned to see what had Paddy up-in-arms.

A long-legged, auburn-haired woman caught up with Michael, linked her arm through his, and tugged him along towards the truck.

"Hello, Paddy, darling," the beauty called out.

Elizabeth felt the tension radiating from Paddy's large body and saw panic in Michael's eyes.

"Well, Paddy, aren't you going to introduce me to your friend, here?" the beautiful woman inquired, her arm still entwined with Michael's. She turned her face up to Michael, "Mick, darling, you didn't tell me we'd have company for dinner." She pouted prettily.

Silence hung in the air, the four of them as still as if carved from Connemara marble.

The saying about silence being deafening was apt. Elizabeth's stomach clenched, bile rose in her throat at the idea that Michael had been toying with her, that he already had someone in his life. It sickened her when the thought he might be married crashed her thinking. *No, I won't believe that of him.* The silence was interrupted by the sound of a horse neighing but still neither man moved or spoke. The silence was painful.

Elizabeth took matters into her own hands, stepped forward, her hand outstretched. "Hi," she said in as friendly a voice as she could muster. "I'm Elizabeth Elliott."

The other woman leaned into Michael, brushing her breast against his arm. She ignored Elizabeth's offered hand.

A clatter from the stable seemed to release both men from the silent tableau.

Michael plucked the other woman's hand from his arm and strode the last few steps to Elizabeth. He took her in his arms and pulled her close. His breath feathered her ear, his words a pleading whisper.

"I didn't know she was here, please Elizabeth. I'll explain everything. Give me a chance to explain, please?"

Detached from the scene surrounding her, a part of her curious, a part of her numb, she nodded well aware she was witnessing in excruciating detail how much she cared for the charismatic Irishman.

"Where did you come from, Shannon?" Michael growled out, keeping his arm banded around Elizabeth's waist.

Undaunted, Shannon answered, "Why from the house, of course. I saw Paddy's truck pull in and came out to welcome him and his guest, as any good hostess would do, Mick." While her words were addressed to Michael, her eyes were on Elizabeth.

"You're not the hostess here, Shannon, and you haven't been for a very long time. It's been over a year since you left."

"I know, darling, and I'm sorry for the pain and misery of it all. But that's in the past. I'm here now," her voice a sultry whisper she moved closer to him.

"You're right," Michael started.

Shannon's chest filled with the air of victory.

"It is in the past." He dropped his arm from around Elizabeth's waist, planted both hands on his hips. "The good and the bad, the pleasure and the pain. It's all in the past now."

Michael turned his back on the now deflated Shannon and held his hand out to Paddy.

"Thanks for bringing her home to me."

Paddy took the offered hand and looked his friend in the eye. "It was a grand and glorious day at New Grange. Ask Elizabeth about it. She knows more than you might think she does." And with that enigmatic statement he turned, reached behind the passenger's seat and got Elizabeth's suitcase out. He handed it to Michael, closed the door, and walked around to the driver's side. As he passed Shannon, he paused and in a low voice said, "Go slowly here, Shannon. If you want anything to do with Mick and his place at all, take my advice and watch your step."

Shannon nodded indicating she'd heard what he said but her eyes never left the couple standing before her. Mick had his arm around this woman; he'd pulled her close to him as if protecting her. He already had her suitcase in the other hand.

"I've got your favorite dinner ready, Mick. It's late, so if you don't mind, I'll stay the night in one of the guest rooms and leave first thing in the morning." Without waiting for an answer, she strode off toward the side entrance to the house.

*What an interesting evening this should be.* Elizabeth leaned her head on Michael's arm suddenly very tired. He put her suitcase down and pulled her into his arms. His mouth was on her seconds later and she melted into him, feeling the surge of passion rise.

Through the haze of passion, she sensed the energy, the spirit of the place surround them. In her mind's eye The Lady appeared, brighter, clearer, stronger than She'd ever been before. She could reach out and touch Her, right here and now—in this place.

Drawing back from the kiss, Elizabeth stepped back and looked around her. The area behind the castle-house glowed with the shimmering light of The Lady. *She's here.* Her expression filled with awe, she looked up at Michael in wonder. When it dawned on her that he knew, he'd always known about The Lady, that She was here in this place, his home, she was unsure if she would faint or vomit from the extent of his perfidy.

"Why, Michael," she whispered, her voice tortured, "why didn't you tell me? Why didn't you tell me The Lady was here?"

Elizabeth picked up her suitcase and started toward the house. Her mind awhirl with thoughts, her body awash in tumultuous feelings it was all she could do to put one foot in front of the other. *I have to get away. I can't stay here with Michael. Even if Shannon leaves in the morning, I can't stay.* Leaving The Lady when she'd just found Her, tore at her heart. Too lost in the enormity of what had happened, she didn't fight him for the suitcase as he took it from her hand. Numb she followed Michael into the house, into the bright and cheery kitchen, where Shannon waited with his favorite meal.

# 10 THE MANOR AND THE LADY

It may have been his favorite meal of corned beef and cabbage with a wonderful rum and raisin cake for dessert but dinner was a subdued affair. Shannon was an excellent cook, but the food Elizabeth managed to choke down sat like lead in her stomach. Conversation was sparse and finally Shannon, the only one who'd made a valiant effort to keep it going, became silent.

It was unbearable sitting there with the two of them, so many words unspoken, tension taut in the air. Elizabeth excused herself and pushed her chair back from the table.

"Show her to her room, Seamus," Michael instructed his houseman.

Elizabeth followed the taciturn man, who just pointed the way, nodding or grunting in response to her few questions. He opened a door toward the end of a hall, "Have a good evening, miss," he mumbled as he turned and shambled down the corridor.

Upon entering the room designated as "hers", Elizabeth found her traveling suitcase sitting open on the bench at the foot of the bed, the other two stacked in a corner. She quickly crossed the room, her mind awhirl with thoughts of someone snooping, perhaps reading her Journals. A quick glance revealed nothing disturbed; everything still as tightly tucked together as when she'd wrestled the bag shut.

The light, emanating from behind the closed drapes, filling the room came from The Lady and permeated every nook and cranny of the room and her being. Inexorably drawn by the magnetic pull, Elizabeth still fought against it, not sure how to stay grounded against the onslaught.

However, the tug from beyond the mullioned glass defied her ability; her will to resist. Stepping between the now partially opened drapes, she gazed out the panes at the scene below. The area down the hill beyond the stone terrace glowed, energy radiating from its center. A canopy of leaves prevented her from seeing inside, but she knew from the dreams and the visions she'd had of The Lady that this place was a sacred grove made up of trees not indigenous to this area. Within the grove, hidden from view were a grassy center circle, an eternally burning fire pit, and a small stone-encircled spring.

Elizabeth slipped toward trance. *I need to ground myself.* Grabbing the red mesh bag of protecting and grounding stones from her pocket, she clutched it close to her heart and took a step back from the view before her. The drapes fell into place, dimming the light and the pulsing energy. Another two steps back—the illumination from the shimmering light dimmed but it still bathed the room. Another two steps and a much needed pinch—she turned her back to the window.

Moving her bag of stones to her forehead, she rested it on the point between her eyes – her third eye. A moment of clarity: Elizabeth strode around the room, flipped on the light switch and turned on lamps, thus dimming the sacred light with that of modern electricity.

Disconnected from the sacred energy, she gasped, her hand over her heart at the scene. The room was larger than her apartment living room; she guessed it at least twenty by twenty feet. A large four- poster bed with an ornately carved dark wood headboard dominated the room and was set against a wall between two sets of floor-to-ceiling windows. She wandered over to look at the bookcases flanking the fireplace to the left of the bed. An eclectic collection of science fiction, mystery, and romance novels as well as scholarly works filled most shelves. Her fingers caressed the velvet covering of one of the two wingback chairs positioned in front of the fireplace. The small table between them matched the dark wood of the furniture in the room.

The wall directly across from the bed held the door to the hall, with a sideboard complete with crystal decanters and glasses on the right and a dresser on the left. Against the wall to the right of the bed stood two large wardrobes, also of dark ornately carved wood, with a door set between them. Elizabeth found herself walking to the door, opening it, and looking into another room - Michael's bedroom. She shivered as his presence, his scent wafted around her. Her knees weakened but her resolve strengthened as she pulled the door closed, stepping back into her space.

Feeling the 'call of nature', Elizabeth started on a quest to find a bathroom. She opened the door to the hallway, looking right and left at the closed doors on either side. Stepping out, she started down the hall to the right.

Seamus materialized in front of her, "May I be of assistance?" he asked with a courtly bow.

"I'm looking for the bathroom. I need to brush my teeth." She blushed.

"This way, miss," he said leading her back into her room. "Over here." He gestured her over to the bookcases. "Right through here." He pulled a discretely placed lever and a section of the bookcases opened, revealing the doorway to another room. "It works like this, miss," he said, showing her where the lever was and how to twist it slightly when pulling down.

"Thank you, Seamus. You've been very helpful." Elizabeth was almost dancing with the need to use the facilities.

"You're very welcome, miss," he replied his countenance placid. "Just ring," he said pointing to a small doorbell in the wall by the bed, "if you need anything else."

"Thank you again." Elizabeth stood very still, resisting the urge to cross her legs.

"Goodnight then, miss," Seamus said as he turned and left the room, pulling the door quietly shut behind him.

Elizabeth hurried into the bathroom and while her need was urgent, the magnificence of the place stopped her in her tracks. The room was covered in an alabaster marble that glowed in the light shimmering through windows that overlooked the Sacred Grove. Elizabeth quickly took care of her needs. When washing her hands, the significance of the details struck her. The bath and sink fixtures were shaped as swans; the beaks where the water ran, the right wing lifted up and down to control the water's temperature and the left controlled volume. The separate shower was of dark blue glass tiles interspersed with varied colored lighter blues, creams, white, and silver tiles in the shape of stars, giving the impression of stepping into the night sky and being surrounded by stars.

The towel she used to dry her hands was warm. The bathroom featured two multi-rung heated towel racks and a towel shelf running along the walls; one by the shower and one by the bathtub. Another smaller rack and shelf were located near the sink. The thick dark blue towels and washcloths contrasted with the glowing white marble floors, counter tops, and shelves.

Luxury. She was standing in the middle of one of the most luxurious bathrooms she'd ever seen. It rivaled the master bath at Lily and Jackson's house. The materials were high-end, the colors opulent, but the understated yet lavish luxury was in the little details: the smaller magnifying mirror built into one end of the main mirror; the silky cushioned bench in a similar blue as the shower; and the semi-private toilet and bidet in a color that matched some of the shower's stars.

Elizabeth's cheeks grew warm as she remembered the passionate love-making she'd shared with Michael in the shower in the hotel. *What would it be like?* She stopped herself from finishing that thought when tears threatened.

Returning to the bedroom determined to do something productive; she cast about for a place to set up her altar knowing the ritual would soothe her raw emotions. *This will work* she noted seeing the small table in front of the fireplace. Gathering her cigar box from her suitcase as well as the necklace still wrapped in red velvet, Elizabeth perched on the edge of one of the chairs and set to work.

The red velvet that had held the necklace became her altar cloth. The necklace with the chain carefully folded underneath it, the center. Each piece was purposefully set in place as prayers of gratitude filled the air. When the last piece was placed where it needed to be, Elizabeth sat back and looked at the sacred space she had created in this room. With everything in place, she lit a candle. Her prayers filled the room along with the smoke from the now lit sage and incense as she cleansed herself, the room, and the altar.

"Universal Oneness, Great Spirit, the Divine in All, help me find my way in this time of turmoil so that my highest good and the highest good of others is served. Light my way, show me signs that I'm on the path that is right for me. May the time I have with The Lady, here in the Sacred Grove, be as it should be. Blessed Be."

As she repeated this prayer three times cleansing herself, the room and her altar, a peace flowed through her. In her heart she knew if she stayed centered, stayed connected with the Divine, her way would be clear, her path lit, and her highest good served. Her prayers completed, she took off her clothes, laying them neatly on one of the chairs, slipped on her gown and crawled into bed.

Just before dawn, Elizabeth woke with a start, the dream of The Lady intense. Getting up she went to the window and looked out on the glow from the Sacred Grove and felt the call to come. *This may be my only chance to experience this sacred place.* The energy seemed to curl around her. *I told Michael I was leaving in the morning.* She stood as if rooted to the spot. *I'll only be gone for a little while. I can be back before anyone notices.*

Through the halls, down the stairs, and out to the back terrace, her feet unerringly stepped. By the light of The Sacred Grove she located the path. By the light of Grandmother Moon, in that soft light that comes just before dawn, she made her way down the overgrown pathway to the bottom of the hill where the trail led her to a small opening between the trees. *Déjà vu: I've been here before.* Going on instinct, Elizabeth plunged forward following the passageway winding through trees eventually emerging into the center circle.

She crossed the clearing, sat on a mossy tree trunk, and faced the fire. Her mind floated free when she stared into the flames. Deep in trance, she escaped her physical self, lost to this world.

Time had no meaning.

Michael woke at his usual four a.m. his restless, sleepless night, over. Restless in part because he knew she was on the other side of the connecting door just visible in the dim light. *If I open the door, I won't be able to resist and I'll go in.* Not sure what the outcome would be, he'd turned over and sought at least to rest.

Dressed for his morning tasks in the stables, he made himself walk past her door. Instead of having breakfast in the large kitchen, he continued on to his office adjacent to the stables where he had coffee and scones. He'd asked Seamus to let him know when Elizabeth was up. Around ten, his house-man informed him Shannon had left and he hadn't seen Elizabeth.

When Michael returned to the main house for his mid-day meal, Seamus reported he'd not seen or heard Elizabeth. Something wasn't right but he took the coward's way out and on his way back to his office, asked Seamus to check on her.

A short time later, the office phone rang.

"Not in her room," Seamus told him adding when he heard Michael's curse, "her things still are."

"Check every room," he instructed. Hope that his worst fears weren't real slipped away as a quick search of the house, paddock area and the front gardens revealed no sign of her.

Dread leadened his steps, as he strode to the back of the house and the only place left.

At the entrance to the path, Michael looked down on the Sacred Grove .The light gently pulsed, the energy calm.

The Lady was pleased.

He wasn't.

Before starting down the path, Michael stooped and moved a rock in the wall surrounding the garden revealing a small cavity. He reached in finding the leather pouch and dagger hidden within. In the belt at the small of his back, he tucked the dagger. The pouch he placed in his shirt pocket. Making his way down the faint path, he followed the fresh trail of bent grasses and twigs.

When he stepped into the center circle, he saw Elizabeth curled in the grass in front of the fire, The Lady standing over her. His breathing stuttered and his heart stopped.

The Lady looked over at him and smiled, looking more content than he had ever seen Her. "She came to me, Michael. She's mine, you know."

"No, she is not Yours. Whether she chooses to serve You or not, it will be by her choice and her choice alone." He quickly crossed the clearing to where Elizabeth lay, her head resting on her outstretched arm, her black hair loose, curling and tumbling around her, her nightgown a slip of silk caressing her slim body.

Gathering her in his arms, he relished the weight of her, her bergamot and more scent, wafted. "If she is to belong to anyone, she'll be mine," he challenged, his voice reverberating in the still air. Urgency permeated his voice as he called her name. She didn't stir. *I have to get her out of the Sacred Grove, out from the influence of The Lady.* The silk gown did not help his hold and he shifted her in his arms to have more purchase as he strode toward the opening.

The Lady shimmered, Her energy pulsing as it surrounded Michael with Elizabeth still in his arms as they disappeared into the trees.

## Fremont, Oregon

Their arms and voices raised in prayer, the women in Elizabeth's circle began their Ceremony. During their sharing time, Lily and Sophia noted something felt "different", "unsettled". Gabriella wondered if Elizabeth was all right and Diana suggested saying extra prayers and sending energy her way.

## The Manor at Kinslow—Three days later

Elizabeth sat at the desk in the room at the front of the house she'd transformed into a study or as it was called here in Ireland, her sitting room. Her experience in The Sacred Grove had fundamentally changed her. Picking up a pen, she opened her Journal and wrote.

> *My soul is magnified. I feel a stream of energy that has no end flowing from my heart chakra. I'm connected to The Lady and to so much more. Words simply can't express what I feel. I do so wish my circle sisters were here to experience this blessed energy with me.*

Four sentences and she was done. One of the things she noticed since her time with The Lady? Her feelings defied her ability to express them verbally or in writing because it was as if she was sucked into a vortex of emotions.

She put down her pen, closed her Journal, and stood gazing across the desk out the windows at the front gardens, admiring both the formal ones along the drive and the more casual ones to her left. Crossing the room to the windows, she threw them open welcoming the light breeze redolent with the scents from the garden perfuming the room.

Hands resting on the sill, Elizabeth leaned out the window and breathed in the fragrance, amazed at the transformation in and around her. This front-facing room, for instance, had been a bedroom. Michael had the bed removed and Seamus had helped her furnish it with odds and ends from other rooms. On either side of the fireplace were matching high-backed overstuffed chairs in a floral print. The room was large enough for two sofas, upholstered in a neutral cream colored silk that matched the background color in the chairs, with room to spare.

Opulent, luxurious were the words that came to mind but didn't really describe the space. The drapes on the floor to ceiling windows were a deep rich red, one of the colors of the floral print. Pillows on the sofas picked up the other colors of the print, a deep blue, a fresh green, and a soft pink. Dark wood wainscoting, dark wood mantel, dark wood moldings— all of the wood matched the dark wood of the floors that were polished to a high gloss and gleamed in the light from the windows.

This room, her retreat was a place to recover her psychic strength. Situated farthest from the energy of the Sacred Grove, it had become a refuge, a place to recover and reflect, a place to rejoice and celebrate finding The Lady.

Her pattern was to set up an altar in whatever room she occupied. In this room, her altar was simple. A piece of cloth from her cigar box lay on the long table between the two sofas. On it a swan feather she'd brought from home to remind her of the strength of her relationships with The Circle, a stone from along a path at Kylemore Abby, a picture of a bank of flowering fuchsias, a polished beach agate from home. A small vase she'd picked up at a shop in Kinslow served as the center and held fresh flowers she'd gathered from the gardens.

Yesterday she'd rearranged pots of herbs into a circle for an altar in the kitchen. Seamus hadn't minded when she'd added a small dish of water in the center and created an outer circle of salt. Usually she used cornmeal but he'd reminded her they were in the country and that would invite rodents or insects into the house.

Her energy higher than it had been for the last couple of days, Elizabeth was restless and needed something to do. She hadn't seen much of Michael because he'd been eating his breakfast and mid-day meal in his office in the stables. Over dinner, their conversation was polite and centered on the weather and his horses.

"How are you feeling?" he'd asked.

"I'm fine," she'd respond.

Today was the day to talk to him, to clear the air, to get things out in the open. However, she knew better than to interrupt him at work if she wanted a productive exchange. So, what was she going to do with herself for several hours?

When the right idea came to her, her whole being lit from within and joy bubbled up from her core. Gathering up things she'd need, Elizabeth left her sitting room, and walked the hallway to the main stairs. Descending to the main foyer, a massive room with its own fireplace, she placed the items on the mantle. A small table tucked away under the stairs suited her purpose and she pulled it out to a more prominent place and went to work.

Culling the surrounding rooms, she collected what she needed: a large Irish lace doily from the back of a settee, a crystal bowl, four bronze statues of horses, and a bowl of tumbled stones. The bowl was a particularly cherished find since it had been hidden from view behind a stack of books on horse breeding. One-by-one she brought the objects back to the foyer and placed them on the mantle. The last addition was the bowl of stones.

Doily in hand, she crossed the hall to the table where she arranged it to cover the top. *Yes, that will do nicely.* Next she brought the small crystal bowl and set it in the middle of the lace cloth. With that done she returned to the mantle, took down the matches, candle, and sage bundle she'd brought with her from the sitting room striking the match and lighting the candle. Using the candle flame, she lit the sage bundle and proceeded to wave it over, under and around the table creating a haze of cleansing smoke. Her murmured prayers released negative energy before calling in the positive.

Elizabeth worked in contented silence interspersed only with the whispered prayers. The statue of the foal in the East, the mare in the South; the two stallions in the West and North: the jumper in the West as she thought that fitting as they jumped into the void, trusting their riders implicitly. That left one bronze and the North. As she built this altar it was obvious to her that horse was Michael's house totem rather than his personal totem. She supposed it could be both, but she was certain the energy of horse protected this land. Several rocks from the bowl found their way to different points on the altar. Not being able to recognize them and guessing they were local stones, she just placed them where it felt right.

After creating the altar, Elizabeth walked around the large room waving the sage bundle, sending its cleansing smoke into the nooks and crannies of the foyer, again saying prayers to release any negativity and call in positive energy. When she was done and the sage bundle snuffed out, she opened the door, stood on the threshold, raised her arms in prayer, and called in spirits of protection for the formal entryway to the house.

"Spirits of protection for this house, hear me. Spirits of protection for this house, hear me. Spirits of protection for this house, hear me. Now is the time for you to come forth and protect this house and the people within from harm."

Elizabeth felt the breeze of energies flow past her. The air calmed. She lowered her arms, took a deep breath, and opened her eyes. When she turned to look back at the foyer, she gasped.

The room sparkled, light catching the crystal bowl refracting rainbows around the room. Calmness surrounded her and she felt weightless in body and buoyant in spirit. She twirled into the hall, her bare feet slipping along the black and white marbled tiles. The dark, ornately carved wooden panels on the walls were the backdrop to her dancing shadow and the sparkling colors of light.

The large grandfather clock against one wall chimed the hour. *Michael should be back from the barn in an hour. Let's see what I can accomplish before then.* She picked up the bowl of tumbled stones, her matches, and sage bundle and started for the front parlor. *I wonder if he'll notice anything different when he comes in today.*

# 11   SACRED SPACE

Michael was hot, tired, and dirty when he came through the kitchen door. He'd mucked out stalls, hauled hay and bags of oats, and worked his horses all in an effort to forget the beguiling woman in his house. It'd been three days since he found Elizabeth unconscious, since his heart stopped, since his confrontation with The Lady. Although She'd been quiet, he knew better than to think She'd given up. She was biding her time, waiting for the right time to come forth again. She was the spirit of this place, as old as time. She was energy manifested in the ancient blue robe of the sacred feminine, the Goddess. No, he was certain She hadn't given up.

From the kitchen he strode down the hall to the back stairs leading up to his quarters. He desperately needed a shower, clean clothes and something to eat - in that order. Thirty minutes later he was showered, shaved, dressed, descending the main staircase for the last item on his list: to satisfy his hunger.

He noticed something different about the place, as he moved down the main staircase the tips of his fingers trailing along the smooth finish of the banister. Before he could identify what that difference was he heard Elizabeth singing.

"She's been waiting ... ."

The purity of her sweet voice, the words of the old song held Michael transfixed.

" ... to return."

Michael remained standing on the bottom step listening to the words of a song he'd not heard in over a year, not since Shannon had left.

" ... alone." She drew out the last word, her voice caressing the last note.

Silence.

Michael stood in the stillness, his heart beating rapidly. *What if we ...* "No," he muttered harshly to himself. "No," he cursed under his breath. He stepped down the final riser to the tiled floor, his boots echoing in the large hall.

She was standing in the doorway to the front parlor, her hair tied back in a blue ribbon he was sure matched the blue of her eyes. A long dark blue skirt swirled around her bare ankles. Even though her hair was tied back, strands had escaped. Fascinated he watched her hand brush the inky tangles away, tuck them behind her ears. The indifference he'd managed the past three days, that is once the panic had dissipated and he knew she'd recover, dissolved in a rush of unrequited lust. His blood surged, his arousal stiffen.

A look of uncertainty marred her features, hesitancy her movements. *She's changed,* flashed through his mind, but he couldn't put his finger on how she was different. He stood staring at this woman, realizing he cared for her not just about her, cared far more than he wanted to. *Hell and damnation. Now what, boyo?*

Elizabeth's senses were caressed by the sandalwood scent wafting across the space. His blue-black hair, still damp from his shower, showed the ridges where he'd combed it. To her, he looked spectacular: tall, dark, and handsome as sin.

Outwardly she remained still under his unrepentant gaze, inwardly a cascade of nerves sizzled. Her gaze steadfast, she straightened her spine, lifted her chin, and took a few steps away from the doorway.

"Hi, Michael, how was your day? How is Brian Boru?" Elizabeth said her voice not as soothing as she'd hoped. Her heart fluttered, her face flushed with heat, and her palms dampened.

From the moment she'd been aware of his presence, Elizabeth had scrutinized his every move and saw the subtle signs of his nervousness. Smiling, she stopped a few feet in front of him.

Michael was mesmerized by her gently swaying hips, her bare feet gliding over the floor. Her scent of bergamot and the indefinable something surrounded him, filled his senses. Her mouth, those luscious warm kissable lips were moving, were saying something. He shook his head.

"...mind, Michael. I can take them down, if you do."

He cleared his throat, ran his tongue inside his now very dry mouth, "Sorry, Elizabeth, I didn't catch all that you were saying." His mouth stretched in a caricature of a smile.

"I was saying that if you mind, I'll take the altars down. I put one up here," she said and gestured to the table to his right, "and one is now in the front parlor. I wanted something to do and thought of creating a specific point of sacredness within each room. Would you like to see them before you make up your mind?"

At his terse nod, she moved to stand by the main hall altar. "As your life here at The Manor revolves around horses, I used them on this altar. As you can see, I put the bronze of the foal in the East as that direction represents new beginnings, spring, birth. The mare is in the South to stand for abundance. I put the jumper in the West as that is the void and from the meets, I now know that the jumper doesn't know what is on the other side of the jump. It's like they are jumping into the void and it is their trust of the rider that allows this miracle to happen. I'm not sure what the significance is of the stallion in the North. It was the only place left so I just trusted that it was the right place for him to be."

"Suleiman." Michael reached out to stroke the bronze stallion reared on its hind legs. "This is Suleiman, the stud that built this place, the ancestor of Brian Boru."

"Then Suleiman is in the right place," Elizabeth's voice was soft, she touched his sleeve with her hand. "Are you all right with this altar, here, in this space, Michael?"

His voice wasn't steady so he remained silent, looking at the altar she'd created from bronze statues, stones, and a crystal bowl. Energy flowed from it. Welcoming and powerful, like being at the races with his horses pounding down the course, straining with purpose for the finish line, focused on the love of running. Their beauty, grace, and power were like an aphrodisiac, beckoning him to indulge in the glory of the win, endorphins taking him higher into the light of joy.

His voice was brusque, "It's fine where it is." He started for the door to the hallway that led to the kitchens. "I'm hungry. I'm going to see what Seamus has for dinner." He called back over his shoulder as he kept going, "Are you coming?"

Elizabeth remained by the altar. He'd been affected by it. The main clue was when he'd absent-mindedly stroked Suleiman. She pressed a hand to her unsettled stomach. *I miss him more than I can say and I've not even left for Fremont.* Catching herself up short she reminded herself this line of thinking wasn't useful. *I'm hungry and dinner is waiting. The right time to talk to him will present itself.* She looked at the wall beyond which lay the Sacred Grove and The Lady. *Trust The Lady. She brought you here for a purpose. Trust.* "Trust," she murmured and started after him.

Seamus was a good cook but tonight's dessert was simple. A dish of fresh peaches and fresh cream capped with a drizzle of Bailey' Irish Cream. As she set down her spoon, he materialized and set down an aperitif glass with more Bailey's, doing the same for Michael. Dinner, a silent affair, due to Michael's rebuffing her efforts at conversation with one word answers, was officially over.

*Now,* her inner voice whispered. *Now is the time, seize it.*

Elizabeth looked up from where her gaze had rested on the table before her into Michael's flame-blue eyes. She'd wanted to see a welcome. What she saw was burning desire. Her pulse quickened as her heart rate rose; her cheeks flushed pink, her breath caught in her chest. She breathed deeply and calmed herself. Without so much as blinking, she raised the small glass of Bailey's to her lips, sipping the smooth, creamy liquid, licking her lips, savoring every last drop. Her eyes never left his as she slowly lowered the glass back to the table.

Instinct, she was going on instinct so was satisfied to see the desire in his eyes go from hot to molten. He slowly, deliberately pushed back from the table and stood. Elizabeth blinked and blinked again as the evidence of his desire strained against the zippered seam as if seeking her.

In two strides he was next to her. "I believe we have some things to sort out," he ground out between clenched teeth.

"We do," Elizabeth raised her eyes from the bulge in his pants to his face. "Where would you like to have this discussion?" she asked in a reasonable tone. Her body reacted to his nearness with its own heat and desire; she felt flushed, heat pooling in her nether regions, her body tightening and melting all at the same time as memories of their love-making roared through her.

"How about the front parlor and you can show me what you did there?" Michael said.

"The front parlor will be fine," she said and rose from the table. Elizabeth preceded Michael to the main hall, crossed it to the front parlor, feeling his intense stare each step of the way. By the time she reached the parlor door, her nerves were stretched. To get his eyes off her, she stopped and gestured him inside. "You go ahead."

Michael stepped into the parlor glancing around room. He stopped half-way into the room; something felt different. Turning slowly, he took in the familiar furnishings, wall color, drapes. He wracked his mind trying to figure out rationally what he sensed: how calm and welcoming the room felt. *It must be the energy of the altar she set up in here, but where is it?*

With Elizabeth out of his sight although not out of his senses, he concentrated on the calm, welcoming energy. The source seemed right in front of him but when he looked all he saw was the table in front of the settee set for tea. *She really is amazing.* His mouth tilted in a smile. *Actually, she's wonderfully amazing.* He turned toward her and pointed to the table. "This is the altar."

"Yes, it is the altar." She moved to sit on the settee. "I wanted something subtle, something that would be natural to this room. I thought in previous generations, this would be the room where visitors and guests were shown, where the lord and lady of the house would greet them, where tea and scones would be served."

"The room did serve that purpose in my great-grandfather's time, I'm sure," his voice was soft now. "Thank you, lu, uh Elizabeth." He looked over at this beautiful woman, sitting primly on the edge of the settee. A vision of her sitting in this same room, on this same settee overlaid the scene before him. Her hair was made up in the fashion of the day with curls tantalizingly arranged around her face, a cameo in the hollow of her neck, her alabaster skin glowing in contrast to the dark blue silk gown she wore. Stunning.

He blinked, the vision cleared, and he was left staring at Elizabeth, her coal black hair escaping the confines of pins and ribbons, the rounded neck of her azure blue blouse showing a hint of décolletage. The midnight blue skirt covering her bare ankles and feet, lending her an air of modesty. Settled into a corner of the opposite settee, he stretched his legs out in front of him. The outwardly casual pose was belied by the tension in his muscles. He wasn't relaxed. He was poised to handle anything that came his way. Waiting, watching her as she nervously licked her lips, fidgeted, took a steadying breath and stilled. *This is it.*

"What sort of things do you think we need to 'sort out' Michael?" Elizabeth met his intense gaze with her own steady one.

*When you will return to my bed.* Instead he said, "I assume you have some questions is all." *And then there's you thinking of leaving.* But he wasn't ready to voice that thought yet.

"I do have some questions, Michael. First and foremost," she said her spine stiff, her chin raised. "I don't understand why you never told me about your connection with The Lady. You knew before the plane landed about my dreams, my sense of being called to Ireland, to Her. But you said nothing. Nothing at all."

"It's a long story, Elizabeth," he began.

"I've got the time," she interrupted leaning slightly forward. "I really want to hear what you have to say for yourself."

His hand rubbed the back of his neck, stroked his chin. Sighing, he stood and crossed to the sideboard along the wall by the door. He poured a snifter of brandy from one of the decanters. "Would you like something?" he asked over his shoulder.

"Another Bailey's would be nice."

Michael rang for Seamus, waiting by the door for him to appear, his back to her. A few minutes later, a knock announced the houseman's arrival. Michael quickly gave him Elizabeth's order, asked for the bottle and a bucket of ice.

Seamus soon returned with a tumbler filled with ice and Bailey's, as well as the requested bottle and bucket of ice which he set on the silver salver on the side board. He then crossed the room to Elizabeth, handed her the tumbler, turned and left the room.

"In case you want another," Michael started.

"Thank you," Elizabeth replied. "You were about to tell me a long story," she prompted.

"Yes, well, this isn't an easy story for me to tell. Actually I'm a bit reluctant," he paused and glanced at her. Somewhere in the past few minutes she'd settled back on the settee, her feet tucked under her, holding her drink cradled in her hands. She waited, no fidgeting, no hesitancy, just quiet, expectant waiting. Here it was—his one chance to explain everything to her, his one chance to win her back. He resumed his place on the settee, took a long swallow of brandy, aware of its liquid heat, and cleared his throat.

"This place has been in my family for hundreds of years. We've always raised horses, served The Lady and protected The Sacred Grove. How it all began is a story for another time. What affects us started with my grandparents. They had one child, my father. My grandfather worked the land and ran horses. My grandmother served The Lady. When he was twelve, my father was sent to boarding school. Other than visits for his birthday and Christmas, he never returned to The Manor.

"My grandparents came to visit us twice a year after I was born. My father never allowed us to travel here. I saw them on my birthday and on Christmas Day. My father did not allow longer visits." He shifted. The emotions tied to these words picked at him...feelings of loneliness, of yearning. He sighed, a subtle shake of his head to dispel them.

"My mother died when I was twelve and my father sent me to boarding school but insisted that I spend all holidays with him. A successful barrister, he worked long hours but when I was in residence he was home by six. The days, however, I spent alone; my activities curtailed to only things my father approved of. So, I read. He approved of my reading but never thought to ask what I was reading about. I filled my days with all kinds of books about horses. *Black Beauty* was a favorite. I then moved on to books on breeding and racing. Dick Francis's books on racing jumpers caught my attention. You get the idea." Michael brought his gaze to her face, raised his glass and took a sip of the brandy, heat slid down his throat, a sardonic smile played across his lips.

"Well, back to the topic at hand," he took another sip, staring into the past, to emptiness, his hand tightening around his glass. "When I was seventeen, my grandparents died within a few days of one another. My father and I came for their funerals. He would not allow us to stay at The Manor although we did spend a few hours here after the service. We didn't even stay in Kinslow. We stayed at a hotel in Killarney, driving out for the service and back the same day.

Half my life-time ago was when I first laid eyes on The Manor. When I was twenty, my father died a young man in his forties. In looking through his papers I found the deed to this place and bills of sale for the horses." Michael leaned his head back, looking up at the ornate crown molding, his gut wrenched, his jaw clenched. He wanted to stop. He' never, ever told it all like this. The pain of his childhood seared his heart and tears threatened. He struggled on hoping, praying he was doing the right thing.

"After my father's death, I decided to take a break from school and come here. Instinctively I knew there was something here my father didn't want me exposed to but I had no idea what. Three years earlier I'd thought the place magical." He smiled sheepishly at the memory. "What I saw on this trip was much different. As I wandered around the place; I saw the barns, stables, paddocks all in shambles. The house hadn't been lived in by humans since my grandparents' death and the mice and rats had set up housekeeping. I'd just come out the front door and was standing on the steps taking everything in, my mind racing with ideas, possibilities, when an old battered truck pulled up. It was Paddy, Padraig O'Cochran.

"We'd met up at boarding school and had become friends. Not the fast friends we are today, but comfortable in each other's company. I don't think we ever felt anything but friendly competition towards each other, perhaps because we liked and respected each other. Whatever it was, I was surprised to see him and then astonished he had a farm nearby. He invited me over for supper and a drink and I ended up not only spending the night but making his place my headquarters while I figured things out." Michael took a long draught of his brandy, held it in his mouth, and let it slowly trickle down his throat.

Elizabeth was mesmerized by the play of muscles as she watched him slowly swallow the strong drink. She took a sip of her ice-cooled Baileys and then another more generous one as she waited for him to begin again.

"When I was looking the place over, I found Journals my grandmother must have written. She wrote about serving The Lady in The Sacred Grove and I wondered what that was all about. It made for fascinating reading as I'd… . " Michael stopped, his voice dropped to a whisper. He took another sip, seemed to take strength from the brandy, and continued in a strong voice, "you see, Elizabeth," he looked right at her, "The Lady had come to me in dreams all my life. I'd just thought She was the guardian angel my mother always told me I had." He glanced away, unable to meet her steady gaze, unable to yet accept whatever solace she offered.

"I made up my mind to leave school and see to fixing up this place. When I returned to Dublin and went through my father's things, I found a letter he'd written to me when I was born. In it he wrote about a promise never to forsake me as he'd been forsaken. He wrote that he'd never felt included in his parents' lives. He wasn't interested in the horses or the land, which were my grandfather's passion. He wrote that my grandmother served The Lady and had no time for him. I could see that whatever he needed to feel important and as if he mattered to them was missing." His tone harsh, he continued. "His feelings toward them were bitter, but he forsook me as much as they did him. He became rigid and distant in his interactions with me."

Another sip of brandy, a shift to cross his ankles, and a deep breath provided a brief respite. "I stayed with Paddy while the place was fixed up, thankful that the inheritance was substantial enough to put things back to rights, knowing and yet ignoring the reality that my father would not approve.

"It took two months to get the stables, barns, and paddocks ready for their first residents. The next six months I lived in the grooms' quarters while the house was renovated. After the rodents and insects had been eliminated, I had the kitchen and bathrooms updated. Most of the house is as it was.

The silver and china was packed away and stored in the cellar. Other than rodents chewing on the boxes, everything survived intact. All the carpets were cleaned, floors polished, the original drapes were replaced with copies, and walls and windows washed and finished off with a fresh coat of paint that matched as closely as possible the same color that had always been on the walls.

"While all that was going on in the house, I worked to build my stud farm and my racing stable by buying the best horses I could afford and breeding my mares to the best studs. I also searched my family's records and found that when they were a force in racing, they had a prized stud stallion, Suleiman. I did my own research and found a stallion of his lineage. He wasn't highly rated but I bought him anyway. I can't explain it, but he thrived here at The Manor and Brian Boru is his son. Because I was learning the business, I set about to hire the best grooms I could find and wooed Dickens, the best head groom in the business away from the best stable in the country with a contract that gives him five percent of the profit."

He looked her straight in the eye. "I'm a very determined man, Elizabeth. I always get what I want because I'm willing to do what needs to be done."

Elizabeth felt her heart stutter and her cheeks flush. The desire in his eyes flashed and her body answered with a pull deep inside. She raised her glass of Bailey's and sipped, her eyes never leaving his. "You haven't really talked about The Lady, Michael. Do go on."

He looked away from the answering desire he saw in her eyes and let his gaze travel around the room coming to rest on the altar on the table before him. "Well, when I moved into the house, I realized that some sort of light shone through the windows on the garden side. I hadn't had any work done on the grounds, and where I slept in the stable ambient light wasn't really noticeable.

Not only was there the light but also this humming sound that at times almost drove me crazy, and The Lady seemed to stand at the foot of my bed at night. It was rather creepy and very disconcerting. Winter finally came and I found myself without as much to do. I was drawn to the back parlor overlooking the gardens and the desk where I'd found my grandmother's writings. I sorted them out by dates and began reading from the first, when she'd come as a bride to this house. She wrote that she'd agreed to marry my grandfather because a vision had come to her, assuring her that all would come right if she accepted his offer.

Michael shifted on the settee, rearranged his long frame, re-crossed his legs and took another sip of his brandy. "When I'd finished reading the journals, I knew what being in service to The Lady meant, at least as my grandmother saw it. I also knew it was important to protect myself from the full pull of Her energy unless I was going to be in service to Her. And while I knew I would not choose to serve Her, I also knew it was a part of my heritage, my legacy to see that She was protected, that The Sacred Grove was held safe.

"I followed my grandmother's directions to the breech in the garden wall, found the stone she'd described and the jeweled dirk and leather pouch inside. The pouch was disintegrating but I wrapped it in a handkerchief and started down the path. I could see the Sacred Grove and the light pulsing from within it. If I hadn't read my grandmother's journal, I know I would have panicked and retreated. As it was, I steeled myself for what lay ahead. I knew I wouldn't die, I was after all, her grandson, and she'd served The Lady well." A wry smile on his face, Michael leaned further back, scooted down on the cushions and rested his head on the arm of the settee.

"It's been a very interesting fourteen years, very interesting indeed." Looking up at the ceiling he continued. "Shannon was also called by The Lady. We lived here, together, for almost a year. Shannon left because she felt she couldn't live up to The Lady's expectations. I hadn't heard from her until the day Paddy brought you here. Since then I talked to her once on the phone. She told me she'd had a "strong urge" to come and just acted on it. Because she'd not felt that urge since she'd left, she'd had no second thoughts or doubts about leaving. She does miss The Lady but does not miss trying to serve her full time."

Michael shifted again on the settee, stood and walked around the table to sit beside Elizabeth. His fingers caressed her cheek, slipping to her chin, tipping it slightly so he could look deep in her eyes.

"I didn't tell you because I didn't want to share you with Her. I didn't want to find you as I did-in the center of the Sacred Grove. I didn't want what happened to my grandmother, to happen to you. She lost herself in The Lady and the Grove to the exclusion of her son and her husband. My grandfather had the horses and the land. My father had nothing. He paid a high price as did I for my grandmother's devotion and service to Her.

"I didn't say anything on the plane because I didn't really know you. Then I realized I couldn't let you go on your journey alone. I wanted you to have some time in Ireland, to see the sights, to meet and get to know the people, so that when you met The Lady you'd have some background, some perspective, and some sense of what you were in for. I always knew you'd end up here with The Lady. I just wanted … ," his voice faltered and he looked down at her mouth. Her lush lips parted slightly in anticipation.

"What, Michael?" Her Bailey's scented breath filled the space between them. "What did you want?"

"More time with you." His lips brushed hers. "More time for this." His lips demanded more. "More, just more." He deepened the kiss as he pulled her onto his lap, his hands roaming over her soft familiar curves. "More of you, Elizabeth, that's what I wanted, more of you."

# 12 THE SACRED GROVE

The mattress shifted; cool air on her back the sign Michael was out of bed. The discomfort from the cold disappeared when he tucked the covers around her, cocooning her. A soft rustling noise – he was dressing.

"Michael?" Her husky voice whispered into the semi-darkness.

"Sorry, luv, didn't mean to wake you." Michael leaned over the bed brushing a kiss on her forehead.

"It's all right." She snuggled under the covers relishing the warmth, his scent on the sheets surrounding her. "You do know I'll be here when you're done with your morning chores, don't you?" In the faint light she felt more than saw the tension leave his body.

"I'll see you later then," he replied. In the doorway he paused, looked back at his siren, her curly black hair tousled from his hands, from their love making, her blue eyes hidden in the shadows of the room, the covers clinging to her form. In

an instant the pull, the sexual desire swelled. He wanted...wanted her, only her. He won the battle, clamping down
on the urge to return to their bed. A rueful smile on his face,
Michael quietly closed the door and left.

Elizabeth sank back into the covers, memories of their loving
flashing through her mind. They'd made love half on and half
off the settee before making it upstairs to his bedroom. Desperate, she'd been desperate for the closeness when he was
deep within her, murmuring ancient words, as lost as she in
their fervor. How was she ever going to survive when she left
in a week? The question more crucial after last night.

The soft glow from The Sacred Grove crept under the
drapes leaving streaks of gold across the floor. *I can either
avoid The Lady for another day or get up now and go to Her.*
She stayed snuggled in the bed for a few more minutes before
tossing the covers aside and stepping onto the soft carpet. Her
steps quickened when she reached the wood floors and the
connecting door to her own bedroom. At her wardrobe, Elizabeth selected an ankle-length purple dress with a random design of stars and the phases of the moon.

Placing a small satchel she'd found when putting together
her sitting room on one of the chairs, Elizabeth set about
gathering what she needed: her bag of protecting and grounding stones and her crystal and copper wand still wrapped in its
red velvet traveling bag; three small sacks containing cornmeal, sea salt, and lavender. On impulse she picked the necklace up from the altar, slipping it on and adjusting it so it
rested against her breasts. The heat from its energy fortified
her and a deep sense of certainty, of knowing, enveloped her:

she was ready to go to The Lady, to step into The Sacred Grove.

First things first though. Lighting a candle, she waved the sage bundle through the flickering flame until a thin column of smoke rose. Thoroughly smudging herself, she took extra care with the necklace. The satchel, the stones in their bag, her wand, and the bags of cornmeal, salt, and lavender were saturated in the cleansing smoke.

Over the last three days, she'd spent time contemplating her experience in The Sacred Grove. It wasn't so much that she hadn't been aware of the power of The Lady, but she'd been naïve, a naiveté brought on by the years of The Lady coming to her in visions and dreams. Now she believed if she was prepared, she could safely enter and leave The Sacred Grove. Preparation meant casting a circle, stating her purpose, and making sure she had the things that would keep her grounded, centered, and psychically safe. Perching on the edge of the chair, she picked up her Journal and scanned the pages where she'd written of her first visit.

> *The first time I bid The Lady's call, I went in innocence, entering from the South, feeling myself walking for the first time over a path that was yet familiar. In the center, I slipped into trance. That is where I was found: where Michael found me.*
>
> *Days passed after I was away from the Sacred Grove before I was myself again. No, not my old self— I have changed. My soul is magnified, a stream of energy keeps me connected through my heart to The Lady and The Sacred Grove.*

Elizabeth set the satchel down outside the East entrance. A faint path led from this entrance and she knew it circled The Sacred Grove's outer perimeter. Three times she traveled that path, reciting prayers and leaving first salt, then cornmeal, and last lavender. Each time she came to the entrance, she sprinkled the substance over her. When she finished her final circuit, letting a handful of lavender buds fall through the air, tangle in her hair, cling to her clothing, she took her bag of protective and grounding stones from the satchel and tucked it into the belt at her waist.

Standing at the East entrance, her wand in her right hand, she raised her arms over her head. Her eyes closed, she stood in silence and let the words rise from her soul.

"I claim this Sacred Grove and all within." She waved her wand in a circle.

"I claim this Sacred Grove and all within." Again she waved her wand in a circle.

"I claim this Sacred Grove and all within." And for a third time she waved her wand in a circle.

"Spirits of this place hear my prayer and grant me safe entrance and egress from this place. May you know that my purpose is peaceful, that I come with a heart full of love, that I wish to serve The Lady this day."

Elizabeth plucked the small satchel up with her left hand and still holding her wand in her right, started along the path leading into the trees. The energy pulsed, her own body responded with lightness, as if she were walking on air and a kind of invisibility, as if she'd lost substance and form. She looked down to make sure she was touching the ground. Her eyes said 'yes' but her feet didn't feel the leaves, needles, or stones on the path.

Once in the center, Elizabeth crossed to the mossy log and set her satchel down before straightening and turning slowly to take in her surroundings. As her eyes passed over the sacred fire, The Lady appeared before her, a luminous being in a long gown in a shade of blue she knew matched the blue of the holy orders that served the Goddess in earlier times. Her head was covered by the hood of the matching cape. As they stood looking at each other, The Lady reached up and removed the hood, Her long blond hair shone in the light emanating from Her.

Silently The Lady glided next to Elizabeth. Together they raised their arms in prayer and the old words were spoken.

*"I am the light*
*"I am the source*
*"Through me love flows to the outer world.*

*"I am the light*
*"I am the source*
*"Through me love flows to the outer world.*

*"I am the light*
*"I am the source*
*"Through me love flows to the outer world. "*

Their energy flowed from the center of The Sacred Grove, through the opening in the canopy of the tree tops, rising into the sky to be carried by the gentle breezes and winds to the outer world to heal, to enlighten, to show a way to be with all that is in peace.

Elizabeth turned to The Lady and smiled. Ribbons of sublime peace and shimmering light streamed through her. Her free hand instinctively rose and stroked the ancient necklace. It was hot but the heated metal didn't burn her hand.

When she grasped it more firmly an awareness brought her back to the reality of The Sacred Grove, to the present. "That was wonderful."

"If you serve me, Elizabeth, you can experience the sublime sense of peace at all times."

The light around her pulsed as these words came to Elizabeth's mind. *"You know I can't stay. I belong in Fremont, to my women's circle. Maybe I can come back next year for a couple of weeks, on my vacation, but I can't stay. I can't serve you as Michael's grandmother did."*

"All things are possible, Elizabeth. Remember to trust that through love all things are possible."

Elizabeth watched in fascination as the shimmering light and the image of The Lady faded until all that remained was a soft golden glow. As she gathered her things together, she oriented herself as best she could. *Which exit should I take?* Taking the necklace's medallion in her hand, she closed her eyes.

"Spirits of The Sacred Grove hear my prayer. I ask in the name of love and peace that you guide me safely from this sacred circle back into the outer world."

She repeated the words three times as was her practice, opened her eyes and looked around. One path leading out of the circle seemed brighter than the others. Without hesitation she crossed the circle and entered the woods. When she emerged from The Sacred Grove, she was in the South. Turning she walked to her left, passing the West, North, and East entrances before she saw the path winding up to the gardens above.

The sun was higher in the sky and while it felt like she'd barely been away, she knew several hours had passed. Hurrying up the hill, she passed the garden, crossed the terrace and entered the house through the kitchen door. Seamus was chopping vegetables, a soup pot simmered on the stove.

"Has Michael come back from the barns yet?" Elizabeth asked in a breathless voice.

"Yes, he has." The familiar deep voice was behind her.

Elizabeth whirled around and stopped in front of him. His masked features did not hide the emotions flickering in his eyes: worry, concern, anger, frustration, and desire. Focusing on the latter, she smiled as she stood on her tip toes and kissed a corner of his mouth.

"Where were you?" His eyes flashed his tone accusatory.

Elizabeth stepped back, raised her chin and shot back, "Where do you think I was, Michael?"

"Damn you, Elizabeth. Don't you think I worry about you when I don't know where you are?" He grabbed her by the shoulders and roughly pulled her closer. "Don't you know anything?" His words were spoken into her hair. The scent of bergamot swirled in the air as he clasped her to him, the last few inches disappearing as her body was crushed to his.

"Michael," Elizabeth tried to talk, her words muffled as her face was pressed into his shirt. She stopped trying to move her head and relaxed into his strength. Her capitulation seemed to reach him as his hold on her gentled, the rough kisses he'd been pressing in her hair stopped, and his breathing slowed.

She didn't move. These past few days she'd really missed him. It felt so right to be in his arms like this. The steady rhythm of Seamus's knife as it continued to chop the vegetables acted as counterpoint to the beat of his heart. She snuggled closer, her arms around his waist, holding him tight.

"Michael, when you have a minute, there's something I'd like to tell you." Elizabeth said in the calmest most confident voice she could muster.

"Come along then, luv." He towed her back through the kitchen door to where the veranda overlooked the gardens.

Elizabeth stumbled when he abruptly stopped. His strong arms caught and steadied her. He stared down at her, waited for her to speak.

"Do you notice anything strange or unusual about me, Michael?" She stood in front of him, her posture radiating her confidence, composure, and calmness.

He took his time, his gaze scanning her from head to toe and back again. He swore softly his eyes riveted on the necklace she still wore.

"I'm fine, Michael. Look at me. Really look at me," she urged.

He stepped to her, ran his hands down her arms, and lightly grasped her fingers in his large calloused hands. *She's all right. She's wearing the necklace and she's all right.* His hands tightened their grip, sliding up to encompass her hands. He bent them back so that his arms were around her waist; her arms trapped behind her, and slowly pulled her close until every inch of her body was pressed to his. Her eyes fluttered closed and she melted against him. Desire rushed through him and he captured her mouth in a crushing kiss.

The relief he felt was palpable, the lust uncontrollable. He wanted to strip her clothes off and take her right here, right now, in the sun with the breeze blowing softly over them. He'd let her hands go and ranged his over her. Trailing kisses from her now kiss-swollen mouth down the alabaster column of her neck to the soft hollow at the base of her throat, he stopped and licked, eliciting a soft moan of pleasure.

"Michael, I want you," she gasped as his hand cupped her breast, his thumb teasing her taut nipple. "Please, Michael." Her breath was coming in shallow gasps as her hand found what it was seeking. She rubbed her fingers over the burgeoning length straining against his jean.

Michael jerked his head away from the soft spot he'd been nuzzling; looking around for any place they could slake their thirst for each other. He spied the window into his grandmother's office: low to the ground she'd used it as a door. Half-dragging Elizabeth the few steps, he reached for the handle and tugged. When it slid open without complaint, he breathed a sigh of relief. They half fell through the window and into the room.

In the relative privacy of his grandmother's sanctuary, their need for each other escalated. Michael pulled her dress over her head. Elizabeth unbuckled his belt. Within moments they were naked, standing in each other's arms, feeling the frantic need to be closer ease as skin rubbed on skin. Michael's hands were trailing flickers of heat up and down her spine until they drifted lower, cupped her buttocks and pulled her against his rampant erection.

Elizabeth wrapped a leg around his and used the extra leverage to press herself more fully against him. Her mouth feathered kisses over his chest, one arm clutched his shoulder the other struggled to slip between them and stroke his hot arousal.

Michael lifted Elizabeth against him and holding her tightly to him, walked the few steps to the couch. He gently lowered her to the cushions, tenderly spread her hair around her, yanked open a foil-wrapped condom he slipped from his pants pocket and after rolling it on his straining penis, eased himself into her hot core.

She sighed in fulfillment as Michael's heat filled her. She wished she could have this man in her life forever, but she had duties and obligations in Fremont. The best she could do was to be with him here and now in every way she could. The present was what they had. With that her last coherent thought, she began to move with him in the ancient rhythm that brought life into the world and filled her heart with majesty.

# 13   THE BACK PARLOR

When comparing any blissful, happy, contented time she'd experienced in her life against now, nothing measured up to what she shared with Michael. They got up at the same time. While he was off seeing to the horses, she prepared herself with prayers, smudging, and her protection before going to The Sacred Grove.

The daily ceremony of casting the circle, the same sense of lightness, of walking on air, the expectancy of entering the inner circle as well as The Lady appearing before her, their chanting the ancient words: the prayer sending the energy of love and peace out into the world. It all had a profound effect on her: more energy, a more solid sense of her purpose, and more confidence in her spiritual power.

The Lady's simple admonition to trust love had worked well for her this past week. Whenever she found herself beginning to feel troubled or questioning what direction to take, she stopped, closed her eyes, brought her awareness within and asked for direction. She trusted the answer she received and acted upon it. It seemed her touch had turned to gold. Every altar she'd created within The Manor sang a song of joy and love. A warm glow enveloped the house; the glow she knew was the energy of love, an energy that welcomed all.

This morning she was in the back parlor, Michael's grandmother, Elsbeth's room. She'd started reading the journals after that day she and Michael had made such passionate love here. Elizabeth sat at the desk and closed the journal she'd just finished. Rising, she walked slowly around the room viewing the paintings on the walls and shelves of books interspersed with objet d'art. Michael's grandmother, Elsbeth, was a complicated woman. Elizabeth's sense of her was growing as she read the Journals and spent time in this room as well as with The Lady.

*I can feel her love for her husband and child even though she rarely mentions them in her writings. Reminders of them are everywhere.* She wandered around the small room, her fingers trailing over the frame of the portrait of Michael's grandfather. And here are three children's books. A silver frame of Celtic design held a photograph of a happy family that she guessed were Michael's grandparents and father when he was a baby. The paintings were of the barns and paddocks and the horses.

Elizabeth returned to the desk and sat looking out the windows, past the terrace, past the rock wall, to snippets of the gardens that could be seen from this room. But beyond that was the clear blue sky streaked with wisps of clouds, a blank palette to paint her thoughts. *I don't think Elsbeth had any idea her son felt so estranged from her.* Glancing around the room, she saw that when Elsbeth was here, her son and husband were with her. *From what Michael has said, his fa-*

*ther didn't feel included. How painful that must have been for him. How lonely and how unnecessary. Elsbeth sent love out into the world but somehow wasn't able to send it to her own son.*

Seated at the desk, her own Journal open, today's entry not yet written. Usually the words just flowed from her onto the page. Today the words didn't come. Sighing, she shook her head, a frown marred her features. *My plane leaves in two days.*

"Elizabeth, luv, where're you keeping yourself?" Michael's familiar voice came from down the hall.

"I'm in the back parlor," she returned. "I'm coming." She rose and headed toward the door. Nerves competed against each other up and down her spine, in her stomach, and her frown deepened. She took a deep breath in an effort to calm them. *No time like the present.* Her efforts failed. Her stomach in revolt, a sharp pain in her heart, she started toward the front of the house.

Elizabeth joined him in the foyer. He'd told her it was one of his favorite places in the whole house. And Paddy, who'd been over for dinner the other night, had remarked on how The Manor felt different somehow. Over the last week, she created a sacred place in each room in the home. That was the difference.

Michael's joy at seeing her faded when he noticed the crease between her brows. Something was wrong.

"Where's my kiss?" Elizabeth demanded an exaggerated pout pursed her lips. "You always give me a kiss when you come in from the barns."

"Ah, forgive me, luv. Very remiss of me. A kiss, is it? Only a kiss? Nothing more?" he teased.

Elizabeth rose on her tiptoes, wrapped her arms around his neck and pressed herself along the full length of his muscled body. "We can start with a kiss and see what happens," she murmured against his lips.

One arm at her small waist; one about her shoulders Michael eased her closer. He lowered his mouth to her upturned face, brushing light kisses across her forehead from one temple to the other. "How about these kisses?" his voice was husky with his growing desire.

She laughed and shook her head.

His mouth trailed down her nose and he nibbled gently on its tip before brushing his lips across her cheek bones, one side and then the other. "Or do you prefer these?" his husky voice deeper.

Her laugh this time was a bit breathless. She relaxed into him. Desire flashed through her body as Michael's gentle seduction seduced her senses and through them her soul. Her hands, tangling in his blue-black hair, pulled his head closer so she could capture his lips with hers. Her tongue eased along their seam. When he opened to her invitation, her tongue darted in. He caught her tongue with his teeth; gently sucked the tip, and she gasped, her breath filling his mouth. He tasted of coffee, strong and black, and heat and promise. She rubbed her body against his and felt his desire surge as his hand dropped from her waist to her buttocks and he pulled her against his growing erection.

With an effort that felt Herculean, Michael pulled back and looked down at her, passion blazing in his dark blue eyes. "Luv, we either need to stop or find a place more comfortable than the marble tiles beneath our feet."

The break from the heated kiss provided Elizabeth with a minute to catch her breath and remember what she needed to do today.

Michael scowled. Elizabeth was hesitating, something racing through her mind. His own frantic need dissipated as the seconds passed. The tenor of the moment shifted, the passion ebbed. They stood in the main hall her arms still around his neck but no longer tangled in his hair; his arms still around her lithe body but now loosely at her waist; a few inches separated their once fused bodies. He felt her take a deep breath as if girding herself for a challenge. *Whatever is coming, I don't think I'm going to like it.*

Elizabeth let her deep breath out slowly, drawing her arms from around his neck, trailing her hands down his arms to his hands. She stroked back up to his wrists, wrapped her hands around them, before gently lifting them away from her waist and stepping back. She took his hands in hers and looked up at this man she knew, respected, cared for and perhaps even loved. The words on the tip of her tongue, a declaration of her feelings a breath away. Knowing she was leaving kept them from being said. He was scowling and she didn't have to guess to know why. She'd never stepped back from the passion. He knew there was a problem, that something was wrong.

"I need to talk to you first, Michael," she said her voice soft, her look pleading.

"Talk then," he said his voice gruff, his look pained.

"Let's go sit in the gazebo. It's a beautiful day out." She tugged him along, his reluctance obvious in his gait. The few minutes it took them to reach the gazebo she filled with chatter about the items she'd noticed in the back parlor, the books, paintings, and pictures.

"So you've dragged me out here to tell me that? That you think my grandmother really did love my father?" Michael's look was incredulous.

"No, that was just something to share with you. The real reason I want to talk to you, I hope will result in a discussion." She fiddled with her clothing, brushed her hair back from her face before she faced him fully, her spine straight, her chin raised.

*Shit, this is serious.* Michael's stance automatically shifted, his feet wider apart; his hands on his hips, his dark blue eyes boring into hers. He met her unconscious challenge, prepared for her assault, or so he'd thought before he heard her words.

"My plane leaves the day after tomorrow, at eight p.m. I need to make arrangements to get to the airport if you can't take me." Her eyes never left his but the defiant light that first lit them had shifted to one that begged him to understand.

"You're not leaving," he growled out and turned to leave. He'd only thought he was ready for the fight. Panic fueled his need to leave, to get away.

"Michael." She grabbed his arm and hung on. "Michael, please talk to me. You know I have to go home."

He stopped and she stumbled, catching herself from falling by clinging to his arm. "No," he said, his jaw clenched, "I don't know that at all." Maybe he was being unreasonable but dread welled inside him and pain seared his chest; he was breaking apart. Camouflaging the terror, he stiffened and scowled.

"Michael, I've a job, people depend on me. Regardless of my feelings for you, I can't stay. Even if I wanted to, Michael, I can't. I've obligations, responsibilities in Fremont," her voice was soft, pleading. "Please try and understand, Michael. Please try." Tears spilled down her cheeks as she turned and walked away, leaving Michael standing alone on the path to the gazebo, staring straight ahead, head high, back straight.

Her footsteps faded.

He didn't move. If he did, he'd collapse, his heart cut out he'd sink to his knees. She was leaving him and the lightness, the joy, the loving she'd brought into his life would leave with her. A shudder trembled through him. He stared down the path for some sign of her. She was gone.

Retracing his steps to the gazebo, Michael sat on the cushioned bench, leaned his head against one of the pillars and closed his eyes. *I'm a very determined man. She'd do well to remember that.* He shifted on the cushion, stretched out his long legs, and crossed his ankles. *I always get what's important to me. Elizabeth Mary Magdalene Elliott may not know it, but she's very important to me.*

He found her in the old still room and stood in the doorway watching her work at the old wooden bench. Light from the windows shown on the flat surface also catching her in their dust-mote-beams; bunches of recently harvested herbs hung drying from hooks around the room, their scents mixing into a pleasant mostly floral aroma. The catalyst for resurrecting the old still room was the recipes she'd found in his grandmother's Journals for salves, tonics, tinctures, possets, and other natural healing potions. She seemed to be working on recreating one of those recipes now. He watched her consult a paper and then go back to the jars of ingredients.

Since she usually knew when he was near, he was confident she was immersed in what she was doing. He leaned against the door frame, took the time to just be with her unnoticed, and studied her engrossed in something that held her interest.

A memory of Elizabeth working in the back gardens flickered in his mind and he grinned. Somewhere in her search through his grandmother's papers, she'd found a drawing of the back gardens identifying different plants and herbs. She'd been determined to bring the garden back.

The picture of Elizabeth, sketch in one hand, searching for remnants of the old garden, her excited cries of discovery peppering the air was vivid in his mind. She meticulously pounded stakes by each find with a code written on the side to help her identify it later. He'd sent one of the lads from the stables to help with the heavier work: digging, barrows of weeds and debris to remove, and part of the rock wall to rebuild. After two days of Elizabeth's hard work, he could see the skeleton emerging of the once glorious garden.

Another gain to Elizabeth being with him was he could send people to the back garden because The Lady and The Sacred Grove were quiet except in the early morning hours when Elizabeth was there. At first he was astounded, because even though things had been quieter when Shannon was there, they were never so peaceful that he could have unsuspecting people in that part of the grounds.

Remembering her determination about the garden, about harnessing the energy from the necklace, about seeing the sacred in every place gave him pause. A small smile crossed his face. *Nope, I'm more determined than she is.*

Michael cleared his throat and watched with amusement as Elizabeth startled a little squeak escaping.

When she turned and saw who was standing at the door, she clasped her hand to her heart. *Goddess, I wish … .*

They stood across the room from each other, the sturdy work bench between. Even with the distance and that obstacle, they connected through their eyes and energy flowed effortlessly heart to heart, soul to soul.

"I found you at last," Michael deep voice reverberated in the stone-walled room.

"Yes, well, yes you did find me." Elizabeth stammered; her nerves stretched taut. She didn't dare look away, so she stood, heart hammering in her chest looking deep into his eyes, hoping against hope he could understand.

"I know you have obligations, responsibilities in Fremont, Elizabeth. I'm not a fool," he began. He watched her carefully for any sign, any reaction to his words and thought he saw a slight softening of her stance but he wasn't sure. "I was hoping I could persuade you to stay a bit longer. You haven't been to Dublin, or to Northern Ireland. We could take a couple of days and go to Dublin and then on to Belfast and Fermanagh. You know, take a tour of the Belleek factory."

"Michael, I really can't afford—" she started desperately wanting him to understand.

"Let me finish," he quickly interrupted. "I've some business I can do in the East and you coming along will hardly cost anything. The only extra expense would be meals and you don't eat that much."

"But Michael," Elizabeth said her high-pitched voice one of anxiety. "My ticket was one of those deals where it can't be changed. I've got bills to pay and, the rent on my apartment. And if I don't get back to work then ... . " The rest of her sentence was silenced by the wave of his hand.

He took a few steps further into the room. "All I want to know is do you have any desire at all to stay with me a bit more. If all of those money concerns of yours, which are reasonable," he added hastily, "were to vanish, to disappear, would you want to stay with me a bit longer?" He stood on the other side of the work bench, his hands flat on the surface and leaned forward, his sky blue eyes focused on her.

Elizabeth could feel his breath feather across her face he was so close. She could see the pulse on the side of his neck. His hands, fingers slightly spread, rigid against the worn wooden bench. Both so strong, so solid, but while the wood was cool she knew his hands were warm. She shivered at the memory of those warm hands growing hot against her bare skin. His face had the look of expectancy; the heat from his gaze warmed her to her toes. *He's offering me a chance to have more time, more of this with him.*

"When the extra time is up, I'll still have to leave," she whispered and felt herself drawn toward him. As if pulled by a series of strings, she leaned across the work table, straining to reach his strength, his warmth.

"Stay with me, Elizabeth. We'll deal with all that when the time comes." His deep voice was husky with restrained desire. He bent down and brushed his lips against hers. "Stay with me now."

The vortex of his heat tugged. If she didn't resist, she'd be sucked in, pulled into the depths, maybe never to surface. He commanded a very large piece of her heart. With a shudder, she straightened, breaking the physical contact, putting the full width of the work bench between them.

"You know," her voice while soft had a ring of strength to it, "how much I love being here at The Manor with you. The reality is, Michael, I have to go home sometime. I'd love to see Dublin and the Belleek factory and all the other wonders of Ireland, but I have a job, an apartment, responsibilities and obligations. My circle sisters and I are hosting The Women of the Fourteenth Moon ceremony Labor Day Weekend. While I do want to stay with you, I just don't see how I can."

"So if I can figure things out so it could happen, you'll stay longer? At least until your Labor Day Weekend?" Michael's hopes soared. It was a start.

"No, Michael, I can't stay until Labor Day Weekend. I have things I'm to do to help prepare for the ceremony," her voice was tinged with exasperation. *He just doesn't understand. I don't know how to make him understand.* "We make things, Michael. Gifts for the women who attend. There's food to buy, the site to prepared. We do it all together."

"So all seven of you go to the grocer?" he asked, his brow knit in confusion.

"No, that's not what I mean," she said her voice strident with frustration. She pushed away from the bench and paced. "But together we decide what to do and who will do it and then we support one another. We all set up the site and cast the circle. And we work on the gifts together." A guilty look flashed across her face. "Well, there are times when we take things home to work on them," she admitted coming to stand before him, the work bench still between them. Lifting her chin in a defiant gesture she added, "Everything is decided together, as a group, a circle."

"Let me see what I can work out. We can talk more at dinner. If we can't work this out, I'll take you to the airport." He hopped up to sit on the work bench, leaned across, took her in his arms, and kissed her soundly on the lips. Letting her go, he slid off the table, strode to the door, calling back over his shoulder, "Don't start packing yet, luv. Remember I'm a determined man."

Michael walked quickly through the house to the library he used as a second office. Inside, he closed the door, crossed to his desk and sank into the leather chair. He pulled a pad of paper toward him and reached for his pen. Quickly he made a list: change ticket; arrange for bills to be paid; talk to someone in her women's circle? He tapped the pen against his chin as he considered whether it would be better to arrange for her to talk to one of them instead.

Job, loss of income. Most of her objections had to do with money and he knew it would be a challenge to get her to accept money from him. With his list completed, Michael swiveled around to the table behind him, picked up the phone, and quickly dialed a number from memory.

"Ian, ole man. How are you doing?" Michael boomed into the phone knowing his business agent was a bit hard of hearing. "I need a bit of a favor, Ian," and he proceeded to outline his plan.

Within the hour the phone rang. Michael wrote down the information Ian had procured for him, a smile of satisfaction on his lips. "Thanks, Ian. Great job. I'll get back to you later. I'm not sure with the time difference I can reach the man now but I want to try." Michael sat for a moment, ran his hand through his already well-tousled hair. "Nothing left but to get to it," he muttered as he picked up the phone and dialed the unfamiliar number in the States. He took a deep breath in an effort to release the nerves jolting through him, clenched and unclenched his free hand, wanting to fidget in his chair but fighting the urge.

"Jackson Montgomery," the masculine voice came over the phone lines.

Michael leaned back in his chair, the tension washed away with relief. He smiled the smile of someone who sees the finish line and no one's in front of him.

"Mr. Montgomery," he started, "Michael Murphy, here. I was with Elizabeth Elliott when we ran into you and your wife at Ashford Castle. I believe you were on your honeymoon. Elizabeth, who has become a very close and dear friend of mine, has run into a bit of a problem. I'm calling in the hopes you or your wife'll have some ideas about how to help her out."

# 14. More Time

Nerves on edge after her encounter with Michael, Elizabeth remained in the still room, the scents from the herbs and the quiet calming. The still room was the pharmacy of the old homes and castles. The women in charge were healers. In some of the historical novels she'd read, the chatelaine or lady of the castle was the healer and oversaw the gathering and preparation of the salves and potions. In other stories one of the characters, either an old woman or a gifted younger one, was the woman wise in the ways of healing. *I'm not a healer, Sophia knows more about plants and their healing properties than I, but I've studied the recipes and am confident I can follow directions.*

Perched on the stool at the work bench, Elizabeth soaked up the room's energy. As in every room at The Manor, a small altar was set up. This one sat in the middle of a chest-high shelf running the length of the rectangular room. A large piece of moss served as the altar cloth. Each direction sported a small pile of herbs and plants. In the East, representing youth, she'd placed sprigs of cowslip, fern, vervain and anise seeds; the South held oak leaves, a geranium flower, and wheat and nuts representing fertility. She'd taken some time figuring out what to put in the West, finally deciding invisibility was her focus. That space held fern, poppy, and mistletoe. Finally in the North, she used herbs and plants for wisdom and spirits. To sweet grass and tobacco, she added dandelion and sunflower petals along with a peach pit. A small jar filled with water from the spring in The Sacred Grove graced the center.

When she considered Michael's offer, the tension in her body increased. Slipping off the stool, she walked the few steps to stand in front of the altar. Immediately a calm energy flowed through her and she relaxed, arms dangling loosely at her sides, head slightly bowed, eyes closed. *What am I going to do? It hurts in my heart to think of leaving in two days. If I stay longer, I'll have more memories of Michael and Ireland but... I wish I could talk to one of my women's circle.* A deep sigh shuddered through her.

In the quiet, an idea flickered. "I brought a calling card to use in case of an emergency," she said to herself. "There isn't any reason I can't use it now," she said her voice strengthening with the energy of purpose. "I'll finish up here and then make that call."

Up in her room, Elizabeth searched her purse finally finding the long distance phone card tucked into a side pocket. She hurried through the house to the back parlor, calculating the difference in time and figuring out who she'd most likely be able to reach.

Thirty minutes later, fighting discouragement, she hung up from her sixth call. *Take a deep breath, E. You've left messages. One of them will call you back.* She chuckled to herself.

*At least you didn't wake someone up at 3 a.m.* Still sitting at the desk, Elizabeth noticed the room fill with pulsing light from The Sacred Grove. She stood and walked to the window Michael's grandmother had used as a door. The intense humming and pulsing light were signals. The Lady was calling her.

The light and sound induced a light trance. Elizabeth lost track of time but she did not answer The Lady's call.

A knock on the door, broke the trance.

"Come in," she invited.

Seamus opened the door, announced, "Dinner's getting cold," before turning and retreating down the hall towards the dining room. Elizabeth looked in the mirror and shook her head in mock dismay at her reflection: hair in disarray, skin pale, eyes bright with remnants of the trance. Taking the pins from her hair, she let it fall free, finger-combing out the tangles. "I'd better get going or it will really be cold," she muttered to herself as she hurried to the dining room.

Michael looked up as Elizabeth came through the door and knew he'd never tire of seeing her. He loved the way the curls of her coal black hair flowed over her shoulders, down her back, the way they looked spread over his pillow as he made love to her. A closer look and he saw the traces of the trance.

He'd heard the hum, felt the pulsing energy, knew The Lady called her. When Seamus came back, he reported she was standing by the barely open parlor window. *Maybe she resisted The Lady's call. Maybe her path, if I can persuade her to remain with me, will be different from my grandmother's. Maybe... .* he stopped himself.

"Hungry?" he stood while Seamus held a chair out for her and she sat.

"Starved," she looked up at Seamus, a grin on her face. She sniffed the air adding, "and I smell something delicious."

Michael smiled to himself as he watched Seamus' cheeks color with pleasure, mumble something unintelligible, and stalk out of the room. His houseman would do anything for her. A chuckle escaped.

Elizabeth turned toward him, a quizzical look on her face. He opened his mouth to say something but stopped as he heard Seamus coming back down the hall. The door swung open and Seamus entered a large tray in his beefy hands. He set it down on the sideboard and began moving the dishes to the table.

"Oh, Seamus, this is wonderful. Fresh bread, still warm from the oven and from the look and smell of things beef vegetable soup. You've outdone yourself again," she gushed as she reached out for a slice of the bread. "Hmmm," she moaned as she took a bite of the yeasty bread she'd already slathered with butter. "A feast," she pronounced. "A veritable feast, this is." These words were directed at Seamus' back as he left the room. Elizabeth dipped her spoon into the soup Michael had ladled into her bowl. Turning to him, she added, "I'm rather famished."

Michael looked at her bright, open face, gazed into her dark blue eyes, and felt himself lean toward her, unable to resist her pull. Her chattering stopped; but she did not look away. "You are... ," he reached out and brushed his fingers across her cheek, "so very beautiful." His fingers trailed a path under her chin, his thumb teased across her slightly parted lips. "So very soft." He stood, leaned across the corner of the table, kissing her forehead. He fought the urge to sweep the dishes from the table, pick her up, lay her down, and surge into her, to ravish her with his body and hands, to feel the completeness that came when they made love. Instead, he sat back down in his chair, purposefully picked up his glass of Guinness, took a drink, and refocused on his dinner.

Transfixed, Elizabeth sat rooted to her chair, unmoving. He took her breath away with his passion, his seeming unending need for her. Was she even breathing? Her skin still tingled where his hand, his fingers and his mouth had touched. From the first moment he'd offered to guide her around Ireland, she knew leaving him would be hard. How hard was becoming more and more evident each hour she remained in his company, each day she came closer to leaving.

Her problem? She'd thought she could keep her emotional distance knowing this was a once-in-a-lifetime adventure, a time-out-of-time from her normal mundane life. *But now? I can't imagine anyone else touching me. I can't imagine making love to anyone else.* She made an effort to eat, her mind still grappling with the feelings roiling within. *I don't know how I will survive leaving him. And if he marries? I don't know what I'll do.*

The war within her continued, the other side of the equation of leaving Michael, leaving The Lady, leaving Ireland was if she chose to stay, she'd be the one who broke The Circle. She'd be the one who left, who changed everything. *We are a sacred women's circle, we've each committed ourselves to The Circle and each other. They are my family. When the seven of us are together, there is something extraordinary about the Energy we create.*

As they continued to eat their simple meal of soup, bread, fruit and cheese, the dinner conversation drifted to safer topics. Elizabeth asked how the training was going in the barns and Michael invited her to come with him tomorrow and see for herself.

"What did you do after I left the still room?" Michael inquired.

"I tried calling my circle sisters but no one was home," she responded, not noticing Michael's arching brows. "I'd gotten an international calling card in case there was an emergency," she explained.

"Is there an emergency?" Michael hoped his voice sounded calm as his heart stepped up its beat.

"No, no, there's no emergency. I just wanted to talk to one of them." Her voice soft, wistful she added, "I miss them and, and well, I just wanted to talk, to find out what they've been doing." Her voice strengthened. "You know, get caught up. I hope you don't mind, but I left your phone number in case one of them could call me back."

"I don't mind, luv. I don't mind a'tall. I'll let Seamus know to expect a call for you. He can get a number and then find you and you can call them back. Use the phone in my office. I've got international dialing on that one." And don't forget to check your desk to make sure Montgomery's name isn't anywhere she'll see it, he reminded himself.

**Nine a.m.**
**Fremont, Oregon**

Ashley's front door was open but Gabriella still knocked and called out as she entered and followed the voices to the backyard patio. All she knew was Elizabeth had called and left messages with everyone. That it had something to do with

Lily wanting them all to meet this morning she was sure. Specifics? She couldn't guess.

On the patio, a mish-mash of lawn and house chairs set around a small metal table, comprised their circle. A small decorative cauldron of sage was lit and passed around so everyone could smudge. Radiating the glow of a new bride, Lily began. "Thank you all for doing what you needed to do to be here." Standing she added, "I think we need to start with prayers." Seeing the concerned looks on everyone's faces, she quickly added, "We need to cast the circle now so if we need it we don't have to stop and do it later."

The other women stood and turned toward the east. One by one they called in the spirits, the essence of the direction. They continued in this manner, turning to the south, the west, and the north, each one speaking as the words came to her. At last they stood, looking into the center, holding hands, arms raised as they called upon the spirits of the air, the ground and the source of all. With their prayers concluded, they sat, and Ashley handed Lily a piece of amethyst to use as their talking stone.

"We all received a message from Elizabeth yesterday," she began. "And we all know that something is bothering her. We could feel it when we listened to her voice and the fact that she said she'd try another one of us." She looked around the circle to gauge the reactions to her words and saw heads nodding. "While I don't know exactly why Elizabeth is calling, I do have some additional information that gives me an idea." She quickly filled them in on the phone call Jackson had received from Michael Murphy and reminded them of their chance meeting at the Ashford Castle. "It seems she's become involved with him enough to be staying with him. Jackson believes he wants her to stay with him but is couching it in terms of showing her more of the country.

"According to what Mr. Murphy told Jackson, Elizabeth's concerns, her reasons for not staying in Ireland longer, center around her job, bills, and 14th Moon responsibilities. He called to ask Jackson for ideas for taking care of Elizabeth's Fremont obligations so she can stay longer." Her blue-eyed gaze traveled around the circle taking in the reactions that showed on each face. "Jackson's idea is to just pay her bills. Gabby has a key to her apartment and has been picking up her mail. She can easily make sure her rent is paid as well as the rest of her bills. Jackson is more than willing to write the checks if he just knew the amounts. That leaves her job and the 14th Moon."

She paused again to gauge everyone's response to what she'd said so far and to let the information sink in. "A critical piece of information we don't have is whether or not Elizabeth even wants to stay." Lily set the amethyst on the small table in the center of their circle.

Diana reached for the amethyst, clasping it gently between her two hands. Absent-mindedly she tucked her dark brown hair behind her ears. "We've each received a card from her with a brief note indicating she was having a wonderful time. I'm not surprised she didn't mention him in her notes. It's very unlike her to get involved with someone she doesn't really know." Diana stared at the stone in her hands as if it held all the answers. Looking up she added, "I, for one, have no problem calling her agency and explaining that she needs to remain in Ireland a bit longer. I can't imagine they'd fire such a valuable employee over extending her vacation." She replaced the stone back on the table.

Hunter picked the amethyst up next. Her green eyes reflected her serious tone of voice. "I called the number this morning. There's an eight hour time difference we need to be aware of. I left a message with the man who answered that I'd call back. The phone number isn't to a hotel or Bed and Breakfast, but to someone's home. That means she is staying with this guy. And knowing Elizabeth, for her to be 'staying with'," she said and hooked her fingers, indicating quotation marks, "some guy—that in and of itself speaks volumes."

"I don't know about y'all, but I do know that I sure sent out prayers she'd meet someone wonderful over there," Ashley drawled. Her gray eyes scanned the circle as she picked up the stone. "I believe we all teased her enough about finding someone tall, dark, and handsome or words to that effect. So, if she has found someone and wants more time with him, I'm all for it. I can help with some of what she's to do for 14th Moon. Isn't she's set to do some of the work with the maidens?"

Sophia took the amethyst from Ashley and held it to her heart. One of the stone's properties was enhancing higher states of consciousness. Her brown waist length hair shielded her face when she bowed her head and centered herself with the calming energy of the stone. Before responding, she lifted her chin, her brown eyes raised to the sky.

"After listening to Elizabeth's message and hearing her voice, I've been more focused about keeping her in my thoughts and prayers. Whatever is going on, it is stressful for her." She stopped and looked around the circle as she lowered her hands, the stone now resting in her lap. "Does anyone have an issue with Elizabeth staying in Ireland longer if that is her desire? If you do, please speak up." Her words were met with silence. "Does anyone have a problem with paying her bills, contacting her agency, and taking on some of her 14th

Moon duties so of she decides to remain longer in Ireland she does so knowing all is well here? If you do, please let us know your thoughts." Again her words were met with silence.

Gabriella, who had not participated in the conversation up to this point, reached out for the stone. "As you all know, Elizabeth asked me to take care of her apartment while she's gone. And last night, when we called each other to compare notes, it seems E called me first. If there are no objections, I'd like to be the one who calls her back and talks to her. I have a feeling there's more going on than just getting her bills paid, talking to her employer, and the 14th Moon ceremony." She looked first to Sophia and Lily and then over to Diana, Ashley and Hunter. "Do any of you have a problem with me making the call?" As she looked around the circle she saw that the job was hers. "To be upfront, I'm involved in a big project at work so with the time difference I may not get her called until morning. Because I'm going in late, I'll have to work late. I want to be able to talk to her for as long as she needs to so don't want to try to call her sitting in my car on my break."

"She knows we've got her messages because Hunter called her back. And, I do think you are the best one to make the call even knowing you most likely won't be calling until morning. Do you know what you want to say?" Lily inquired.

"First I want to listen to what she has to say. Then if it is as we suspect, based on Jackson's conversation with Michael Murphy, I can assure her that between us we can take care of everything until her return." She turned to Ashley. "How about a potluck here tomorrow night? I can let everyone know what Elizabeth had to say. There'll be enough food for the kids and Art, if he's home. Would that be okay with you?"

Hunter added, "I'll bring Logan and she can entertain the kids while we talk."

"Y'all are more than welcome. Ya know I love having you here." Ashley's silver blond shoulder length hair swung with the energy in her nods. "It's supposed to be another hot day so I'll have plenty of lemonade and ice tea."

With everything settled, the women stood and said prayers to release the spirits who'd held the circle's energy. Arms around one another, they bowed their heads and whispered blessings for safe journeys.

## The Manor, Kinslow, Ireland

Elizabeth rose early as always, to serve The Lady in The Sacred Grove. Together they said prayers that sent love out into world, and then she returned to the house to busy herself with refreshing the altars or a project in the still room.

It was evening when the phone rang.

She heard Michael's voice speaking briefly. A knock on her sitting room door and a moment later he stood in the entrance, running his hands through his rumpled hair, a slight smile on his face his eyes narrowed, the blue deepening, as he caught her gaze from across the room. "It was for you, luv. A Gabriella Montcriff, I believe was her name."

Elizabeth jumped up from the window seat. "Gabby called?" She started for the door. "Is she still on the phone?"

"No. She apologized for taking so long to call, something about work. I asked if you had her number and when she said "Yes", I told her you'd call her right back. Use the office phone." Michael stood in the hall the scent of bergamot and Elizabeth swirled, the result of her race down the hall, down the steps to his office.

The next few minutes were critical to whether he had more time with her. Her plane left tomorrow evening. Slowly with a heavy heart and heavy tread, he followed. As he approached the office door, he heard Elizabeth's excited voice, "Gabby, is that you? Oh, Gabby, it's so good to hear your voice. How is everyone?"

There was a pause he interpreted as Gabriella's response. He remained just outside the door, hidden in shadows, unable to tear himself away, listening to Elizabeth's voice shift from excited to serious.

"Gabby, I'm in such a pickle here. You see, I've met someone," a pause and then her voice again, "Yes, Michael. He's really very special and then there's The Lady and The Sacred Grove. They're really here in Ireland, actually here at Michael's. I don't know what to do, Gabby. I feel so torn, so conflicted. There's the rent and the bills, you know. And my job and then the 14th Moon and all of you. But then there's The Lady, The Sacred Grove and Michael."

Michael felt a myriad of emotions as he listened to Elizabeth describe him as very special and then place him at the end of the list, behind The Lady and The Sacred Grove. He turned and made his way up the stairs to his quarters where he poured himself two fingers of Irish whiskey. His mood was darker after downing the liquor in one gulp, the burning in his throat mirroring the anger raging through him. Shaking his head to dispel the bleak images of a life without Elizabeth, he knew he was in no shape to hear her plans to leave the next day or stay because of The Lady instead of him.

He slammed the glass back on the tray, grabbed a jacket from the wardrobe, and stalked out the door. Taking the back stairs, he charged through the kitchen and outside. Without looking back, he stormed to the garage, opened the door, and got in his car. *I can't stay here right now. The pub or maybe Paddy's.* Backing the car out of the garage, he gunned the motor. The car fishtailed spewing gravel when he tore off down the drive.

Elizabeth, momentarily distracted when a car sped off, refocused on her conversation with Gabby. Her friend would go through her mail and sort out her bills: rent, utilities, car insurance. Arrangements made to talk again tomorrow, she hung up. *Maybe everything will turn out okay. With The Circle's help I can stay with Michael for three more weeks.* Being back at least two weeks before the 14th Moon Ceremony would give her time to put the finishing touches on the dress she wanted to wear, and for Gabriella and her to decide on some of the final details for the Maiden Ceremony.

Hugging herself, a grin on her face, Elizabeth hurried out of Michael's office. She stopped at the bottom of the stair and slowed her steps, prolonging the feeling of joy at being able to spend more time with Michael in this old castle-house she loved, and see more of Ireland in the process. Her hand glided over the silky wooden banister as her feet glided over the carpeted risers. It had been a bit overwhelming at first, but she found comfort in knowing that generations of women who served The Lady had lived here, had worked in the still room, had walked the path to The Sacred Grove. There was tradition, a history here she'd never felt or found anywhere else. She sighed. *At least I'll have a bit more time here with Michael. Maybe we can come to an understanding so I can come back every year to serve The Lady — and see him.*

She stopped outside Michael's bedroom; smoothing her skirt, fingers combing her hair, knocking once before opening the door and stepping in. The room was empty. The sound of a car driving away poked her memory. *He's left. Where has he gone?*

Her confusion was immediately overwhelmed by the humming, the pulsing energy, the shimmering light: the call to come to The Sacred Grove. She could see The Lady's arms outstretched in invitation; but she'd never been to The Sacred Grove at night, never served The Lady in darkness. With Michael gone, nothing kept her from doing so now.

Returning to her room, Elizabeth donned a long skirt and her necklace, picked up her bag of protective stones and tucked it in her waistband. The light emanating from The Sacred Grove lit her room as if it was daylight. The call, the pull to come was stronger than she'd ever experienced. She walked out of her room and down the hall, stopping at the top of the stairs. It'd been less than an hour since Michael had told her about Gabriella's call; less than an hour since she figured out she could stay; less than an hour and her world was in turmoil. *Where was Michael? Why did he leave without saying anything?* An idea flashed and she hurried down the stairs to the foyer table. *No note.*

Standing in the foyer, the house acted like a buffer lessening the impact of the energy assault from The Sacred Grove. That respite allowed her time to focus on what she wanted to do. She took three deep breaths and went within, into the quiet center, to ask for direction. *What do I do now?*

Moments passed before the answer came to her. She felt a confidence flow through her as she hurried down the hall leading to the kitchen, detouring down the short passageway to the still room. Once inside she searched for rosemary and sage, tucking these herbs into her blouse and bra. She smoothed some lavender lotion on her hands and arms and again on her feet. She filled a small bag with a combination of the herbs she had on the still room's altar.

With preparations as complete as she knew how to make them, she left the still room and walked outside to the back garden. At the top of the path she stopped, took some of the herbs from the small bag, and sprinkled them on the posts on either side of the gate as well as the ground between. As she traveled the now well-worn path she continued to sprinkle a few of the herbs every few feet, conserving most of them for the work she needed to do at The Sacred Grove.

This time she made only one circuit around The Grove, but still said prayers at each of the directions. At the East gate, she stated her intention, "I've come in peace to serve The Lady," and started along the path to the center. The familiar feeling of lightness and buoyancy surrounded her.

The Lady was waiting, her robes the blue of the priestess' who've served The Goddess throughout time. Elizabeth saw the white light of pure energy streaming from the blue crescent tattoo at the place of her third eye. Raising her hand, Elizabeth tossed herbs in the air where they drifted down into her hair and on her gown before stepping closer. The power surging through her rocked her back on her heels. Instinctively her hand grasped the necklace, the energy so potent it felt as if it scorched her hand. Although the urge to drop it was intense, her hold on the pendant firmed and it pulsed with an answering energy.

That special communication, mind to mind, flared and she could hear The Lady's gentle command to come, stand beside her. She complied, and as she moved closer, felt the energy infiltrate every cell of her being.

> *I am the Light*
> *I am the Source*

*Through me Love flows to the outer world.*

*I am the Light*
*I am the Source*
*Through me Love flows to the outer world.*

*I am the Light*
*I am the Source*
*Through me Love flows to the outer world.*

The ancient words flowed from her lips. Her arms, at first raised in prayer, lowered as the words came to an end. She turned now, facing The Lady. She looked deep into her luminous eyes. "Come, say the words with me again," she communicated to The Lady. But instead of raising her arms, she held out her open palms. The Lady touched her outstretched hands. As intense and dazzling the sensations of their merging energies were Elizabeth did not falter.

*We are the Light*
*We are the Source*
*Through us Love flows to the outer world.*

*We are the Light*
*We are the Source*
*Through us Love flows to the outer world.*

*We are the Light*
*We are the Source*
*Through us Love flows to the outer world.*

As the ancient prayer ended, Elizabeth was the Light, the Source as her whole being shimmered with the ancient energy of this sacred place.

# 15   SOMETHING'S CHANGED

"Tis four o'clock, Mick." Paddy's booming voice assaulted his throbbing head. Michael cringed at the cold air when his friend yanked the blanket off, stumbled as he was hefted up and hauled cursing and grumbling into the bathroom. Four came early, too early for Michael's whiskey fogged mind. *Maybe taking that bottle of Jamison's to the apartment and getting drunk wasn't my best idea.*

"We've been through a lot boyo, and in a few minutes ye'll be thanking me for this," his friend continued as he dumped him in the shower and turned the water on hard and cold.

"Shit!" Michael felt the stinging cold water from the shower hit him like bullets of ice. "What the hell are you doing?" he tried unsuccessfully to stand. "Cochran," he bellowed, "you're a dead man, you are."

"Ah, Mick, you're alive then," Paddy's voice was jovial as he eyed his friend, now soaked to the skin, shivering under the onslaught of the freezing shower. Knowing Michael was furious, he kept his distance as he turned the water off and backed up against the counter. "Need some help getting up?" Paddy's mild voice queried his friend who sat in the shower, head in his hands, shoulders rounded in defeat.

Michael shook his head and wished he hadn't. "I could use some aspirin. In the kitchen, right of the sink." It hurt to talk, it hurt to think, it hurt to move. He'd done it to himself. But knowing that didn't make it better, only made it worse.

Paddy returned with a glass of water and four aspirin in hand. Michael grimaced as he swallowed them down. He handed the glass back to Paddy and leaned his head back against the cold shower wall. "I really did it to myself this time. I haven't gotten this drunk in ... I don't remember when. It hurts to think," he groaned out the last.

"I've never seen you so wasted either, Mick. You're tied up in knots over Elizabeth. Love does that to a man," he said, his voice thoughtful, Paddy still held the glass as he resumed his former position leaning back on the counter.

Michael startled, grabbed his head as the pain shot through it with the sudden movement. "Love? You think I love her?" He ground out between clenched teeth. "I can't love her. I can't marry her. I can't take the risk. Oh God," he moaned. "What have I done?"

"Mick," Paddy's voice was gentle. "Mick, let's get you showered. It'll help with that head you've got." He reached down and wrapped one of his large hands around Michael's arm. "Come along now, Mick." He coached as he helped a shaky Michael to his feet.

Michael leaned against the shower wall, fumbled with his clothing. The wet clothes stuck like a second skin. He tossed each soggy item on the bathroom floor as he managed to get them off.

Paddy adjusted the water to warm, but after Michael washed and shaved, slowly turned the temperature back down until Michael begged off. A bit more sober but with a head filled with jack hammers, he got out of the shower, dried himself and dressed in a set of spare clothes he kept there.

"Thanks, Paddy," Michael growled, as he struggled to pull on his boots. "I feel better. Not good, exactly, but better."

"Good to hear, Mick," Paddy started for the door. "Got to get going." He stopped and turned back in the doorway. "Some words of advice, Mick," seeing the frown cross his friend's face, he quickly added, "you owe me after last night and this morning."

"Be quick about it then," Michael grumbled.

"She's a special one that Elizabeth is, Mick, but then you already know that. You've made a lot of rules about what can and can't happen. Don't deny it, because I spent the night listening to your list." He stopped, wanting his words to be the right ones, wanting his words to help Mick figure things out.

"Sometimes we can have all we want, Mick. You say you're a determined man. My advice is don't limit yourself with rules. Remember you're a determined man. You can have what you want if you go after it." He turned and left closing the door softly behind him.

Michael sat, listening to Paddy's footsteps recede as he trod down the steps, hearing him call out to Peter. Paddy's words echoing in his mind, he waited for inspiration to strike, to find a way out of the mess he'd made of his personal life. When there was nothing but the pounding in his head, he stood, grabbed his jacket, and went down to the pub for a strong cup of coffee before driving to his place to begin his morning routine.

Elizabeth woke alone. She glanced at the clock; it was seven. Michael hadn't come to bed. Either he didn't come home last night or slept somewhere else in the house. She wasn't upset and was no longer worried. Somehow she knew he was all right. After her time with The Lady last night, she felt different, more confident in her sense of self. She got up, dressed, and noticed a peaceful look on her face. A healthy serene glow, similar to what she imagined an aura looked like, surrounded her.

Down in the kitchen, Seamus had scones and tea waiting for her. Watching him chop, dice, slice, knead, stir, blend—all without a recipe in sight was a joyful experience. While he prepared something for either the noon or evening meal, she sipped her tea, nibbled on her scone, and made occasional comments on what he was fixing. Something was different today because several times he glanced in her direction.

Upon finishing her breakfast, she brushed her crumbs onto her plate and took it and her cup to the sink. After washing them and setting them in the rack to dry, she thanked Seamus for the food, and went about her day.

Instead of going to The Lady and The Sacred Grove or working in the still room, her plan was to explore. Generally she remained in or near the house but since Gabby's call wouldn't come until seven this evening she wasn't concerned about missing it.

There was much about this place, Michael's home, she'd yet to discover because of her pre-occupation with The Lady and The Sacred Grove and the house. Starting at the beginning, she crossed the entry foyer, opened the imposing oak door, and stepped out onto the wide terrace-like porch made of a local stone, with eight risers of the same material leading down to the graveled path from the drive. A slight curve in the road, barred the stone-pillared entrance from her sight. To her left the ornate woodworked gazebo, where she had talked to Michael about leaving, perched on a small rise before vacant green fields crisscrossed with stone fences. Straight ahead, between the house and the curve in the drive, was a large lawn flanked by flower gardens and dotted with old oak trees. Benches, strategically placed, offered views of the gardens, fields, and the house itself. Graveled paths meandered through the grassy lawn connecting benches and the main path from the drive to the house. Fields to her right were sectioned by stone fences or white wooden one. These marked the paddocks, her destination this morning.

On her way to the barns, she looked toward the garage that once had been the carriage house. Michael's car was there. She stopped a moment, centered herself, and reassessed her feelings. She was both glad he was here and that nothing had happened to him, and upset that he'd left without a word. With that settled in her own mind, Elizabeth continued to the barn.

At the large doorway, she paused until her eyes got used to the dimmer light. The noise and smell of horses and the men working with them brought back memories of the races and the time she'd spent with Michael and Paddy at the barns there. She began strolling down the aisles of horses, conscious of the work around her, keeping out of everyone's way.

Dickens stopped in mid-sentence as he was giving directions to one of the grooms when he saw Elizabeth in the barn. As soon as he finished his instructions, he stepped across the aisle and waited. Within a few minutes she'd progressed to where he stood. "Morning, Miss Elizabeth," he said quietly.

"Good morning, Dickens." Elizabeth said.

"You've come to see the horses? Mick's got a fair number of good uns, he does."

"Well, they all look beautiful to me, Dickens. But I must admit I particularly like the grays or the black ones. The gray back a couple of stalls, you know, Ghost Rider, is almost dappled. Michael's horse Brian Boru is gorgeous too. I don't think there's a white hair on him." Her nerves stretched as she chattered away. Dickens was giving her an appraising look similar to the glances she'd seen from Seamus. "Michael invited me to come to the stables yesterday but I was waiting for a phone call. I thought to come today but if I'm in the way, I can come another time."

"Nah, Miss, you're not in the way. Just surprised I am to see you as Mick didn't say nothing. If'n you go out those doors," he pointed to her right, "you can see the lads takin' some of the horses through their paces."

"Oh, I'd like that, Dickens. Thank you." Relief rushed through her and the nervousness dissipated when she turned in the direction Dickens pointed. At the opening, seeing a large paddock with a number of jumps set up, she stopped. One by one the riders were taking their mounts through the course. She stepped up to the rail but her view was hampered as the top rail was at her eye level. Remembering how she'd handled the same situation at the races, she climbed up the two bottom rails, hung her arms over the top, and settled in to watch the workout.

Michael knew she was there before Dickens informed him of the fact. He'd felt a shift in the energy, the noise, the feel of the place and knew she was near him. He hadn't gone in search of her because he didn't know what to say or do. Dickens, who'd added that she seemed different and the horses were acting a bit off, told him she was over watching the jumpers work out.

Dickens was right. She was clinging to the rail, watching the horses go through their paces, enthralled with their strength, their beauty, the effortless way they lifted themselves and their riders over the obstacles. He didn't think she'd cause a scene here with all the lads around, so he strolled over to where she stood, put his foot on the bottom rail, and began watching the training session.

In silence, they watched the horses. The first group finished and a second group came into the practice area starting through the jumps.

"I'm sorry, Elizabeth," he said his voice soft and low.

"For what?" she asked.

"I – I - uhm," he started and glanced her way only to meet two icy blue eyes boring into him. *Hell!* He looked away; better to get the words out. "Well, I don't believe I let you know I was meeting Paddy last night at the pub."

"No, Michael, you didn't let me know nor did you leave a note," her voice was decidedly frosty. Another glance and he saw her, chin raised, eyes looking daggers at him.

"Well, that's what I'm apologizing for," he heard the note of defensiveness in his voice and hoped she didn't. One look...she'd heard.

"Really. And is that *all* you're apologizing for?" her voice now had that calm, sweet tone most men knew meant they were in deep trouble.

She moved to get down but before she could fully untangle her arms from the top rail and step down, Michael, his hands on her waist, lifted her gently to the ground. He pulled her back against him, rested his chin on her head breathing in her familiar scent of bergamot, feeling her remain stiff in his arms.

"We have to talk, Elizabeth. I know I screwed up last night. I know I don't have any claim on you. I just — hell and damnation. Please. Just come back to the house with me," he said, his voice a mixture of exasperation and pleading. He didn't care if she heard him begging, he just wanted to make things right with her. To have her soft body mold to his, to feel her arms around his neck, her leg wrapped around his to pull him closer to her, to have the chasm between them bridged at worst, gone at best.

Elizabeth listened with her heart instead of her mind to the sincerity in his words, sensed the underlying fear and vulnerability. His arms held her tight.

"Let me go, Michael," she ordered. His arms immediately dropped to his side.

When she turned and looked, his face reflected a blend of pain and panic. Reaching out she took his hand. "If we're going to talk in the house, we'd better get going," she tugged. "Come along, Michael," her gentle voice commanded.

Michael trod beside her. He wasn't fully recovered from his night of drinking; he wasn't sure he had the ability to talk her into forgiving him. Paddy's advice "you're a determined man" lifted his spirits, so by the time they reached the kitchen door he felt more himself.

"Where do you want to talk?" Elizabeth turned and looked at him.

"My study, unless you'd prefer someplace else," he responded, hoping he sounded reasonable, conciliatory, not condescending.

"Your study is fine," she started through the kitchen into the hall that led to Michael's study. Once there, she sat on the settee with the view of the barns and paddocks.

Michael crossed to the sideboard, took one look at the decanters of alcoholic beverages and thought twice about pouring himself a stiff drink. "Do you want tea?" he asked Elizabeth.

"No, I'm fine."

He sat beside her, took her hand in his, and looked out the window. "What do I have to do, to make it up to you?" he asked, his voice soft, his thumb stroked her palm.

"I can't answer that, Michael." She felt him stiffen. "Don't do that, don't withdraw from me. I don't know what happened last night. One minute everything was as it has been for weeks, and the next thing I know you've left, gone off with Paddy, and don't come home all night. Why, Michael, why did you leave?" She had shifted on the settee and was looking at him, her brow wrinkled with confusion, hurt in her dark blue eyes.

"I heard you talking to your friend. I didn't mean to listen," he held up a hand as she started to interrupt. "I'd come downstairs, and heard only a few minutes. I just lost it, Elizabeth, I had to get away, to try and think things over. I know I have no right to be first in your life, not really. I just thought I was a bit higher on your list than I am. I didn't deal with it very well, I know."

"What list are you talking about, Michael? I don't have a list." Elizabeth's mind raced back to her conversation with Gabby, trying to figure out what she'd said that had hurt Michael so deeply.

"You told her that The Lady, The Sacred Grove and Michael, me, in that order, were your conflict in Ireland. I come after them, Elizabeth. Just like my father," his voice broke; he dropped her hand and stood, striding to the window. He stood his fist against the glass, his head bowed.

Rushing to him, Elizabeth wrapped her arms around his waist, her forehead resting on his back. "Oh Michael, I am so sorry you overheard that part of the conversation and not the whole of it. I do not see you as less than The Lady and The Sacred Grove. Without you, they would not be. Don't you know that? You are the keeper, the protector of The Lady and The Sacred Grove. I can only serve Her. You keep Her safe." She tugged on him insisting he turn so she could look him in the eyes; convince him of the truth of her words.

With great reluctance he turned.

Elizabeth flung herself against his chest wrapping her arms tightly around his neck. "Without you, Michael, I don't think I'd have found The Lady and The Sacred Grove. Without you, I don't think I would have learned to be in my power. Without you ... I don't want to think about being in Ireland without you." She rose on her tiptoes and slipped one hand from around his neck to his cheek. She kissed his chin and feathered kissed across his mouth. "I am here, Michael. I'm here with you. I missed you last night. The Lady and The Sacred Grove can only feed my spirit, but you, Michael, you feed my heart, my body and my spirit."

The bands constricting his heart broke under the gentle onslaught of her words and kisses. His hands roamed her body, delighting in its familiar curves. *Will I ever get enough of her taste, her scent, her feel?* She arched into him and his ardor flamed. He carried her to the settee, pulling her blouse from her skirt as he laid her down. Kneeling he pressed hot kisses to her now bare abdomen.

"Michael, please slow down," Elizabeth gasped, her hand tugging his head away from her body. "Please, Michael," she gazed into his darkening eyes and struggled to sit up. He sat back on his heels and watched as she slowly undid the buttons on her blouse, took it off, and dropped it on the other side of the settee. "You next." She licked her lips and smiled; heat danced in her dark blue eyes.

"Ah, luv, you drive a hard bargain," he watched her eyes travel to his now obvious erection as he took off his shirt.

"I can see that," she grinned and then giggled as he grabbed for her, unfastening her bra and slipping it from her body before she scooted out of his way. She wriggled closer to him, felt his calloused hands stroke her body, shivers of arousal marking their path. She shifted as he unbuttoned her skirt and pulled it down her legs and felt herself slip into that passion-glazed trance that he so easily induced. She nibbled on his ear lobe, "Love me, Michael. Love me now," she whispered. "Take me to see the stars of the Universe."

## Fremont, Oregon

"Well, I talked to Elizabeth," Gabby reported to the other women sitting in the circle. They'd first smudged and said prayers and now sat eager to hear the news. "She certainly has met someone special in this Michael guy. It isn't so much what she says about him, it's how she says it. You know what she doesn't say and the tone of voice."

While they were sitting in a circle, they were not involved in Ceremony and were not using a talking stone. Anyone could ask a question and Hunter did so at this time. "So from what you understand, she wants to stay?"

"Very much so," Gabby replied. "And if he's as crazy about her as she is about him, I wouldn't be surprised if he asked her to stay forever. And that brings up a conflict for her. Having to choose between a life in Ireland with Michael, The Lady and The Sacred Grove, maybe having that family we all know she's dreamed about versus her life with us, with The Circle. She talked a bit about how we are all more as seven than we are as our individual selves.

"Anyway, I went by her apartment today, got her mail, wrote out the amounts of her bills, and the name of her supervisor and agency phone number. She's okay with you calling Ms. Renfrew about an extension of her vacation," she turned to Diana. "She'll return August 16th and be able to start back to work on the 18th if that's okay with them." Gabby directed her attention to Lily. "She also said to tell you she'd get a check to Jackson as soon as she got home. And, Lily," Gabby leaned forward for emphasis and said, "she wanted me to be sure to ask you to thank him for her."

"Consider it done. I have many ways to thank Jackson for his generosity." Lily's cat-who-drank-the-cream smile left little to the other women's imagination as to how she might fulfill her task. "And," her look now serious, "there is something special between Elizabeth and that young man. Jackson and I commented on it when we chanced upon them in Ireland. He or perhaps it is Ireland draws out her strengths. You'll see when she returns that she has changed in subtle ways."

"She knows we're meeting now," Gabby clarified, "but with the eight hour time difference, it's very early in the morning in Ireland. I'll give her a call during my lunch break and let her know everything's been taken care of.

Sophia shivered as she half-listened to the flow of conversation around her. She knew what Elizabeth was talking about. Since they'd reconnected as a circle of seven women, she'd felt the spiritual connections, their spiritual power strengthen. *What would happen if Elizabeth left? Or if one of the others left?* Remembering the year Hunter had lived in California, Sophia thought about how that had worked. What stood out in her mind was they always celebrated the major holidays together. The sharing of these special times on the Wheel kept the connections strong enough to withstand the separation. Because the commitment was there, somehow they'd made it work.

The thought that they could become a circle of five flitted through her mind as she remembered the attraction that sizzled between Gabriella and Jackson's friend, Giovanni Migliori who lived in Italy. Not please with where her mind was going, she stopped. *What is that question Diana always asks when the problem seems unsolvable? Ah yes, "if there is a way to have _________________ and ____________ are you willing to work for it?" In this case, if there is a way for Elizabeth to have her life in Ireland and for us to remain a circle of seven, am I willing to do what is necessary to gain that end? My answer? A resounding 'yes'!*

While there was always a chance when Elizabeth returned to her life in Fremont her attraction to Michael Murphy, The Lady and The Sacred Grove might wane, Sophia did not believe that was a realistic outcome. Her attention turned back to the animated conversation speculating whether Michael would propose to Elizabeth before she came home.

# 16   THREE WEEKS MORE

Michael sat on the settee that after yesterday was his favorite piece of furniture in his study and listened to Elizabeth's side of the conversation with her friend, Gabriella. He'd alerted Ian to expect a call this evening and quick action was needed to change Elizabeth's flight. At least that was his hope.

"All of you are in my prayers, Gabby. Tell everyone I love them and be sure to thank Diana and Jackson for me." Elizabeth's voice tight with emotion reverberated through the room.

From Elizabeth's side of the conversation Michael had pieced together that everyone missed her and wished her well. He heard the emotion in her voice as she made comments to Gabby's updates on everyone. *And there are six of them and only one of me.* He returned his gaze to the dark outside the window, seeing the room reflected in the glass, realizing the odds were against him. Lost in his thoughts, he didn't hear her end the call, or see her stand and walk over to where he was sitting. The touch of her hand on his shoulder startled him.

"Sorry, Michael. I didn't mean to surprise you." She bent over and kissed his ear. "You've got me until the 16th if we can get the plane reservations changed." She nibbled on his other ear.

"Miichaaeell," she squealed as she flew through the air. "What on earth are you doing?" she gasped as she landed half in his lap the other half of her sliding toward the floor.

"This," Michael growled as he caught her before she landed on the floor hauling her back onto his lap. "And this." His lips sought hers in a soul-searching kiss. "Ah, luv, for sure you won't regret staying. I'll make sure of it."

Elizabeth felt her blood warm as she succumbed to his touch. Confusion replaced arousal when he halted the kisses. Although his hands continued to caress her, they now gently massaged her neck and shoulders, stroked her back, fingers lightly trailed up and down her arms. He pressed soft kisses in her hair and held her close. She melted in his arms, her bones dissolving. She felt ... At first she couldn't identify, couldn't name what she felt when he held her like this. Then a word came to her. Cherished, she felt cherished by this man. Wonder and awe filled her, blended with the feeling of being cherished.

First the tears threatened.

Then the tears fell.

Michael's heart soared when Elizabeth relaxed in his arms, melted against him as he held her, stroked her, caressed her, and willed the moment to stretch until he noticed his shirt was wet. Tipping her face up, he saw tears streaming down her face. What the hell is going on? "What is it, luv?" His tone of voice betrayed his anxiety.

Elizabeth wriggled, freeing her arms and wrapping them around Michael's neck. "I just feel so special right now. They're tears of joy. I have three more weeks to spend with you, here in Ireland. I have no doubt you'll find a way to fix my plane ticket."

She was babbling but words poured out when the dam of her constraint broke open. "Gabby said everything is taken care of there, Diana called my supervisor and got an extension for my leave, Lily's husband will see that my bills are paid until I get home and can pay him back. Everything has worked out so I can stay with you, stay in Ireland a little longer."

Michael saw the truth of her words mirrored in her eyes. *I've got three more weeks with her.* "Well, luv," he said and gently pulled her arms from his neck, "I've got a call to make then." He shoved her off his lap with a light slap on her bottom and stepped purposefully to the desk and dialed Ian's number. "The 16th," he said. "Yes, that's right," he responded to something Ian said and hung the phone up.

He swung back toward the settee and saw Elizabeth watching him, her arms resting on the back, her dark blue eyes luminous in her pale face. *She's mine. For three more weeks she's mine.* Grinning he strode across the room, knelt, and took her hands in his, his thumbs already stroking her palms. "It's all taken care of, luv. All that's left is for us to decide what to do with each other for the next three weeks." He waggled his brows, licked his lips, and leered. "Got any ideas, or do you want to leave it up to me?"

"I've got a few ideas of my own." Elizabeth scooted so she knelt on the settee, leaned forward, and kissed him. "Of course, if you don't like my ideas, you'll have to come up with some of your own, luv," she mimicked his Irish lilt to the best of her ability before nibbling on his bottom lip, slipping her tongue along his teeth, and extricating her hands from his to run them through his thick dark hair.

"I rather like your ideas, luv." He kissed her back. "In fact I like them just fine."

The next three weeks passed in a blur of activity. When at The Manor, Elizabeth rose with Michael and spent time in The Sacred Grove where she prayed with The Lady. When Michael returned from the early morning workouts, they breakfasted together and planned their day. The sixth day, they packed up and traveled to Dublin where they spent two full days seeing the sights. While Michael took care of some business, Elizabeth toured Trinity College, saw the Book of Kells and purchased scarves her circle sisters could use as altar cloths. Together they browsed along Grafton Street, strolled along the River Liffy, and sat on a bench in St. James Park.

Next on the agenda was Belfast in Northern Ireland. Michael had arranged a private tour of the Belleek China Factory and Elizabeth purchased small vases for her circle sisters, debating over which colors and designs would go to whom. Since these were gifts for Winter Solstice, she made the decision to have the delicate Parian china shipped home.

The night of the fifteenth came swiftly. That morning Elizabeth said her prayers, spent an hour in the still room, and packed. It was a challenge to fit everything in her luggage. She was swearing under her breath from the stress of leaving combined with the difficulty packing. Seeing her on the verge of tears, Michael stepped in, directing Seamus to bring a box.

"Trust me on this, luv. It's easier to go through customs when all you need do is open a suitcase for them to check. It doesn't mean they won't look in the box. But this way, they can see when they look in the suitcase you don't have much in the way of clothes." She'd agreed, set aside the clothing to go into the box, and Seamus deftly completed that part of her packing.

She and Michael ate dinner in the back garden, the energy of The Sacred Grove pulsing around them, the air shimmering with the light from The Lady. Seamus outdid himself, preparing Irish stew, fresh baked bread, fresh butter from a neighboring farm, salad with his own blue cheese vinaigrette dressing, and homemade garlic and parmesan cheese croutons. For dessert he'd baked a deep dish cherry pie with fruit from their own orchard.

*Check-in for her flight is tomorrow at 4 p.m. In less than twenty-four hours, I'll be gone.* The thought struck like a physical blow, her stomach churned with nausea and she struggled to overcome the debilitating sense she was going to lose her meal. Her last hours with Michael and The Lady would not be affected by her roiling stomach, she vowed. Slipping her hand in his, she tugged, "Come with me, Michael, please come with me."

"Where are we going?" he grinned down at her, not sensing her physical discomfort.

They were at the garden gate now. Elizabeth bent down, pulled the rock aside, uncovering the secret cache. She took Michael's dirk and leather bag out and handed it to him. She reached back inside and took out her necklace and her protection bag. Tucking her bag in her skirt's waistband, she put the necklace around her neck feeling it pulse with energy as if in anticipation of what was to come.

The energy from The Sacred Grove strengthened, the shimmering light glowed with intensity, Elizabeth stood, reached out to Michael, took his hands, looked deeply into his eyes, "Please come with me this time."

Even though he saw how important it was to her, Michael's impulse was to resist. She stood before him, her gaze holding his, and waited. His eyes wander down her lissome body, the necklace hanging easily around her neck. A memory of the day he'd found her at the dance, unconscious, lost in trance, unable to withstand the power, or the energy from the necklace flashed through his mind. Every morning she went to The Sacred Grove and served The Lady. He might not know the details of what they did but he knew they did energy work because he felt it. Another memory surfaced: Elizabeth puttering in the still room or with the many altars that now adorned his house, or more recently out in the barns and paddocks with him.

*She's come into her own, she has. Something profound happened since she's been here.* Michael's gaze traveled back to her face. "All right." He gestured toward the gate. "After you."

Elizabeth exhaled slowly. She'd been holding it, waiting for his answer. This, her last time with The Lady, was going to be with Michael. They would share this experience at least once. The reality that he'd agreed stunned her. She'd been prepared to go alone.

Preceding Michael down the path, sprinkling herbs as she went, Elizabeth softly chanted prayers of gratitude. At the bottom, he followed her as she circled the outside of The Sacred Grove, stopping to raise her arms and voice in prayer at each gate. His original idea was he'd be an observer but her power was too great. He was drawn into her energy, heard the words of her prayers reverberate through him, touching his soul.

When they had completed one circuit, Elizabeth continued on until she stood before the South entrance. She waved her right arm above her head in a circle then stood with both arms raised in prayer. "I come this time from the place of abundance, of enough, of fulfillment. I come with purpose, to share the love that emanates from this sacred place with Michael, the one who guards and protects this place."

Elizabeth lowered her arms and stepped onto the path. She felt Michael's presence behind her as she walked through The Sacred Grove, following the faint path through the trees. Her practice had been to enter from the East but this time, her last time, she came from the South, in celebration of the fullness of her life. The same sensation of walking on air as she did when entering from the East assailed her, but this time the path seemed longer, the trees thicker.

Never hesitating, she moved forward, until at last, she reached the edge of the center circle. While she could see the shimmering light and feel the pulsing energy, the image of The Lady did not come to her. She stepped into the circle, reached behind her for Michael's hand, and drew him to stand beside her.

Together they made their way across the grass, past the bubbling spring, to the sacred fire and the mossy log before it. Elizabeth looked around once more for The Lady. A moment of doubt crept into her mind when The Lady did not appear. She quickly pushed it aside. In her soul she knew what she was doing was right.

Michael stood in front of the sacred fire in the middle of The Sacred Grove. He could feel the energy of The Lady, see the shimmering light, but he could feel Elizabeth's energy more. He looked down at her, standing so straight beside him, and waited. As if she read his thoughts, she turned to face him, looked up, and smiled.

Her arms raised in prayer, her head tilted so her dark blue luminous eyes looked directly into his she began.

>*"I am the Light*
>*"I am the Source*
>*"Through me Love flows to the Outer World."*

>*"I am the Light*
>*"I am the Source*
>*"Through me Love flows to the Outer World."*

>*"I am the Light*
>*"I am the Source*
>*"Through me Love flows to the Outer World."*

Elizabeth lowered her arms, reached out and took his hands in hers. She held them firmly; her gaze remained locked with his.

>*"We are the Light*
>*"We are the Source*
>*"Through us Love flows to the Outer World."*

>*"We are the Light*
>*"We are the Source*
>*"Through us Love flows to the Outer World."*

>*"We are the Light*
>*"We are the Source*
>*"Through us Love flows to the Outer World."*

Michael felt the pull, the energy flood his body, his feet rooted to the ground as if they were planted. His hands fused with hers as the old words came through him. He held her gaze, knowing that he was lost in the power of this place at this time. He heard his voice, its deep tones in a contrasting blend with her lighter ones,

>*"We are the Light*
>*"We are the Source*
>*"Through us Love flows to the Outer World."*

>*"We are the Light*
>*"We are the Source*
>*"Through us Love flows to the Outer World."*

>*"We are the Light*
>*"We are the Source*
>*"Through us Love flows to the Outer World."*

He watched Elizabeth transform, the shimmering light radiating from her and illuminating the circle. He watched her drop his hands, step toward him, and reach around him as she pressed against him. He watched as she rose on her tiptoes; felt her kisses rove from one corner of his mouth across his lips; felt her tongue flick the opposite corner; felt her kisses trail down his jaw, and felt her nibble his skin from one side to the other.

She slid her arms up the front of his chest, entwining them around his neck, brushing the hair along the nape of his neck. "Make love with me, Michael. Make love with me here and now," her whispers commanded, she wrapped one ankle around his leg pressing herself closer, her kisses more urgent, her hands roamed up and down his back pulling his shirt from his trousers.

Michael's control vanished; flames consumed him as this bewitching woman's hands left flickers of heat over his bare back. He bent his head, covered her mouth with his, his tongue plunging into her wet heat. His hands were pulling and tugging at her clothing, as hers were his.

The last garment tossed they were naked, tumbling to the ground, the grass cushioning their bodies as they sought to slake the thirst their bodies brought to each other. Her hands reached for his rigid erection; his hands teased her taut nipples; their tongues tangled. They came together, the energy pulsing in an ancient rhythm, the shimmering light enveloping them. Higher and higher they soared, seeking the stars until they climaxed as one, the brilliance of the outer edges of the Universe blinding them as they clung to each other.

Elizabeth felt the light shift within and without of her. The force of their climax shook her soul. Michael was stretched out beside her, one arm thrown around her, his hand cupping her breast. She felt drained and energized; complete and fragmented; whole and broken. She stirred and felt Michael's breath on her neck.

"Michael," she whispered. "Michael," her voice held more urgency.

"I'm here." He shifted pulling her closer.

"Michael," she said and squirmed, shifted so she could see him. His hair was tousled; his sky blue eyes heavy lidded, his chin stubbled with a night's growth of beard, his lips turned up in a sated grin. He was magnificent.

"Ah, Elizabeth, let me look at you. Shh, now." He kissed her on the nose. "You're a sight, you are. A beautiful, wanton sight." He took in her long disheveled hair, skin reddened from his kisses, her lips rosy red and imminently kissable. He could feel her nipples pucker against his chest. *I could take her again, right here, right now.* Michael leaned forward and kissed her on the forehead, breathed in the scent of bergamot, felt her softness pressed against him, and released her. There was a plane to catch.

He rose and her breath caught as she looked at his naked body: the taut muscled buttocks and thighs, the broad shoulders and long legs. He was the most beautiful man she'd ever seen. Her body tightened with need as he bent over and retrieved her blouse and skirt, tossing them to her. He found his own pants and shirt, quickly dressing. Together they found his dirk and leather pouch and her necklace and bag of protective stones.

Standing in front of the sacred fire, they repeated the prayers that sent the energy of love to the world. They came together, arms around each other, Elizabeth's head resting on Michael's chest. With a sigh, Elizabeth stepped back, took Michael's hand. Their time here was over. Hand in hand they found the South path.

The Lady appeared as they stepped on the path. Surrounded in the brilliant shimmering light, Her blue robes flowed around Her ankles, Her feet bare, the blue crescent of Her rank glowed. She raised Her arms and the words of Her blessing filled them.

> *May you go in peace.*
> *May you find your heart.*
> *May you know that all you desire is within your grasp.*

# 17 APART

Leaning against the window frame, Michael watched the jet pull away from the gangway. To a casual observer, he looked to be relaxed with his arms folded and ankles crossed. The firm line of his jaw, the furrowed brow reflected in the glass spoke of a different story, of emotions churning inside. *How could I let her go?* One side of his internal debate followed by: *Nothing you could do to keep her here, boyo.* The practical Michael knew that but the other Michael struggled with the reality that Elizabeth was gone.

The plane taxied to the end of the runway, stopped and gathered power before hurtling down the asphalt. As the plane rose into the air, he started to turn away but stopped, leaned back against the window frame, watched the plane grow smaller and smaller, disappearing into the sky. Even after the plane was out of sight, Michael stood, staring at nothing. The internal debate continued.

Shaking his head, he straightened, turned from the window, and walked through the airport. He was surrounded by people, a few who called out in greeting; abstractly he nodded in response. Over the last twelve hours they'd made love, she finished the final packing, all the while talking about staying connected through emails and phone calls. She promised to call when she got home so he'd know she'd arrived safely.

He knew she cared about him and knew her ties to her women's circle were strong. His feelings? They were complex. He cared about her, already ached with missing her, felt a hollowness inside with her gone. And, it'd been less than an hour since he'd held her in his arms, kissed her goodbye, waved as she disappeared down the gangway.

A wave of memories engulfed him when he reached his car. He unlocked the door, slid behind the wheel, and sat, staring ahead at nothing in particular, one thought echoing in his mind. We never talked about seeing each other again. He closed his eyes, leaned back against the headrest, the reality of her leaving sinking in.

Back at The Manor it was worse. Reminders of Elizabeth were everywhere he looked; her altars in every room, her favorite flowers in the main hall, one of his grandmother's books on the desk in the back parlor, the bookmark holding her place. His bedroom felt empty. He picked up her pillow the faint scent of bergamot wafted as he held it to his chest. His heart ached. Still carrying her pillow, he wandered into her sitting room and sat in the chair she favored. Resting his head on the high back, he let his mind drift with the memories. The first time he saw her on the plane; the awe on her face upon seeing the swans at The Hotel Lir; the vision of her at her altar in the hotel; the manifestation of her power in her interaction with the River Shannon swans.

She'd grown stronger in her own spiritual power and he thought she was stronger than his grandmother. Was it her boundaries? Whatever it was, she seemed able to serve The Lady and yet disengage from those duties to go on with other aspects of her life and to be with him.

"Ah, luv," he said, his quiet voice resigned, "you are sorely missed. I don't know what I'm going to do without you here, how I'm going to get on with things."

The light shimmered. The Lady stood before him, a slim column of blue, a gentle smile on her face. *You will need to decide, Michael, how much you want her here with you. You will have to name your feelings for her. You will need to make a commitment to her before you will have her in your life. If you want her enough, you can make it happen.*

The Lady's presence dissolved and all that was left was the shimmering light. When that dimmed and was gone, he was left alone, in Elizabeth's sitting room, with his memories, and a decision to make.

Elizabeth sat in her first-class seat, courtesy of Michael's upgrade, her forehead resting against the window. She wished she could see him, could hold him close, could smell his sandalwood scent one more time. The heaviness in her heart told her she'd run out of "one more time". Closing her eyes she visualized Michael walking toward her, his face wreathed in a boyish grin, his dark hair in its familiar tousle, his sky blue eyes alight with desire for her. Never had anyone wanted her the way Michael did. Her time in Ireland, her time with Michael was in the past; a dream, a memory, something to hold fast to as she went forward with her life.

She tried to relax, enjoy the amenities of first class, the effervescent champagne, the piece of dark chocolate. Feeling the effects of the champagne, she stopped after her second glass. The plane had long since taken off. Out her window, between the banks of clouds, she caught glimpses of the Atlantic Ocean, Iceland, icebergs floating on the green white-capped water. This flight was going over the North Pole which meant she'd clear customs in Seattle, change planes, and fly on to Fremont. She glanced at her watch noting the time; counting at least one hour in customs; another before her connecting flight left figuring almost nine hours before she walked in her own front door.

Gabby was picking her up and Elizabeth looked forward to some time with her and hoped to be able to see all of the other women within the next day or two. *I have to find a way past all this, to get my life back.* She shook her head and sighed and wondered how to make Michael nothing more than a memory. *Oh E, you miss him too much right now to figure anything else out. Just close your eyes and rest.*

Sometime later, Elizabeth opened her eyes and although she didn't really feel rested she did feel calmer, the incessant chattering in her mind gone. As she looked out the window into the darkness, she saw a glowing light and realized Grandmother Moon was just beyond her sight. *No matter where I am, my circle sisters and I see the same moon.* She felt tears well and struggled to keep them from falling. *Michael may be looking at this same moon but that brings me no comfort.*

She got up and walked up and down the aisle to stretch her legs. Returning to her seat, the flight attendant offered her a meal of chicken and rice with broccoli as the vegetable; chocolate cake with raspberry filling, and champagne. Once the dishes were cleared away, she settled back into her seat determined to rest, to stop thinking until she arrived in Seattle.

As soon as her eyes closed, The Lady appeared in her inner vision, surrounded by the shimmering light, her arms tucked into the sleeves of her long blue robe. *Always remember, Elizabeth, all things are possible. You have the power to create the life you want. Remember that above all things, You are the Light, You are the Source, through You Love flows throughout the world.* In a flash of light, She disappeared. In Her place was a dark-tousled-hair boy with sky-blue eyes.

*Finally.* The familiar sight of Fremont from the air welcomed her: the majestic Mt. Hood with dark patches of rock interspersed by glaciers and snow, the Willamette River meandering through the countryside and the city below her. Checking the seat pocket, under her seat, and gathering her bag from the overhead bin she exited the plane, stretching her legs as she walked up the inclined gateway to the concourse. Not really expecting to see Gabby here as the plan was to meet outside baggage claim, nonetheless she found herself looking for a familiar face as she neared the exit.

She flashed a big smile and waved, her mood lifting when she caught sight of her auburn-haired friend. Startled when a hand grasped her shoulder, Elizabeth looked to her right and smiled when she saw Lily's husband, Jackson. "Thought you were going to walk right by us." He stepped to the side revealing Lily, Diana, Hunter and Sophia.

"You're all here!" Elizabeth greeted and hugged everyone, thankful to be home. "Oh, where's Ashley?"

"Ashley and Logan are fixing breakfast for us." Sophia reached for Elizabeth's carry-on.

"I'll get that." Jackson pushed Sophia's hand aside as he picked up the suitcase and set it down again. "What do you have in here? Rocks?" he grumbled good-naturedly.

"Yes, but they're Irish rocks," Elizabeth retorted in her best Irish brogue. "They're lucky rocks, Jackson. Or don't you believe in the "luck o' the Irish"?" She laughed and the shadow of Michael's loss dimmed. *I just need to keep myself busy, distracted and it'll get better.* Taking the lead, she called out over her shoulder, "I'm starved!"

At different times while waiting for her luggage or traveling to Ashley's, she was drawn to watching Lily and Jackson's easy interaction. *We were like that too.* Lily and Jackson seemed to fit, were comfortable and at ease with each other. *Michael and I… . If only we… .* Ruthlessly she quashed the wayward thought.

Jackson brought her luggage into Ashley's house but declined sharing breakfast with them because of an appointment that morning. She watched Lily walk him to the door, smile, and kiss him gently on the lips. She watched Jackson's arms band tightly around his wife as he lifted her off her feet to deepen the kiss. She watched Lily's arms wrapped around her husband's neck as she kissed him back. She watched as Lily whispered something in Jackson's ear, hearing him chuckle. She watched his hands slip down to Lily's buttocks, giving her a quick pat before releasing her. She watched as he gave her a quick kiss on the forehead and turned to leave.

So caught up in the scene before her, the scene that elicited memories of Michael's arms around her, his kisses, his closeness, his strength, his scent, she was startled when Jackson called out, "Good to have you back, Elizabeth." He was out the door before she could form a simple answer.

Breakfast was a feast of Eggs Benedict, fresh orange juice, and pecan sticky buns. She was reminded of Seamus' breakfasts of fresh baked bread, fresh butter, and scrambled eggs once he knew they were her favorite. *Not better or worse, just different, E. Remember that. Here things are just different than they were at Michael's.* She banished the troubling thoughts and joined everyone in chatting and eating.

"I imagine you're anxious to get home." Sophia deftly shifted the focus back to Elizabeth. "However, I have a request." The other women became silent and Logan took the children into the family room to watch a movie.

"What is it?" Elizabeth felt more than a little nervous as everyone's focus was centered on her.

"Just that we take the time to smudge and sit in circle together. It's been almost two months since we were all together. And, while we are sitting together, perhaps you'd share with us a bit about your trip. You are the same, Elizabeth, but yet I sense you are different."

"If that suits everyone, it's fine with me." Elizabeth rose and began clearing her dishes.

"No, no, no, you naughty girl." Hunter gently tapped her hands and pushed them aside. "You are the guest of honor this morning so get out. Go with Sophia while the rest of us make short shrift of these dishes." Hunter flapped her hands in a shooing motion until Elizabeth backed away from the table.

"May I please have my tea cup?" she asked sweetly.

"Yes, you may." Hunter picked up her cup and handed it to her. "Looks like you need a refill."

"Here's more hot water." Diana walked towards her carrying a carafe. "And here're bags." She reached into her pocket and pulled out several colorful foil wrapped packets.

Selecting and opening one, Elizabeth put it in her cup. She waited while Diana poured the hot water, letting the tea bag steep a few times before taking it out and doctoring her tea the way she'd come to like it with milk and sugar. She thought of her morning prayers with The Lady and looked out at Ashley's backyard. The flower beds were in full bloom, the patio sheltered from the summer sun, and she could see several chairs. She turned to Sophia. "How about sitting on the patio?"

"Great idea. We'll need two more chairs from, no make that three more chairs from inside," Sophia called out over her shoulder, "we're meeting outside so be sure you bring three more chairs." She reached for Elizabeth's hand and together they went outside.

Quickly the chairs were arranged in a circle with a small table in the center. Elizabeth darted back inside, returning a few minutes later with a piece of Irish linen, a souvenir from her trip. She placed it on the table as an altar cloth before walking through the yard, picking several flowers. Noticing an empty sand pail, she rinsed it out with water from a nearby hose, wiping off the pail with her hands, and partially filling it with water, she arranged the flowers inside. When she turned back, everyone was gathering around the small table adding items to the impromptu altar.

Ashley looked up to see Elizabeth carrying the pail and looked down at the beautiful piece of linen a look of horror flickered in her grey eyes. "Don't y'all let her put that down, ya hear?" she said and dashed inside. A few minutes later she returned with a trivet and towel. The trivet with the design of a deer was placed in the center of the cloth. Ashley took the pail from Elizabeth and efficiently wiped its outside. "Now you can put it down," Ashley said handing the pail back to Elizabeth. "But use the trivet, E. No sense messing up that beautiful piece of linen."

Following Ashley's instructions, Elizabeth set the pail on the trivet and took her place in the circle. Smudge was lit and the altar cleansed before each in turn took the small cauldron of smoking sage and moved it up, down, and around her body. Some even put the cauldron on the ground and stood over it, letting the smoke drift up under their skirts. When everyone was done, the cauldron was put to the side and a lid placed on top.

"Elizabeth, would you be willing to lead us in prayer?" Diana asked.

"Yes, I'm more than willing." She turned to face the East, lifted her arms and set her feet a little wider and began. "Spirits of the East hear my prayers. Watch over, bless, and guide us as we start this day. Keep our eyes and hearts open to the many gifts and miracles each day brings. Blessed Be."

She turned to the South and stood in the same manner. "Spirits of the South hear my prayers. Watch over, bless, and guide us as we move through this day. May we feel abundance surrounding us; may we always be generous to others in every aspect of our lives. Blessed Be."

Standing facing West, she prayed, "Spirits of the West hear my prayers. Watch over, bless and guide us through this day. May we find the moments of peace, even in chaos, to connect with our souls; for it is in that connection that we find the answers, the way forward. Blessed Be."

Now facing the North, arms raised, feet spread, she said, "Spirits of the North hear my prayers. Watch over, bless, and guide us this day and always. May we be able to hear the wisdom of voices other than our own. Blessed Be."

She turned back to the center, a serene smile on her face, she reached for the hands of Gabriella and Diana, who stood on either side of her. "Now I'd like to teach you the prayer that The Lady and I did each morning." She looked around the circle. "That is if you are willing," she quickly amended.

The women shared looks between themselves before as one turning their gazes on her and nodding their agreement.

"Every morning when Michael left to work with his horses, I'd get up and go to The Sacred Grove, cast my circle, call in protection, and then enter. After traveling a path, I'd come to the center where a spring bubbled, a sacred fire burned, and The Lady awaited. Together we would stand, hold hands and raise them up," she demonstrated as she held Gabby and Diana's hands. The other women immediately followed her lead.

"Then we'd pray together. At first the prayer was "I am the Light; I am the Source; Through me Love flows to the outer world." The outer world is here, in this place, in this time. The Sacred Grove is like a place out of time, not of this world.

*"I am the Light*

*"I am the Source*

*"Through me Love flows to all the world.*

"Can you remember the words?" she asked as she looked around the circle noting all heads nodding. "Good, then let's begin. Oh, yes, and we repeat it three times to honor maiden, matron, crone." She widened her stance slightly, raised her head to the sky, and closed her eyes.

*"I am the Light*

*"I am the Source*

*"Through me Love flows to all the world.*

*"I am the Light*
*"I am the Source*
*"Through me Love flows to all the world.*


*"I am the Light*
*"I am the Source*
*"Through me Love flows to all the world."*

Elizabeth felt the energy shift as they prayed. The final word said, she opened her eyes and looked around. By the looks on their faces, the other women had felt the shift too. "Now, for the change. Insert 'we' for 'I'." She smiled and closed her eyes. "We'll do this three times three so everyone becomes comfortable with the rhythm of the words.

Arms lifted overhead and holding hands with the person on either side, they began.

*"We are the Light*
*"We are the Source*
*"Through us Love flows to all the world."*


*"We are the Light*
*"We are the Source*
*"Through us Love flows to all the world."*


*"We are the Light*
*"We are the Source*
*"Through us Love flows to all the world."*

The first time was a little rocky as her circle sisters stumbled over the 'us' in the third line. But before they were through with the second repetition, she felt the energy shift and could see the light shimmering from behind her closed eyes. As they began the prayer for the third time, a golden glow bathed them. Silence permeated the air at the prayers end. Keeping hold of their neighbor's hands, the women lowered their arms to their sides.

Elizabeth watched as one by one her circle sisters opened their eyes and looked in her direction each reflecting a look of dazed delight, a trance-like glaze ... a seeing but not seeing. She continued to stand quietly as they individually came back to the present. Without words they sat down as one.

Taking the piece of Connemara marble off the altar, Elizabeth handed it to Diana.

"That was amazing, Elizabeth. I felt surrounded in golden white light with more light shooting from me." Diana looked around the circle and saw her other sisters nodding. "And you did this every morning?" her voice was incredulous.

"Once I was staying at The Manor, Michael's place, yes. From the beginning I thought it rather magical myself. With the seven of us praying as one, it was more than magical," Elizabeth spoke softly, a gentle smile on her face. "The Lady taught it to me as I told it to you first. But as I was preparing to leave, we stood facing each other, and held hands. We looked into each other's eyes as we said the prayer, changing the words from 'I' and 'me' to 'we' and 'us'."

As the stone traveled the circle, the women shared their experiences and asked Elizabeth questions about The Sacred Grove, The Lady, New Grange, and other sacred places in Ireland. She talked about the almost hidden well at Kylemore Abbey; the stone dance; the necklace that Paddy had found there; and the young women she'd met at New Grange.

Gabby now held the stone. "When are you going back?"

"No, Gabby, I won't be going back. It was a dream-of-a-lifetime trip, but my place is here—in this circle." She felt tears threaten and fought to hold them back. Her voice shook with the force of pent-up tears. "I won't be going back. What

I have here with all of you is too precious to give up. We are so much more when we are together like now. While I know we all feel the power of our prayers, this is special. My time in Ireland has strengthened me spiritually and that is a gift from the Goddess that will never leave me. For that alone I am grateful." Elizabeth looked around the circle at the women she'd missed so much. "I really didn't sleep well on the plane, so if you don't mind, I would like to go home and get some rest."

The women were quiet as they stood, said closing prayers, and began to dismantle the altar. Elizabeth folded the altar cloth and handed it to Ashley. "For you, Ashley. You guarded and protected it, so it must be yours."

"Oh my," Ashley's face wore a big grin. "Y'all don't get jealous now. I'll let you look at it whenever you come on by." She took the linen from Elizabeth with reverence. "It's all the more precious because we used it today. It'll be a powerful addition to my sacred space." She looked at Elizabeth, a slight frown on her face. "I don't think y'all have heard about my new sacred space."

"I know that I haven't if it came into being since I left."

"Come with me," she said taking Elizabeth's hand and pulling her into the house, through the kitchen to a set of doors that housed the pantry. Ashley opened the doors and pulled out a box marked household cleaners. "I knew Art'd never open this one," she said quietly as she set the box on the kitchen table and opened it. Inside Elizabeth saw dragonflies on various items, stones of all shapes, sizes, and colors, a candle, matches, small carved animal figures, and a piece of red cloth. Ashley gently placed the white linen in the box. "See here?" She pointed to small fasteners at each corner. "I can just unhook these here," she demonstrated as she talked, "and the sides fold down so I have a base for my altar."

"What a great idea, Ash," Elizabeth said as she helped Ashley put the sides up, top on, and stow the box back on the shelf. "I created altars in all of the rooms at Michael's and came up with some ideas that might work for you without Art ever knowing what they are. That is if you're interested."

Ashley called out, "Elizabeth has more to share, everyone." And within a couple of minutes, they were all standing in the kitchen, replenishing coffee and tea mugs and nibbling on the last of the pecan sticky buns. "Go ahead, Elizabeth. This way we'll all know what you did."

Elizabeth described the altar she'd made for Michael's kitchen by placing four herb pots in the four directions with a small candle in the middle. She'd cleansed everything, said prayers, and charged the altar with the intention of flavorful, healthy food from that kitchen. "Anyone coming into the kitchen would see the herbs, but would not necessarily see a sacred altar. As we know, it is the intention we charge the objects with after we've cleansed them that creates the sacred space. In the front parlor, I created an altar out of the tea service; in the still room out of moss and dried herbs; and in the main hall I used statues of horses, Michael's house totem, on a lace doily. And, as Ashley has demonstrated, an altar or sacred space can be enclosed or hidden and then brought out into the open when it is safe."

Sophia held out her arms. "I think it is time for our group centering since I know there are things we all need to do."

As they came together, arms around one another, Elizabeth looked at each of her circle sisters. The connection, already strong between them, was strengthening. Hope surged as she remembered The Lady's words. *Everything is as it should be.*

"We're meeting tonight at Sophia's." Gabby had a twinkle in her eye and a mischievous grin on her face. "Then you can tell us all about this Michael Murphy. I know I wasn't the only one who prayed you'd meet a tall, dark, handsome, and sexy as sin man over there. From the little Lily shared, I think you did. So be prepared, E, to 'fess up' tonight. And do bring your pictures. We want to see what this man looks alike."

"Anyone who can convince you to remain in Ireland for another three weeks must be something else." Hunter laughed as she broke from the circle, crossed the center, and gave Elizabeth a hug. "Glad to have you back with us."

"Did y'all keep that journal? Bring that along too so we can read about what you did." A bang and a shout came from the family room. "Keep it down in there, ya hear? We're almost done."

"Everything's okay, Ashley," Logan called back. "Don't worry."

"I'm not worried, Logan, just don't want to miss anything that's said in here 'cause y'all are being too noisy."

Lily, Diana, and Sophia, who had been watching the exchange and interplay between the younger women, exchanged a look.

*Something happened over there. And something else is going to happen. I can feel it.* Lily's thoughts brought her a slight sense of unease. She turned to Diana. "I'll drop you off at your house so you can pick up your car." Looking beyond Diana to Sophia, she asked, "Are you coming with us?"

"I am, yes," Sophia replied. Waving at the still chattering younger women, she followed Lily and Diana out the door.

# 18   Together

"Thanks again, Gabby. I'll pick you up tonight." Elizabeth leaned out her window, calling to Gabriella who had just reached her car.

"See you around seven then." Gabriella smiled and waved in reply. "It's good to have you back, E."

Elizabeth watched as her friend eased away from the curb before ducking back into her living room and taking inventory of the chaos. She was very grateful her friend had helped her haul her three suitcases up the two flights of stairs. And as she looked around she was equally glad for Gabby's organizational skills. The boxes she'd shipped back were stacked by size on the floor by her dining table; her mail was arranged in three neat piles on the uncluttered tabletop. Regardless of how Gabby had arranged things, between the mail, the boxes, and her three pieces of luggage, her small living area was overflowing.

"First things first," she said, as hands on hips she surveyed the area. "My bills are paid so I can ignore the mail until later or even tomorrow." She smiled brightly. "I know, I'll get things organized for tonight. Now where is that box from Galway crystal?" Elizabeth sorted through the boxes, easily spying the Galway box from the dark green insignia on the side and the Belleek box from its distinctive markings.

She'd sent three medium-sized boxes home from Michael's along with a smaller box of her pictures and one completed Journal. She was very glad she'd taken the time to label the pictures and coordinate their identification with her Journal so she'd always know exactly where and when she'd taken them. The box from Belleek, with her Winter Solstice gifts, was quickly stored in her office closet.

Pulling the Galway crystal box aside, she slipped the kitchen knife through the packing tape before putting it next to her front door. The three similar boxes were moved to the floor in front of her couch and the box of pictures placed on her table.

She carefully cut the packing tape on each of the three boxes in front of her before she opened them and sorted through their contents. The first box, containing clothes she'd sent home when she was first scheduled to leave; only needed to be unpacked so she took it down the hall to her bedroom, placing it on the bed.

The second box held seven multi-colored scarves with varying Celtic designs. Each scarf's recurring design was in multiple hues of different dominant colors, each chosen with a specific circle member in mind. She smiled to herself as she reached to take the scarves out of the box. Below them, in their own presentation boxes were seven Celtic crosses. Three were carved from soapstone, two were porcelain, and two were cast and beautifully painted in the Book of Kells' tradition. "I'm so glad all of these crosses came through unscathed," she murmured as she set the seventh one on the small coffee table in front of the couch. Gathering up the scarves, she scattered them around the couch and over the backs of chairs.

Elizabeth stood in the middle of her living room. Her view of the colorful scarves and Celtic crosses blurred. Absentmindedly she rubbed her breast bone to ease the ache in her heart. Tears welled in her eyes. A deep, painful longing for Michael overwhelmed her.

"This will never do, E," she chided herself, while wrapping herself in an enveloping self-hug, "you're made of sterner stuff than this." She closed her eyes and prayed for the strength to do what she needed to do.

Stay here.

In Fremont.

When she felt calmer, she opened her eyes, and took a deep breath. "I need to stay busy," she muttered. Taking her suitcases into the bedroom, she set them on the bed beside the box. Since she'd done laundry before she left, everything was clean so she put things away as she unpacked.

Whether they were clothes from the box or from her suitcases, everything reminded her of Michael. Fighting her tears and steadfastly pushing memories away, she shook her clothes out, hung them up or refolded them and put them in her dresser. Coming to the long skirt and top she had often worn when visiting The Lady, she set that aside to wear tonight. Thoughts of The Lady and The Sacred Grove were easier for her than thoughts of Michael.

With her suitcases unpacked and things put away, Elizabeth decided to finish that process by putting them in storage. It took three trips to cart her three pieces of luggage and dismantled empty boxes down to her storage unit in the basement and the box from Galway Crystal to her car. Although she'd asked Gabriella to use her car at least once a week to keep it running, she decided to check it out herself. It started right up, ran smoothly, and now had a full tank of gas.

Next came restocking her kitchen. She turned off the car, went back upstairs for her purse, and after checking the cupboards and refrigerator, made a quick list of items she needed.

A few hours later, everything from her trip to the grocery store was put away and her potluck contribution set aside. Once again she surveyed her living area. One unopened box with various souvenirs from her trip remained. Treasures included a small piece of wool sealed in a plastic bag. She knew it was still well-sealed since the malevolent odor of dirty sheep's wool had not escaped. Other treasures were pebbles and rocks she'd collected on her various walks, and the swan feathers which were protected in their own box, and with permission from The Lady, seven twigs, dried leaves, and cones from The Sacred Grove.

Elizabeth returned the six crosses to their boxes and placed them in the carton with the scarves on top. The brilliantly painted multi-hued blue and green cast cross and similarly colored scarf she took to her bedroom and placed on her dresser. Taking off her clothes, she climbed into bed, pulling the throw from across the foot up over her shoulders.

*I think I'll rest a bit before finishing things up, see if a bit of sleep will help this despair.* She snuggled down and closed her eyes against the threatening tears, trying to blank her mind. He was so real she smelled his scent and felt the back of his hand caress her cheek. Various images of Michael sitting by her at the dining room table, Michael across the workbench in the still room, Michael leaning over her shoulder as she sat in the back parlor, Michael tucking the covers around her when he left the bed consumed her. Holding herself tightly, she gave in to the tears, letting them fall as the loss consumed her.

As her tears faded so did the feeling she'd lost everything of value. Opening her eyes, she stretched and sighed. *I should have expected this.* She got up, wandered into the bathroom, and recoiled at her reflection in the mirror. *Maybe if I look better I'll feel better.* But the steamy shower only brought more memories – memories of showers with Michael. Washing quickly, she toweled her hair and body dry, and dressed in the long skirt of muted blues and greens with the pale blue blouse she'd set out to wear.

In her office, she booted up her computer. Sometime during the last hour she decided she couldn't call Michael, couldn't hear his voice, couldn't maintain her composure if he said he missed her. But she had promised to let him know she'd arrived home safely, so she accessed her email account and typed: *Home safe. Uneventful trip. More later.* and clicked send.

With an hour to go before leaving to pick up Gabriella, Elizabeth went through her emails, responding to some, saving others, deleting most. She still had twenty minutes so she quickly went through the pile of newsletters and magazines, tossing out the few solicitations that had slipped past Gabby. By the time she'd finished, her paper-recycling bag was almost full.

After a quick trip to the bathroom to dab on a bit of mascara, she stopped by the kitchen to gather her contribution for the evening's potluck which included three bottles of champagne. Tucking the champagne in to a small cooler she kept in her trunk, she added a couple of gel-packs to keep them cold. Finally it was time for her to leave to pick up Gabriella.

She made sure her door was locked before going down to the garage and her car. Even that simple act brought the memory of being able to leave Michael's house without worrying about break-ins flashing through her mind. Settled in the car, she laid her head against the headrest and sighed. *Memories are all I have so I'd do better to embrace them than fight them.* Tears welled and she struggled to hold them back. *It'll all be better tonight when I'm with my circle sisters.*

"I knew I'd miss him—I just never realized how much it would hurt," she whispered to herself as she backed out of her parking space and drove to pick up Gabby.

Elizabeth and Gabriella were the first to arrive at Sophia's. After setting their potluck contributions on the counter, they joined Sophia on her patio. "Sophia," Elizabeth said, giving her circle sister a hug, "I would like to be last in our talking circle tonight."

"I don't think that will be a problem, Elizabeth." Sophia returned the hug, holding her close for a minute before letting her go, stepping back, and gently grasping Elizabeth's arms. She looked searchingly at Elizabeth's face, deeply in her eyes before she pulled her back into her embrace and whispered, "Trust in the Goddess, Elizabeth. All will be as it should be if you trust."

Emotions clogged Elizabeth's throat making speech impossible. Even breathing was a struggle. With tears shining in her eyes, she nodded.

A bell chimed, the front door flew open and in came the other women laughing and chatting. Sophia and Gabriella walked inside to greet them, giving Elizabeth a few moments to compose herself before she was surrounded by her circle sisters.

"Let's start right away, I'm starving," Hunter spoke up over the chatter. "Let me put it another way, does anyone object to our starting? If you do, now is the time to speak up," she added and grinned. When no one raised any objections, she moved to where the small cauldron of cleansing sage was kept, lit it, and began to smudge herself. By the time she'd finished, voices were subdued, demeanors more solemn. One by one they smudged and took their places on the floor in Sophia's living room. From pockets and bras they removed personal talismans and placed them on the center altar cloth.

"Will you be willing to do prayers, Elizabeth?" Sophia asked.

"Of course I will," she responded and stood. She turned to the South and stood with her legs slightly apart, arms raised and began. "Spirits of the South, Universal Source of All, Great Spirit, Great Goddess, we thank you for the abundance that graces our lives each day. Especially we are grateful for the blessings of the great friendships we share with one another. Thank you for leading us to this circle and to each other. Blessed Be."

She turned now facing the West. "Spirits of the West, Universal Source of All, Great Spirit, Great Goddess, we thank you for the quiet understanding we receive from each other, the compassion, the time for our own reflection as we travel our paths individually and together. Blessed Be."

Facing the North she began again. "Spirits of the North, Universal Source of All, Great Spirit, Great Goddess, we thank you for the wisdom you share with us each day and for the wisdom we share amongst ourselves, wisdom we've learned from our own life's journey and wisdom passed down to us from our own ancestors. Blessed Be."

Elizabeth slowly turned so she was facing East. Taking a deep breath, she centered herself as she began. "Spirits of the East, Universal Source of All, Great Spirit, Great Goddess, we thank you for the opportunity to begin again each second, each minute, each hour, each day. We come to you replete with the certainty that we are ready to start anew at this time. We ask you to watch over, guide, and protect us from stagnation, to keep your bright light shining so we can see our paths clearly. In love and light, Blessed Be."

Elizabeth lowered her arms and turned to face the center of the circle. She reached out to either side, taking Sophia and Gabriella's hands, raising them skyward, motioning with her head and eyes for her circle sisters to do the same. Tilting her head back, and closing her eyes, she let the words come.

"We are the Light," her voice was strong and clear. "We are the Source," she could feel the energy flow around the circle. "Through us Love flows throughout the World," the light from the energy shimmered behind her closed eyes. The voices of her circle sisters joined with hers. "We are the Light, We are the Source, Through us Love flows throughout the World." She felt herself floating, merging with the shimmering light, and beheld the faint image of The Lady. "We are the Light, We are the Source, Through us Love flows throughout the World. Blessed Be."

The women lowered their arms and for several minutes stood standing, looking at one another, soft smiles on their faces, dazed looks in their eyes. As one they settled to sit on the floor.

Sophia picked up the talking stone. "We are gathered to-night to welcome Elizabeth back with us." She'd purposely not used the word 'home' and while she was uncertain as to the "why of it", instinctively she knew she'd done the right thing. "She has asked to speak last. I suggest that we each find time to spend with Elizabeth this next week to catch her up on our various adventures. Having said that, if you have news to share of things recently past or soon to come, please tell us. I thought I'd fix a big salad on Sunday with vegetables from my garden if Elizabeth is free to come, that is. And, anyone else could come also. Children would be welcomed because it would be a social time. Who thinks she might be able to make it?" Sophia looked around and saw that Elizabeth had raised her hand as had Gabriella, Hunter, and Ashley. "So it's a plan then." She passed the talking stone, a large piece of amethyst, to Ashley.

"I'll bring dessert, Soph. The kids and I'll make cupcakes or maybe some homemade ice cream. I think ya like fresh peach ice cream, right E?"

Elizabeth nodded and smiled. "It's one of my favorites, Ash."

"Not much going on in my life," she continued, "other than the children are growing. I swear they've each grown an inch a week." She laughed and passed the stone to Diana.

"What are you doing tomorrow, Elizabeth? I thought maybe we could have lunch. I start a new class on Monday and I've let things slide so I'll be finishing things up on Sunday. It's possible I'd be done in time, but I'd rather not count on it. You know Murphy's law and all that," her laugh caught abruptly when she saw the stricken look on Elizabeth's face. "Oh Elizabeth, what did I say? I'm so sorry to have upset you." She reached across Sophia and took Elizabeth's hand, gently squeezing it. "Please tell me, Elizabeth."

Elizabeth sat like a stone statue unable to talk, to think, and wishing she couldn't feel.

Lily, who was sitting on Diana's right, whispered in her ear, "His name is Michael Murphy, D."

"Oh, Elizabeth, I'm so sorry. I didn't know, didn't remember. I'm not sure I ever heard it." She stopped as she felt Lily's elbow jab her side. Recovering from the sharp but short-lived pain, she added "I'm truly sorry for saying something that upsets you so, Elizabeth. We can talk later about a good time to get together." She looked ready to cry as she passed the stone to Lily.

Elizabeth heard Lily's voice and then Ashley's and Hunter's but it wasn't until she heard Gabriella's voice right next to her that she was able to wrench her mind from the overwhelming memories back to this circle. She felt the smooth textured, faceted stone in her hand, and knew she had to do something other than sit here. "I have something to get from the car," she stood and tucked the talking stone inside her bra. "I'd appreciate it if you wouldn't talk while I'm gone." She stepped from the circle and jogged to the door.

Outside she stopped and breathed deeply, once, twice, three times. Some semblance of calm rose within her. She hurriedly went to her car and got the Galway crystal box from the trunk. Back at the entryway to the living room she stopped. Her circle sisters sat quietly.

Elizabeth carried the box to her place in the circle setting it behind and to the side of her place before she sat. Swiveling to open the box, she began taking out the presentation boxes passing them around the circle. "One of the first places I visited was Galway," she said amazed at how calm her voice sounded as she began to share the story. "I went to the Galway Crystal factory and watched master craftsmen making beautiful intricate cuts on the glass. It was fascinating and wondrous. There were many things I thought we could use in our ceremonies. However, these," she opened her box, "goblets were what I chose." She smiled and felt joy as she watched her circle sisters open their boxes. "They are all in the Lismore pattern."

"I don't have a goblet, Elizabeth," Hunter spoke up. "I have this." She held out a beautiful crystal bell ringing it softly.

"Oh Goddess, please help me," Elizabeth clamped her hands over her mouth. Rivulets of tears flowed down her face, leaving dark wet blotches on her light blue blouse.

Gabriella looked into the carton, brought out another box, and handed it to Hunter. "This must be your goblet, Hunter."

Hunter gently placed the bell back in its box, passed it to Gabriella, who noticed a piece of paper tucked into the lid.

"Elizabeth, there's a note. Do you want to read it?"

Arms wrapped around her middle, Elizabeth shook her head.

"Do you want me to read it to you?" Gabby's voice was soft and gentle. She rested her free hand on her friend's arm. On Elizabeth's other side, Sophia lightly rubbed her back, offering comfort as best she could. Her other circle sisters sat quietly, bearing witness to her distress, ready to act if asked.

"What does it say?" Elizabeth choked out.

Gabriella opened the piece of paper and glanced over the words. She looked around the circle and then back at Elizabeth. "Do you want me to read it out loud?"

Elizabeth nodded.

"Luv," Gabriella began. Elizabeth buried her face in her hands, her shoulders shaking with sobs. "I want you to have this bell, the one you held in your hands. When you ring it, remember the man from the plane that slept on your shoulder, and showed you some of Ireland's sights. Mick Murphy known to you as Michael." Gabriella folded the paper, tucked it in the box and pushed the larger carton out of the way. She gathered Elizabeth in her arms and rocked her.

Sophia's softly murmured prayers closed the circle. The women got to their feet, leaving Elizabeth sobbing in Gabriella's arms, the deep gut-wrenching sound following them from the room.

Gabriella sat, rocked, and held Elizabeth. Not knowing what words Elizabeth needed to hear she said nothing. The quiet voices of the other women and the muted sounds of getting things ready for their meal were a backdrop to her friend's sobbing. Wonders about the relationship Elizabeth had with this man, what he meant to her buzzed in her mind. She'd never seen her friend so distraught. When Elizabeth and Jeremy broke up, she was sad but nothing like this. She wasn't even sure E had cried. If she had, it was because her dream for children and her own family had left with him. As these thoughts popped up in her mind, Gabriella quickly banished them, focusing her attention on her friend.

They were "of an age", she smiled at the thought, both thirty-two years old and both Gemini. She was born in May and Elizabeth in June so she was the older 'sister'. Ashley was next at 33, followed by Hunter at 35. Diana, Lily, and Sophia were the oldest approaching or just passing the big 4 – 0. As she pulled her errant thoughts back to the present one more time, she realized that while Elizabeth's tears were still flowing, she was no longer sobbing.

"Elizabeth," she spoke quietly. A movement caught her attention, she looked up to see Diana and Lily at the door, one with a washcloth, the other a box of tissues. They paused a moment before exchanging glances and coming into the room. Lily pulled the altar cloth to one side and sat cross-legged in front of Gabriella and Elizabeth. Diana sat on Elizabeth's right.

Lily reached out and touched Elizabeth's shoulder, gently massaging it a moment before she spoke. "Elizabeth, it's Lily. Diana and I are here with a cool washcloth and some tissue.

Diana pulled a couple of them from the box; tenderly uncurled Elizabeth's fisted hand and placed the tissues there.

The kaleidoscope of emotions tumbling through her eased. With a sigh, Elizabeth shifted to sit on her own and Gabriella's arms dropped away. She swiped at her eyes and blew her runny nose.

Diana put her arm around Elizabeth's shoulder and scooted a bit closer. "If I'd known, if I'd remembered, Elizabeth," she started and her own voice broke. "I'm so very sorry."

"It's all right, D," Elizabeth's voice was hoarse from the crying. "I know you didn't mean anything by it. It's just that I never thought it would hurt so bad to leave him. It's like I've lost a piece of myself." She took a shaky breath. "When Jeremy left, I was sad, but not like this. I know the few tears I shed then were not because of him but because of what he represented to me. Michael." She sighed, swiped once more at her watery eyes and nose, and whispered, "With Michael it's different. My soul aches."

Sophia's voice came from the doorway. "May we come in, Elizabeth? If you need us to stay out, we will. But if it is all right with you, we'd like to come in."

Fresh tears fell at the words, but Elizabeth nodded, looking up to see Sophia, Hunter and Ashley come in arranging themselves to complete a semi-circle around Elizabeth and Gabriella.

"This isn't how I thought tonight would go," she said her laugh shaky, her smile tremulous. "I brought champagne, envisioned laughter, toasts, and stories about sheep. Of course, I knew I'd have to mention Michael. I figured Lily'd told everyone about him." Her wobbly smile firmed. "You know one of the last fights we had," she said and smiled ruefully at the astonished faces of the women's around her. "Yes, Michael and I fought, I even yelled at him."

"So what was this last fight about?" Lily asked the question on everyone else's mind.

"Well, he only heard a part of my conversation with Gabriella and thought that he was last on the list behind Ireland and The Lady. He left without telling me, went to his pub, got drunk, and spent the night with his friend. He was cold and distant and I couldn't figure out why because I'd just decided to stay longer.

"The irony is that memories of The Lady and Ireland in general only remind me of him. When I think of Michael, he stands alone in my mind. I don't immediately think of Ireland or The Lady. But I can't think of either of them without Michael coming to mind.

"I'm so confused right now. I missed you all so very much while I was gone. There were so many times I wished I could talk to you, sort out my thoughts and feelings with you." Elizabeth sat, her hands clasped in her lap, her head bent as she talked. She took a deep, shaky breath and looked up at Lily, a look of understanding on her face.

"I remember when I was so confused about Jackson. I relied on everyone here to help me sort things out so he and I could be together. Is that something we can do for you too?" Lily smiled and reached out, handing Elizabeth the wash cloth.

"No," Elizabeth's voice began to tremble again. "No, I need to find a way through the pain. Michael and I can't be together like you and Jackson. It can't be."

Sophia leaned forward and cupped Elizabeth's chin in her hands, speaking softly. "E, perhaps the best thing for now is to be here, with us, right now and let the future, whatever it might be, stay out there," she said gesturing vaguely with her free hand. A smile on her face, she straightened, her hands dropping into her lap. "I believe I heard the word "champagne" earlier and we do have those beautiful crystal goblets to christen." Her voice turned brisk. "I don't know about the rest of you, but I think it's a good idea to finish our evening with food and champagne." She looked around at the other women, saw nods of agreement, and turned back to Elizabeth. "Elizabeth?" Sophia's voice was gentle as she put the question out.

"I'll go get the champagne, then." Elizabeth wiped her face with the washcloth and blew her nose. Her voice was still hoarse from crying but the tears had stopped, at least for now. She stood and one-by-one gave each woman a hug and a whispered "thank you". Gabriella she held the longest while the tears threatened again. When she had them under some semblance of control, she stepped back, looking her friend in the eyes. "Thank you for everything, Gabby. While I know I hurt more because I stayed, I have more memories now to sustain me and for that I'll always be grateful."

"What I don't understand, E, is why you think you'll never see him again? You can go back to Ireland; you can meet him when he travels here to the U.S. You said he races his horses in our country." Gabriella's face showed her puzzlement and concern in her frown.

"If it hurts this bad now, Gabby, I can't even imagine what it would feel like to leave him or have him leave me if I grew to care even more for him."

"It isn't like he doesn't care about you, Elizabeth." Gabby took Elizabeth's arm and they started walking to the family room.

"What do you mean by that?" Elizabeth asked as they joined the others.

Gabriella looked at the other women, an intent look on her face. "I think it's time to get everything out in the open," she started, paused, took a deep breath. "Did you know that Michael called Jackson and asked him to help figure things out so you could stay with him?"

"He what?!" Elizabeth shrieked as she spun around to face Lily. "Michael called Jackson?"

Lily, her face calm and neutral, nodded. "Yes, he did. He told Jackson that he cared about you and wanted you to stay longer but you had bills to pay and other obligations. He asked Jackson for his help in working things out so you could stay."

Gone was the weeping woman. Elizabeth was furious. "How dare him! Just like that! Taking things into his own hands. Thinking he has all the answers. He's demanding, obstinate, oooooo," she growled in frustration.

The other women stood, mouths agape as Elizabeth stormed. Where was the quiet almost shy young woman they'd known for almost eight years? Gone ... and in her place was a raging woman whose eyes flashed, her cheeks pinked with emotion, her dark hair tumbling down from the horse-shaped clip that held it high on her head. They saw a new Elizabeth, a woman whose passion was exposed for all to see; a passion that had been carefully hidden away—until Michael.

Within minutes the flare of anger dissipated. Although Elizabeth still steamed, she no longer ranted. She turned to face the other women. "Anything else I need to know?" her tone held vestiges of her anger. She watched as each woman shook her head. "Thank you for telling me that, Gabby. I truly did need to hear how conniving that man can be to get what he wants." She smiled but it was not one of pleasure. "He calls himself a determined man and says he always gets what he wants. We'll see about that," she snapped. "We'll just see about that." She turned on her heel and stomped down the hall to the front door. "I'm going to get the champagne."

The other women heaved a collective sigh, looked at each other, noting the amusement dancing in each other's eyes.

"I don't envy him, when she gets a hold of him," Hunter chuckled.

"Wow," Ashley drawled. "I never woulda believed it if I hadn't seen it for myself. Our Elizabeth can be hell on wheels."

"She's always shown fierce passion for the children and the families she works with, but I've never seen her show it for herself. I must say that while a part of that display was disconcerting, overall, I'm glad for it," Diana commented.

"She loves him but doesn't know it," Lily added.

"I agree," Sophia turned to look at everyone. "But there's more to it than that."

"She loves us too," Gabriella spoke up. "She doesn't know how to love us here in Fremont and love Michael in Ireland.

And, she sees it as an "either – or" decision and she's chosen us."

The sound of Elizabeth coming through the front door stopped further speculative comments. Sophia and Diana began washing and drying the crystal goblets, passing them around. Gabriella stepped up to help Elizabeth open two bottles of champagne.

When everyone's goblet was half-full, they raised them, the light sparkling in the prismed glass.

"May the blessings of our friendship be strong in our lives forever and our circle unbroken," Elizabeth started.

"May we know with certainty we are connected wherever we may be; physical distance does not break our connection," Sophia added.

"May we see ourselves as a source of good in the world," Ashley spoke next. "I love the prayer ya brought back with you Elizabeth."

"May the light of love flow through us," Hunter smiled. "May we always be surrounded by the light of love."

"May that light of love be with us always and strengthen out ties to others," Lily added.

Diana sang, "May we always know we have each other. May we always know when we feel alone we are not. We see the same sun, the same moon, the same stars in the sky no matter where we are in the world."

"Blessed Be," Gabriella clinked her goblet to those of her circle sisters as they repeated again "Blessed Be."

"Let's eat," Hunter said after a sip of champagne. "I'm starved." Picking up a small plate, she began putting bits of everyone's potluck contribution on it creating a spirit plate. Ashley said the prayers of gratitude and thanksgiving to the plants and animals who gave of themselves for their meal. After the spirit plate was set outside, the women picked up their plates and served themselves from the plethora of dishes on the counter.

Sophia stood to one side, Gabriella nearby, and watched her smiling, chattering circle sisters. By this time, Elizabeth's despair and anger were gone. To everyone's amusement, she was laughing and talking about her obsession with sheep.

Sophia took a sip of her champagne. *I think that Elizabeth's connection to Michael is as strong as mine still is with Jonathan and he's been gone five years. I can't imagine once she decides she wants both The Circle and Michael she won't be able to find a way.* "Well, Gabriella, we'd better join in or there'll be nothing left."

An unladylike snort greeted that statement followed by a chuckle. "That'll be the day, Soph. We may run out of champagne, but we'll never run out of food."

The two women stepped forward and immediately were surrounded by the other women. As they filled their plates, hoots of laughter rang through the room as Elizabeth regaled them with another story about Irish sheep.

# 19 14TH MOON PREPARATIONS

The next two weeks Elizabeth was busy with getting back into a routine of work, spending time with one or another of her circle sisters, and preparing for The Women of the 14th Moon Weekend. Her partner in the Maiden Ceremony was Gabriella and they spent hours making altar cloths for the eight young maidens by hand-sewing delicate Irish lace trim around the twelve-by-twelve squares of Irish linen.

The weekend before Labor Day, everyone met at Ashley's to put the finishing touches on each handmade gift. It was important to The Circle that every gift was touched by each one of them so they spent the afternoon painting, beading, embroidering, and gluing decorations making each unique.

"Well, we have them finished," Gabriella sighed as she carried her box of supplies toward her car. "I'm glad this workday happened so we aren't trying to finish things up as we set things up."

"I know what you mean. It's one of the reasons I was worried about staying in Ireland longer," Elizabeth said following with the basket of altar cloths and glad they'd carpooled. "I worried we'd not get everything done in time."

"But we did get everything done with time to spare," Gabriella added, opening the trunk. "Of course it helps that our schedules meshed."

"That's because you took time away from your writing. If I'd come back sooner, you wouldn't have had to for us to be finished." Elizabeth glanced at her friend but was not surprised to see her frown. "I truly am sorry, Gabby."

"Oh, E, it isn't that. I'm not behind because we've been working on the Maiden's Ceremony. You see, I've these goals for myself, you know like my own self-imposed deadlines. I don't always meet them because I have these other goals too. I'm committed to being in service to others so my checking on your place while you were away helped me meet that commitment to myself.

"And I want I want to feel happy, joyful even when I'm writing so some days when the words don't come and it isn't fun anymore, I stop. Sometimes it's hard to keep thinking positively. I know I'm doing what I'm supposed to do, but... ." her voice trailed off and she looked into the distance."

"You know, Gabby, I spent several hours in a little book store in Kinslow and got to know the owner, Maura. Between all of us, we have contacts and resources to help market your book once it's finished and published. You have a wonderful story, you have our support now, and you'll have it when you're published. Remember Giovanni? Jackson's architect friend in Italy? I'm sure he's got contacts all over that country, too. And when the time comes, we've the women who attend the 14th Moon to call upon. You could write something up, asking for ideas, contacts to market your book. You've talked about your writing in the past, someone may ask about it and you can hand them something that asks them for ideas; something more than asking them to buy your book."

Gabriella's voice was excited, her face animated. "That's a great idea, E." Her chin went up as she added in a formal tone, "I'd rather not involve Senor Migliori.  He's trouble."

"Giovani? Trouble? He's very polite," Elizabeth paused, "Actually come to think about it, he's been very friendly the few times I've seen him. Why do you think he's trouble?"

"He's a consummate flirt, E, a 'ladies man'. A couple of centuries ago, he'd be called a rake. He's the kind of man who relishes "notching his belt" with his conquests," Gabriella's tone was harsh as she continued. "I don't want anything to do with him. He's trouble, trouble, trouble."

"You've made your point, Gabby. I guess some men are so much trouble they aren't worth the risk to reach your dream." Elizabeth placed the basket in the trunk. As she straightened a picture of Michael, a little boy in his arms, a little boy with dark hair and blue eyes, flitted through her mind, she could hear their laughter. "I actually understand what you mean," she said a rueful smile tugging the corners of her mouth. "I know full-well that some men come with lots of risks attached to being involved with them."

The loss of Michael and the little boy laughing in his arms or the loss of these women; she'd made her choice and she wouldn't be sorry for it. As she opened the passenger door, the laughing image of the little boy, arms outstretched to her shone brightly; she turned the gasp of surprise into a cough as she slipped into the seat.

# 20  14TH MOON

In a separate area of wooded land, Elizabeth, Gabriella and eight young women gathered for the beginning of the Maiden's Ceremony. It was Friday evening and the other women were sitting in a talking circle sharing what they wanted to experience tomorrow. Elizabeth was glad that Kris and Heather, women in another sacred circle, had added this special time for the Maidens, a time to explore what it means to be a woman, to be a giver of life. Did these young women have any idea of how powerful women were in earlier times? How their wisdom and counsel were sought by others, even men? The foundational goal they'd set was these young women would not only know but have experienced what that felt like by the closing of the circle tomorrow night. Her attention wandered, Gabby's voice brought it back.

"Who knows about smudging?" Gabby smiled in encouragement as she took in the sight of the eight young women sitting in the circle. She and Elizabeth had agreed on who would take the lead in the different areas they wanted to explore with these young women as well as the sequence of those areas. However, they also agreed that if an opportunity presented itself, they could veer from their outline and still cover everything by the time they joined the other women in the morning.

As she and Elizabeth sat in comfortable silence, another agreement they'd made, they continued to look encouragingly at the young women, who ranged in age from thirteen to nineteen-years-of-age. Finally one of the young women tentatively raised her hand, and with Gabby's nod to go ahead, quietly said, "My aunt says you use the smoke to clear away bad energy."

"Good. Any other thoughts?" Gabby continued to look around at the others until another hand rose. "Go ahead. Just chime in. No one needs to get permission. Just make sure the other person has stopped talking."

"My grandma told me that smudging is used to cleanse. I'm not sure exactly what, but that's what I remember her telling me."

Elizabeth and Gabriella continued to sit quietly as another other young women spoke. "My mom said smudging is about protection."

They looked across the circle at one another, slight smiles on their faces, but kept silent until the fourth contributor had finished.

"You are all correct." Gabriella's gaze met that of each of the young women who'd spoken. "Smudging has been used since ancient times to cleanse, purify, and protect. Depending on where people lived, different substances were used. We are using sage to smudge. But you can also use cedar, which was the choice of the indigenous people in this area because sage was hard to get since it isn't native to the valley."

Elizabeth had stood while Gabby talked, retrieving from a small chest the items they'd brought to share with these young women. First was a basket lined with cloth to protect tuna cans decorated with bits of wood, small stones, and paint. Small holes had been punched on either side of the can and a piece of wire fashioned to make a handle. Each can contained sprigs of sage and a small box of matches.

Gabriella demonstrated how to light one or two sage leaves and when the flame caught, how to gently blow out the flame leaving a thin wisp of rising smoke. Standing, she continued to show the young women how to move the smoke over and around their bodies in order to cleanse and protect themselves. Within a few minutes all eight of the young women had their smudge 'pots' going and were smoothing the wisps of smoke over and around themselves. When the smudging was complete, everyone resumed her seat and, following Gabriella's example, placed their smudge 'pot' on the ground behind them.

"You'll notice the white cloth on the ground in the center of our circle," Elizabeth began. She withdrew a piece of hematite from her skirt pocket, held it to her heart as the power of New Grange thrummed through her. Saying a silent prayer for the wisdom and grounding she'd need for this weekend, she held it in her hand as she spoke. "You were asked to bring something to contribute to our sacred altar. If you need to get that from your things, feel free to so that now." She nodded and smiled when two young women got up and hurried to the tent, returning shortly.

"First we smudge ourselves, then our altar. How many of you have altars in your room?" She saw no hands raised. "If not in your room, what about elsewhere in your home?" One of the young women who'd shared about smudging raised her hand.

"Creating altars and sacred spaces brings me great joy," Elizabeth said her voice ringing with the truth of her words. "You really can set one up anywhere. If you want it to be personal but it's in a public place, you can arrange it so people who are not familiar with altars or sacred space don't recognize it." She went on to explain, much as she had to the young women on New Grange how to talk about an altar to someone who would disapprove of the practice and she gave them examples of the altars she'd set up at Michael's: the herbs in the kitchen, tea set in the front parlor, even the arrangement of horses in the foyer.

Indicating the cloth in their midst, Elizabeth asked them to think about where the item they'd brought would best fit as she went on to explain about the four directions.

"You'll see that the center of this altar has a pottery bowl. A few years back all of the women in my circle, made bowls out of clay. I made this one. Tomorrow you'll see the one Gabriella made because we'll change some things on this altar in the morning."

"The center of the altar represents the 'center' direction. In some traditions instead of four directions, they hold to seven: East, South, West, North, Above, Below, and Middle or Center. The Center then represents 'the whole' or everything as one. 'Below' represents our connection to the Mother, the Earth and 'Above' is our connection to the Father, the Sky.

"I'd like you to bring your smudge back in front of you. Relight it if that is needed. Gabriella and I have more sage and matches if you need them." She and Gabriella got out their abalone shells, lighting a few leaves of sage until smoke rose. When everyone was ready she continued, "Now, take the item you brought with you for the altar and cleanse it." She demonstrated with her hematite stone and then with a piece of turquoise how to draw each through the smoke, turn each around and around ensuring all sides were thoroughly coated in smoke.

Rising, she placed the piece of hematite in the North and the turquoise in the East saying, "put your item on the altar where you believe it should be." She stepped back and watched as the altar filled: a piece of rose quartz the size of her fist, a six-inch statue of Kwan Yin, and a four-inch porcelain robin. The youngest, a girl of thirteen, placed a rabbit carved of soapstone in the South next to the rose quartz. Kwan Yin was in the North, the robin in the East and Gabriella's small figure of a wolf sat in the West.

The two oldest, at ages eighteen and nineteen, were cousins brought by their paternal aunt. The last to arrive, they showed no sign of excitement or pleasure at being here. Their aunt had whispered to Gabriella she'd had a difficult time convincing them to come but knew in her heart they needed to be there given the challenges they faced. Both, she'd muttered, were involved with young men who were users on many levels. Elizabeth noted they remained seated, showing no signs of joining in.

A multi-hued glass float had been placed in the West, the many shades of blues reminding her of the blues in the Irish sky and light sparkling on the stream flowing through Michael's farm. The memory was fleeting, her emotions were not.

The fourteen-year-old daughter of one of the matrons who was also attending her first 14th Moon Gathering stood before the cloth on the ground, a crystal cluster in her hands. Chewing on her lower lip, she appeared uncertain about where to place it. Giving her time to decide before stepping in, Elizabeth waited several minutes before walking the few steps to stand next to her.

"When I was talking about the directions, which one felt right to you?" she said her voice soft but still loud enough others could hear.

"I don't know," the young woman replied. "I've never done anything like this before."

"You aren't alone in that as others in this circle are here for the first time as well. And, I'll remind you that while I've been in many circles and created numerous altars, I had my first time too." Elizabeth waited a minute before continuing. "When you look at this altar, where is your eye drawn?"

"The place where you put the black stone, the North. But what if I'm wrong," she whispered.

"That's what's so wonderful about creating an altar; there is no 'wrong'. Wherever you place your beautiful crystal city will be just where it needs to be." Elizabeth placed her hand on the young woman's shoulder and gave it a gentle squeeze. "Trust me, it'll be perfect," she whispered and then stepped back. She met Gabriella's gaze as she did, noting Gabby's nod in the direction of the two oldest girls who were still sitting, bored sullen looks on their faces. *Right now I wish Logan was here but she made the decision to stay at Sophia's with Ashley's children so their mom could come.*

She saw the crystal cluster now sitting in the North and looked over to see the young woman's relieved face as she sat down again. "Does anyone else have something to contribute before we move on?" she asked brightly, looking at the two who had yet to place anything on the altar. They stared back at her with blank looks. "Well, then," she started when she saw a hand begin to rise. "Yes?"

It was the thirteen-year-old who asked "Why aren't they doing it?" as she pointed to the two older girls.

"I don't know," Elizabeth's answer was matter-of-fact. "If it is important to you, you could ask them."

"So why aren't you?" the question was one of confusion not one of accusations.

"We don't want to be here," the eighteen-year-old replied.

"Then why are you?"

"Because our aunt made us come," the nineteen-year-old retorted.

The fourteen year old chimed in, "How did she do that?"

"She just did, that's all," the two said almost in unison. "It's hard to explain."

"Please try." This request came from one of the two sixteen-year-olds. "I came because I knew it was important to my Mom for me to be here. She came last year and was so excited that she could bring me. I'm not sure I believe all this stuff, but when I think back to how my Mom changed after coming last year, I figured I'd at least come and see why she wanted me to be here."

"My grandmother wanted me to come," one of the fifteen-year-olds added. "She's been a couple of times and thinks being a crone is the greatest. I don't know why because that means she's old. And for my grandmother, letting anyone know she's old is really strange."

"I've been waiting and waiting to come," the thirteen-year-old spoke up. "I had my first period a month after last year's 14th Moon. My Mom has come and talked about it forever. We go to activities in the community on the solstices and equinoxes and try to live softly on the land—you know, recycle, grow vegetables organically, that kind of stuff. Mom says her life would have been different in lots of ways if she'd had a 14th Moon to go to when she first had her period and had been able to see the power of being a woman."

"What do you mean the power of being a woman?" the eighteen-year-old snarled. "It's a man's world, haven't you heard?"

"Actually in ancient times, the Earth was seen as sacred, the bearer of life," Gabriella spoke directly to the eighteen-year-old. "And because women have children, they were seen as having power. In those days, people lived in accordance with the seasons, worshipped the Goddess, the divine feminine. Men were the hunters and protectors; women were the gatherers, the keepers of the hearth who bore and raised children. They were the healers, the wise women who taught herbal lore and how to live within the rhythm of the Mother, or Earth.

"If we lived in those days, we would have lived in a matriarchy where the women were sought out for their wisdom; where the feminine was sacred, where the feminine was revered. Men did not have the power to berate women, to beat them physically, mentally, or emotionally. To do so would result in their banishment or death.

"We are the givers of life, and in those days we were seen as powerful, with our power at its peak when we were bleeding. In many traditions, the women were separated from the clan or tribe when they had their monthly flow. Only other women or children could be in their presence at that time. Men did not even look at them for fear of being weakened."

The young women were a rapt audience, even the two oldest were no longer looking bored and sullen, just skeptical.

"When a woman's body releases the blood from her womb, cleansing herself before beginning another cycle, it is a time for rest and reflection. Just think if each month as your menses began, there was a special place for you to go; your responsibilities to your family and home were taken care of by others. In this place you had nothing to do except rest, dream, sleep, and think until your flow stopped. Someone would do your cooking, cleaning, bring you food, water. How would your life be different if, when your period began, you were honored as being powerful?" Gabriella let the silence fill the space.

"That possibility, the possibility that even if no one else honors us as women, we can honor ourselves and our power as givers of life, that is why your grandmothers, mothers, aunts, nieces, cousins, friends, whoever it was who encouraged you or perhaps drug you here, made the effort. They wanted you to have the experience of living for a weekend in your full power, to see what your life could encompass, to know when you leave here Sunday you have the choice to continue to honor yourself and your power or not. But to understand in a different way that it is a choice."

Silence.

Gabriella and Elizabeth sat quietly, alert for signs of questions or concerns. The nineteen-year-old was the first to speak. "Do you really believe all that crap about women having power?"

"Yes," Elizabeth replied. "I know that many things make it seem as if we don't. All over the world women are sexually and physically enslaved, beaten, threatened, exploited, mutilated, raped, and murdered. It doesn't seem like we have any power at all," she paused. "But we do." She let the words hang in the air. "Who has some ideas about how we still have power when all these things are happening?"

Her question was met by silence but as she looked around the circle she could see brows furrowed in thought, quizzical glances being shared. She looked across the circle at Gabriella and by silent agreement they decided to move on and finish creating the altar.

Gabriella turned to the two skeptical young women sitting close to her. "If you'd like to add to the altar now or at some time over the weekend, it is your choice." She looked across the circle at Elizabeth, saw her right brow lift slightly. Out of the corner of her eye she espied the two slowly rise. They stood before the altar, and while she did not discern joy in their hearts, still the nineteen-year-old placed a blue and green cloisonné butterfly in the West and her eighteen-year-old cousin put her yellow and peach colored butterfly in the East. They stood together, just for a moment, looking at the altar before turning and clomping back to their places grumpy looks on their faces.

"Thank you," Gabriella said softly.

"A couple more things about altars," Elizabeth now spoke. "Notice the small dark stones on the corners?" She looked around to see heads nodding. "Those are apache tears and are stones of protection for the altar. Before you all arrived, Gabriella and I called in different spirits or energies to charge these stones to protect this altar. I called upon The Lady, a servant of The Goddess. She protects the Northeast corner. The Eagle protects the Southwest corner because the Eagle has the power of sight, of vision which is a good energy to have as one enters the West."

"I called upon the power of Frog for the Northwest corner and the power of the Buffalo or Bison for the Southeast corner," Gabriella shared. "Frogs symbolize transformation and the ability to change. After a time of reflection, of going within in the West, we can transform ourselves as we move to the North. The Bison or Buffalo's energy leads us to find the right combination of thoughtfulness, which is a form of prayer, and action that allows us to move into abundance with little effort."

"If you were to create an altar for yourself, who or what would you call upon to protect it? Think about it. When you registered, you were given a notepad and some colored pencils. Use them to write down your ideas or maybe draw pictures. Gabriella and I will be around to answer questions.

"Now, last but not least, you can 'charge' your altars with particular powers. For example: you might want to create an altar of protection, or perhaps one of love; some people create altars of welcome or prosperity. So the question is if you were to create an altar, what would your focus be? If you are willing to share your thoughts at this time, please do."

"I'd want two altars," the fifteen-year-old who hadn't spoken up yet responded quickly. "First I'd want one of protection. I don't like feeling scared. The other altar I'd want for friendships because I don't do a very good job at picking good ones," her voice faltered at the end, her last word whispered.

"Finding good friends, ones that are on your side and don't betray you is hard," the eighteen-year-old contributed. "People are usually bad. You just gotta accept that as a part of life and make the best of it."

"I don't think that's true," chimed in the fourteen-year-old. "I learned something from my Mom about picking friends. The hard part is when I'm feeling lonely and just want someone to hang with. I just want to be with someone and I don't think about if I want to really be friends. This last year at school I tried to be better about it. But this summer someone new moved into my neighborhood and I really want us to be good friends. My Mom says to take it slow and not rush into it because it takes time to be really good friends."

"Well, who wants to feel lonely and left out?" This question came as a verbal challenge from the nineteen-year-old. "Who wants to sit home alone and have people pity them because they don't have a date?"

"I'm too young to date," the thirteen-year-old replied, "so I may not really understand what you're talking about. But I think people pity us when we are hooked up with people who treat us bad too. My neighbor's husband beats her and I know I feel bad for her. I wish she'd leave or make him leave because I'd rather see her alone than bruised."

The group was silent after that interchange. Elizabeth and Gabriella let the silence extend until all the young women were looking at the two of them for direction. They stood and motioned to the other young women to do the same.

"When you are ready to close the circle or stop the ceremony and take a break it is important to say prayers. This is how Gabriella and I do it," Elizabeth said demonstrating how they stood, feet slightly apart, arms raised in the air.

"We start by facing east," Gabriella turned so she was fully facing in that direction and began. "Spirits of the East hear our prayers. We thank you for being with us while we contemplated the opportunities for new beginnings presented to us in this circle."

"Next we turn to the South," Elizabeth continued. "Spirits of the South hear our prayers. We thank you for being with us while we explore the abundance currently in our lives and look for ways to share more of your bounty."

"West?" Gabriella looked around to ensure everyone was turned to face this direction. "Spirits of the West hear our prayers. We thank you for the time to reflect on what has been said and what has not yet or may never be said."

Without prompting, everyone turned to face the North. "Spirits of the North hear our prayers," Elizabeth's voice was clear, "We thank you for the wisdom shared in this circle this evening and for the wisdom to come."

"Now we turn back to the center," coached Gabriella. "Take hold of your neighbors' hand on either side and lift them high. It's okay to move in to make it more comfortable if the stretch is too much. Close your eyes and think in your mind of white light surrounding us all."

As a group they stood, hands held, arms raised, and envisioned themselves surrounded in white light. Elizabeth felt the pulse and heard the low hum before the shimmering light and image of The Lady appeared before her. She opened her eyes and looked around at this group of young women, eyes closed, faces lifted to the sky. She caught Gabriella's gaze across the circle. She too had opened her eyes. They shared a smile. "Blessed Be," they chorused together and lowered their arms. "Blessed Be," was murmured by at least some of the others.

"Now, who is hungry?" Gabriella was already moving away from the circle toward the area set aside for eating. Neither she nor Elizabeth heard any complaints as they led the way to the tables and coolers. The two women smiled, laughed, and chatted with their charges as food was set out.

"Who knows about spirit plates?" Elizabeth asked.

"I do," piped up the thirteen-year-old. "We put bits of the food we are eating on a special plate which is our spirit plate. Then after saying a blessing, we put it outside for the spirits." She smiled and added, "but I know it's our neighbor's cat who eats it."

Everyone pitched in and the spirit plate was quickly prepared. "It's like saying 'grace', isn't it?" queried one of the sixteen-year-olds when they were told about saying a prayer of gratitude.

"Yes, it is," was Gabriella's response, quickly followed by, "do you say grace at home?"

"Not all the time. We do on Sundays and when we have big celebrations and lots of relatives are there."

"Would you be willing to say prayers over the spirit plate? I'll stand right beside you and help out if you stumble," Gabriella moved as she spoke.

"I—I—I'll try," the young woman said taking the offered plate.

Gabriella leaned over and whispered a few words in her ear before straightening and giving a thumb's up sign.

"Spirit of the Earth. Thank you for the food we have to eat tonight. We are grateful for your bounty." She looked worriedly at Gabriella who mouthed two words. The young woman grinned. "Blessed Be."

"Great job," Gabriella exclaimed. "Let's eat." She and Elizabeth stood back as the young women crowded around the table helping themselves to bits and pieces of the various foods before them. "That went well," she whispered to Elizabeth.

"Very well," Elizabeth whispered back. "This weekend promises to be a learning experience for us all. We may learn more from these young women than they learn from us."

"You may be right," Gabriella agreed in a low voice. In her normal tone she added, "Let's get in there Elizabeth before they've eaten everything and we have to lick the plates for sustenance." The young women turned and laughed as Elizabeth and Gabriella joined them.

## Sunday

Even though the 14th Moon Ceremony ended with the closing of the circle Saturday night, most of the women chose to stay the night and leave Sunday morning. Around noon everyone had packed, cleaned up their spaces, and checked out the common area for any overlooked pieces of trash. Elizabeth and her circle sisters were saying their good-byes to the other women when she noticed the two oldest maidens hanging back. She excused herself, grabbed Gabriella's hand, and together they approached the two young women.

"I am so very glad you came this year," Elizabeth said beaming.

"I guess we're glad we came too," the eldest said, studiously watching her toe scuff the ground. "We wanted to apologize, Elizabeth. To you and you too, Gabby." She glanced up and caught Gabriella's eye. "We know we were real fuck-ups."

Elizabeth's hand shot out but she gently grasped the young woman's chin, raising her face until their eyes met. "While we appreciate your apology, tell me how referring to yourself in that manner honors you?"

Gabriella had also stepped forward mirroring Elizabeth's position with the younger woman. "I'd like to know the answer to that question, too."

Both young women tried first to pull away, then to lower their eyes, to avoid answering the question. Elizabeth and Gabriella remained firm yet caring bending to maintain eye contact, preserving the connection until both young women closed their eyes. Still, they stood, hands lightly holding the young women's chins, silent as they waited.

"Guess it's just habit," the younger one said looking up at Gabriella, her cheeks stained red with embarrassment, tears welling in her eyes.

"Here's the deal," Gabriella countered. "It's a habit you need to break." She watched both young women turn to her, startled looks on their faces. "I know Elizabeth and I didn't tell anyone what they needed to do all weekend. But, for the two of you, we'll make an exception." She calmly laid her free hand on the 18-year-old's shoulder. "When we hurt ourselves, we aren't honoring ourselves. Do you agree with that statement?" She looked again at each young woman and saw their nods. "So here's what you do when you catch yourself saying something that dishonors you. Stop. Immediately when you hear the words come out of your mouth or run through your mind, Stop. Then say either out loud or in your head "cancel, cancel, cancel". Say it at least three times and if you still feel the negative energy, say it another three times. You can also add a neutral statement such as "that's not like me" or go even further and say something positive about yourself."

Elizabeth spoke next. "Instead of the negative statement about yourselves, what positive statement could you say instead?" She waited for a moment but spoke before the silence became uncomfortable before suggesting, "That's not like me to be so rude. I can do better than that when I feel pushed or threatened."

Gabriella stepped closer and put her arm around the younger of the two as Elizabeth did the same with the older. "I'd like to hear those words or something like it from your lips," she said softly. "From both of you, actually."

The words came as broken whispers, "It's not like me to be so rude. I'm sorry for being so disrespectful."

Elizabeth whispered back, "I can do better?"

With trembling lips in quirky smiles and threatening tears, both young women looked at Elizabeth and Gabriella as they stood taller and held their shoulders back. "I can do better," they both spoke clearly now. They looked at each other and then back at Elizabeth and Gabriella, "I will do better when I feel pushed or bullied or threatened."

"What about a hug?" Elizabeth asked.

Without words the young women threw themselves into Elizabeth and Gabriella's arms. Elizabeth had noted their aunt standing off to the side. She released one arm to motion her to join them. "I've invited your aunt to join us," she whispered into the middle of the hug.

"Girls," their aunt's voice was soft and gentle. "Thank you for coming with me. It has been a gift I'll treasure the rest of my life."

Elizabeth and Gabriella gave the two young women brief hugs and then stepped back so the young women and their aunt could talk in private. Arm-in-arm they walked back to where their five circle sisters stood and joined them in waving good-bye. The last to leave were the aunt and her two nieces. The young women ran up to Elizabeth and Gabriella saying breathlessly that their aunt had just promised to bring them again so they'd see them next year.

With the only sound the breeze soughing through the trees, they moved into a circle. This was the time for sharing.

"You two were inspired," Hunter began, looking at Elizabeth and then Gabriella. "Having the Maidens decorate half-masks and all of them dance."

"Since no one had been to a 14th Moon before, it seemed the best plan." Gabriella looked at Elizabeth.

"The only real challenge was the music. I'm just grateful they finally decided to drum and dance with no words. That was definitely the best option." Elizabeth sighed. "They all changed before our eyes, didn't they Gabby."

"They did," Gabriella said, a note of serious in her voice, a thoughtful look on her face she continued. "I don't think our two oldest maidens would have made the changes they did if they'd remained with their aunt throughout the time. They really benefited having the time Friday night with the other maidens."

"We were able to create a safe space because we accepted each and every one of them exactly where she was," Elizabeth added. "And the time spent decorating their masks, listening to their chatter—so much wisdom in their souls, so much to share with one another, so much—well, suffice it to say, they each brought exactly what was needed for everyone to learn and grow."

Both the Matron and Crone ceremonies were successful from the feedback they'd received. The Matrons loved the exercise that guided them through why they said "yes" to a more successful understanding of when it was right for them to say "no". And the Crones talking about their life experiences, passing their wisdom on to the younger women was always a highlight of the 14th Moon Ceremony.

"While I could sit and talk about this year's Gathering for hours," Lily said as she rose, "I believe it's time to finish dismantling things and go."

The women rose, folded their chairs and took the last of their items from the altar. After stowing them safely in their cars, they returned to remove the masks they'd made to represent the spirits of each direction as well as the lights that hung from each gate. With everything dismantled and the masks and lights packed in their cars, the women turned back to the space that had held this year's Women of the 14th Moon Ceremony.

Elizabeth walked forward a few steps and surveyed the grassy area surrounded by trees. The natural bowers would remain, the cedar they'd spread on the ground in a circle would decay. By next year there would be little trace of this year's gathering.

Gabriella appeared on her right. "It's always a special time but this year seemed more so," she said softly.

Elizabeth took her hand and as she began to raise it, she felt another of her circle sisters take her left hand. The seven of them stood with hands held and arms raised, facing the now empty space that held vestiges of the magic of their Ceremonies.

> *"We are the Light*
> *"We are the Source*
> *"Through us Love flows throughout the world.*
>
> *"We are the Light*
> *"We are the Source*
> *"Through us Love flows throughout the world.*
>
> *"We are the Light*
> *"We are the Source*
> *"Through us Love flows throughout the world."*

The air around them hummed and pulsed with energy as three times three they repeated the prayer. Elizabeth saw the shimmering light surround them as they connected to the source and sent the light of love out into the world. The Lady stood before her, a beatific smile on her face. *You are doing well, Elizabeth. I will see you soon for we have much to do.* An instant later she was gone.

# 21  In Ireland

Michael studied his horses as they went through their early morning workout, his assistant beside him writing notes as each went through its paces. My Wild Irish Rose was looking particularly good, which pleased him to no end as she was scheduled to run in the Breeders' Cup Distaff next month. Traveling to the U.S. and being that much closer to Elizabeth brought the now familiar sense of loss rushing through him. He shifted, rolling his shoulders in an attempt to dislodge the tightness that seemed to be in permanent residence.

He hadn't talked to her in the four weeks since she'd left, although they had exchanged emails several times a week. The first week after she left, Michael searched his in box several times a day in hopes of getting mail from her. After four weeks, he checked twice a day, once in the morning and again before he went to bed. Before replying, he waited at least twenty-four hours. Ridiculous or not, his pride wouldn't take the chance she'd see how eager, or maybe it was desperate, to hear from her. *And, it's not like she answers right back.* A frown creased his brow, his mouth turned down as he stood, one foot on the bottom rail, murmuring comments to his assistant.

The morning workout over, Michael returned to the main house and breakfast. Seamus, ever taciturn, was out of character this morning. Pots and pans banged and Michael's plate of eggs, scones, bacon, and potatoes was slapped down on the table before he stalked over to the sink where the banging continued amidst the sounds of running water. Michael just tucked into his breakfast, ignoring the discordant sounds. He heard Seamus stomp back to the table and caught a glimpse of him standing to the right out of the corner of his eye.

He looked up, cocked an eyebrow, but said nothing. He sat and waited a forkful of potatoes held in mid-air half-way to his mouth.

Seamus glared, made an unintelligible noise and stomped back to the sink where he commenced with the racket of clearing up after breakfast. It seemed to Michael that it was taking longer than usual to finish the chore, but again, he chose to say nothing. Within a few minutes he heard the unmistakable sounds of Seamus's booted feet tramping back toward him.

"What?" Michael's voice was tinged with exasperation as he looked up at his long-time houseman.

"Yer stupid, that's what ye are," the older man growled before clomping to the sink.

Michael watched Seamus looking out the window before noticing him puttering with something on the sill: the pots of herbs. His houseman was meticulously caring for the pots of herbs Elizabeth had placed in the window. Michael surreptitiously watched as Seamus picked up, fussed with, and then replaced each pot exactly from whence it'd come. Finished, he turned and caught Michael's eye, before he ordered, "Put yer dishes in the sink when yer done." Shaking his head, he left the room.

Sitting at the kitchen table, Michael perfunctorily ate his breakfast, the aromatic scents and rich tastes of the food lost on him. He still wasn't eating well, but after he'd lost weight and grown weak and light-headed, he heeded Seamus and Paddy's nagging and made himself start the day with a hearty breakfast of three eggs, scones, bacon or sausage, and fried potatoes along with several cups of tea with milk and sugar. He shook his head. Why he was drinking his tea just the way Elizabeth liked it defied his understanding. He'd tried going back to his old way and even tried coffee but the next break would find him with a mug of tea stirring in the milk and sugar.

Evenings were another time when the feelings of loneliness overwhelmed him. Sometimes he'd go to the pub or sometimes Paddy'd drop by and they'd have a bit of whiskey and talk horses. But most of the time he sat, staring at nothing, thoughts of Elizabeth, memories of their time together flashing through his mind.

Morning, evening, any time of the day when his routine had included time with Elizabeth was hard. Mornings they talked, showered, made love, and talked some more. He missed having her to talk to about his horses, his dreams; more than that he missed her softness, the scent of bergamot and Elizabeth, the silk of her skin, the heat of her body, and the passion of her kisses. He halted the flow of memories, a rueful smile on his lips. It was hard not to think of her, and when he was being honest with himself, he admitted it was impossible.

Seamus came back in the kitchen and seeing Michael still at the table, dishes surrounding him, stomped over, picked them up, and noisily prepared them for the dishwasher.

"So, you think I'm 'stupid' do you?" Michael leaned his elbows on the table.

"Aye," was the reply.

"May I ask why you think that?" As soon as the words were out of his mouth, he regretted having extended the invitation. "Don't answer," he bit out between clenched jaws as he stood and strode toward the door.

"Yer stupid because you love her and let her leave," Seamus rumbled.

Michael stopped mid-stride, his mouth gaped. "What do you mean; I love her and let her leave? She is an adult, you'll remember," he spat back, anger infusing his words and posture. "Did you want me to chain her up?" The sarcasm was lost on Seamus.

"Yer stupid because you haven't got her back." Seamus continued to clear the last of the breakfast dishes during this exchange. Turning the dishwasher on, he glared at Michael. "I've better things to do than stand here with a stupid...," his last words trailed away as he moved down the hallway toward the main hall leaving Michael standing, temper blazing, anger written in the flare of his nostrils, the thin line of his lips, the set of his jaw. But his eyes, his eyes showed the dark of despair. He reined in his temper, tamped down his anger, but the despair was beyond his control.

When he could move without picking something up and hurling it across the room, Michael walked across the kitchen to the back door. Once outside, he strode quickly to the barn and saddled Brian Boru. As they galloped away from the barns, the wind whipped around his face. He urged B.B. on the sound of pounding hooves a balm to his soul. Through fields and woods man and horse charged on. From time to time, Michael dismounted to open and close gates but within minutes he was back in the saddle.

At the top of a rise, he slowed his horse, knowing B.B. was tiring. He was breathing hard, his horse even more so. As he looked around, his heart stuttered. The stone circle, the dance where he'd found Elizabeth unconscious was just to his left. The memory of the terror he'd felt came unbidden. He sat atop his horse, head bowed, fighting the emotions, the tears that overwhelmed him.

Minutes passed.

Michael slowly dismounted and walked, leading B.B. down the hill to the dance. He dropped the reins, knowing his horse would rest without being tethered, and walked the circumference of the stone circle.

The circle was quiet, no humming, no shimmering lights, no Elizabeth. She brought life and energy to wherever she was and whatever she did. *After I found her here, she changed, grew stronger—strong enough to leave The Lady, to leave me.*

He stopped before the largest of the still standing stones, leaned forward, and rested his forehead on the rough surface, his arms hung down, hands fisted by his sides. *What am I going to do about this?* He took a deep breath and eased his hands open. *I miss her so much it hurts. Hell, sometimes it hurts to breathe.* A wry chuckle escaped sounding more like a choking sob. Michael straightened and returned to B.B. who now munched grass. He stood and wrapped his arms around the horse's neck gaining comfort from his warmth and familiar smell.

"I'm a sorry excuse for a man, boyo." He stroked the horse's nose. As if in answer, the black stallion tossed his head and nudged his dismounted rider. "You don't have to agree." Michael's hands caressed the horse's neck as he gathered the reins and prepared to mount.

"Let's go back through town," he said as he swung into the saddle. "Maybe stop at the pub for a pint. Seamus will kill me for sure if I get something to eat." The thought of Seamus's frowning face if he came home and announced he'd already eaten brought a cautious grin to his face.

They found a gate to the road a few miles further along. Michael dismounted, opened the gate, led B.B. through, shut and secured it before he remounted. They cantered down the road toward Kinslow. At the pub, Michael saw Paddy's truck and looked forward to a pint with his friend. Dismounting, he handed the reins to one of the young boys. "Take him to the back, see that he has some water, a couple of apples, and rub him down," Michael told the boy as he ruffled his hair. "There'll be a reward for you if you do a good job."

"Right, Mick. You can count on me," the young lad said over his shoulder as he led B.B. toward the back of the pub.

"Mick" shouted out in several voices greeted Michael as he stepped through the door into the dimly lit pub. He responded with a general greeting as his eyes adjusted to the lowered light. Then espying Paddy, he waved, and made his way through the tables to where he sat in a back booth.

"What brings you to town today," Paddy asked as he lowered his glass and motioned Patrick to bring him another pint. Michael slid into the booth and turned so he was propped in the corner, his long legs stretched out on an angle, a mirror image of Paddy. This way their long legs didn't get all tangled up and they could see what was happening in the pub.

"Feeling a bit restless is all." Michael shifted to get more comfortable.

They sat in a comfortable silence. Patrick brought two pints, handed one to Paddy and set the other down at the edge of the table. He stood with his hands on his hips and a scowl on his face. "Anything else?"

"Making me work for my pint, eh?" Michael arched a brow and looked at the pint just beyond his reach.

"Thought it wouldn't hurt if you had to work for something," Patrick shot back as he turned and sauntered back to the bar.

"Hell," Michael muttered. "What was that all about?"

"Do you really want to hear an answer or was that one of those rhetorical questions?" Paddy continued to look straight ahead seeming to find something of interest in the couple of regulars who sat at the bar and the two couples at one of the tables.

"What do you mean by that?" Michael challenged.

"Nothing." Paddy still didn't look at him. "Just asking a simple question is all."

"Hell," was Michael's reply as he shifted enough to reach his glass. He lifted his pint and took a deep swallow.

The two men continued to sit, sipping their pints of Guinness, watching the others do pretty much the same. They'd just ordered another pint when Michael heaved a long, deep, heart-felt sigh. "Come on upstairs, Paddy. If you're going to lecture me I'd rather it be a private one." He shifted in the booth and slid to the end of the seat. When he stood, he motioned to Patrick they were going upstairs. He heard Paddy exchange a couple of comments with Patrick but wasn't paying enough attention to make out what was being said.

At the top of the stairs he stopped, fished for his keys, and unlocking the door stepped inside. Memories of Elizabeth assailed his every sense. He swore he smelled a hint of bergamot in the air. One of her simple altars remained on the small table by the door; the furniture was still as she'd rearranged it. He ran his hands over the rough texture of the blanket he'd wrapped her in after finding her unconscious at the stone circle. Now it was folded neatly over the back of the couch. *Not that many weeks ago.* He forcefully stopped the thought. *It won't help anything, keeping on like this. I need to get over her. Maybe another woman?* That thought brought an unpleasant sensation in his stomach. He heard the door close and turned to see Paddy standing with a couple of bottles of Guinness in each hand.

Paddy walked across the small apartment and handed two of the bottles to his friend. Michael took the bottles, put them on the table, and rummaged through a drawer looking for an opener. "Hell, where is the damn thing," he muttered.

"Right here." Michael turned at the sound of Paddy's voice and saw him holding a bottle opener.

"Hell and damnation, where was it?"

"Right here on the table," he said innocently before his face broke into a grin. "Brought it up with me. Patrick stuffed it in my pocket."

The two men opened their bottles, sprawled in the matching chairs, propped their booted feet on the table and took a swig. Both swallowed noisily and then plopped their bottles down on the wide arms of the chairs.

"So, you want to hear what I think?" Paddy began in a soft almost gentle tone.

"Not really but this seems to be my day for it." Michael stared sullenly at a spot on the floor.

"So, Patrick's not the first?" It was hard to tell if this was a question or a statement from Paddy's tone.

"Seamus started on me at breakfast," Michael grumbled.

"That's a bit out of the ordinary for Seamus, I'd say. Want to tell me about it?"

"Not really." Michael sighed and leaned his head to rest it on the chair's high back. "He thinks I'm stupid."

The sound at that statement was a cross between a snort, a cough, and a chuckle. Michael turned his head to look more fully at his friend. "Glad to amuse you." The sarcasm dripped from every word.

"Stupid in general or stupid about something in particular?" Paddy's look was neutral and held a hint of curiosity.

"Something in particular. No, that's not right either. A more accurate statement would be 'someone' in particular." Michael took another swallow of his Guinness and rested his head again on the back of the chair.

"And that someone would be Elizabeth, if I'm guessing right," Paddy's voice was gentle in tone. He sighed softly. "That'd be the source of Patrick's problem with ye also, Mick. The lass was well-liked by everyone around here. They miss her."

"I didn't force her to leave and I didn't make her go. I even asked her to stay." Michael sat up in the chair and gestured wildly. "You know how strong-willed she can be. What was I supposed to do, chain her up? She's one of a circle of seven women. How can I compete with that?" He was on his feet now, striding back and forth across the small room. The energy from his anger quickly burned out and he stood in front of his friend. "Doesn't everyone know that I miss her too?" he said, his voice dark with emotions.

"Ye love her, Mick. Of course you miss her. Everyone around here knows that. What they don't understand is why you haven't done something about it. Why you haven't gone and gotten her. Brought her back?" Paddy was also standing. He put his bottle on the table and his hand on his friend's shoulder. "Where is the man who has more determination than anyone? Where has he gone?"

"He sees no way to win her over. The odds are too great." Michael stood, head bowed. *They're right. I've done nothing to get her back. They all think I can do something because they see me as a determined man and seen me prevail when faced with long odds.* Something shifted. He raised his head and turned to face his friend. "I've nothing to lose, have I?"

"If you fail, Mick, you'll only be where you are now but at least know you've tried." He quickly added, "It isn't that you won't be hurting, but I think if you know you've tried everything you can think of it'll take some of the edge off." He squeezed Michael's shoulder, his expression serious. "You only have to ask, Mick, and I'll help in any way I can."

"When I wanted her to stay longer and she was fighting it, I called upon the husband of one of her friends. He seemed more than happy to help then." Michael's voice had the energy of hope as he looked Paddy in the eyes, clasped his shoulder, and smiled. "Let's finish these beers, boyo. I've got a campaign to plan."

The men grabbed their bottles, clinked them together and chugged the contents. Gasping for breath, they set the empty bottles down. "Good thing they were almost empty," Paddy laughed.

"We're a bit out of practice," Michael chuckled. He picked up his unopened bottle, crossed to the mini-refrigerator and placed it inside. "Go ahead and take yours along if you want," he looked over his shoulder at Paddy.

"Don't need another one if you don't," he handed his unopened bottle to Michael who placed it beside his own. "I've got to get going."

"I've got some strategy to plan if this is going to work out like I want. I want it all, Paddy. I want Elizabeth here in Kinslow at The Manor as my wife. She'll be skittish so I have to go slow." Michael took a last look around the small apartment.

Paddy preceded him out the door and started down the stairs as Michael turned, closed, and locked the door before following him.

In front of the pub, the two men shook hands and clapped each other on the shoulder. "Why don't I drop by for a glass of your fine Irish whiskey tonight and you can tell me your plans?" Paddy grinned. "Maybe I can help?"

"Oh, I've got a few ideas now. But, come on by tonight. How about dinner? I'll let Seamus know."

"About seven?"

"Seven it is," Michael turned to go, his step now eager to get B.B. and head home to work out his plan. He turned and took a few steps, walking backwards as he called out to Paddy, "Thanks, boyo." And then he turned, striding toward the back.

Paddy stopped before he got into his truck and watched his friend's energetic stride. "If you can bring Elizabeth back, boyo, you'll have all of our thanks," he said to himself. "She brought something with her and we all miss it. The connection she has to the spirits of this place is lost and I don't know that we'll get it back without her."

# 22  MICHAEL'S PLAN A

"Thanks again for the ride, Gabby," Elizabeth said bending down to speak to her friend.

"Not a problem," Gabriella replied.

Elizabeth closed the door and waved as the red Honda Civic pulled away from the curb. She stood watching the car, sending thoughts for a safe trip, until it turned the corner two blocks away. It was only then, when her attention was pulled away from the retreating car and back to the sidewalk where she stood, she realized she was not alone. The familiar scent of sandalwood assaulted her. *When will it be over? I can sense his energy, smell his scent, feel his warmth.* She turned toward her apartment and collided with a hard, masculine chest; her yelp of surprise smothered by a kiss.

She shifted in an attempt to unman her attacker.

"It's me, Elizabeth," Michael whispered against her lips. "It's me, luv." His mouth found hers again and he kissed her with the finesse that comes from being lovers over time, knowing what your partner likes, and giving it to them to please you both.

"Mmmichael?" Elizabeth stammered reeling as waves of pleasure rolled through her.

"Hmm," he nuzzled her neck, kissing her with little nibbling kisses wherever there was bare skin.

"Michael? Wh—wh—what?" She stammered out stagger by the feeling of being in his arms. "Michael?" She managed before his mouth took hers again.

"What are you doing? What are you doing here?" She said struggling to move away when the kiss ended. "Michael, let me go!"

"Just let me hold you," Michael's voice was soft, soothing.

Elizabeth recognized his tone as one he used with a fractious horse. "I'm not one of your horses, Michael. Just let me go." She emphasized the last word by shoving against his solid chest. Frustration that he didn't budge boiled.

"Promise me, Elizabeth, if I let you go, you'll hear me out." His arms were banded around her; the breath from his words ruffled her hair.

She quieted in his arms, let her forehead rest on his chest, and felt the tears threaten. He'd come all this way, and he wouldn't leave without saying his piece. Her hope was it wouldn't hurt so bad when they parted. She'd made her choice: The Circle, a life here in Fremont and in time adopting a baby.

"What do you want to say to me?" she asked her words muffled in his shirt.

Michael loosened his arms and stepped back. She hadn't invited him in but she had given him an opening.

"Well to begin with, I bring you greetings from Paddy, Patrick, Seamus, actually from the whole town. They all miss you." He paused, leaned forward resting his chin on her head, and cradled her gently against him. "And then there's me," he said in a soft voice. "Ah, Elizabeth, how I've missed ye." The whispered words full of the Irish brogue always thicker when emotions ruled.

*Do I really want to hear what he has to say on the sidewalk in front of my apartment? No. Whatever he has to say, I'll hear him out in private.* "Come inside, Michael. You can talk to me there." She tried pushing him away but his solid body didn't move. "Michael, did you hear me? Come inside."

"I heard you," he said quietly as the weight eased from his chest. *There is a chance.* He released her, stepped back, and bowed low. "After you." With his step light with potential possibilities, he followed her to the stairs and watched with obvious male appreciation as her gently swaying hips preceded him. He hoped before morning came he'd see those rounded hips bare and feel them tucked against his groin as they slept. Of course he hoped to do a lot more than sleep, but if that was all she'd allow tonight, he'd consider himself a lucky man.

As Elizabeth walked up the stairs to her apartment, her mind was awhirl with thoughts, her body awhirl with feelings. Just his touch, his kiss, his scent and she was aroused, her body betraying her mind's determination to forget him. She unlocked her door, walked in, put her keys and purse on the small hall table, and turned on the salt rock lamp welcoming its soft peaceful light. Kicking off her shoes, she walked into the living room.

Elizabeth felt Michael right behind her. While he wasn't touching her, his heat, his scent engulfed her.

"Have a seat if you want, Michael," she said as she crossed the room, busying herself by fussing with the drapes. "Would you like something to drink? I can quickly make a cup of tea," she said as she turned and smiled. "I've some Bewley's Irish Afternoon tea."

"A glass of water will do me just fine." Michael stood in the doorway, casually resting his shoulder against the frame, his intent gaze never leaving her. "If you want some tea, I can wait to finish what I came to say."

In the kitchen, she hurriedly filled two glasses with ice and water. *Goddess, be with me. Help me be with this man who makes my knees weak without losing my resolve.* She stopped, took a deep breath, put the glasses on a small tray. *What is wrong with me?* She turned to the small altar of herbs similar to the one she'd created at Michael's house. She focused her intention, bowed her head, and whispered, "Goddess, may whatever happens be for my highest good. Blessed Be." Picking up the small tray, she retraced her steps to the living room where Michael stood by the table between the windows that held her main altar. He turned at her approach.

"Please sit down, Michael," she said and gestured to the couch. Once he seated himself, she set the tray down on the coffee table, handed him a glass of water, and sat in the chair placed at an angle to the couch. "What is it you want to say to me?"

Michael took a drink of the cool water not so much because he was thirsty but to give himself a moment to gather his thoughts. He'd been looking at the altar she'd set up in her living room. The cloth was one of those she'd purchased in Ireland. Several stones were ones he'd swear she'd picked up along the road or the shore when they'd traveled. The leaves in the north he knew were from The Sacred Grove because he could feel a faint familiar hum in the air from their energy. He lounged in the corner opposite her, his right arm stretched along the back of the couch, legs extended before him, ankles crossed. While he looked physically relaxed, the tension emanating from him told a different story: the story of a predator having sighted his prey, waiting for the right moment to pounce.

Elizabeth remained in her chair, silent. *What is he waiting for?* She licked her dry lips and fought the urge to say something, to break the silence. *He's just staring at me; like he's hungry. Maybe I should offer him something to eat?* At that thought, her cheeks flamed. She narrowed her eyes and concentrated on his expression. *Oh yes, he's hungry. I know that look.* She shifted in her chair, took another drink of her water, and visualized the cool glass rubbing over her heated cheeks and forehead.

*Has he noticed how he affects me?* A glance told her he had; his look more intense, his pants bulged at the crotch. Her eyes were drawn to that now growing area and as she looked it grew even more. *Oh Goddess, what am I going to do?* The prayer, said like a chant, brought no answer. The voice that so often provided her with direction, with answers, with options was silent. She was alone, in the living room of her apartment with the sinfully handsome, devil incarnate, Michael Murphy.

Michael saw a moment of panic flash across Elizabeth's face. It was quickly hidden but he'd been paying close attention to her so he was sure of what he'd seen. He shifted again, steeling himself to keep from covering up. It'd be so easy to cross his legs instead of his ankles. But he wanted her to know, in a very primal way, how much he missed her. He thought the evidence spoke for itself as his pants were now nicely tented in that particular place.

"I believe you asked why I was here and what I wanted to say?" His eyes locked with hers. "I don't believe I've answered yet."

Elizabeth slowly shook her head.

"I'm here because this is where you are and what I want is you. You are the only reason I'm here." Without breaking eye contact, he shifted and stood. In two steps he was kneeling in front of her, his hands on the arms of her chair, his chest pressed against her knees. "I want you, Elizabeth. I'll always want you," he declared as he leaned forward and pressed soft kisses on her face.

The lyrical Irish brogue sifted over her senses like the lightest powdered snow. Her arms wrapped around his neck, her hands wound in his hair, her legs spread in invitation. His tongue slid into her mouth and she welcomed the intrusion as she tangled her tongue with his.

His hands pulled her closer, his arms banded around her, one at her waist and one at her shoulders. "Ah, luv, I want you so bad but I'll not be taking you on the floor. I want you, Elizabeth." His hands had already unclasped her bra and were massaging her breasts. "I've missed you so." He pushed her top up to bare her to his sight. He bent and placed a reverent kiss on each nipple and then stopped to lick and suckle playing no favorites.

"Bed, Elizabeth. I'll not take you here," he gritted out as he moved back pulling her with him. She sat perched on the edge of the chair. He, still on his knees, held both of her hands. In one easy, graceful motion, he stood pulling her up with him. Striding across the living room, towing Elizabeth behind him, he stopped at the hallway. He looked to his left, cocked his head, and raised an eyebrow. "Your bedroom?" He swept her into his arms and made his way down the hall.

The cool sheets and firmness of the mattress beneath her; the heat and hardness of Michael above her was all that registered in Elizabeth's passion drenched brain. Her body ached and arched as Michael's fingers deftly undressed her, taking his time, kissing and nibbling his way around and down her body as he divested her of top, bra, skirt and panties. She reached for him but he evaded her touch.

"Just let me love you," he whispered against her stomach. "Just let me do this, luv." He rose on his arms, made his way up her body, and kissed her fully. "I need you, Elizabeth. I need you now."

His erection nudged the entrance to her heat. "Michael," she said and arched up trying to take him in. "I want you," her final word slid slowly out of her mouth as Michael slid slowly into her. He filled her and her body sighed at the rightness of being together, with him, like this. She opened her eyes and saw his questioning look. Smiling, she wrapped her arms tighter around his neck and pulled his head down for a kiss as her hips rose to press urgently to his. As they began to move together, tears fell as she was consumed by the power and passion of Michael's loving.

He held Elizabeth tenderly in his arms, stroked her back with one arm, held her close with the other, pressed soft kisses in her hair. "I've missed you so. I don't have words to tell it," he whispered in her hair. "Don't cry luv, we can work this out."

"You don't understand, Michael. I can't live in Ireland with you. I can't leave everyone. It's not that I don't want to be with you, it's just that I can't," Elizabeth's voice broke and tears flowed freely down her face.

"Remember, I'm a determined man," he growled playfully.

"I haven't forgotten, but sometimes, well, sometimes there are things we want that we can't have because the price to have them is greater than we can pay."

His hands brushed her sides finding a particularly sensitive spot, his mouth trailed kisses from her hair to her ear where he gently sucked its lobe. "I'm willing to pay the price for this," he said and moved his lips to nibble her neck. "What's the price for this?" he asked as his fingertips skimmed from one breast to the other. He grinned and lowered his head, his lips trailing kisses from her neck along her collarbone before taking a detour south toward her breasts. "I'm waiting to hear what I'll have to pay, luv. Cat got your tongue?"

The heat from his kisses, his touch swirled through her as her brain slowed and then stopped thinking, caught in the sensations Michael wreaked on her body. The waves of passion subsided and she opened her eyes to see him watching her, waiting it seemed, but for what? She couldn't imagine. The question must have been in her eyes because he bent over her again. "I think I know the price, Elizabeth. The price for all of this is to hear you scream my name when you come." And then his mouth and body claimed hers and once again she was lost in the moment, in Michael, in the passion that they created when they were as one.

Light flooded the room, waking Elizabeth with its brightness. She wanted to stretch but a weight kept her pinned down, a weight with a name ... Michael. Deep even breathing, he was still asleep. She snuggled closer, her eyes shutting against the light, relaxed into his embrace, and let sleep claim her again.

Noise and the aroma of bacon and eggs awakened her. Stretching, she opened her eyes. From the sounds and smells, she surmised Michael was fixing her breakfast; or at least she hoped he was because she was starving. Elizabeth got her robe and pulling it on, padded to the kitchen.

"Hey there, sleepy head." Michael grinned as he stirred the eggs. "Scrambled, just the way you like them." He kept stirring with one hand as he poured her a cup of tea with the other. "Have a seat; they'll be ready in a minute."

"I could," she started.

Michael interrupted, shoved a cup of tea into her hands.

"Go. Sit." His grin turned serious. "Let me finish this for you. It's almost done. We can talk over breakfast."

"Okay," Elizabeth said. Sitting at the dining room table, she watched Michael efficiently put bacon, eggs, and toast on plates. *How could I sleep through his getting up, taking a shower, dressing. Goddess, he looks wonderful. I've missed him so.* Tears welled. *Enough of this, E.* She forced a smile on her face as Michael brought her plate to the table.

"One moment." He turned back to the kitchen, quickly picking up his own cup of tea and returning to the table. Settled in his chair, he grinned at Elizabeth still sitting, hands in her lap. Something was bothering her and he had a good idea what it was. He purposely chose to ignore it. He had plans for today and beyond and he wasn't going to get derailed now. "Aren't you hungry?" He asked, concern lacing his voice.

Shaking her head as if to clear the fog, Elizabeth's attention was refocused on the man and the meal before her, "Starved," she said smiling at him, "just waiting for you to join me."

"Well, I'm here now."

They ate in companionable silence. Michael was a decent cook and Elizabeth's scrambled eggs were perfect, a little on the dry side, just the way she liked them. Her bacon was, by some standards, half-cooked, just the way she liked it. Milk and sugar were on the table and she doctored her tea so it, too, was just the way she liked it. *A perfect meal with a perf—* she stopped herself in mid-thought. *Stop it, stop it, stop it.*

Michael watched the emotions flit across Elizabeth's face as he ate his breakfast. When he noted a calmer look, he shifted in his chair, kept his eyes on his plate, and cleared his throat. "What are your plans for today?" He hoped the question came across as casual.

"I've a report due so I'd planned on finishing it today and my circle is meeting this evening. It's a potluck so I've got to fix something to take." Elizabeth's voice was business-like as she struggled to find a way to put some distance between them.

"I've some errands to run this morning and hoped you'd be able to spend time with me this afternoon. Will you? Will you spend time with me?" He glanced up to see Elizabeth frown before returning his gaze to his plate. "I promise I won't interfere with your meeting. And, I'll make sure you have something to take for the potluck." Looking up again, he saw tears in her eyes.

"Elizabeth, tell me what's wrong," he said in his soft Irish brogue as he reached across the table and laid his hand over hers.

She battled the tears back, shook her head to indicate there was nothing wrong.

"I'll let you get to your report then." Michael rose, took two steps to stand beside her chair and bent down to kiss her cheek. "I'll be back about one and we can see how things are then, okay?" Noting Elizabeth nod of ascent, he picked up his dishes and took them to the kitchen. After rinsing them off and putting them in the dishwasher, he came back to her side. He ran his hand down her arm to her hand. Raising it, he bowed his head and placed a chaste kiss on its back. "See you later."

Hearing her front door close, Elizabeth let out the breath she'd been holding. Her eyes filled with tears, a few slipped down her cheeks. Unable to finish the last bite of eggs, she took her dishes to the kitchen, rinsed them, and placed them in the dishwasher next to Michael's. It was a simple sight: their dishes side-by-side in the dishwasher. The sobs held deep inside struggled to break free. In the shower, the tears ran free as memories of showers with Michael flowed through her.

Tears and memories resolutely held at bay, she dressed, fixed a fresh cup of tea, and sat down at her desk determined to finish her report. She booted up her computer and as it went through its process, opened the file cabinet and took out the family's paper file. When the screen blinked it was ready, she clicked on the family's computer file, read what she'd already written, and began to type.

After leaving Elizabeth's, Michael stopped by Jackson's friend, Daniel O'Donnell's and changed clothes. He'd actually arrived yesterday morning, been met at the airport by Montgomery and O'Donnell, who'd taken him to the real estate agent's office they'd recommended when he'd put his plan in motion.

For the past couple of weeks, he'd been in email contact with the man, narrowing down options. In their meeting, with Montgomery and O'Donnell adding to the discussion, the possibilities were narrowed down to four houses. When that meeting was over, Daniel had taken his suitcase to his home as the plan included Michael staying there.

Michael met with the real estate agent and toured four homes, selecting two to see again in the afternoon, he hoped with Elizabeth by his side. Part of his plan included purchasing a home in Fremont where Elizabeth would live and from where he could run his business when he was in town. The two men's help meant he was further along with his plan than he'd expected to be.

This morning when he'd left O'Donnell's, he'd considered taking his suitcase with him because he wanted to keep it at Elizabeth's. But, he also knew he needed to move slowly because while he wasn't sure what the problem was, he knew there was one, at least in Elizabeth's mind.

Just after noon, he knocked on Elizabeth's door. The plan was for them to meet the real estate agent at the first house at two. Michael tried the door. It was locked. He tapped again and waited. The lock click, the door opened.

She had the phone to her ear, a frown on her face when she saw him, frantically motioning for him to be quiet as he came through the door.

"Okay, Lily. Thanks for letting me know there is a change in plans. I'll be there at five." Elizabeth risked being rude in an effort to get off the phone before Lily heard Michael's voice.

"I'll be quiet," Michael whispered in her ear, nibbled on the lobe, and then chuckled when she shivered.

"Who's with you?" Lily asked.

The phone eased from her ear as Michael nibbled along her neck. She pulled away, glaring at him before pushing him in an effort to put distance between them. "Uh, Michael's here," Elizabeth managed to get out.

"Well, invite him along. With the change in plans with all the children here and Jackson is making his famous spaghetti dinner you know there will be enough food," Lily said, her cheerful voice not quite covering the underlying command.

"I think he has plans for tonight," Elizabeth started. Michael grabbed her from behind, pulled her close. She could feel his erection pressing into her backside.

"I do have plans for much later tonight, but nothing after you come with me this afternoon." He wiggled his hips and nuzzled her neck. "I've great plans for later."

"Michael, please," she said, frustration was clear in her tone.

"Since I don't have any plans until much later, what are we going to be doing?" He stroked her breasts, trailing his fingers from one to the other while he pressed against her back.

"Stop it, Michael. Stop it right now, or I won't go anywhere with you and you won't go anywhere with me." Elizabeth fought the rising passion, turning it into exasperation.

Michael's hands immediately dropped and he stepped back.

His movement caught her by surprise and she staggered catching herself with a quick shuffle. Turning she glared at both Michael and the silence on the other end of the phone.

"Okay, Lily. You can stop smiling now. I expect that by the time we get there everyone will know that Michael's coming with me."

"You can count on it," Lily laughed. "It'll make it much easier since you won't have to really do introductions or anything. And, he and Jackson can hang out and help Logan with the kids."

I'll let him know that if he comes, he's volunteering to baby-sit." She looked over her shoulder at Michael who was leaning against the wall, his intense gaze giving her no doubt as to what he was thinking. When he saw her looking in his direction, Michael straightened from the wall and gave her a thumbs up sign.

"Not a problem," he mouthed.

Elizabeth walked back into her office as she concluded her conversation with Lily. She hung up the phone and sat at the computer. She'd just finished the report when Lily had called informing her of the change in plans. Jackson's now famous spaghetti dinner with garlic bread, salad, and something fabulous for dessert was a welcomed treat given his cooking expertise. After all the work she'd put into the report, she saved it again just to make sure, before opening her email. The cover letter composed, the report attached, she sent the report to the agency with a quick click. Shutting the computer off, she turned to find Michael lounging in the doorway watching her.

"It sounds as if I don't need to fix anything for dinner?" he inquired cocking his eyebrow.

"No, it's all taken care of," Elizabeth replied not moving from her chair.

"If you're hungry, I'll fix us some lunch." Michael straightened from the doorway and stood with his hands now shoved in his back pockets.

Elizabeth drank in the sight of his lean, muscular body, the easy stance, the intense gaze focused on her, the growing bulge in his pants. Her gaze traveled over every inch of him and finally made it back to his face and his eyes. He stood now, with a shoulder planted on the door jam, ankles crossed, a grin on his face, heat in his eyes.

"Like what you see, luv?" his Irish brogue was thick with desire.

Elizabeth stood and strolled across the room reaching him in a few steps. She purposefully brushed against him as she went through the door into the hall, her hands tingled from touching him, her nipples hard from his touch. Sauntering down the hall towards her bedroom, she looked over her shoulder and smiled as she went through the door saying, "I think I'd like it better with a little less covering it."

Michael pushed away from the doorway and started down the hall after her. "I think we can manage that."

"What's at this address? Why won't you tell me what we're doing?" Elizabeth's frustration was more evident than her curiosity although she did admit it was difficult to be truly frustrated after such an amazing romp with Michael less than two hours ago. Just the thought of what they'd done, how he'd felt deep inside her had her body rousing. She drove, at Michael's direction, down a street not too far from Lily and Jackson's.

"Up on the right," Michael directed. "The stone one."

Elizabeth pulled her car into the driveway of an old stone house with grey trim and accents in a cobalt blue. "What are we doing here?" she asked but Michael was already out of the car and striding toward the front door which was now open. She could see him shake hands with someone, then turn and motion her to follow. *I guess it's follow him or sit here and wait until he comes back.* Sighing, she got out of her car and walked up the slightly winding path to the partially-opened front door. She peeked in, no one was in sight.

"Michael?" her voice was tentative as she stepped across the threshold. Before she uttered another word, the door closed behind her. Michael, a grin splitting his face, stood there with another man.

"I'd like you to meet James Weston. James, this is Elizabeth Elliott," he said, stepping forward, taking her elbow in an old familiar gesture.

Weston stepped forward, hand out in greeting. "I'm pleased to meet you Ms. Elliott." He turned back to Michael. "Are you ready to see the place?"

"We are," Michael replied, his hand still on Elizabeth's elbow. "After you, James."

James started the tour, commenting as they went on the size of the rooms, the upgrades in the kitchen and bathrooms, the additional storage inside the double-car attached garage that sported a mudroom between it and the house. Somewhere along the way he also mentioned that the trim had recently been painted, the deck stained, and it had a new roof. They were back at the front door and while he normally would have asked questions to gauge what the interest was, he'd been cautioned by Michael Murphy to say nothing. So, he did as he'd been instructed, locking the house up as they left.

"Do you want to ride with me or follow?" He asked Michael as he started toward his car, also parked in the driveway.

"If you don't mind coming back this way, I think we'll take you up on the offer of a ride." Michael still had her elbow firmly in his grasp and steered her toward Weston's car where James stood holding open the passenger side door. He escorted Elizabeth to the car door and assisted her in. As he did so, he leaned down and whispered, "Just bear with me on this. I'll explain everything soon." He kissed her cheek and then backed out of the car, turned, opened the backdoor, and slid in. To his amazement, Elizabeth sat quietly, answering Weston's questions with brief answers. For his part, Weston kept the conversation light and superficial.

Thirty minutes later they were pulling into another driveway. Michael quickly hopped out, opened Elizabeth's door, and assisted her out. The three of them walked up the slate steps from the driveway to the large, wrap-around porch. While this house did not have the views of the first, it had a large expanse of well-manicured lawn. Lush flower beds lined the house's foundation and the perimeter of the yard.

Weston unlocked the front door and the tour began. This home was a little larger than the first and in addition to the large front lawn; it had a backyard to match. Again, the house's amenities, upgrades, and features were touted by the real estate agent. The tour over, they returned to the car and Weston drove them back to the first house. This time, Michael sat in the front seat and chatted amiably with Weston about sights to see around Fremont.

Elizabeth, sitting in the back seat, watched houses pass by, half-listening to the men's conversation. The only conclusion she could draw was Michael was purchasing a house in Fremont. The thought both terrified and thrilled her. She knew his horses were his passion; she knew how hard he'd worked to build his stud farm and racing stable; and she knew his commitment to protect The Lady. But the idea of Michael being so close had her mind racing.

Soon enough they were back at the first house, had said their good byes to Mr. Weston, and were back in her car. They sat in silence each waiting for the other to speak. The impasse was broken when Michael shifted towards her, cupped her chin in one hand, and gently turned her to face him. He studied her face looking for signs of distress or perhaps signs of welcoming joy. He was disappointed she remained neutral. To disguise his disappointment, he dropped his hand, cleared his throat, looked at his watch, and nodded toward the house.

"Do you think we've got a few minutes to sit here before we leave for Montgomery's? I know you don't want to be late."

Elizabeth glanced at her watch. No, she didn't want to be late but sorting things out here was better than showing up distressed. Whether any one said anything or not, there'd be looks. She griped the steering wheel, took a deep breath, let it out slowly and said, "What's going on?" She prided herself on her voice sounding composed.

Michael, on the other hand, was concerned. He didn't know this Elizabeth. The one he knew, whose passion shone, who said what she thought, challenged him on every level. His answer was guarded. "I'm looking to invest in some property. I'd narrowed it down to these two houses and wanted your opinion."

Elizabeth turned the key in the ignition and backed out of the driveway. *Ha, you just want my opinion* she sing-songed in her head. *I'll bet.* "My opinion?" she said, her voice oozing with sugary tones as she kept her eyes on the road.

"Aye, your opinion. If I were to have a place in Fremont, which one do you think I should get?" *This is not going as I'd planned.* A sliver of panic churned in his gut. *Remember to go slow.* "Guess we're at Montgomery's, right? So, we can talk some more later." He was already unbuckled and getting out of the car.

"Later will be just fine." Her words were spoken in a matter-of-fact manner that gave no hint of her inner turmoil.

Before getting out of the car, Elizabeth took a moment to close her eyes and find the peaceful center she easily experienced during her time with The Lady. She held herself in white light, until the upset faded to nothingness. When she opened her eyes, gathered her purse, and got out Michael reached to take her elbow. She shrugged out of his touch and strode ahead of him to the front door. Before she even knocked, the door opened. Lily, an expectant look on her face, stood there.

"Come in, you two," she said, reaching out to take Elizabeth's hand while motioning Michael in behind them. "Jackson?" she called out. "E and Michael are here."

"Bring 'em in the kitchen. I'm in the middle of mixing my special salad dressing," the decidedly male voice replied.

Lily took their coats, hanging them in the closet beside the front door, chatting as she led them to the kitchen. As the three of them strolled into the great room, they could see Jackson at work. He looked up and smiled at his wife. "Come here, darling," he murmured. "Don't you think the cook needs a reward or something? You know something to keep him going? So he can finish fixing the meal?" He waggled his eyebrows and winked.

Lily sauntered over to him, reached up and pulled his head down toward her. She rose on her toes and kissed him. "You mean something like that?"

Jackson dropped the hand mixer, barely remembering to turn it off as he did, grabbed his wife and hauled her against his broad chest. "You are such a tease, my dear. I was thinking of something more along these lines." He backed her against the counter, held her with one hand by the nape of the neck, pulled her close, and brought his mouth down to hers in a decidedly passionate kiss.

"Excuse us, folks," he drawled as he let Lily go. "Newly married and all that." He grinned at his wife who was straightening her blouse. "Sometimes I have to remind her why she married me." He turned and winked at Michael who hadn't blinked an eye during the whole proceedings.

"Understandable, Montgomery," he commented. *I, too, have that passion with Elizabeth. Now to find a way to have it all. To, at least most of the time, have her with me.*

The doorbell rang.

Lily, still flushed from her encounter with her husband, grabbed Elizabeth's hand and pulled her along as she went to answer the door. They opened the door and the house filled with women and children. As Michael was introduced to and chatted with the other women, Ashley's children, and Hunter's daughter, Logan, he knew he wasn't the only one doing the appraising. *These people are my competition.*

Within fifteen minutes of everyone's arrival, dinner was served. Jackson's sumptuous spaghetti dinner and homemade salad dressing lived up to expectations. As always, when the women were together, even if they'd just seen each other, the conversation flowed. Michael was an unknown quantity but because of Elizabeth they tempered their curiosity and questions and instead just including him in the general mix of things as they did Jackson and the children.

After dinner, the women decided to meet first and have dessert later. Jackson's variety of homemade ice creams complete with sauces, nuts, whipped cream, and cherries would be used to create sundaes or banana splits for dessert. Everyone wanted to have lots of room for this special treat.

Michael decided now was the time to put Part 'B' of his plan in place. He stood and tapped his knife against the water glass in front of his plate. "If I can have your attention for a moment, please."

All conversation came to a stop, all eyes turned to him. "As you all know, or at least I think you all know," he said, his blue eyes shining with amusement, his boyish grin splitting his face. "I met Elizabeth when she came to Ireland this past summer. I believe she's told you about The Lady and The Sacred Grove." He looked around the table and saw heads nodding. "I'd like to invite you all to The Manor, my home, to celebrate Samhain at The Sacred Grove with The Lady. I've plenty of room for everyone."

His invitation was met as he'd hoped, with excited chatter from the women. When he glanced in Elizabeth's direction, instead of the expected gratitude or perhaps astonishment, all he saw was her furious countenance. The room went silent as everyone felt the air crackle between the two of them.

Elizabeth slowly pushed back her chair from the table, rose to her feet, and turned to look at her circle sisters. "I think it's time to meet." She turned and strode toward the living room and plopped down on the couch, her arms folded across her chest, her back to the others. Her temper raged and entrance to the center of peace she'd accessed a short time ago eluded her. She sat, foot tapping the floor, fingers tapping her arms, and waited.

As the other women rose and began clearing the table, they were waved away by Jackson. Without saying a word, they made the decision to join Elizabeth in the living room.

Michael began helping Jackson clear the table, taking the dishes to the sink. Within a few minutes the table was clear, dishes rinsed and stacked in the dishwasher.

"They'll be awhile," Jackson murmured to Michael. "I've an office upstairs. Come on along. We can discuss the details of your plan."

"Right." Michael closed the dishwasher door. "Will they let us live long enough to leave?"

Jackson's laughter drew looks from the women seated around the fire. "You stay to my left and I'll protect you as we pass by." He was still chuckling as he led Michael across the great room to the stairs. He stopped on the bottom step and turned. "Lily, do you have a copy of the financial report or should I print one off and bring it down to you?"

"Thank you for the reminder, Jackson. I already have a copy of the report right here," Lily replied in a cool-toned voice.

"Shit, Montgomery," Michael whispered as the two men walked up the stairs. "She sounds really pissed, sorry about that."

"Nothing to worry about. She's just protecting one of her own. We've lots of practice at making up. In fact it's one of the things I like most about being married to someone with spunk — lots of opportunities to make up."

# 23   Decision Time

Lily lit a sprig of sage, placing it in the abalone shell she used as a smudge pot. After wafting the fragrant smoke around herself, she passed the shell to her left as was their tradition. Within minutes everyone except Elizabeth had finished smudging themselves and their items for an altar they were quickly setting up.

Elizabeth held the smoking shell, breathing deeply of its calming essence. The flash of anger at his announcement dissipated, replaced by a deep ache of despair. Since she'd crashed into him yesterday on her sidewalk, Michael had continually surprise her. Why was she surprised at his invitation? It made sense if she viewed it as another tactic, one in what she guessed was a long list, to get her back.

What he didn't realize? He never really lost her. But that didn't mean they could be together. She finished smoothing and soothing the wisps over and around her paying special attention to her head and her heart.

Lily took the still smoldering shell from Elizabeth, tucked it in the fireplace, and shut the doors. She stood for a moment watching the wisps of smoke drift up the chimney before turning back to the group and the tasks at hand.

Sophia stood, and using the small crystal and amethyst wand she sometimes wore as a necklace, circled it three times around the altar while saying a short prayer. "May the words we share, the time we spend, and the decisions we make be for our highest good. Blessed Be."

When Sophia was seated, Diana leaned forward. "I would like to suggest we start with the financial report, so we know where we are with The Golden Cauldron fund. This is really the first time we've taken stock of our endeavors since setting The Fund up in June. I know I've no idea how much is in it." She turned toward Lily saying, "From what Jackson said, you have a financial report?"

Lily shifted and slipped a piece of paper out from behind the cushion on the chair in which she sat. "I have it here." She smoothed the piece of paper on her lap as she looked around. "From the 14th Moon we have a balance of $253.72. In the past we've kept whatever was left over to use as seed money for the next year or to give to other groups who wanted to put one together. I'm assuming from the general conversation we've had over the last month we want to do the same this year." She looked around the room at the confirming nods.

"But as we all know, the house totems are why we have a business and bank account. We've averaged four a month since July for a total of twelve; at $5000.00 each so our gross total is $60,000. Since 50% goes to the woman who senses the totem, that leaves $30,000.00. Our actual balance is closer to $90,000 because we had money from earlier ventures. I know you all remember we agreed to keep a contingency fund, something that would pay taxes, etc.

"The end of the year is coming and at this point we've very few expenses to go against this income. We can invest some of these monies and as you can see, we've funds to spend if that is our decision." Lily, in her formal,  precise business mode, added, "And, just so you have full disclosure, we have three appointments for October and Jackson thinks we'll be very busy in December and January because this makes a unique and unusual gift. I think we could spend most or all of the $30,000 and be okay." Lily stopped to give everyone a chance to digest her report. As she looked around the room she saw thoughtful looks on each face.

"I think the Goddess is telling us something," Diana spoke first, letting her gaze rest on each woman as she looked around the circle and took a deep breath. "This may be hard for you to hear, Elizabeth, but I think we need to seriously consider Michael's offer and spend Samhain with The Lady at The Sacred Grove. As I heard his words, a shiver of awareness, of acknowledgement—it's hard to put into words. I have that certain knowing that this is something I need to do." She looked expectantly around the room.

Gabriella rested her hand on Elizabeth's arm giving it a gentle squeeze of support. She knew her words would be difficult for her friend to hear but she also knew in her heart they were the words she needed to say. "I agree with Diana. I felt a sense of rightness about all of us being with The Lady on Samhain. And, we have the funds to pay for it."

Elizabeth half-listened to the voices of her circle sisters. As soon as she'd heard Michael's invitation, she knew the die was cast and her circle sisters would want to accept. They wouldn't if she said 'no' because this was something they would do together. But it was beyond her to say 'no', in part because the prospect of spending time with Michael and with The Lady at The Sacred Grove was something she hadn't allowed herself to imagine ever doing again and in part because she didn't want to deprive the other women of the experience.

What a gift for each one of them to experience the power of prayer with The Lady in The Sacred Grove. She cherished her daily practice of standing every morning in front of her main altar, the one with the stones from Ireland and the leaves from The Sacred Grove, and calling upon The Lady to be with her as she chanted the words three times three sending love out into the world.

*That peaceful center source where I go when angry or upset, where I find my balance is another gift I brought home. I'm more grounded in my power and I still have a connection to The Lady and the Sacred Grove. What I don't have and, truthfully, what I'm afraid to have, is a connection to and a relationship with Michael.*

Silence.

They waited as everyone except her had spoken.

"If it is The Circle's wish to go, then so be it." Emotions she'd held at bay surfaced, tears welled in her eyes. "It's a beautiful place and Michael is right, there is plenty of room for everyone." She turned toward Ashley. "Artie, Anthony, and Amanda will love it. If you'll allow it, Michael will see to it that they have horses to ride. The stable hands are gentle and will be wonderful teachers." She closed her eyes and shimmering light and a shadowed form filled her inner sight. "The Lady would be delighted to welcome all of us to celebrate Samhain with her," she whispered.

"Are we all agreed then?" Diana asked in her formal manner. She looked around to see all heads nodding in agreement. "What's left then is to decide when we'll leave and return."

Lily rose. "I'll be right back," she said as she dashed down the stairs. Moments later she returned, her appointment book in hand. "Samhain is on a Friday. And while I'd love to spend a week in Ceremony, we have the children and school as well as our own work to consider." She paused in thought. "If we travel on Wednesday, we can recoup on Thursday and be ready to do ceremony on Friday. Perhaps taking a flight back Sunday? That gives us Saturday to recover from being up almost all of Friday night." She looked up. "What do you all think?" Her gaze traveled around the group stopping briefly on each one. She looked at Elizabeth last. "Elizabeth, if this is something you don't think you can do, we need to talk about it."

"No, I can do this. It's just that… ." her emotion choked voice broke. She stopped, took a deep breath before she continued. "I had convinced myself I'd never be able to return, ever."  She looked at each of her circle sisters as she said, "To be there with all of you, to celebrate Samhain, it's more than I'd ever dreamt possible. I can't tell you the number of times I stop this summer and think "I wish" and the wish was that one or all of you was there with me. Now, it won't be a wish, it will be a reality." Her eyes watered, her smile wobbled, her chin trembled; she struggled to control her emotions enough to finish. "And the children will have such a good time. You'll all see for yourselves the magic of Ireland."

Lily had seen how well they fit together, seen the power of the attraction. In some ways it reminded her of her struggle with committing to a relationship with Jackson—easier said than done. There may be magic in Ireland, the sacred grove, and The Lady but the real magic is with Michael.

Upstairs in Jackson's study, the two men sat in overstuffed dark leather chairs, glasses of Irish whiskey in their hands. "So that's my plan," Michael finished.

"You think it'll work?" Jackson said his voice and face neutral.

Michael interpreted the lack of affect as Montgomery having doubts. "I'm open to any suggestions you might have now or later if they come to you." He took another sip of the whiskey, his eyes never leaving his host's. "She's mine, Montgomery. The only problem I have is getting her to understand and accept that." He smiled. "Knowing Elizabeth that seems to be a bigger challenge than I first thought."

"Do you know what's keeping her from staying with you?" Jackson's curiosity was piqued.

"Something to do with The Circle. Best I can figure out she's afraid something will happen to them if she isn't here. I know it doesn't really make any sense but it's all I can come up with," Michael's voice held evidence of his exasperation and frustration.

"I'll see what I can learn from Lily," Jackson offered. "I can't just ask her outright or she'll feel she can't answer because of her loyalty to Elizabeth, but I can ask some general questions and maybe glean something that'd help you."

"Anything would be appreciated." Michael put his glass down on the table between the two chairs, stood, and walked to the windows. Hands in his back pockets, he stared out at the inky darkness. "She belongs with me. I've known that from the beginning but when she left I… ." He turned back and caught the eye of the man who was an ally and becoming a friend. "Anything you can do to help me would be appreciated. But," he cautioned, "You've got yourself a great woman so watch it." He chuckled, "I know you said you enjoy making up, but these women are special to one another. I'm not sure how strong our relationships with them are in comparison to their relationships with each other."

"I do know what you mean, Murphy. I'll be careful." Jackson put his glass down and stood. "Lily is more important to me than I can put into words. I won't do anything to jeopardize that. I think you have the same thing going with Elizabeth. I know what Lily means to me and I'll do what I can, within reason, to see that you have that with your woman."

Michael was elated at the news that the women would join him at The Manor for Samhain. Another piece of his plan had fallen into place. It hadn't escaped his notice that while everyone else was chatting animatedly about the trip and asking questions about what to expect; Elizabeth was not participating. He had to admit that was worrisome. Jackson's voice boomed as he announced the four different flavors of ice cream and a longer list of sauces as he placed the makings for sundaes or banana splits on the counter. Michael took this opportunity to approach Elizabeth.

"Elizabeth, what are you having? A sundae or a split?"

"I'm not very hungry," she muttered.

He'd asked Jackson where he could talk to Elizabeth in private should the need arise and was now very glad for his foresight. Reaching out, he took her hand, pulling her from her seat by the fire. When she didn't resist, he took that as a good sign. "Come with me, please. There're things I need to say to ye."

Elizabeth looked deep into his eyes, saw the vulnerability and longing he tried valiantly to hide, and relented. "Just for a minute or two," she agreed, going with him when he took her elbow, led her to the stairs, and started up. Glancing back over her shoulder, she saw no one looking their way, at least not in an obvious manner. She had no illusions; resigned to the reality her circle sisters knew exactly what was happening, Elizabeth continued up the stairs.

At the top of the stairs, Michael turned to the left and led her down the hall to Jackson's office. Once inside, Michael released her and watched her take several steps into the room before stopping. He closed the door and leaned back, his hands on the doorknob.

"What is it, Michael?" She asked and turned to look at him.

"Ah, Elizabeth." She looked so very serious, her blue eyes wide and wary. He knew he couldn't go to her or he'd act rather than speak and this was his chance to try to explain everything to her. She was here, they were alone, and she was listening. He kept his hands behind him, clutching the door knob to keep from reaching for her. "About this evening," he began. "I hope you can forgive me for extending the invitation without talking it over with you first."

"While I do wish the whole episode had been handled differently, I know everyone will have a wonderful time. To have us all together with The Lady at The Sacred Grove on Samhain is truly a gift. I just wish...." her voice trailed off and she turned to look out the window into the darkness.

The silence exacerbated his discomfort and he blurted out, "About this afternoon, which of the two houses do you think is the better bargain?"

"I don't understand why you'd buy a house here in Fremont to begin with." Her hands fisted at her side, her tone challenging, she turned back to face him. "You can't seriously think to sell off The Manor. It's been in your family for generations and you have The Lady and The Sacred Grove to think about."

"I know all that, but just tell me which of the two houses you think would suit best. If you're going to be in Fremont, I want to spend time here, too."

Elizabeth's heart caught in her throat. He wasn't giving up and was offering to spend time here, in Fremont, to be with her. It wasn't just about getting her back to Ireland. Tears welled, her stomach lurched, and for a moment she thought she was going to be sick. She shook her head to clear her thoughts. "I would think the first house would be easier for you since there really isn't much of a yard. The second house is beautiful but sits on almost an acre and those lawns would need tending weekly during the spring and summer. But really, Michael, you can get a small condominium to stay in when you're in town. You don't really need anything that large."

"I'd go stir-crazy in a small place, Elizabeth. You know how large The Manor is. The large yard reminds me of the space in Ireland but you're right about the upkeep. The first house, being of old stone and all, also reminds me of home. That's why I was trying to decide between those two. I'd looked at two more this morning and even more online." He kept his gaze fixed on her not daring to look away and miss something. She wasn't on guard and he caught emotions flitting across her face as he talked.

A wry smile on his face, Michael leaned away from the door, surreptitiously flexing his fingers now cramped from their death grip on the door knob. "I'll call Weston in the morning; make an offer on the first place." He reached for her. "Thanks for helping me make that decision." He took a step in her direction, captured her hands, and bent down brushing a chaste kiss on her forehead.

"You know I'll have to rely on you to help with everything here. I've got the Breeders Cup coming up so I need to get back to the farm." He chuckled, "and I've got to give Seamus time to get everything in order for company." He stepped to the side, slipped his arm around her shoulders. "Do you think Ashley's kids would like to learn to ride a horse?" He blew softly against her ear and kissed her hair.

Elizabeth locked her knees before she swayed. "You could ask them." She hoped her voice sounded unaffected from his sensual onslaught. She stepped away to protect herself. "I'd check with their mother first, to make sure she's okay with that." Another step followed the first. "I'll help as best I can Michael, but I do have a life here."

"I know you do. I'm just asking to be a part of it when I'm in town."

Elizabeth looked at the man who made her blood heat and surge through her body. He looked innocent but there was something about that innocence she distrusted. She dreaded going to Ireland and she welcomed it. To be with The Lady in The Sacred Grove again, to see the friends she'd made, to spend time in the back parlor and still room—this time with her circle sisters was a dream come true. A dream come true connected to a nightmare. The nightmare of leaving Michael and The Lady again, the nightmare of finding her balance again here in Fremont. How was she ever going to manage if he kept coming back into her life? She might be better able to protect herself spiritually but she did not delude herself in thinking she could protect herself from the pain of leaving him after Samhain.

"I'm sure by now they've missed us," she said to Michael as she opened the door.

"I don't care about that. I just hope there's some of that ice cream left for me to make myself a banana split. I haven't had one of those in half a lifetime."

"Well, if I know the people we left downstairs, there won't be much." Elizabeth smiled over her shoulder. "And since my appetite has returned and I'm ahead of you, there'll be even less for you." With that she sprinted to the stairs, clattered down, and laughing, when she hit the bottom, raced across the great room to the kitchen.

Michael, right behind her, caught her as she reached the counter now devoid of ice cream. He picked her up in his strong arms and swung her around, kissed her thoroughly, and set her back on the ground behind him. He looked up, caught Jackson's eye. "Where'd the ice cream go?"

"It's in the freezer. Didn't know when you two would re-appear and didn't want it to melt," he said amusement was evident in his voice. "Go ahead and help yourself. The cartons are marked."

"Yoouu," Elizabeth started. "You think you can go first because you kissed me?" Her hands were fisted on her hips, sparks flew from her eyes. "You've got another think coming, boyo." She advanced slowly, her blue eyes blazing, her gaze never wavering.

Without taking his eyes from hers, Michael called out, "Hey, Montgomery, is there enough for both of us or do I have to challenge her to a duel, winner takes all?"

"There's enough for both of you."

Jackson's voice sounded muffled but Elizabeth wasn't go-ing to look over at him to find out why. She knew how good his homemade ice cream tasted and loved his vanilla bean flavor. As every one of her circle sisters favored this flavor she wasn't sure if there'd be any left.

Michael grabbed her upper arms and hauled her to him, shifting so his back was to the great room. He leaned down and tried to kiss her.

She ducked her head. He was not going to seduce her over a banana split, she vowed to herself.

One arm banded around her waist while the other hand found her chin and gently tilted her face so he could see into her eyes. "He said there's enough for both of us. So give me a kiss so we can fix ourselves some dessert."

Trapped, like a deer caught in on-coming headlights, entranced, she watched Michael lower his head, his lips brushed the tip of her nose, one cheek and then the other before coming to rest like a feather on her lips. He nibbled and teased her lips until she softened and answered him with a kiss of her own. His hand left her chin, traveled to the nape of her neck and then shifted through her hair, holding her still as he plundered her mouth and her senses; until her knees weakened; until she reached up and wrapped her arms around his neck and melted into him.

As the kiss ended, Elizabeth could hear vague murmurings in the background. She blinked to clear her vision and stepped back. Cheeks flaming, she knew with a certainty everyone in the great room had paid very close attention to that kiss. They might pretend not to notice but she knew that for a lie.

Michael softly whistled to himself as he rummaged through the cartons in the freezer. "What flavor do you want?"

"Vanilla, just vanilla."

"Got it," he handed her a carton and straightened from the freezer, his arms holding three more. He stacked them on the counter, reached for a bowl, and began to build himself a gigantic banana split.

Elizabeth took a sundae glass, dumped a spoonful of peanuts in the bottom covering them with chocolate sauce and proceeded to create her ice cream sundae.

Across the great room by the fire, Jackson, Lily and the others watched fascinated by the scene playing out on the other side of the room. Lily, her ice cream finished, leaned her head against her husband's shoulder.

Sophia caught her eye, smiled and whispered, "Looks like there's more going on there than we thought. Reminds me of someone else I know," she winked.

# 24  IRELAND

Twelve of them made the trip: Lily and Jackson, Sophia, Diana, Ashley and her three children, Hunter and Logan, Gabriella and Elizabeth. Michael and Seamus met them the Wednesday morning before Samhain at the Shannon airport. Each man drove a van that held seven people plus luggage. Hunter, Logan, Ashley and the three younger children rode with Michael. Elizabeth, along with Lily, Jackson, Sophia, Diana and Gabriella, rode with Seamus. His rough hug and growled, "ye've been missed, lass" surprised her.

Memories assailed her at every turn. This was where she and Michael or this was where Michael or this was where she...
. Even though the drive to Michael's took three hours, she convinced Michael and Seamus to stop in Limerick. Once so everyone saw the swans on the Shannon River and a second stop at the hotel to view the Children of Lir statue. The rest of the trip was uneventful and they drove through The Man-

or's stone gates mid-afternoon. Elizabeth's breath caught and she pressed a hand to her stomach.

Overwhelmed.

She was here at The Manor.

With Michael.

The door opened as the van came to a stop in the front drive. Michael stood silhouetted for a moment in time before his purposeful strides carried him to her. He opened her door and the door behind her, welcoming everyone, helping Seamus with the luggage. Before she knew it, they were all in the main hall, luggage piled around them, Michael handing everyone what looked like maps. Hunter and Logan had already disappeared up the stairs obviously eager to see the room they shared. Ashley's children, each with a backpack slung over their shoulders, trudged behind their mom.

Elizabeth stood in a daze of memories and emotions. Michael's voice filtered through the fog. She felt his presence, smelled his sandalwood scent, his breath feathered across her cheek.

"You know where your room is. I'll check in with you after I've made sure everyone else is settled in."

Elizabeth left her suitcase and carry-on in the hall and walked slowly from room to room. Other than the fresh flowers were different, everything was just as she'd left. Approaching the back parlor, the hum she'd heard since they neared the village grew louder. She stepped into the small room and was instantly surrounded by shimmering light.

The Lady appeared before her, resplendent in her blue robe, her long hair shinning with a golden light as her hood was thrown back, a smile of welcome on her face. She lifted her arms and held them wide in an invitation. Elizabeth walked toward the outstretched arms, her own mirroring The

Lady's. The energy thrummed between them. The shimmering light, peace and joy in equal measure flowed through her.

*"We are the Light,*

*'We are the Source*

*'Through us Love flows throughout the world."*

The familiar words of the prayer were repeated three times three. The Lady smiled, the shimmering light flared and faded. The Lady was gone. Elizabeth was alone, the pulsing of the sound from The Sacred Grove echoing in her veins.

She returned to the main hall to get her things only to find them gone. Slowly she trod up the stairs turning left at the top. She wanted to see what Michael had done to the old wing she told herself. But deep inside she knew she wanted to avoid being alone with him a bit longer.

The chattering of familiar voices told her she was near the rooms her circle sisters and the children would occupy for the next five nights. They'd decided to travel Tuesday night, arriving in Ireland on Wednesday, returning home on Monday in order to see some of the local sights in addition to celebrating Samhain in The Sacred Grove with The Lady.

Each room had been scrubbed until it was spotless. Windows gleamed, furniture polished to a shine, curtains cleaned and hung, and rooms aired until any vestige of mustiness was gone. Elizabeth had picked up one of the maps so she knew who was in each of the rooms. She checked with everyone, making sure they had what they needed. Although everyone was tired, the excitement of being there, of actually being in a castle, gave each of them the energy to unpack and settle in.

Gabriella's room was the last one Elizabeth looked into. Her friend was sitting in a dark blue velvet chair by the fireplace, a notepad in hand furiously scribbling away. Hearing Elizabeth's soft knock, she stopped writing, put her pen down and grinned. "Wow, Elizabeth. This place is great! I've so many ideas for the location of my novels. That is such a bonus for me. I think we're all just overwhelmed." She gestured toward the fireplace. "Come over here and sit down."

Elizabeth crossed the soft peach, cream, and dark blue carpet to sit in the matching chair. This room was done in peach, with cream moldings and plaster work and dark blue accents in the chairs, drapes, and bedcovers. She toed off her shoes, tucked her legs underneath her, and gazed into the cheery flames. The women sat in comfortable silence, the only sounds that of the crackling fire and the scratching of Gabriella's pen moving across paper.

A bell ringing brought both women back to the present. "What was that?"

"A reminder that dinner will be served in fifteen minutes." Elizabeth rose, slipped on her shoes, and crossed to the door. "I'll see you downstairs. The map will show you the way." She hurried down the hall, crossed the landing at the top of the main staircase, and entered the right wing. Two doors down she stopped and opened the door on the right, the door to her sitting room. An overwhelming sense of relief flooded through her. Everything was as she left it.

Elizabeth slowly backed out of the room, shutting the door quietly behind her. Across the hall was the door she dreaded most. 'Her room.' The room with the connecting door to Michael's, the room she'd claimed as hers for almost five weeks, and the room that overlooked The Sacred Grove. As Elizabeth stepped inside, she saw him slouched in the chair by the fire, long legs stretched out in front of him, ankles crossed. She couldn't see his eyes in the dim light but she could feel them bore into her, raking up and down her body, setting her on fire.

"The dinner bell rang." She stilled in the doorway, her hand on the knob.

"I heard." The rightness of seeing her here, in this room, the rightness of her being here with him filled his heart. He uncrossed his ankles and gracefully rose. Glancing down to ensure the fire screen was in place he took note she hadn't moved before crossing the room and stopping in front of her. The fingers of one hand trailed down the side of her face to her chin, pausing for a moment before continuing their trek down her throat to the fabric of her blouse. He stopped before the urge to pop all those buttons and ravish her against the door took control.

"Our guests are waiting," he said and stepped to the side, reached out for her elbow, and guided her into the hall and toward the stairs. "We don't want to keep everyone waiting now, do we?"

"No, Michael, you don't," Elizabeth responded. "Your guests are looking forward to something other than airplane food tonight." She heard Michael's soft chuckle as they started down the stairs.

Thursday, Elizabeth slipped into her routine of morning prayers with The Lady while everyone else slept in. After breakfast Elizabeth took everyone on a tour of the still room and the back parlor; Michael took them on a tour of the barns and paddocks. In the afternoon they all went into the village; Gabriella remained talking with Maura at the bookstore, while everyone else continued looking in the small shops. At three o'clock they all gathered at The Winner's Circle for a pint of Guinness for the adults and sodas for the children. They returned to The Manor and by five the women were seated in the front parlor. Jackson was working in Michael's office. Logan and Michael took the children to the barns to check on the horses since there were two hours until dinner.

Everyone smudged. The front parlor altar Elizabeth had made from the tea set was moved over to the sideboard. One of the Irish lace doilies was removed from the back of a chair and placed on the table in front of the couches. Each woman contributed something to the altar, a small china bowl served as the center, and candles in crystal holders were placed in each direction.

"This is a magical place," Sophia said from where she sat at the end of one of the couches.

"It really is," Gabriella agreed as she settled in next to her.

"Wow, y'all will think me stupid or something because that's all I can say when I look around this place." Ashley slipped in beside Gabriella and took her hand. "This time here with the kids, well, y'all know how much it means to me." She sighed and snuggled deeper into her corner of the couch. "Have y'all seen my kids? They're so happy." Tears welled in her eyes.

"Elizabeth," Lily began, "what ideas do you have for Samhain? Does Michael's grandmother have any suggestions for ceremony in the notebooks she left?" She sat on the couch across from Ashley.

"We'll come up with something," Diana said and settled in next to Lily. "We always do."

"Having some ideas from Michael's grandmother, would be awesome," Hunter added. "But you're right, D, we'll come up with something and you'll pick the songs."

Elizabeth stood and watched everyone find a place to sit. They filled the two couches leaving the chair that faced the fireplace for her. "Sophia? Why don't you sit here and I'll take the couch," she began.

"Because my place is here," Sophia said with a smile, "and your place is there," she pointed to the chair. "This is your time, Elizabeth. We are all here to celebrate this special time together because of you. Take your place. You know you're ready. You know it's your time."

Elizabeth sat on the edge of the chair and looked at everyone's expectant faces. She scooted back, closed her eyes and let the energy come to her, flow through her, and spread out from her to envelop the entire room. She didn't question why she felt the energy of the Goddess infuse her so strongly in this place in Ireland. She accepted it as her reality. The presence of The Lady was strong. When she opened her eyes, the image of The Lady shimmered before her and then dissipated and was gone.

"As we all know, Samhain is the time to honor our ancestors, when the veil between the worlds is thinnest. For pagans it is the beginning of their new year, when bulbs and seeds are planted to bear flowers and fruit in the spring.

"While I'm not sure exactly what we will do, I do know something will unfold for each of us individually as well as for the seven of us as a whole. I do know we need to take extra precautions to ground ourselves before entering The Sacred Grove. We also will circle The Grove three times, saying prayers at each of the four direction's entrances, and finally stepping through the gate, onto the path that leads to the center. Tomorrow during the day we need to prepare ourselves."

"So we should enter from the North?" Sophia asked. "I'm asking because I think of the North as the direction of our ancestors, of wisdom."

"Yes," Elizabeth responded. "We will enter from the North. It really is The Sacred Grove so we will need very little other than our protection. A spring and a fire are already there. Once we enter The Sacred Grove, we won't be leaving until our Ceremony is over."

"I'll ask Jackson to see to the children tomorrow so we can have from noon on to ourselves," Lily offered.

"Logan will be thrilled to join them. She's still intimidated by the power of this place. She hears the humming noise, says she sees lights, but she doesn't see herself as strong enough in her own power to join us," Hunter said her brows furrowed in a frown.

"That's all right, Hunter," Elizabeth hurriedly interjected. "The first time I entered The Sacred Grove, I wasn't prepared. Several hours later Michael found me on the ground, unconscious, because I'd fallen into such a deep trance. The power here is strong. If we prepare ourselves, determine our purpose, keep ourselves grounded, it is an exhilarating and sublime experience. Without all of that, it can be dangerous.

"Maybe before we leave, Logan will come and do morning prayers with us. And actually that will be the first order of business tomorrow. I used to get up at four, prepare myself, go to The Sacred Grove, do morning prayers with The Lady and return between eight and nine o'clock. I don't know how so much time passed because it never seemed like I was gone that long.

"Since we're still adjusting to the time difference, we'll meet tomorrow morning in the back parlor at eight. We can do prayers on the back terrace so everyone has a better feel for the energy of this place before our Ceremony tomorrow night." Elizabeth looked from one circle sister to the other until she'd caught the eye of everyone. "How does that sound to everyone?"

Sophia's smile was brilliant as she looked across at Diana and Lily. They smiled back with almost imperceptible nods. A frown crossed Elizabeth's face as she realized they were all looking at her, radiant smiles on their faces.

"What's everyone smiling at?" Elizabeth's brows knit in confusion.

Gabriella stood, stepped over Sophia's feet, and stopped when she was directly in front of Elizabeth. Reaching out she placed her hands on her friend's shoulders. "You have a glow, a shimmering light that surrounds you in this place. You have a confidence, a clearness of sight. We can see it, hear it, sense it—you come alive here, Elizabeth. We've," Gabriella looked around her to see her circle sister's nodding in agreement, "we've never seen you this way. What you see is our rejoicing to see you this way now."

She pulled Elizabeth to her feet, moved to her side, and put her arm around her waist. Holding her other arm out, she invited the others to join her. They came together, heads bowed in silence, the table with the altar in their midst, drinking in the essence of the moment, of this time together.

The bell rang announcing dinner would be served in thirty minutes, a change from yesterday's fifteen since getting the younger children washed and ready took a little more time. The seven women stepped back, letting their arms fall to their sides.

"I've the utmost confidence that we'll get things just right tomorrow. But right now, I'm hungry and I've got kids to round up before we sit down to eat." Ashley started for the door. As she turned the handle and opened the door, she called back over her shoulder, "Logan and the kids are going to prepare a spirit plate. I'm going to check the kitchen, make sure they are washed up and aren't bugging Seamus too much." She trotted off across the main hall and down the side hall to the kitchen.

"I'm coming, too," Hunter called out as she followed Ashley.

"I'm going to find my husband," Lily said grinning, "and see if I can disrupt, oops, I mean interrupt whatever he's working on." Her look was one of pure mischief.

"I, for one, am going to hang out in the back parlor until it's time to gather for our meal. I trust that Seamus, even with the help of the kids, can manage without me," Gabriella said and held out her hand. "Anyone want to join me?"

They chatted as they left the front parlor and headed toward the smaller back parlor. "Not much time to scout out anything," Diana said and slowly turned in the middle of the room. "What's this?" she asked reaching for a small book sitting askew in the otherwise organized bookcase.

Elizabeth looked over her shoulder. "That's a book of recipes," she replied when she saw the small volume in Diana's hand. "I had it out and experimented with some of them this summer."

"Oh, let me see," Sophia said peering over Diana's shoulder.

"There are more of them." Elizabeth stepped to the bookcase and perused the shelves as she spoke, quickly plucking two other smaller books from the shelves. They were eagerly snatched up by Sophia and Diana.

Gabriella had found one of Michael's grandmother's diaries. "I'd like to take this to my room to look through tonight, if that's all right." She held the book up for Elizabeth to see.

"Of course it's all right," Elizabeth said glancing at the clock on the mantel. "If we don't hurry, we'll be late." She opened the door and stood to the side while everyone passed before pulling it shut and slowly followed her chatting circle sisters to the dining room.

"I hope you ladies had a successful meeting." Jackson blocked the doorway to the dining room, his arm around Lily, a smile on his face. Lily, a glow of happiness surrounding her, looked a little dazed. The sound of clattering feet from the hallway announced the three younger children followed by Logan, Hunter and Ashley.

Elizabeth knew exactly when Michael stepped into the anteroom off the dining room. She sensed his coming closer but still shivered when he wrapped his arm around her and pulled her tight against him. His breath stirred her hair, his hard muscular chest and burgeoning arousal pressed against her back.

He hadn't come to her last night and she hadn't heard him leave to check the horses this morning. "I missed you," he whispered in her ear sending frissons of heat coursing through her.

Amazed she didn't stagger when he let her go, Elizabeth observed him greet his guests ushering everyone into the dining room, joke with the children, compliment the women, and banter with Jackson. Through it all, his eyes seldom left her. There was no doubt in her mind, tonight would be different. The only question was whether he would come to her or she would go to him. While it was true flames leapt inside her at the touch of his hand, it was obvious he was aroused being in the same room with her.

Elizabeth took her place at the table and joined in the conversation that consisted right then of the children sharing their day with the horses. When someone asked Jackson about his day, he was vague, offering only he'd crossed some things off his "to do" list. The meal of Irish stew, fresh bread and butter, salad with lettuce and tomatoes fresh from the small hot house behind the garden, and a dessert of apple crisp with homemade ice cream filled everyone to the brim.

As was their habit, everyone cleared his or her own dishes from the table, trooped into the kitchen where they were stacked on the counter. Two people scraped and rinsed, another loaded the dishwasher, while the others finished clearing the table, putting any leftovers in storage containers in the refrigerator. In less than fifteen minutes the kitchen was turned back over to Seamus to "finish up".

"If we're meeting at eight, I need my beauty sleep," Sophia said as she closed the refrigerator door. "I'm off to bed. See you all in the morning."

"Me, too," Diana added as she followed Sophia down the hall to the main stairs.

Ashley, Hunter, Logan and the younger children were already gathering things up and heading off, saying "good nights" over their shoulders.

"I think I need to take my wife to bed." Jackson said and winked at Lily. "She's looking exhausted."

"If that's what you think, Jackson," Lily said with a wicked smile, "you'll want me to go right to sleep." She sauntered across the kitchen and down the hall, Jackson's chuckle trailing back to Elizabeth, Gabriella, Michael, and Seamus who still remained in the kitchen.

"See you in the morning, Elizabeth." Gabriella gave her a hug and turned to give one to Seamus as well. The taciturn houseman ducked his head, his cheeks reddening with embarrassment. He nodded to Gabriella's now retreating form.

"An excellent meal, Seamus," Elizabeth said and started toward the door. "I think I'll check a few things in the still room before I go up to bed."

"Good idea." Michael's voice was close, his arm slipped around her waist. "I'll go with you in case you need some help."

Seamus smiled to himself, picked up a towel and began wiping down his countertops.

# 25   Samhain In Ireland

The women gathered in the back parlor at eight Friday morning before stepping through the low window to the terrace. Dressed warmly, they wore shawls around their shoulders, long skirts, wool socks and slippers on their feet. A pot of Elizabeth's special blend of potent grounding herbs: lavender, primrose, ash, clove, and sage sat on the wall within easy reach. Heeding her caution, they sprinkled the herbs over their heads, tucked a pinch into their pockets, and adding another bit to their bag of protecting stones. Elizabeth set out additional grounding stones of hematite, jet, and black tourmaline small enough for the bags but also had placed larger stones along the wall to act as a barrier between them and The Sacred Grove.

Hands folded in the prayer position they touched their foreheads while saying "The Gifts of the Goddess are to Think", moving their hands to their lips "to Speak", placing their still folded hands between their breasts, "to Feel", and inverting and slightly opening them over their womb "to Create". Spreading their arms wide "To Give" and then crossing their arms across their chests "To Receive the Gifts of the Goddess" they began again with "Which are To Think." They repeated the words of this prayer and their accompanying movements three times ending with a low bow "For I am the Goddess, For I am the Goddess, For I am the Goddess, Blessed Be." Joining now raised hands, the prayer Elizabeth had taught them flowed from their lips as they sent love throughout the world.

Back in the front parlor, with tea and scones for sustenance, the women shared how they'd experienced the energy of The Sacred Grove. Each had seen a shimmering light, heard the hum of sacred energy, and easily slipped into an altered state.

"You are right, Elizabeth," Sophia commented. "We must be well-protected tonight so all goes well."

The rest of the morning was spent in quiet contemplation. Michael, Jackson and Logan took charge after breakfast and by noon the men and four children were packed up and off on an adventure. The details were a secret but the two men assured the mothers they had everything under control. The plan was to return around noon the following day, but that was just an estimate. If they were a little later than that, no one should worry. Seamus was off to see a friend and would also not return until later the next day.

The women had the next twenty-four hours to themselves.

In the past each woman had been in her own home as she prepared for their Samhain ceremony, but today they congregated around the kitchen table while Elizabeth brewed a pot of tea.

"This is different for us," Hunter began. "How do you all want to do this?"

"Why don't we each share a bit about how we prepare for ceremony," Diana suggested.

"Great idea, D," Lily chimed in. "I make an effort to spend the day in silence. I think and read, especially about the holiday. In preparation, I brought a small book on Samhain I planned on perusing."

"I eat lightly," Sophia commented. "I drink different liquids such as the tea Elizabeth is making. But in all honesty, I have been known to taste whatever I'm preparing for our feast afterwards."

"I have a routine where I do some yoga and then a belly dance. You might think that belly dancing doesn't go with ceremony but remember belly dancing came about as a woman's dance for other women. I find that dancing brings me closer to the feminine which is where I want to be for ceremony," Hunter shared.

"I sort of mix quiet time and light sustenance," Gabriella said in a thoughtful tone. "I may read or listen to music. I keep journals. Sometimes I go back and review what I've written about my experiences with other ceremonies I brought my journals for the last two years and planned on reading the entries on Samhain."

"I do something similar, too," Elizabeth added. "Not the journals, but I do read and find time to be quiet and thoughtful about the meaning of the ceremony. As our ceremonies mark the changes in seasons and life, I think about what the change we are celebrating means in general but more specifically in my own life."

"With the children and all, I don't find extended quiet time easy to come by but I do find time for bits and pieces of it. I guess I'm more mindful on these days to make sure I find those moments for contemplation," Ashley said in her soft southern drawl. "The last couple of years, I just focus on what I've got to be grateful for no matter what season or ceremony. It's one of the ways I've kept myself sane. While a lot is wrong, I do have things to be grateful for." She smiled as she looked around the room. "Y'all are at the top of my list, right behind my kids."

"I make an effort to keep my schedule light on ceremony days. When I can, I spend time meditating and thinking of the significance of the time of year, the ceremony, the celebration of change." Diana's serious face broke into a smile. "When I can't keep that schedule light, I'm more like Ashley taking a moment here and there to contemplate. I'm grateful for red lights and slow traffic on those days."

"We should be able to do all of the above," Elizabeth said bringing the tea pot to the table. "You all know where things are in the kitchen if you want something to eat. Seamus asked me yesterday what we would want to eat and spent time this morning preparing things so we'll have very little to do when we get back from The Sacred Grove."

"He fixed us a wonderful vegetable soup," Sophia started. "I watched him prepare it and it looks delicious."

"It smells delicious too," Gabriella interjected.

"Looks like all the bases are covered," Lily said and took a sip of her tea. "When do you think we need to start tonight?"

"If we meet around ten in the back parlor, we can finish anything we need to do and be in The Sacred Grove by eleven," Elizabeth said looking hesitantly around the table, "that is if that's okay with everyone."

"Does anyone have an objection to gathering in the back parlor at ten?" Lily looked around the table seeing various expressions of amusement but none of disagreement.

"What other ideas do you have, Elizabeth," Sophia inquired. "You do seem to know the place better than all of us put together. I, for one, would welcome your suggestions."

A chorus of agreement followed that statement.

"I don't know if they're really suggestions," Elizabeth's self-consciousness showed in her voice and her hands as she played with her cup. "It's just that I know time seems to warp in The Sacred Grove so I have no idea what time it'll be when we return to the house. As you know from our morning prayers, it's very important to be well-grounded before we enter and to take extra protection with us in order to leave, to return here."

Gabriella poured herself a bit more tea adding cream and sugar. "And I'd like to see Lily's book on Samhain."

"Perhaps we can take turns reading it out loud?" Lily offered. "Anyone who wants to participate can join us in the front parlor this afternoon. What would be a good time Gabby?"

"How about three?"

"Would you be willing to share your thoughts from the past on Samhain?" Diana asked Gabriella.

"Yes. I'll bring my journals along if anyone is interested."

"Looks like we've got a plan," Sophia said smiling at everyone still sitting around the table. "We've free time until three and then time together until we're done with the readings." She laughed. "You don't think I believe any one of us will miss this coming together, do you? Because I don't."

"The gift of ceremony with The Lady in The Sacred Grove is huge," Ashley added, "but the extra special gift for me is the gift of private, solitary time. With three young children, I don't get much of it at home." She grinned. "But y'all see me at three."

The women cleared up after themselves, rinsing their cups and placing them in specific spots in the kitchen. These were 'their' cups and as such would be reused during the day. They were smart women and did what they could to keep the mess to a minimum. There would be time for dishes after ceremony.

By ten o'clock everyone stood, sat, or perched in the back parlor. The day had passed swiftly, with each person taking solitary time to walk, meditate, contemplate, write, or some combination thereof.

Sophia had been right. No one missed coming together at three. The time together with Lily's book on Samhain and Gabriella's journal entries had been followed by thoughtful discussion of what this holiday meant: the thinning of the veil between this world and the next; the connection to the ancestors; the beginning of a new year for those with certain pagan beliefs.

Elizabeth wore the necklace from the dance and carried the stones of protection she wore at New Grange. She checked each of her circle sisters, adding stones of hematite to Ashley's pouch, and giving them each a small bag of protective herbs. The hall clock began chiming eleven when Elizabeth opened the window that also served as a door and led them out.

Stopping before the gate leading down to The Sacred Grove, they held hands, bowed their heads and prayed, "May our highest good be served here this day. Blessed Be."

Elizabeth led the way.

At the base of the hill they paused. The shimmering light and pulse of energy engulfed them. Elizabeth held her hands high drinking in the essence of the place. Taking Lily's hand, she motioned for everyone to do the same. With all hands joined, Elizabeth started forward again. It was more awkward this way, but she knew they needed their combined power to withstand the onslaught of this night's energy.

How long has it been since a group of women have come to serve The Lady and celebrate in The Sacred Grove? "A very long time," floated through her mind, "too long."

The women trod the path around The Sacred Grove three times, lifting their arms in prayer at each direction's opening. At the North entrance, the direction of the ancestors, Elizabeth's voice rang clear in the still night.

"Spirits of the North, ancestors, those who have gone before, hear our prayers. We come to this sacred place to celebrate Samhain and through ceremony, you. We come to honor you, your wisdom, your place in our lives and the lives of others. Come with us as we enter this sacred place; be with us as we celebrate Samhain and reach through the veil to you. Blessed Be."

Shoes were left outside the entrance. Single file they walked along the path, approaching the center, the pulsing energy strengthened, the light grew brighter.

Elizabeth entered first, standing to the side, her hand outstretched. She grasped Gabriella's hand as she stepped from the path onto the grass. In turn as each woman passed from the leaves and needles of the path to the grass of the sacred center, she took the hand of the woman who had entered before her. When everyone was assembled, Elizabeth started forward toward the spring. As a group the other women matched her steps.

The light shimmered before their eyes as the vision of The Lady, resplendent in her blue robes, the crescent of her calling on her forehead, materialized.

"Welcome, I have waited so long for you to come to me." As always her words were heard in the mind. The women remained holding hands in a semi-circle facing The Lady.

Elizabeth let go of Gabriella's hand and stepped forward. "We are here to celebrate Samhain. We have our own traditions but are also here to serve You. What do You wish us to do?

"I wish for you to join me in prayer."

As one, the women raised their arms, palms toward the sky. The Lady stepped forward to complete the circle.

*"We are the Light*

*"We are the Source*

*"Through us Love flows to the outer world."*

As was their tradition, the prayer was said three times. At the conclusion, The Lady smiled and lowered her arms. Now it is for you to go forward this night.

Gabriella's voice rang clear as she began to recite the names of her family and friends who were beyond the veil. This tradition started many years ago and stemmed from a tradition with the Women of the 14th Moon Ceremony where the women spoke of their matriarchal lineage as far back as they knew. The change they'd made for Samhain was they included men and friends as well as their female ancestors who beyond the veil.

One by one they called out the names of those who were gone. They spoke as they were called to do, not because of their place in the circle. Sophia was last. In a strong voice she called out to family and friends who'd been gone for a long time. Her voice trembled with emotions as she called out the last name, Jonathon, her husband who died five years ago. Tears fell when she said his name. "I'll always love you, Jonathon. Always. I miss you so much. I still have a hole in my heart, in my soul because you are gone." A sob wrenched from her as she sank to her knees, her head bowed.

Elizabeth saw the sobs cease and what looked like peace settle over Sophia who had raised her head and stared as if looking at something. The tears still flowed but a look of sublime joy lit her face. Her lips moved but Elizabeth heard no sound.

The others drifted off to sit in different places on the grassy center.

Shadowed light grew brighter and glowing images surround each woman as she connected to friends or family members beyond the veil. When an older woman came to her, Elizabeth communicated with her in the same way she did The Lady.

Slowly the energy brought by the ancestors dissipated. In silence the women reformed their circle, hands raised to the sky. Once again The Lady appeared in their midst.

> *"We are the Light*
> *"We are the Source*
> *"Through us Love flows to the outer world.*

> *"We are the Light*
> *"We are the Source*
> *"Through us Love flows to the outer world.*

> *"We are the Light*
> *"We are the Source*
> *"Through us Love flows to the outer world."*

The shimmering light that enveloped The Lady now spun around each of them, the effervescence of the light swirled within their bodies, and the light emanated from them in a soft glow.

"Blessed Be." They lowered their arms, continuing to stand in the circle looking around at each other. Elizabeth grasped the medallion of her necklace tightly, the metal digging into her hand helping her come back to the present. She had much to think about from her interaction with Michael's grandmother tonight. But her first task was to make sure everyone was all right and able to leave The Sacred Grove.

With both hands on her heart, she bowed to The Lady. "Thank you for allowing us to be with you this night."

The Lady smiled, shafts of light streaming from her. "May you return many times to celebrate the old ways in Ceremony. Always know you are welcome here." The light around her began to fade, She was gone.

Elizabeth turned to her circle sisters. "It's time to go," she whispered. "Come," she took Gabriella's hand and led her to the opening. "Go through here; let your feet follow the path. As soon as you reach the outside, put your shoes on and wait for me. Go now," she encouraged. As Gabriella started down the path, Elizabeth turned to Diana and then Lily with the same instructions.

Hunter was standing with Ashley and Sophia, both of whom were still deep in trance. Elizabeth stood in front of Ashley and took her hands. Taking Ashley's pouch of protection from her pocket, she placed it in her palm, folding her fingers around the pouch, squeezing them shut. Calmly and quietly, she spoke to her about her children, how they needed her, and how they would be back soon. She watched Ashley's face carefully as she talked, finally seeing the signs of the trance beginning to fade. Leading Ashley to the path's opening, she gave her the same instructions she had the others. Hunter, who had followed was standing close, nodded to Elizabeth.

"I'm right behind you, Ash," her soft voice drifted in the stillness. "Take a few steps, Ashley. Remember, the children will be back soon. We need to leave here for now." She nudged Ashley's shoulders until the young woman took a few steps. Murmuring encouragement, Hunter followed Ashley down the path.

When Elizabeth was certain Ashley and Hunter were on their way, she turned back to Sophia. "Let's go now, Soph," her voice was firm but soft. "It's time."

Sophia did not respond.

Elizabeth took her hand and led her to the opening. Retrieving Sophia's bag of protection as she had done with Ashley, Elizabeth also used herbs from her own bag, sprinkling them over her as she quietly talked to her friend. Even with these ministrations, Sophia remained deep in trance. Elizabeth's concern deepened. She needed to get Sophia out of The Sacred Grove for the trance to wear off, but she had to be the last one to leave.

As she was standing there, talking softly to Sophia, and thinking of her options, she heard a male voice.

"Come along, Sophie love. It's time to go."

Still deeply under the influence of the trance, Sophia began to move down the path. "I'm coming Jonathan," she whispered, her face streaked with falling tears.

Elizabeth waited until Sophia had disappeared down the path before she turned back, let her eyes roam over the grassy center and rest for a moment on the bubbling spring. She shuddered, not because of the cold, but from the awareness of how very thin the veil was here. The spirits, the magic of The Sacred Grove were strong. There was one more task to complete before her job tonight was done. She turned back to the opening and started down the path to the outer world.

Outside The Sacred Grove, Elizabeth joined the other women, raised her arms to the sky and said, "Thank you spirits of this place and beyond for being with us tonight. Thank you to those of you who chose to join us and share your thoughts and wisdom with us. Thank you for staying connected to us here on this side of the veil. May you find peace until we meet again. Blessed Be."

# 26 MESSAGES

Elizabeth remained standing, arms up-raised, eyes closed until a shift in energies signaled the spirits had left The Sacred Grove. When all felt calm, the women returned to the house. The jubilant noises that usually followed ceremony were missing. Instead of chatting and laughter, she heard quiet murmurings. As she left the back parlor, Gabriella was waiting.

"We're going to camp out in your sitting room, Elizabeth, if that's all right."

"Of course. How is everyone?" She asked as they started down the hall toward the main hall.

"Lily is staying with Ashley and Sophia in your sitting room and making a fire. Diana and Hunter are gathering blankets, pillows, cushions from our rooms, and you and I are bringing up the food," Gabriella informed her friend.

The two women turned down the corridor to the kitchen where Gabriella picked up a tray and began stacking it with bowls, plates, utensils and napkins adding salt and pepper shakers, the pot of fresh butter and another of jam. Gabriella hefted the tray and grinned. "Reminds me of those years as a waitress when I was working and going to college; I can manage but we need to get going."

Elizabeth removed the bowls to lighten Gabriella's load. "I'll be right behind you."

At the top of the stairs, they could hear low murmurs coming from the sitting room. As Gabriella nudged the door open with her hip, the load was immediately lifted from her arms. "Thanks, D," she said as she moved into the room so Elizabeth could get by.

"We're going back for the food now," Elizabeth said in a lowered tone.

"We'll come and help," Diana and Hunter offered.

"We can do it in one trip then," Gabriella said and stretched her arms over her head working the kinks out.

With all four of them carrying things, they were easily able to transport the food upstairs. By the time everything was set up, Ashley was moving around, only vestiges of the trance remained.

Sophia, however, remained deep in trance, sitting in front of the fire, arms around her knees rocking gently to and fro. Tears streamed down her face. Lost to the present, she made no sound. Lily sat beside her, one arm around her shoulder, one hand on her arm, talking quietly, continuously. She glanced up at Elizabeth, the anxiety and concern clear on her face. Elizabeth crossed the room and sat on Sophia's other side, putting her arm around her waist, gently rubbing her arm.

Diana, with a bowl of cool water and washcloth, knelt in front of Sophia. She began to sponge the cloth over her face, her arms, her hands, and her feet. Again and again Diana started with Sophia's face and worked her way down until she'd finished each foot while Lily continued to talk about things from the present; her high school classes, her home, and especially her garden. Hunter came over and began to lightly massage Sophia's shoulders. Ashley and Gabriella brought everyone a glass of champagne.

"To our ancestors, may they know how we cherish the gifts they gave us tonight. To Michael for inviting us to celebrate Samhain with The Lady in The Sacred Grove. To Elizabeth for leading us through a powerful ceremony. Blessed Be." Ashley's soft voice said the words of the prayer and toast. "And may y'all find peace in the gift, Sophia." Ashley leaned forward. "Have a sip, Soph, I know this is a favorite of yours." Ashley slowly lifted the glass to her lips. "Here you go, Soph, take a sip. You know Jonathan would want you to rejoice and celebrate now. That was his way."

Sophia managed a sip. Her trance-glazed eyes fluttered open; she blinked, looked at Ashley and in a gravelly voice whispered, "Did you see him?"

"No, Soph, I didn't see Jonathan. I was too busy with my granny. But I know you saw him. I know that with all my heart. And, Soph, I know it's hard to do, believe me I know, but we really need you to come back to us. At least a little ways tonight."

"Take another sip of your champagne," Lily encouraged, as she continued to sit with her arm around Sophia's shoulders.

The seven women sat in silence, looks of contemplation on their faces sipping their champagne. Time was passing and Elizabeth knew from experience they needed food and water to be able to shake off the last remnants of the trance. She shifted away from Sophia and rose. "We need food now."

"The spirit plate is fixed," Gabriella said standing. Crossing the room, she picked up the small plate and returned to where the other women were sitting. She held the plate at heart level. "Great Goddess, the one who sustains us all, thank you for sharing your bounty with us tonight. Blessed Be."

One by one the women rose, fixed a bowl of soup and a plate of salad and bread, and returned to sit in a semi-circle before the fire. Someone was always with Sophia. Lily and Diana fixed her food. Everyone was pleased to see Sophia eat a few spoonful's of soup.

Time was spent in quiet contemplation during the meal. An internal signal passed between them as the women turned as one to look at Elizabeth. She sighed, a slight smile playing on the corners of her mouth. "Guess I'm still 'it'?" she queried. All heads, except Sophia's, nodded.

"This is our time for sharing our experiences of this ceremony. And, of course, if you do not want to share, that will be respected. When we've all had a chance to share, we'll take time for general conversation if that is what everyone wants to do." She let her gaze travel from one to the other. "So, who wants to go first?"

"I'll go first," Hunter shifted on her pillow and carefully set down her bowl of soup. "My friend, Jorge, from Los Angeles came to me. He and I became friends when I was attempting to break into choreography and dance in Hollywood. He died of AIDS a year after I left. I'd stayed in touch, but not as much as I knew he needed," her voice trembled with emotion. "He came to tell me it was okay and that he was proud of me, proud of my dance studio, proud of what I've accomplished in Fremont."

Tears streamed down her face, the wetness darkening the green of her blouse. "He was the first person who reached back when I reached out. He was the first person to cheer me on, to encourage my ideas for a dance studio. He was the first person to honestly tell me that while I was really good; I wasn't good enough to be a star in Hollywood. And he made that okay because he told me it was because I was a great mom and that is why I couldn't and shouldn't dedicate myself more to dance than I was already."

Hunter reached for a tissue and wiped her eyes. "I told him I was sorry I hadn't been there for him at the end." Her voice broke as sobs welled up from deep within. "He told me he had other people who were with him and he knew I was where I needed to be because I'd send him cards with notes and pictures of the dance studio, and more importantly, Logan. You see, he loved her very much and wanted the best for her. He knew I was taking care of someone he loved and he said that was why I had nothing to be sorry about." She handed the talking stone to Gabriella.

Holding the piece of Connemara marble, Gabriella began. "A college friend, Amelia, came to me. We were roommates and worked at the same diner. She committed suicide our junior year. I never understood why. She was smart, beautiful, and talented, she had everything, or so I thought. Amelia came and told me why she'd taken her life. The mystery of it is now gone but the sadness I feel for the loss of her friendship still remains." Gabriella cheeks reddened and she looked down at her hands. In a quieter voice she said, "She said she's proud of me and knows I'll be a best-selling author. All those romantic stories I'd tell her when we were working. You know, you see the couple in the booth?" She grinned. "Well, I used to make up stories about them. Were they really married? Were they living together? Had they just had a night of wild sex? As you know I have an active imagination."

Her chuckle, meant more for herself than the others, she went on. "We'll just leave it at that. Amelia did what she did and at least now I understand her reasoning. I do wish I'd known then what I do now, but I'm not sure in the end it would have made any difference." Gabriella looked around the circle. "I am so very fortunate to have you all in my life. I think it's because I was so devastated when Amelia died I know life can be short and friends can leave you without any notice." She passed the stone to Lily.

"My parents came to me," Lily began. "I never thought they understood what happened in my marriage, why I wasn't happy. Tonight I learned that while they did understand what was happening, you know his affairs, his hitting me; they believed it was my duty to remain in the marriage. I know that comes from their foundational religious beliefs that a wife belongs to her husband.

"While I don't think anything really changed because of tonight, that disquiet I've always felt is gone. My myth was that if they really knew, really understood they would have accepted the divorce. Well, that myth is just that, a myth and it has been replaced by the reality that because of whom they were, and their belief system, they never would have accepted it. As some of you know my parents were not very demonstrative in their affections so the greater gift is they both told me they loved me and hoped I was happy in my new marriage. I was able to assure them that I loved them too and that I was very happy in my marriage; and in a way I was grateful to Paul because I learned some lessons I needed in order to find true happiness this time around."

Diana took the stone. "My aunt Dorothy came to me. We had a long talk about philandering husbands. I'd had suspicions my Uncle Walt had affairs, but he was discreet, or so I thought. My aunt was very clear he was not discreet and she should have left him. But at that time, getting a divorce was very hard and she'd never worked outside the home so had no job skills. While they had enough money, she knew they didn't have enough for separate households at the standard they currently lived. So, she stuffed the anger, hurt, betrayal, and at times, despair. She told me at one point she'd contemplated suicide. She didn't go through with it because it would not hurt him but it would devastate the people she loved and who loved her back.

"I thanked her for not doing that," Diana's voice was strong but as the next thought came to her it softened, "she told me that I was one of the main reasons she didn't. I loved going to her house and staying the night. We'd talk and make cookies." The expression on her face changed again to a somber one. "She sees me on the same path she was in her marriage. Losing pieces of myself with each discovered affair, compromising my soul for appearances. There is truth in those words but... ." Tears slipped down her face as she took a deep shuddering breath and added, "And then she said, "You know, Diana, I love you still." She handed the stone to Ashley.

"My grammy was a feisty old lady and someone who loved me unconditionally. That didn't mean she never got in my face or anything, 'cause she sure did. I've missed having her to talk things over with. She always knew what to say, just the right amount of push mixed with just the right amount of support with a dash of independence. I'd leave her place thinking I'd come up with a really great way to solve the problem and then later, looking back on it; I could see her hand in it all along the way.

"She didn't like Art. Never could stand him but was always polite and respectful because he was my husband. Things weren't as bad as they are now when she died. She told me she's very disappointed that I'd stay with "the bastard". And she's concerned about the kids, what will happen to them if something happens to me. I've worried about that myself. She thinks I need to have a Will, try to protect the kids 'cause she doesn't trust him at all." Ashley's smile was faint but there nonetheless, "she reminded me that I'm her granddaughter; I'm full of grit and determination and I can be feisty when I need to be." Ashley still held the stone, resting lightly in her hands, but remained silent. Shrugging, she looked around at her circle sisters. "Lots to think about but I'm grateful for the reminder of where I come from."

Ashley handed Sophia the warm marble. Sophia took the stone and laid it gently in her lap. Tears welled in her brown eyes and began a slow journey down her cheeks to fall on the rose-red blouse she wore.

"You all know Jonathan came to me. I hadn't told him I loved him that morning and then he was gone and I couldn't tell him to his face. The pain, the ache in my heart has eased but in another way it has intensified. He knows, because of tonight, that I loved him then and love him still. I know that he loves me through all time and watches over me. He thinks I'm too young to close myself off from other relationships and even brought up the idea of my marrying again,"

Sophia choked on these last words. "I can't imagine sharing my bed or my life with anyone else," she whispered, too overcome with emotion to speak. She sat, head bowed, letting the tears fall, before taking a deep breath and looking around at the faces of these women who were her dearest friends. "When I said I'd see him next year on Samhain," her voice broke but she gathered herself to blurt out the last, "he told me "no", this was the only time he could come to me like this. I've lost him again." She hugged herself and sobbed, rocking back and forth.

The other women bore witness to her pain, placing the box of tissue within her reach, sitting in silence. Eventually the sobs lessened and Sophia reached for the tissues. Without speaking she dabbed her tear swollen eyes and handed the stone to Elizabeth.

"Michael's grandmother came to me," her quiet voice quavered. "She wanted to meet me because I've been serving The Lady and reading her journals, trying her recipes in the still room, and I've captured the interest of her grandson. She wants me to stay here with The Lady and Michael," Elizabeth's voice broke. "She said I'm stronger than she was and can serve The Lady and still be a wife to Michael and a mother to our children. She was very sorry she'd failed Michael's father, repeating that she wasn't strong enough to shut herself off from The Lady."

Tears fell, her voice a whisper, "I can't stay." Her eyes stared at an unseen spot on the floor in front of her. "I tried to explain it to her but she didn't understand. You are my family and I've made a commitment to this sacred women's circle. I can't break it. I can't break The Circle." The tears rolled down her face, she struggled to speak but gave up, held herself and cried. "Leaving hurts so bad," she finally choked out. "But I know I can't stay."

"Why can't you stay?" Lily asked her voice gentle. "I'm a bit confused right now so it would be helpful if you could try and explain it to me."

"We had a commitment to this sacred women's circle. You remember the ceremony?"

Lily nodded.

"Well, that's why I can't stay here. If I did, I would break my commitment and break The Circle. Don't you see, we are Seven. Together we are The Circle. If one of us leaves, then we are six. Seven is sacred. I can't take that away from us. I know six is about love and family, but it isn't magical like seven. I know you all feel it. When we're together, especially when we're doing Ceremony we are blessed, it is a sacred, magical time.

As Elizabeth's passionate voice listed the reasons she couldn't stay, Lily exchanged glances with the other women. When she'd stopped talking, Lily took the lead, assured that the others would also chime in.

"It seems to me, Elizabeth, that you've put a lot of thought into this situation."

Elizabeth nodded.

"But," Lily quietly continued, "you've only been looking at it from one point of view."

"Have you thought about how each of us would feel if you sacrificed a life with Michael and service to The Lady for us?" Diana asked in her formal tone. She watched with some satisfaction as she saw Elizabeth's slowly shake her head. "I, for one, would feel a burden for your loss, exacerbated by the reality that I wasn't even asked if I wanted to carry it."

"I too would feel bad if you made that decision without talking to me about it," Lily added. "What would the rest of you feel, knowing Elizabeth was sacrificing a life here to remain in Fremont with us?"

"I'm confused," Hunter spoke, bewilderment evident in her voice and on her face. "Why would you ever give up a hunk like Michael? He obviously loves you. And a place like this with the opportunity every day to serve The Lady? I must have missed something somewhere because that doesn't even make sense to me."

"Y'all are just trying to be true to us, aren't you Elizabeth?" Ashley reached over and touched Elizabeth's knee with her hand. She smiled reassuringly when she noted Elizabeth's agreement. "But, ya see, E, the way you're looking at this, to be true to us, you betray yourself. That's not a good thing."

Sophia listened to the exchange. While she barely followed the discussion, she knew she needed to speak up. When Elizabeth first returned from Ireland she'd seen it. Elizabeth was conflicted between her circle sisters and the man who'd won her heart.

"Do you love him, Elizabeth?" Sophia knew that was the critical question and what would come after depended solely on her answer.

"Yes," Elizabeth whispered. "I do love him. I tried so very hard not to, but somehow it just happened."

"Elizabeth, answer this question. 'If there was a way to keep the circle unbroken and have all this," she gestured widely, "is this something you'd want to strive for?"

"But I don't see how… .

Gabriella quickly interrupted, "That isn't the question, Elizabeth and you know it. You've heard it asked of others in the circle any number of times. The question asks us to shift our thinking from one or the other to having it all. It asks us to change our point of view, in other words, eliminate the conflict. So, Elizabeth, the question remains. Do you want to figure out a way to have Michael and The Circle?"

"If there was a way to have both, then yes, I would want that." Elizabeth straightened her spine and looked around at the other women. "If you can help me figure it all out, I'd be most grateful."

With that invitation, the women discussed options and the challenges of maintaining The Circle with one of their members living so far away. Ideas flew fast and furious at one point but when all was said and done they had decided on a plan. While they didn't know exactly when Michael planned on using the house he'd recently bought in Fremont, they were fairly sure he did plan on being in the States from time to time. They were fairly sure he wouldn't object to Elizabeth occasionally spending additional time in Fremont.

They also had the Golden Cauldron fund and could come to see Elizabeth and celebrate some of the holidays here. And while it wouldn't be the same, they would stay in touch with emails and for a time at each meeting, they'd have Elizabeth on the speaker phone. Something imbued with her presence; her energy would hold her place in The Circle when they met. They weren't sure how it would work, but they were all excited to try it out and to tweak this plan or even scrap it and start over if they needed to.

"And then there's something called instant messaging and Skype that we can look into," Diana said. "We'll all be on the lookout for other ways to stay connected."

"An idea just came to me," Elizabeth started and then paused, "actually it's more of a remembering." She took a deep breath. "It may sound a little crazy but I remember when I first came to Ireland and I was missing you all, I'd remind myself that we were all looking at the same sky, at the same Sun and Moon, standing on the same Mother Earth, and it would help that feeling of loneliness. Maybe we could set a time when we'd all think of each other, send each other energy, hold each other in 'the light'?"

"I think that's a great idea," Lily's voice held excitement as she remembered her and her son, Charlie's agreement to think of each other on the full moon. "We all get so busy sometimes we do disconnect from each other even living in Fremont."

"I don't know about y'all but I need some sleep before my kids get back." Ashley's statement was a reminder that their everyday lives were about to begin again. "I see daylight creeping in between the drapes. Now, I don't want to know what time it is, but if we all pitch in we can get the food cleaned up and get in a few hours."

Before she'd finished speaking everyone was up and gathering plates, cup, bowls, and the remnants of the remaining food. One trip had everything downstairs. In less than twenty minutes everything was done and the women were back in the sitting room settling down on pillows, cushions and blankets.

Gabriella suddenly sat up. "We forgot one key question, everyone," her voice was excited. She waited a minute listening to the sleepy voices murmuring their discontent.

"What is it, Gabby? We're all so tired now," Elizabeth's sleep-drugged voice asked.

"When's the wedding?" Gabriella laughed. "Since everything's been worked out, there's a wedding to plan. How about Winter Solstice?"

"First things first, Gabby, I can't get married without a proposal," Elizabeth murmured.

# 27 FINALLY

The sound of excited, chattering children's voices interspersed with deeper male responses filtered under the sitting room door. Elizabeth yawned, stretched and was about to get up when the door burst open and Ashley's children ran in, Logan close behind.

"Shhhh," Ashley's oldest child, Artie, said, "they're still sleeping."

"Oops," the youngest, Amanda, added, "we'd better go."

"Ya better not go without me, ya hear," Ashley's voice still held traces of sleep but her meaning was clear. She tossed off the blanket she'd been wrapped in and struggled to stand. "Guess I'm not as young as I used to be 'cause getting up off this floor is harder than it should be."

Immediately she was surrounded by her children who were tugging on her arms, helping her to stand. With a laugh, she tumbled back down pulling them with her while kissing and hugging them. "I missed ya. Did y'all miss me? Were you good for Logan?" Ashley looked up at the three men standing just inside the door. "Giovanni? Where did you come from?"

"I hear my friend is in Ireland so I come." The Italian, a boyish grin on his face, shrugged. "The little ones were *molto buono.*"

"What are you men doing here?" Lily pointed her finger in the direction of the door. "Out now!" she ordered.

"Lily, my love, did you miss me?" Jackson started toward his wife.

"No, Jackson, don't come any closer. You all have to leave this room. If you want to wait in the hall, that's fine, but this is not the time or place for you to be in here."

Lily's prim voice and starched posture brought a grin to her husband's face, a smile to his eyes. "We'll be just outside the door if you need any help," Jackson turned and ushered the other men out, pulling the door closed after them.

While they might all wish they had more time to sleep, more time to reflect, more time to just be, those wishes were not to be manifest today. Their time-out-of-time Samhain Celebration in The Sacred Grove was over. It was time to embrace their real lives and be grateful for the gifts they'd received from those who'd gone before them. The women quickly put the room back in order deciding to gather in the kitchen in a couple of hours.

"Let me help you with these," Jackson reached out to take the pillows and blankets from Lily as she entered the hall. "Do these go back to our room?"

"Yes they do," she stood on her tiptoes and kissed his cheek. "Thank you for taking them for me." She saw his brow raise in question. "I'm helping Sophia with her things, Jackson. I'll see you when we're done." She smiled and mouthed "later".

"Here, I help with the blankets and pillows." While Giovanni's words addressed the women now in the hallway, his eyes were on only one.

The object of his interest held her blankets and pillows tight to her chest. "I don't need any help, thank you Migliori," Gabriella's spine was stiff, her chin raised, her voice frosty.

Giovanni chuckled.

"Givani?" Ashley's daughter tugged on his hand.

"*Si?*"

"Will you pick me up?"

Giovanni sighed as he saw Gabriella's retreating form. She'd used his momentary distraction to get past him. Resigned for the moment, he bent down and picked up the little girl.

"Like this?" he asked as he held her upside down; "or like this?" he tossed her over his shoulder. Already she was squealing with delight. "Or maybe you like this?" he held her under his arm like a sack of sugar. "Ahh my little pigeon, I think you like to be held like this." He shifted and held her as if to rock her and looked deep into her blue eyes that always turned so serious at this point in their little game. She snuggled closer to him and he thought it would be good to have children of his own, ones he didn't have to put down and send back to a doting papa.

"Senor Migliori, I hope my little girl isn't a problem for ya." He knew the soft southern voice belonged to the mother.

"No, no *problema* at all." He kissed the little one on the forehead and gently lowered her to the floor. "Children, they are gifts from God, *si*? So, they cannot be problems. Trouble, *si*? But problems, no." He smiled at the serious young woman, taking her blankets and pillow from her. "I help you with these," he said and started down the hall

As soon as Elizabeth was within arm's reach, Michael's hands claimed her. He tugged her with him as he backed down the hall in the opposite direction of the others. Amusement danced in his eyes, a seductive smile on his lips, he continued walking backward, pulling her along. She looked delicious and he planned on seeing her naked, sample her flavors, and love her to distraction. He released one of her hands to reach behind him to open the door at his back. Stepping inside, he guided her until they were both inside. He swiveled, closed the door with his foot, leaned against it, and pulled Elizabeth tight relishing the way she fit against him.

Elizabeth rose on her tiptoes, pressing kisses to his chin and then slowly, nibbling and kissing traveled up one side of his jaw to his ear before slipping to the other side and working her way down. His mouth waited for hers to claim it, his arms tighten until there was nothing but clothing separating them.

Michael's arousal pushed against Elizabeth's soft body. When he shifted to ease the pressure, he felt her answering response. Scooping her up in his arms, he quickly crossed the room and dumped her on the bed. No finesse, no grace.

His long hard body followed her down, pressing her into the mattress, preventing even a slight bounce as his hands roamed over her, enticing, exciting, enthralling her with every touch. The fingers of flames flared as his hands touched, stroked, caressed.

"What's all this?" Michael's muffled laughter belied his attempt to be serious. He sat up and gazed down on the nearly naked object of his desire who had several stones on or around her. "You look like a rock store."

"It's my protection," she huffed, her tone indignant. "You know I wear protection when I go to The Sacred Grove and The Lady."

Michael smiled as his gaze took in the assortment of stones tucked between her breasts, one having slipped down to her navel, as he considered a way of removing the stones with his teeth. He nuzzled her breast, seeking the stone caught under its fullness. His tongue snaked out and traced the outline of the rock, easing the small object out from under her fragrant flesh until it rested on her rib. Making sure to breathe on her skin, he picked up the stone with his teeth, depositing it at the indentation at the base of her throat. On the third stone he added running his jaw over her breasts and toying with the curls at the apex of her legs. Seven stones later, her breathing shallow, her gaze intense he stopped fighting the surge of desire.

"I've missed you so," he whispered in her ear as he slipped inside her heat. "God, I've missed you." His mouth clamped over hers, his tongue ruthlessly invading her mouth as he moved in and out, in and out until she was frantically raising her hips to meet his thrusts, her hands grasping his buttocks, her legs locked around his thighs. They reached the peak together, their voices mingling as they called out to one another at the height of the glory.

They lay quietly, gathering breath and energy to move. Elizabeth's arms had slipped from Michael's back, lying boneless at her sides. Michael, his full weight crushing her, lay unable to move.

Moments passed before he shifted to bear some of his weight on his arms. Her face relaxed, her eyes drowsy, he placed a gentle kiss on each of her eye lids, the tip of her nose, her chin, her forehead, and then her mouth. He sighed into her mouth as it opened to him. He felt his penis stir, begin to harden again. Remembering her telling him when they'd left

The Hotel Lir that there was a difference between people thinking they were lovers and knowing it, he pulled away.

"Time to get up," he nuzzled her neck where it met her shoulder, rolled off her, and onto his back. Holding her hand, brushing his thumb over her palm, looking up at the ceiling, he knew the bone deep, soul deep sense all was right in his world.

Elizabeth was quiet, basking in the afterglow. *This isn't just mind-blowing sex. It's soul sharing. We love each other and this love-making comes from a deep and abiding love.*

Michael gritted his teeth, rolled off the bed, gathered up his clothes, and started dressing. Elizabeth eyed him, her gaze slipping over his body. She smiled when she saw his penis twitch and begin to rise. She chuckled as he turned away from her.

"You'll pay for that later, luv." He tugged the zipper up over the slight bulge in his pants. "You'll pay dearly." He sat on one of the chairs to put on his socks and boots, his eyes automatically finding her.

Elizabeth half-sat and half-leaned on the bed, her generous breasts hung free, gently swaying with her movement, the covers pooled at her knees. He dragged his eyes from her breasts to her face, saw the laughter in her eyes. "You're definitely paying. And the price is going up."

Her laughter interrupted him. "How high?" she teased, her eyes drifting to his crotch. "How much will it rise?" When she saw Michael begin to get up and start toward her, she scrambled off the other side of the bed, grabbed her clothes, and made a dash for the bathroom.

His hand on the knob, he heard the soft click of the lock falling into place and her muted laughter through the door. Michael stood on his side of the door, his hand on the handle, his forehead resting against the smooth wood. In his mind images of Elizabeth naked, Elizabeth in the shower, Elizabeth stroking mascara on her eyelashes flashed. *Get a grip, boyo. She's here for two more days. You'll see her over New Years in Fremont. Things are progressing according to plan.*

On her side of the door, Elizabeth mirrored Michael's stance. Her body was cooling from their ardent love-making and her mind was clearing. *He'll go to the airport with us so I've got two days to get that marriage proposal.*

Two o'clock in the afternoon and Seamus's kitchen was filled with the scents of the early preparation for tonight's dinner: Roasted leg of lamb with a homemade mint relish, his fresh baked bread, fresh butter, and a salad all preceded by an appetizer of basil, tomato, fresh mozzarella cheese, crusty bread drizzled with olive oil—one of Elizabeth's favorites. He was debating over what to make for dessert when his kitchen was filled with nine adults, three children, and Logan. He didn't growl or fuss; he just turned his back and went about his business.

He heard Mick clear his throat and ignored him. Seven people had turned into thirteen; of course one of them was his boss and although he did find the children a joy he'd never let on. He hoped it was practice for when Mick had children. His thoughts were interrupted by a knock on the kitchen door. It opened before anyone could respond and in walked Paddy and Shannon.

Michael, surprised to see Shannon with Paddy, made the introductions as he crossed the kitchen to greet his visitors. He lowered his voice when he neared Seamus. "Everyone's hungry. What can you make to hold us until dinner?"

Sophia heard Michael's statement. "Michael, Seamus doesn't have to make us something to eat. There are seven women here, eight including Logan, nine counting Amanda, ten counting Shannon. I think we're capable, with Seamus' permission, of course, to put something together to tide us over."

Seamus glowered at her and shrugged his shoulders.

"Or," Elizabeth came to stand next to Seamus. "We could all go to the pub and let Seamus finish what looks and smells like a fabulous dinner. And while we made an effort to put things back where we found them, I'm sure he'd like some time to sort through his kitchen on his own. Why don't we go to the pub?"

Seamus just looked at her, his face blank. Then he turned and leveled the same look at Mick.

"I think that's a great idea. Let's get jackets. I'll call Patrick and let him know we're descending on him." Michael was almost across the kitchen when he turned and caught Paddy's eye. "You two going to join us?" At Paddy's nod, Michael left the kitchen to make his call.

Amid much chatter and a bit of chaos, they got their things together and left the house through the front door so they wouldn't disturb Seamus again. Elizabeth found herself walking with Shannon toward the cars. She wanted to be friends with the young woman. Once again it struck her that since the first time she and The Lady changed the words of the prayer to "we", she viewed people differently. She more easily saw the other person's point of view, looked past possible differences and curbed her suspicions.

Since she hoped to be living here soon, she made idle conversation about this part of Ireland asking about winter weather, signs of spring, and what Shannon did with her time. She wasn't surprised to learn Shannon worked with adolescents who were struggling with family issues at a nearby special boarding school.

At the pub, they pulled tables and chairs together so they could all sit in a group. Trying their first Guinness, relishing the pub's specialty of potato skins, playing a boisterous game of darts, joining in singing when a couple of the local lads started playing fiddle, guitar, and bodhran passed the time. It was getting dark and they were in high spirits, laughing and talking amongst themselves when they left to return to The Manor.

Elizabeth again found herself walking with Shannon and thought this was a sign. "We do morning prayers in The Sacred Grove with The Lady. Would you like to join us tomorrow?"

Shannon stopped. Elizabeth walked on before realizing Shannon was no longer beside her. Turning, she faced Shannon, a questioning look on her face.

"You're inviting me to join you for prayers?" Shannon looked stunned.

"Yes, if that's a problem because of my relationship with Michael, I do understand. But I'd hoped that we could find a way past that and if not become friends at least join together in serving The Lady." Elizabeth stepped closer and laid her hand on Shannon's arm. "I really hadn't planned to ask you in such a way." She looked and saw Shannon's face still registering shock. "Of course if you don't want to, I'll understand."

"No." Shannon shook her head and smiled. "I'd be honored to join you. What time?"

"We gather at 5:30 a.m. If you want to spend the night, you're welcome to. As you may already know, Michael opened the other wing so there are plenty of bedrooms. There is certainly room for you."

"I don't live far and can be there at 5:30." Shannon took Elizabeth's arm and stepped to face her. "Thank you, Elizabeth. I miss serving The Lady. I know I'm not cut out to do it full time," she said, a soft and rather sad smile on her face. "Thank you for including me."

There was an air of nervousness in the back parlor as the women came together for morning prayers. Logan and Shannon were joining them. What had nerves on edge? It was the first time they'd been back in The Sacred Grove since their Samhain ceremony. To feel more confident, they took extra grounding protection. Last night they'd met and talked, coming to a quick agreement that all they'd do this morning were the prayers.

Elizabeth checked everyone out and was glad that Shannon was with her because she was also familiar with the energy. Last night Shannon had easily incorporated the change in the prayer from "I" to "we".

For different reasons both Logan and Sophia needed experienced support. It was Logan's first time and Sophia, while recovered from their Samhain ceremony, was a little tentative, not her usual 'take charge' self.

Single file they walked down the path, circled the grove, saying prayers at each of the four entrances. They entered from the East, the direction of new beginnings. Once in the center, The Lady appeared and prayers were said. Even though they did nothing more, it was almost nine o'clock when they returned to the house and had breakfast.

The day passed quickly and since their flight left Monday in the late afternoon, they all planned to pack in the morning. Shannon drove Gabriella, Diana, Hunter, and Logan into town so they didn't have to worry about which side of the road they were on. Lily was taking a nap. Ashley and her children were out at the barns, the children getting another riding lesson. Elizabeth and Sophia puttered in the still room. Together they experimented with another of Michael's grandmother's recipes. The men, who had become fast friends, were off doing something. Michael had mentioned meeting up with Paddy.

It was late when they'd finished dinner and retired to their beds. Michael had mentioned nothing about her staying longer. She was beginning to doubt whether she'd have a Winter Solstice wedding. *If he doesn't ask me to marry him on this trip, I may just have to ask him when he comes to Fremont for Jackson's New Year's Eve party.* While her thoughts were confident and positive, her feelings were a little less so. She'd been so sure he'd try to keep her with him.

Morning came too soon. She and Michael had barely slept. Over and over again he'd pulled her into his arms; held her tight after their loving; and whispered words in the old language to her. She'd had no idea what he was saying and when she'd ask him to tell her, he just smiled and said the words weren't important; what was important was how she felt when she heard the words. Her heart translated the old language – he loved her and she was the most precious thing on earth to him.

Overcoming her embarrassment, her shyness at being so forthcoming about her feelings, she told him she loved him. She'd hoped if she went first, he'd propose. His reaction? He kissed her on the forehead, tucked her head on his shoulder, and wrapped his arms around her. In a matter of seconds she heard and felt his breathing slow and deepen as he fell asleep.

After breakfast, Elizabeth packed her things and went to see if anyone else needed help. She found her circle sisters in

Sophia's room; packed luggage in the hall waiting to be taken downstairs. The children, including Logan, were off to see the horses one last time. The women were sitting around talking, actually speculating about her and the upcoming wedding, when Elizabeth walked in.

"Well?" Gabriella's expectant look told volumes.

"No, he hasn't, Gabby. And he may not ask me. Or at least not ask me now." Elizabeth tried to look accepting but knew her resolve was weakening.

"It's obvious to all of us that he loves you very much." Diana reached over and put her arm around Elizabeth's shoulders.

"I know," Elizabeth's voice was a whisper and she fought the tears that threatened to spill. She would not cry over this. She would not. She bit her lower lip and stiffened her resolve and her knees.

She heard footsteps in the hall and then saw Michael filling the doorway. "Everyone ready?"

"Yes. Is it time?" Hunter asked.

"Tis time to get things loaded up." Michael looked at Elizabeth. She looked pale and a little sickly he thought. "Are you all right Elizabeth?"

She took a deep breath before replying, "I'm fine. I'll just go get my things." She started toward him and out the room.

"Already taken care of, luv." He turned and picked up Sophia's suitcase and followed her out.

The women looked at each other, shrugged their shoulders, and rolled their eyes their looks ranging from "what is going on here?" to "what the 'f---' is going on here?" Sophia picked up her carry-on and tote; slung her coat and scarf over her shoulder and walked out, the other women following her.

Gabriella found Giovanni in her room, her belongings in hand, his perennial grin on his face. She reached for her suitcase, her hand brushing his. The hot sensation shot up her arm. She steeled herself and managed to not jerk her hand away. "I can manage," she snarled, batting at his hand. "Go help someone else."

"But, *mia caro*, I want to help you."

"But, Senor Migliori, I don't want your help," her tone was frosty, her glare icy as she tugged to free her suitcase from his unrelenting hands.

Amusement danced in his eyes. "We share, you and I. You take this." He dumped her coat, scarf, and hat over the hand clamped on his. "And here," he said holding out her tote.

Her coat began to slide to the floor and as he had planned, she let go of him to catch it. With her nicely distracted he whisked himself out the door with her suitcase and carry-on in tow. His walk was jaunty and his whistle lively as he traversed the hall to the stairs. He strolled down and outside where Michael and Jackson were loading the luggage into the vans.

From where he stood next to Michael, Giovanni turned to see Gabriella storm out the front door.

She looked around the assembled group, fury blazing from every pore. Stomping down the steps, she strode down the walkway toward the van, her finger pointing straight at him. In a threatening voice she said, "When do you plan to marry?"

"You want to marry me?" Giovanni, startled but not terrified, imagined himself married to this passionate woman. His grin began to spread across his face but another look at the rage-filled countenance had him sobering immediately.

"Not you, you idiot," Gabriella sputtered. "Him." And she pointed at Michael.

Stunned, Michael gripped the edge of the door. "What? What are you talking about? You want to marry me?" he managed to utter the words though he felt numb from head to toe.

"No, you—," Gabriella rolled her eyes skyward. *How could two educated men be so stupid?* She glared at the men in front of her. One man was looking at her cautiously, questioningly. The other wore an expression that could only be described as "dumbfounded"."

Diana stepped forward and put her arm around Gabriella. "It's all right Gabby." Lily came to stand on her other side. Sophia moved to stand with Elizabeth as did Hunter and Ashley. Elizabeth face reflected stunned horror.

"It's just that we've planned a wedding for Winter Solstice," Diana began. "And we had thought that you and Elizabeth might be the bride and groom."

"It's obvious you both love each other. There was a time when you wanted her to stay," Lily continued her eyes never leaving his face.

"She didn't want to leave The Circle," Michael felt the pain afresh as he said those words. In some ways his situation with Elizabeth reminded him of the conflict his father felt with his own mother. He couldn't compete with The Lady and Michael couldn't compete with The Circle.

"There are many ways to be together, Michael." Lily now stood less than a foot away from him and spoke in a low voice only he could hear. She stood on her tiptoes, her hand resting gently against his chest for balance, her eyes locked with his. "If you want to hear "yes", then ask her."

Michael looked at the familiar faces that were watching him. His gaze locked with Elizabeth's and without thinking he walked toward her. Never breaking eye contact, he took her hands in his. He wanted Elizabeth more than he'd ever wanted anyone else in his life, but he wasn't ready to commit or ask her to until he was sure they were on the same life path.

He tossed the van's keys to Jackson. "We'll meet you at the airport," he called out over his shoulder as he drew Elizabeth along behind him toward the house. His expression grim, he strode to the kitchen door, he reached inside and grabbed his car keys before continuing on to the garage. Stopping by the passenger door; he turned, effectively caging her against the car.

They were being watched.

He hadn't heard doors slamming and engines starting. The decision? Here or along the road to the airport? He didn't have the answer to even that simple question.

One thing he was clear on. He loved her and had yet to tell her in a language she understood.

"We need to talk." His intense gaze met her questioning one. "I do love you, Elizabeth. I do want to marry you but… ." He paused before going on unsure which words to say; to let her know what was in his heart.

"But…?" Elizabeth whispered. Her knees were shaky and she could feel her heart beat in every pore.

Michael shifted, easing his hand behind her to open the car door. He now knew where they needed to go. "Trust me." He held the door for her and she got in.

The car pulled onto the verge of the road. Elizabeth had known their destination when Michael pulled off the main road. The river Shannon flowed serenely within its banks, the bare branches of the willows wispy reflections in the calm waters. The trees in the grove they'd picnicked in that July day were bare but the bushes would provide some privacy.

A misting rain fell muting the scene as they strolled toward the grove. No dry place to sit, they stood, his arm around her shoulders, her head resting on his arm.

"Ye know how me father felt about his mother." Michael's gaze rested unseeing in front of him. He felt Elizabeth's head nod against his arm. "I know ye are stronger than my grandmother when it comes to serving The Lady. You've already shown me you can serve her and still have time for us."

She shifted to stand in front of him, looked up into his serious face and saw the truth of his words in his intent look.

He lifted his hand, his fingers brushing her lips. "I need to know I'm first." He took a deep breath and exhaled. "For you it isn't The Lady, it's The Circle. I know how important the other women are to you. I also know I cannot complete with what you have with them."

Elizabeth slid her arms around Michael's waist and stepped into his warmth and strength. What he said was true. Until two days ago, she'd always chosen The Circle over everyone. Remembering his reaction a few months ago when he overheard the tail end of her conversation with Gabby, it was critical to explain that now things were different now.

"You are right, Michael. The Circle has come first, before you. Until now." She brought her hands to his face, pulled him to her, lightly kissed him on the cheek. "Now it is different. Lily, Sophia, Diana, Hunter, Ashley and Gabriella all want me to be with you. We talked about ways to stay connected, to keep The Circle whole if I'm here with you and we all believe it is possible."

Elizabeth stepped back, her hands now resting on his chest. "It will take work and at times it will take compromise. There are times I won't be here with you because I'll be in Fremont. And there will be times when everyone will be here with me." She felt the shimmering light flood her and knew she glowed. "I love you Michael Joseph Patrick Murphy. I love you with all my heart and soul. I love you with every breath I breathe. My love for you flows throughout the world."

"Elizabeth Mary Magdalene Elliott, will you marry me?" This woman who had filled his nights with passion and his days with laughter was the same woman who now filled his days and nights with passion and laughter. When he looked again, he saw tears streaming down her face. "Marry me, Elizabeth." He wrapped his arms around her and held her close. "I want you in my life. It's as simple as that." The way she fit in his arms was perfect. Her scent of bergamot and more filled his senses. Picking her up, he held her pressed against his body, her eyes now on a level with his. "I was told that the answer'd be "yes", but I've yet to hear it, Elizabeth."

"Is that what Lily told you?" She flung her arms around his neck and grinned. "There is one condition." She wrapped her legs around his waist.

"What?" His breathing was strained as his body remembered what it felt like to love her.

"We marry on Winter Solstice." Her eyes never left his.

"That's it?" He grinned and shifted her, letting her slide a few inches down his body.

"Yes," her voice soft she began to feather kisses along his jaw.

He let her slide the rest of the way down his body. "Will you stay now?"

"I need to go home and put in my letter of resignation and finish things up with the families I work with." Her smile lit up her face, as she added, "when that's done, I'll come back."

"Don't forget the house in Fremont. I want us to live there when we're there. So, we'll have to get your things moved in and see what else is needed to furnish the place."

"So, I'll need to give notice on my apartment. Another reason I need to go home now."

Arm in arm they returned to the car. Michael bent and kissed her lightly before closing her door. Elizabeth leaned over and kissed him thoroughly before he started the engine.

Everyone was waiting for them at security. Michael saw smiles on every face. "You're invited to our Winter Solstice wedding," he announced. "I'm sure I'll be informed of the details so I can show up and do my part." Laughter greeted those words.

"I can tell you from experience, that's about all you have to do with this bunch in charge," Jackson commented.

"Winter Solstice." Sophia held out her hands to Elizabeth. "You'll be a beautiful Winter Solstice bride."

Elizabeth turned back into Michael's arms and saw the love she'd waited her whole life for shining back at her.

"I want a dozen children," he whispered as he nibbled on her ear. "After the wedding the condoms are gone."

"Deal," she pulled his head closer so she could kiss him. Through the haze of building passions, she vaguely heard people talking and laughing.

Michael broke the kiss. "We've a life time ahead of us. You'd better get going so you don't miss that plane."

# 28   THE WEDDING

Elizabeth Elliott soon to be Elizabeth Murphy pinched herself. She was on the plane heading for Ireland, heading for her new life. Shifting in her seat, she looked out the window. Memories of her first trip just under six months ago cascaded through her mind. June twenty-second, the day after Lily and Jackson's Summer Solstice wedding, she'd been excited about the adventure of a five week summer vacation. Now, in ten days she would embark on the ultimate adventure for the rest of her life: marriage to Michael on Winter Solstice.

She rested her head against the back of her seat, closed her eyes, and listened to the familiar voices. Lily and Jackson, Eleanor, Jackson's mother and his business partner and friend, Daniel O'Donnell as well as Diana, Sophia, and Gabriella were traveling with her. Diana's husband, Dennis, Ashley, her husband, Art and their three children, along with Hunter and Logan would follow on December eighteenth when school was out and Hunter's dance studio's Holiday Recital was over.

Elizabeth regretted missing the Recital but there was so much to do and as it was she had less than ten days to do it in.

Gabriella slipped into the seat beside her. "Are you nervous?"

"No, not really. We got so much done before we left Fremont I can put that all behind me. It's just that I don't know for sure what all will need to be done in Ireland."

"Whatever is needed we'll get it done before your wedding and our Winter Solstice ceremony." Gabriella sounded confident. "I don't know that I've really thanked you for inviting me to live in that gorgeous house in Fremont. The lower level with its own entrance is like an apartment. I just love it."

"Well, Michael and I are very glad you were willing to share the house with us otherwise it would be empty most of the time. It seemed a shame to have the place sit vacant when there was so much room. Even with the three of us, there's lots of space. I don't know what Michael was thinking when he bought such a large place."

"He was thinking of you and lots of children," Gabriella said and laughed. "He's made that very clear."

Elizabeth chuckled remembering Michael's plans for turning the room they'd first decided to use as their office into a nursery. He wanted to paint it blue and decorate it with horses. It had taken talking and a bit of loving to distract him from going out right there and then and buying a large wooden rocking horse.

"It only took us five days to move, unpack, and settle in," Gabriella was saying.

"If it had only been the three of us, we'd still be unpacking," Elizabeth countered. "Sophia organized the kitchen, made lists of what was where and taped them on the cabinet doors and drawers. Michael went out and bought bedroom furniture for our room and living room furniture for the main living area and negotiated until it was delivered the day we were moving in. Lily and Jackson came over to help and then Diana, Ashley, and Hunter showed up with food. It was a group effort."

"Most of the major things we do become group efforts," Gabriella sighed, resting her head on the back of the seat.

"You're right, and I'm glad that's the case. I don't think I'd be on this plane, flying to Ireland to marry Michael if it wasn't for the groups' efforts," Elizabeth's voice held a serious tone. "I was so stuck in seeing my relationship with Michael from one point of view, I couldn't see the possibilities available from any other. I'm ever so grateful to have you all in my life and to know that even when I am in Ireland we are still connected."

"Where are you in your planning for The Golden Cauldron's Retreat Center?" Gabriella asked. "Last I heard Michael was supportive of making the changes to the old wing so you'd have a meeting room there."

"Yes, he is supportive and even offered a couple of the bedrooms in the family wing. I told him it was important to keep them separate and the only thing I could see was if Shannon agreed to help out and would want to spend the night she'd use one of those rooms. I've lots of ideas but don't have it all sorted out yet. I thought that would be something we could talk about when we're all together."

"Elizabeth, when we're all together, you'll be getting married. Don't you think that will take up your time?" Gabriella's look of amazement brought a smile to her friend's face.

"I'm sure there will be time for us to gather, to sit in circle together before the wedding, before Winter Solstice. The worst that will happen is it will be a topic of conversation at breakfast or dinner." Elizabeth sighed and shifted in her seat. "I want everyone's input, all of your ideas so I can work on things while I'm in Ireland. I won't be coming back with you. I won't see you until the end of January. I'd like to have something to present by then because I'd really like to begin having the Retreats before Beltane."

"You're rather determined about this project." Gabriella laid her hand on Elizabeth's arm. "I know you'll find time for us to discuss this idea more fully." She looked at her friend who stared out the window. "You've come into your own since you first came to Ireland. I have no doubts that you'll accomplish this and more."

"Was I really so 'undeveloped' before?" Elizabeth continued to look out the window at the clouds below and the bright blue sky above.

"I don't think you were 'undeveloped'. I'm not even sure why I think you've 'come into your own'. It's just that you've changed. You seem more confident in your spirituality. I know you and I are the youngest and often acquiesce to Sophia, Lily, and Diana but that has changed. I see them looking to you now. There is something about you or in you that is different."

"What I feel is a stronger connection to the sacred." Elizabeth turned to look at Gabriella. "It started with answering The Lady's call and then having to figure out how to protect myself from the overpowering effects of the energy, the trance. I can't explain it; I walk into a room and I see the sacred space where the altar should be and the words just come to me. I really feel so blessed to have so much joy in my heart."

Elizabeth turned back to the window. The sense the plane was suspended in the air, the racing clouds the canvas for the vision before her. *Who is next?* She saw the shadow of a woman, head bent in despair. Another woman in The Circle's life would be changed by love.

"I, Michael Joseph Patrick Murphy, do take thee, Elizabeth Mary Magdalene Elliott to be my lawfully wedded wife, to have and to hold from this day forward until death us do part," Michael's voice rang clear in Kinslow's packed church. He was well-known in the area and well-known in the world of horse breeding and racing. The fact that he was thirty-four and had evaded the matrimonial machinations of many women for so many years had the society columnists and photographers clamoring for news.

"I, Elizabeth Mary Magdalene Elliott, do take thee, Michael Joseph Patrick Murphy to be my lawfully wedded husband, to have and to hold from this day forward until death us do part," Elizabeth's voice carried throughout the church. She was nervous and thought it showed in her voice but those who witnessed the couple saying their vows commented on how composed the bride was.

Some of the two hundred witnesses criticized her dress, a simple floor length gown of blue with a scooped neck, long sleeves, and a simple white veil of Irish lace that fell past her waist and covered her flowing black curls. But even those who thought her dress too simple for a wedding to so important a man could see that that man was enthralled with his bride and she was obviously in love with him.

Standing in a circle of colored light from the sun streaming through the large stained glass window over the altar, the groom kissed the bride, a long, slow kiss of promises to come. They turned to the congregation, arms linked, smiles of wonder on their faces.

There were those who saw the image of another woman in a similar blue gown standing before them, her arms raised in prayer, a radiant smile on her face. The shimmering light emanated from her enveloping the couple merging with the colored light before outshining it.

*You are the light*
*You are the Source*
*Through you love flows throughout the world.*

"Come to bed Michael," Elizabeth's voice was full of invitation. "Come to bed and hold me."

"When I get to bed, I'll do more than hold you." Michael stood at the foot of the bed, his gaze taking in the enchantress who a few hours before had become his wife.

"Sooner rather than later would be nice," her voice, with the beginnings of a pout in it, sounded sulky.

"Ah luv." Michael sauntered to the side, lifted the covers and slid in. Before he could reach out she was in his arms, pressed against him, kissing him, her hands roving over his already aroused body. "Elizabeth?" He was losing the battle for control as her warm soft mouth worked its way down his body. "Ah luv," he groaned as she flicked his nipples with her tongue.

Elizabeth stopped her assault on her husband's sexy body. She could feel his arousal, the heat pouring off him. She leaned on his chest resting her chin on her folded arms. "Well, Michael. I thought you had plans for us now." She gave him a wicked smile. "Of course, if you don't really have anything in mind, anything you want to do, we can get some sleep."

The words were barely out of her mouth when she found herself flipped onto her back, Michael's weight pressing her into the mattress, his mouth crushing hers, his hands relentless in their quest for her most sensitive places. He filled her, moved in her, and her world exploded. The shimmering light from The Lady, the pulsing energy from The Sacred Grove were nothing compared to the myriad of stars, the glory of the galaxy that burst behind her closed eyes.

The adventure she started on six months ago would continue. She knew it in her soul. She'd taken a chance, followed the vision of The Lady and her instincts, and had found this man who made her heart sing. She snuggled in his arms. He stroked her back. She pressed soft kisses on his chest. "I love you, Michael Joseph Patrick Murphy," she whispered. *The most sacred place is here.*

## New Release Mailing List:

You have just finished the second book in The Sacred Women's Circle series. Be the first to learn about future releases, any pre-release pricing or sales and special events by signing up for my mailing list at http://eepurl.com/NWgIH

## For More Information:

My website: www.JudithAshleyRomance.com
My blog: www.JudithAshleyRomance.blogspot.com

## A request:

If you enjoyed *Elizabeth*, please consider telling your friends and family and writing a review on Amazon and Goodreads. Goodreads reviews are important because Barnes and Noble, Kobo, and other places use them to help their readers find books they'll love.

# ABOUT THE AUTHOR

Judith, in her real life, has been a part of sacred women's circles for over twenty years and knows first-hand how important spirituality is when dealing with life's challenges.

Her imagination has always been active and through books she's been a princess rescued from the tower by the handsome knight, a missionary in India, explorer in the Amazon jungle, a priestess of the Goddess, and a nun to name a few. She's lived with people from all walks of life including different tribes of indigenous people on five continents in tents, wood cabins, igloos, castles, mansions, high-rise apartments, penthouses, dungeons, basements, and cottages.

Then one day in Judith's real life, the stories that make up The Sacred Women's Circle series flooded through her in daydreams, lucid dreams, and conversations so real at times she wondered about her sanity. It was a compelling experience! An experience that was a catalyst to starting her journey to tell these stories and see them published.

Judith's prayer for you:

***Each and every day of your life may you find joy, may you see beauty, may you experience wonder, and may you know you are unconditionally loved.***

For more books from the heart in fiction and non-fiction please visit Windtree Press

http://WindtreePress.com